NO PLACE TO DIE

Also by Clare Donoghue

Never Look Back

CLARE DONOGHUE

NO PLACE TO DIE

Minotaur Books
New York

NO PLACE TO DIE. Copyright © 2015 by Clare Donoghue. All rights reserved.
Printed in the United States of America. For information, address St. Martin's
Press, 175 Fifth Avenue, New York, N.Y. 10010.

www.minotaurbooks.com

Library of Congress Cataloging-in-Publication Data

Donoghue, Clare.
  No place to die / Clare Donoghue. — First U.S. edition.
     p. cm. — (Mike Lockyer novels ; 2)
  ISBN 978-1-250-04608-6 (hardcover)
  ISBN 978-1-4668-4626-5 (e-book)
  1. Women detectives—England—London—Fiction. 2. Missing
persons—Investigation—Fiction. 3. Police—England—London—Fiction.
4. Murder—Investigation—Fiction. I. Title.
  PR6104.O553N6 2015
  823'.92—dc23

2015007164

Minotaur books may be purchased for educational, business, or promotional
use. For information on bulk purchases, please contact the Macmillan Corporate
and Premium Sales Department at 1-800-221-7945, extension 5442, or write to
specialmarkets@macmillan.com.

First published in Great Britain by Pan Books, an imprint of Pan Macmillan,
a division of Macmillan Publishers Limited

First U.S. Edition: June 2015

10 9 8 7 6 5 4 3 2 1

To my family and friends.
Your support means everything.

NO PLACE TO DIE

After ten years in London, working for a City law firm, Clare Donoghue moved back to her home town in Somerset to undertake an MA in creative writing at Bath Spa University. In 2011 the initial chapters of Clare's debut novel, *Never Look Back*, previously entitled *Chasing Shadows*, were long-listed for the CWA Debut Dagger award. *No Place to Die* is Clare's second book.

You can say hello to Clare on
Twitter @claredonoghue or Facebook
www.facebook.com/claredonoghueauthor

NO PLACE TO DIE

PROLOGUE

Maggie tried to run, but she couldn't feel her feet. Her breath felt warm against her cheeks as each step pushed air out of her lungs. He was behind her. She could smell him: an earthy, feral scent chasing her through a labyrinth of hedges, trees and bare brick. She saw a door up ahead, its red paint peeling away from the doorknob, as if repulsed. As she reached out, it shook, shivered and vanished. She screamed herself awake until she lay panting, her lungs burning.

She arched her back and let out a low groan, expelling the nightmare. Not even a street light penetrated the inky blackness of her room. Her tongue felt swollen and heavy in her mouth. Memories of the previous evening began to flit through her mind like a magic-lantern display. Had she had a lot to drink? She didn't think so. She had been to his house. They had eaten dinner. He had been angry. They had fought. Then nothing: a void. She allowed her muscles to retract and draw her body back into a foetal position as she felt around for the duvet. Her hands felt heavy. Sleep was pulling at her, dragging her back under. She wanted to give in, but she was cold and yet she was sweating, her skin clammy beneath her cotton pyjamas. As she ran her hands over the freezing bed sheet she became conscious of a familiar odour. It was earthy – the smell of her parents' front lawn after the rain. Her heart began to beat faster, a pain spreading and gripping her throat.

This wasn't her bed.

She sat up, staring into the darkness. She reached up and touched her face. Her skin felt cool, slick, alien. 'What?' She turned her head from side to side, but there was no light to soften the darkness. 'I can't see. Please, help me.' She stopped, her chest heaving. Her words sounded muted, almost lost by her leaden tongue. She listened. 'What's happening to me?' Maggie tasted bile. It filled her mouth as adrenaline flooded her system. She tried to stand, but her head struck something solid above her. Her whole body was shaking, her teeth biting down on her tongue. She sat back and reached up, inching her hands higher and higher until they rested against a flat, marble-like surface. She pushed against it: no movement. She snatched her hands down and began rocking back and forth. 'It's all right. It's okay.' She drew her knees up to her chin, put her arms around her shins and held herself. Her head ached as she tried to pull her thoughts into focus. This wasn't real. She was still dreaming. She began to count, slowing her breathing with each number, ignoring the aching in her bones and the slur in her voice.

When her shivering body had settled enough for her to move again, she turned, until she was on her hands and knees in the empty space. God, she hoped it was empty. The counting was helping, but she needed more – she needed to break the silence. She began to sing as she crawled, crab-like, to her right. 'One little elephant came out one day, upon a spider's web to play,' her voice trembled. She closed her eyes and forced out the words, 'He – he had such tremendous fun that he called upon another elephant to come. Two . . . two little elephants came out one day, upon a spider's web to—'

She stopped, her head pulsing in rhythm with her voice as her hip struck something solid. With her palm flat, she crawled forward, running her fingers along the cool surface until she came to one corner, then another, and another, until she reached the fourth: the final wall enclosing her. She leaned closer, her nose pressed against the freezing surface. She took a deep breath. Soil, mud – it was earth, compacted earth, smoothed to a slick finish. 'No, no . . . ' Panic silenced her, like a shard of glass in her throat, tearing at the delicate tissue. An image of a grave flashed into her mind. She began to scream, all rational thought lost.

She screamed until she didn't know if she was screaming at all.

CHAPTER ONE

22nd April – Tuesday

'I know,' she said, waiting for the next line in what was a well-rehearsed piece. 'Yes, Mother, I'm aware of that.' Jane looked at the clock on the bottom right-hand side of her computer screen. 'I agree. I'll call as soon as I leave.' The seconds ticked by. 'Yes, clean ones are in his room.' She resisted the temptation to drum her fingers on the desk. 'That's right, where they're always kept.' Jane could sense other people in the office beginning to tune into her conversation. 'Nothing. There was no tone. Sorry – yes, you're right. I'll be home soon.' Almost there. She hoped. 'Before eight. Yes. Okay. Yes. Good. Thanks, Mum. Bye.'

Detective Sergeant Jane Bennett put the phone back in its cradle, closed her eyes and let her head drop onto her desk with a thud.

Her mother didn't object to looking after Peter. Far from it. She was 'happy to help'. Jane would have the words engraved on her mother's tombstone: 'Celia Bennett, beloved wife, mother and grandmother. "Happy to help".' The image relaxed Jane's shoulders and she smiled. The ten-minute ear-bashing she had just endured was routine. The caveat to her mother's favourite phrase was full entitlement to bitch and moan whenever the mood struck. Jane didn't mind. Her working life didn't allow for routine, something that her son craved. She couldn't be there all the time. So every pick, veiled dig, subtle criticism or direct assault that her mother levelled against her was worth it.

She lifted her head off the desk, using her fingertips to pull her fringe back into place. The heat of the day had all but gone. She turned and pulled her jacket off the back of her chair and slipped it on. Peter would be eight in June. When Jane looked at him she still saw the chubby, red-faced baby who was always hungry. That was before his autism had been diagnosed, before the invisible barrier separating mother and son had been explained. Eight years old. She couldn't believe it. She would have to organize a party, get his friends over. Her mother would help. Jane rolled her eyes. It was an involuntary action, or rather a pre-emptive reaction to what her mother would say. She pushed the power button on her laptop and waited for it to shut down.

One quick meeting with department heads, a briefing with the team and then she should be able to head home. She slipped her laptop into her bag, surveying the files on her desk, deciding what she needed to take home with her. She wanted to be ready the second the briefing was over. Peter had already picked out a book for tonight's bedtime story. A bedtime story that Jane had promised to read to him. Her eyes settled on the most current file on the Stevens case. She shook her head. A serial killer in Lewisham. Five women dead. She couldn't get her head round it. The man responsible was behind bars, had been for two months, but it wasn't over. Not yet.

She still had one girl to find.

The young woman's face had been a shadow, following Jane wherever she went. She picked up the file and two memory sticks and pushed them into her bag. It would take months – years – to erase the images that she and the rest of the team had witnessed. The killer's two-bedroom semi could have been wallpapered with all the photographs found in his home-made darkroom. The majority were shots of his victims, names and faces Jane knew well, but there were a handful of pictures showing girls that no one knew. It was her job to identify and find them, to make sure they had been photographed – and nothing more. Two girls had been found safe and well, but the third? Only time would tell. Jane looked up and spotted her boss, DI Mike Lockyer, walking towards her. He returned her smile, but his pale skin and shadowed eyes didn't match his expression.

'Jane,' he said, resting his arms on the partition that separated her desk from the rest of the open-plan office. 'How are you getting on with the Schofield case?'

'We're pretty much there, sir,' she said, reaching for the corresponding case file on her desk. 'The husband's with the custody sergeant downstairs. I don't think it'll take much to get him to talk.' She watched Lockyer nod, rubbing his eyebrow, his fingers tugging at the skin around his eye. He had lost weight. He had the look of a sheet that had been left in the dryer too long: crumpled.

'Are you leaving him for the morning then?' he asked, no longer looking at her, his eyes no longer engaged.

'Yes, in fact I was going to suggest Chris ran the interview,' she said, putting the file back in its place, straightening the edges with her palms. She could see that he wasn't really interested. In fact he had just about got by doing the bare minimum, since his return to the office three weeks ago.

He was shaking his head, staring across the office. 'I don't think that's appropriate, Jane, do you?' he said. 'Once Schofield's admitted it, maybe; but to send Chris in at this stage – before we know we've got enough evidence to convict, with or without a confession – is just a risk. A risk I'm surprised you're prepared to take, considering the mess the guy made of the wife. Have you even looked at the crime-scene images?'

Jane sat back in her chair. His words didn't bother her, and neither did the disapproval and judgement in his tone. But the look in his eyes made her stop and think about how to respond. She knew he was struggling to come to terms with what had happened on the Stevens case, but what more could she do? He wouldn't talk to her; hadn't talked to her. He hadn't trusted her, and that hurt. More than she was willing to admit. She had always assumed that their relationship went beyond being mere colleagues; that he respected her, considered her a friend. His actions had proved her wrong on both counts. Now he prowled the office like some phantom from a horror movie, his eyes black, empty of reason. Most of the staff had taken tongue-lashings. But Lockyer was the boss. It wasn't unusual to hear his shouts reverberating around south-east London's murder-squad offices. But now he seemed to be going off the deep end about nothing, while overlooking something vital. She had been covering for him for weeks, but his behaviour had not gone unnoticed. Roger, the Senior Investigating Officer for the Lewisham squads, had already pulled Jane into his office and told her to keep an eye on him.

'Not a problem, sir,' she said now, her voice quiet, her words measured. 'I'll take Chris in with me on the initial interview and, if Schofield confesses, I'll let Chris take over, under my direct supervision.' She waited for some kind of response, or at least recognition, but there wasn't any. 'Are you happy for me to do that, sir?'

He shrugged his shoulders. 'It's your case, Jane. Do what you like – you don't need me to babysit you. I don't need the details, just get it done. I've got enough on my plate.' He ran his hands through his hair before dragging them down his face, his sallow skin pulled out of shape by the action. 'I'll see you in the briefing.' With that, he turned and walked back across the room, into his office, closing the glass door behind him. The sun was setting outside his window. He sat motionless, his face silhouetted by the fading light. Jane couldn't take her eyes off him. She wondered how long her boss could subsist on anger and regret.

As she stood to leave, her mobile started to ring. She glanced down at the name on the screen. It was Sue, a fellow copper, albeit a retired one. They hadn't spoken in months. Jane glanced at the clock mounted on one of the pillars in the centre of the open-plan office. It was ten past seven. Peter would be going to bed soon. The ringer on her phone seemed to increase in volume as if it could sense her indecision. 'Oh, all right,' she said, dropping back into her chair. 'Sue, hey. How are you doing?' Silence greeted her. 'Hello,' she said, straining to decipher the muffled sounds coming from the other end of the line. It was then that she heard a sniff. 'Sue, are you okay?'

'It's Mark,' Sue sobbed, more than said, down the phone. 'He's gone.'

Jane felt a flood of relief that she had answered the call, but a tug of guilt that she wasn't going to be reading Peter his bedtime story after all. She might just make it home for lights out. 'Oh, Sue, I'm so sorry. What's happened?' she asked, sitting back in her chair. 'I didn't realize you guys were having problems again.'

'What? No, Jane, it's not that. He's just gone. There's blood, Jane . . . Mark's gone.'

CHAPTER TWO

22nd April – Tuesday

Three hours later Jane was standing in Sue Leech's kitchen, surrounded by terracotta-coloured walls and ceramic wall hangings from trips abroad. Worktops lined the room, but there wasn't an inch of space. Every surface was covered in ornaments, numerous glass paperweights, cookery books, sunglasses, paperbacks and drawings by the children. There were two noticeboards on the wall opposite the fridge overflowing with scraps of paper, receipts and more drawings, all held in place by a few coloured pins. In the centre of the room was a large pine dining table with six wheelback chairs. On any other day Sue's kitchen would have been a perfect representation of a bustling family home.

The forensic team was working in the utility room.

Initial testing had revealed extensive blood-spatters on one wall. Scene-of-crime lights seemed to illuminate the entire rear of the house, as well as half the garden. Jane could see Mark's herb garden, just beyond a small patio. It was his pride and joy, but somehow it looked spoiled by the glow cast over it. Whether the blood found was his remained to be seen. The lab had a major backlog from a gang-related incident that had happened over the Easter weekend. Three young lads had lost their lives, and another four had been injured. The side-street in Camberwell where it all happened was still a mess. Baseball-bats-versus-machetes was never going to be a fair fight. Jane turned away from the harsh spotlights and refocused her attention on her friend.

Sue was sitting at the kitchen table answering questions in a monotone. She had lost weight since Jane had last seen her. The grey jumper she was wearing hung off her frame, her slim-fit blue jeans no longer tight. Her face looked gaunt, framed by an unkempt greying bob. Her appearance was understandable, given the circumstances, but Jane couldn't help wondering what else was going on in Sue's life. She looked like a woman who had been under a considerable amount of stress for months, not hours. The constable conducting the interview was a new recruit to the Missing Persons team and couldn't have been more than twenty-two. She looked pained to be at the centre of such emotional turmoil. She kept reaching over and touching Sue's arm. The gesture showed a vulnerability that Jane wasn't accustomed to witnessing from her own, more seasoned team. The majority of the DCs and DSs in the murder squad had been recruited by Lockyer – herself included. His position was clear: allowing personal feelings into a case clouded your judgement and led to mistakes. Not that he had observed his own rules. His behaviour on the Stevens case had made him a poster child in Lewisham nick for 'what not to do'.

The sound of the young constable's voice brought Jane's thoughts back into focus.

'When did you arrive home?' the constable asked.

'Today, about six-fifteen,' Sue said. 'We spoke last night, Mark and I, about what time me and the kids would be home – what we should have for tea. He was going to cook a lasagne.'

Jane replayed her own conversation with Sue when she had arrived at the house in Bromley three hours ago. On the drive over from Lewisham she had run through as many scenarios as she could think of, trying to find an explanation for Mark's disappearance. In Catford, with the dregs of the rush-hour traffic slowing her progress and horns blaring, she had toyed with the idea that Mark might be having some kind of mid-life crisis, arriving home with a new haircut and a Porsche. She had dismissed the idea as stereotypical and stupid. Mark was an ex-copper: 'rational' was his middle name. As she had passed Beckenham Hill and negotiated her way around a three-car shunt, she had thought about the obvious scenario: that Mark had found someone else. Again, it hadn't felt right. Mark and Sue had been together for thirty . . . thirty-five years. They had met on the force in their early twenties, married within two years and then spent the next fifteen working their way up in their respective departments. Thomas, their eldest son, had been born on Sue's fortieth birthday, and George had arrived two years later. By the time Jane passed Millwall training ground she was running out of ideas. She knew that Mark had suffered from anxiety attacks since his retirement from the force five years ago. The transition from a detective chief inspector in the murder squad to stay-at-home dad and retiree had been tough. Sue had told Jane on several occasions that Mark felt redundant – without focus, emasculated somehow. She rubbed her eyes, resisting the urge to shake her head.

From the second Jane had crossed the threshold into Sue and Mark's home she had known something was wrong. Despite the welcoming lights in the hallway, the plush Persian rug beneath her feet and the warm honey-coloured walls, there had been something ominous, a coldness. She thought about the blood in the utility room. Was it possible that Mark's mental state was worse than Jane, or even Sue, had realized? Could this be a suicide? Sue's eyes told her that the same thought had more than crossed her mind. It was a potential reality that seemed to be crushing the very breath out of her. Jane had pulled out a chair, sat down and taken her friend's hand. 'We'll find him, Sue,' she'd said, surprised by the assurance in her tone.

'Can you take me through what happened after you arrived home, Mrs Leech?' the constable asked, giving Jane a nod. She recognized the gesture from her own experience as a fresh-faced recruit. It was a silent thank-you from a young DC who felt way out of her depth.

Sue took a deep, shuddering breath. 'Thomas and George went straight upstairs to play on their Xbox and I came into the kitchen, made a pot of tea and opened my mail.' She gestured to a pile of half-opened post on the table.

The constable scribbled in her notepad, nodding. 'And did you notice anything out of place, out of the ordinary?'

Jane watched as Sue looked up at the ceiling, as if searching for information. 'No, not really,' she said, squeezing Jane's hand. 'The boys called out when we first came in and, when Mark didn't respond, I just thought . . . I can't remember what I thought, but I wasn't concerned. I guess I just assumed he was in his shed or out at the shops.' A single tear rolled down Sue's cheek and came to rest at the edge of her lips.

'I know this is difficult, Mrs Leech, but anything you can tell us will help.'

The reference to 'us' didn't escape Jane's notice. Part of her was tempted to intervene, give the girl a break and push on to the more salient information, but she resisted. The constable was right. Even the most insignificant detail could be crucial in cases of disappearance. Given the evidence in the utility room, treating this like a standard 'missing person' seemed ludicrous.

'It's all right,' Sue said, her tone almost soothing. She had been a senior DI before her retirement, working in the family unit. Cases like this would be all too familiar, but no amount of experience could help when it involved your own family. Jane knew that she herself would be a wreck if anything happened to Peter, but despite Sue's tears there was a calmness to her demeanour that Jane couldn't help but admire.

'At what time, approximately, do you think you entered the utility room?'

'About six-thirty,' Sue said, looking down at her hands. 'The cat needed feeding, and I wanted to put the boys' football kit on to wash. That's when I saw the blood on the floor.'

'What made you think the substance was blood, Mrs Leech?' the constable asked, her pen poised over her notebook.

'I'm a retired police officer, not to mention a mother. It's a familiar site in a house full of boys.' The carefree comment seemed to catch her by surprise. Jane could almost feel the atmosphere shift in the room, as if the normality of Sue's words had disturbed some negative ether surrounding them. 'I just knew it was blood.'

'Could you describe it, Sue?' Jane asked, before she could stop herself.

'It was about the size of a ten-pence piece,' Sue said, holding up her thumb and forefinger to demonstrate. 'It was to the left of the doormat. I was bending down to put the boys' clothes into the machine. At first I thought it might be from one of the boys: a nose-bleed, or Mark had cut himself in the garden, but there was something – I don't know what – there was just something about it that scared me. I didn't even notice the marks on the wall until you guys got here.'

Jane turned to look at the doorway to the utility room. There seemed to be a constant murmur from the SOCOs as they photographed and documented the scene. She wondered what she would have thought in the same situation. Sue wasn't prone to panic, any more than Jane was. The job gave you gut instincts. Time and experience taught you how to interpret them. If Sue felt frightened when she saw the coin-shaped drop of blood, it was because somewhere deep inside she already knew what was to come.

Jane listened as the constable changed tack with her questions, steering Sue back to the more mundane aspects of her discovery. It would be a technique she had been taught, to keep the witness talking, to keep them calm. Jane waited for Sue to respond, before standing and walking over to the utility room where all the activity was centred. She leaned into the small side-room.

It was no more than eight foot by six. She stared at the nearside wall, above the peninsula where the washing machine and tumble dryer were kept. It looked as if someone had loaded a paintbrush with red paint, flicked it at the wall and then tried, in vain, to wipe it off. The result was numerous brownish smears. There were a few spots on the countertop, but the concentration of the staining was on the wall. As Jane looked, she wondered again about Mark's mental state. Sue and the boys had been to Sue's parents for the Easter weekend. They had only arrived back tonight, which meant that Sue must have taken the boys out of school for the extra day. Mark had chosen to stay home. Why? Sue hadn't said. Could the amount of blood fit with a suicide? She shook her head. Mark was an ex-copper. He would have been to his fair share of suicides over the years. They were, without exception, horrendous. Not because of the body; the blood, vomit, faeces and urine. That was expected, part of the job. It was because of the face of the wife, mother, child, brother or whoever had been unlucky enough to discover the body. Jane couldn't imagine Mark doing that to Sue or his boys. But it might explain why the blood had been washed off.

She walked further into the room so that she could look at the wall face-on. She closed her eyes and imagined Mark standing next to the peninsula, maybe even leaning on it, cutting into his own flesh, testing the sharpness of the blade. Most suicide victims showed evidence of numerous cuts: nerves, uncertainty about the pain or how deep they needed to go made practice incisions common. If Mark had thrown his arm out, in shock at the pain or the resultant bleeding, he might have created a blood-spatter consistent with what Jane was looking at. It was possible.

'We're almost done in here, Jane,' one of the Scene of Crime Officers said. It was difficult to tell exactly who was who on the SOCO team, when they were working on-scene. They were in the full get-up: hooded white paper suits, boots and face-masks. One of the team flicked off the lights and turned on the four UV lamps positioned at each corner of the room. The smears of blood on the wall were unmistakable. They stood out like black scratches across the paintwork.

Sue's sobs dragged Jane from her thoughts. She walked out of the utility room. Sue was sitting alone at the kitchen table now, crying into her hands. Thomas and George had been taken back to Sue's parents. Thomas was thirteen, George only eleven. They were both too young to see this – too young to support their mother or be exposed to this amount of grief. Jane thought about Peter. She had missed putting him to bed this evening, like so many other evenings. Then she thought about Lockyer. She needed to call him, to let him know what was happening. Since Sue's call, Jane had only been able to brief him with the bare essentials. Mark and Lockyer were close, or had been, and given his current demeanour she knew Lockyer wouldn't let up until Mark was found.

She let her head fall back, relishing the pinch as her neck muscles pushed against her tired shoulders. It was then that she realized she wanted the blood to be Mark's. She wanted his wounds to be self-inflicted. She was trying to force a suicide to fit the scene in front of her because the alternative was worse, much worse.

CHAPTER THREE

22nd April – Tuesday

I can't feel my legs. The numbness is spreading.

At first it was just my feet. I reached down with cold fingers, stroking the soles, pinching my toes, but I felt nothing. It was like touching someone else's freezing flesh. Even now the thought makes me shudder. I don't know how long I have been here, but at the beginning – at the start of this nightmare – I would have given anything not to be alone. I screamed and cried out, hoping to hear an answer. Someone else in the dark with me. Someone to save me. But there is no one. I am alone. I don't cry any more. There isn't enough moisture left in my body to create tears. I'm empty.

I curl up in a ball, reach down and run my hand over my left thigh. Nothing. I try the other leg. No feeling at all. Death is leaching under my skin, sliding into my bones, slithering up towards my heart. I roll my head back and forth on the hard ground. Coloured lights dance behind my eyelids. I think about my routine. Routine – it feels like an alien word down here, but it is the only thing I have to stop the madness. Before the numbness started I would crawl back and forth, my hands searching every inch of the space, touching the smooth mud, feeling for any inconsistency. I know the layout of my tomb better than I know my own face. The thought comforts me, though I don't know why. I have tried to dig my way out. I dug until my fingers ran with blood. To know you are bleeding, without being able to see. A sensory game I am unaccustomed to playing. The pain familiar, but dulled by the cold. The smell metallic and sweet. The sensation as the slick warmth bathes my hands, dripping onto the floor of the space. There is no way out.

I sleep, but there is no rest. Hours, or maybe days, ago I awoke to find I couldn't crawl any more. I couldn't move. My body had become a dead weight, pinning me down. I wailed and pleaded with the darkness. My routine was gone. Without it, madness would return and envelop me. As I rocked myself, I pushed my tired mind to find another escape, another regime I could follow. The numbness has been my answer. I use it to mark the time. Like the hours on a clock, it creeps inch by inch over my body.

My time is running out. I can see the hourglass in my head. I can visualize each and every grain of sand dropping through the centre, as if in slow motion. Each grain is a nerve ending, an electron, a neuron – a basic-level gene that makes up my life. It is pouring away faster and faster. I remember my bed. I can almost feel the warmth of my duvet, thick and heavy on top of me. It's pulled up over my head, my breath heating my face. I know I should get up. I know I need to get on, keep living, but the heat keeps me there, fixes me to the spot. I feel *a pain in my stomach, dull and cramping. It travels up to my chest, squeezing my lungs.*

The numbness is spreading.

CHAPTER FOUR

23rd April – Wednesday

Jane stared across the open-plan office at Lockyer. He was hunched over his desk studying something on his laptop. He hadn't spoken all morning, not since she had told him about Mark's disappearance. She had prepared herself for a barrage of questions, but instead he listened and nodded, before returning to his bubble of apathy. He didn't even react when she told him that the DNA results on the blood wouldn't be back until Friday, at the earliest. 'You'll just have to be patient,' he had said in a monotone. Patience – a word no one in this office would associate with Lockyer, let alone hear him say aloud. She shook her head and put her hands over her ears, trying to block out the revving of engines and car horns invading the office from Lewisham High Street. She wasn't sure she had the capacity to be patient as well as dealing with her caseload, her boss's bad attitude and the constant noise of Lewisham traffic.

She turned in her chair and looked out of the window. The station car park was the only view that greeted her: police vans and squad cars lined up in precision-spaced rows. The sun bounced off the windscreens, creating disco-ball patterns over the expanse of concrete. It wasn't a green field with oak trees swaying in the breeze or an ocean view, but, like a lot of other things, she was stuck with it and it could be worse. She rubbed her eyes, remembering too late that she was wearing mascara. She peered into her computer screen and attempted to wipe away the black smudges on her cheeks. She felt like crying. There was still no movement on the missing girl from the Stevens case. The girl whose photograph Jane had memorized, though not from choice. Missing Persons were yet to come back with anything, and no one had called in after the press release. Cases were piling up around her: half-started, half-finished, half-arsed. She slumped in her chair and spun back around and resumed checking her emails. When she saw one from Lockyer, she pressed 'Delete' without thinking. He had withheld evidence relating to his brother – evidence that might have a serious impact on the Stevens case. That was bad enough, but it was the brother part that really stung. All the years they had known each other, worked side by side, Lockyer had never even told her he had a brother, let alone that he was autistic, like Peter. Didn't he trust her? Her phone started ringing.

'DS Bennett,' she said, snatching up the receiver.

'Hi, Jane, it's Dixie. I'm working the front desk today and wondered . . . ' There was a pause. 'I wanted to see if . . . Are you dealing with Mark Leech's disappearance?'

Jane sat back and pushed her fringe off her forehead. 'Well, officially it's not a disappearance yet, Dix,' she said, 'but I guess the jungle drums are working. What can I do for you?' This was the first call about Mark, but given how long he had worked in Lewisham, Jane knew it would be the first of many. In fact she was surprised it had taken this long for word to get around.

'A call just came through. I thought it might be . . . relevant.'

'Hang on,' Jane said, reaching across her desk and snagging a pad and pen. 'Go on.'

'Derek Small, phone number: zero, double seven, three, nine . . . four, one, three, six, seven, eight. He lives at the southern end of Elmstead Woods. He's found a trainer – brand unknown – in the woods. He thinks there might be blood on it.'

Jane noted down what Dixie was saying. 'Right. Anything else?' She wanted to ask why this would be of interest to her, but sensed that Dix had more to say.

'I told Mr Small to leave the item where it was and that an officer would be in touch. His dog picked it up, tried to take it home apparently, so Mr Small can't be positive where in the woods the shoe was. Anyway he's gone home now, but he said he's happy to come back out whenever we can get a squad car over there.' Dixie paused, it seemed, for Jane to say something, but what could she say? A call-out about an unidentified trainer – blood or no blood – was a bit beneath Jane's rank. 'Anyway, I know you're probably wondering why I'm bothering you with this,' she said, as if Jane had spoken aloud, 'but I just thought you ought to know that . . . I thought you might not know that Mark used to walk his dog in Elmstead Woods. He went there a lot. I mean, it would be a while ago now, as Barney died a few years back, but . . . I'm sorry, you must think I'm nuts. Mark was so good to me when Jason was ill. I wanted to help, if I could?'

Jane took a deep breath and looked down at her pad. She had doodled crazy S-shapes all around Mr Small's name and phone number. 'It's fine, Dix, I understand. I'll get a car sent over there.' She paused. 'I'll let you know if anything comes of it.' She listened to Dixie apologize several more times, before hanging up and dialling through to Despatch. She relayed all the information and was about to hang up when the officer stopped her.

'Actually, looking at the system, we've just had another call relating to Elmstead Woods,' he said.

'About the shoe?'

'No. A caller – no name given – phoned in to say that a man . . . Hang on a second, let me get into the full phone log.' Jane waited, drawing her pad closer to her, with her pen poised. 'That's right. A man, mid- to late fifties, dark hair, well built, about six foot, was hanging around the park and, quote, "walking funny"; seemed to be, and again I quote, "injured",' the officer said, with an air of disinterest. Jane figured he was angling for her to take both calls off the sheet. An image of Mark flashed into her mind. He wasn't far off six foot. His hair was dark; thinning, but still dark. And he was certainly well built.

'Assign the call to me,' she said, logging on to her computer. 'Email me the full sheet and I'll deal with both calls.'

'Doing it now,' he said without hesitation.

As she hung up the email pinged into her system. She opened it, pressed 'Print', pushed away from her desk and walked over to the printer. Until the DNA came back from the Leech house, Mark's case would be in limbo between her and Missing Persons. She could waste days waiting, or she could follow up on the calls. There would probably be some grumbles from the MISPER contingent, but Jane could handle that. If two unconnected calls did, in fact, relate to Mark, then any aggro would be worth it. She went back to her desk, filled in a decision log, shut her laptop and headed for Lockyer's office.

As she approached she wondered whether it was worth disturbing him. He was in the same position, but his eyes were closed. He could be thinking, but Jane was pretty sure he was sleeping, sitting up, in his office, in the middle of the day. 'Sir?' she said, hoping the rest of the office hadn't noticed Lockyer resting his eyes. He stirred and then jolted awake, his arm jerking, scattering paperwork all over the floor. 'Sir,' she said again, trying to act as if nothing had happened. 'Despatch have had a couple of calls about Elmstead Woods. Old guy's dog found a shoe, possible blood-splatter. Another caller saw a man who seemed to be unsteady on his feet, possibly injured. Thought I might head down there and check it out . . . just in case. Description sounds a bit like Mark. He used to walk his dog there, apparently.' She finished and looked at Lockyer, who was staring back at her. 'Tenuous, I know, sir,' she said, feeling a blush start at the base of her neck. 'But I think it's worth a look.' She tried to put as much confidence into her last statement as she could muster. He didn't look impressed but then he didn't look unimpressed, either. He just looked.

'Want some company?' was all he said.

'Sure,' she said, restraining the shrug in her shoulders. 'I mean, yes, sir. Thank you.'

CHAPTER FIVE

23rd April – Wednesday

Jane stepped over a fallen branch and followed the line of officers in front of her. Twenty of the outdoor unit were walking, a few feet apart, their heads bent, each wearing an all-in-one, white disposable suit. They had been searching Elmstead Woods for the past four hours, but so far had found nothing. Nothing but the bloodied trainer. It belonged to Mark. His name was written in black felt-tip pen inside the heel. A remnant from his days on the force, before anyone bothered with lockers for their personal items. She looked over the officers' heads at Grove Park Cemetery. It was only twenty yards away: lines of headstones nestled in the grass. What were the chances that today's search would end with a cemetery and a grieving family? She fell into step with the final officer in the line.

The indoor unit was at the station in Lewisham, trying to piece together a timeline to establish how Mark might have ended up in Elmstead Woods – or at least how his trainer had. Eighty per cent of the woods had already been searched, although it was difficult. The undergrowth was thick and overgrown. Finding anything in such a wilderness was going to be difficult. She pushed a stone over with her heel. It felt odd to be surrounded by grass and trees, rather than concrete and a plethora of takeaway shops, like the ones that lined Lewisham High Street. She tipped her head back and let the waning sun warm her face.

She tried again to imagine Mark taking his own life. It wasn't unusual for people to return to a familiar place. The fact that Elmstead was an old haunt – a place Mark used to come to when he was still on the force – could have a bearing on his motivation. It wouldn't be the first time an officer, retired or not, hadn't been able to cope with the pressures of the job. Some cases ate you up and spat you out. For the most part you had to suck it up and move on, but some officers weren't that lucky. Jane had already taken a look in the archives at some of Mark's old cases. A couple stood out. There was a house fire in Peckham: a mother and three children had died in the blaze; a fourth child, aged ten, had been left badly burned. Mark arrested the father, Stanley Pike, after his fingerprints were found on two oil canisters. The canisters had been thrown in a skip two streets away, but the case fell apart during the trial. The defence was able to prove that the chain of evidence relating to the oil canisters had been compromised. Mark and his team were publicly reprimanded for the error and it delayed his promotion by two years. The other case was one that Mark handled a year before his retirement. The victim was a young girl, Amelia Reynolds. She was raped, beaten and then strangled, before her body was dumped in an allotment shed. She wasn't found for two weeks. The evidence trail was non-existent. Her killer was never found.

Jane remembered both cases. The first because Lockyer had told her about it on a number of occasions, and the second because she had been in the unit at the time. Both cases were traumatic. Both could have affected Mark's emotional state – along with many others, she was sure – although she still didn't believe it. She ran her hands through her hair and closed her eyes. It didn't matter how she looked at it. Suicide just didn't feel right.

She walked away from the line-up and leaned her back against a tree. As she pushed her fingers into the base of her spine she wondered when spring had been replaced by summer. The Easter weekend had been a blur. Her mother and father had taken Peter on an Easter-egg hunt over in Blackheath on bank-holiday Monday. Jane remembered cooking roast lamb with all the trimmings, but she couldn't recall eating it. She had been working flat out for so long that even the seasons were passing her by. As she moved her head from side to side the sun heated her face. Peter loved sunshine. As soon as the sun shone he would be out in their tiny back garden, sitting cross-legged on the lawn, running his hands back and forth over the blades of grass, as if hypnotized. It was the warmest April that Jane could remember. Her shirt was sticking to her back beneath her light jacket. She listened to the murmurs of the team as they talked back and forth. She wondered if they felt out of place in such a rural setting. She listened as they joked and laughed, taking the mick out of Ashford, who seemed to be today's target. It broke the tension, helped them to concentrate. Jane understood that. As long as the press weren't watching, she didn't mind. How the murder squad's presence there had been kept quiet this long was a miracle. Mind you, while they were just searching, there wasn't much to see; but if, and when, a white tent was erected, every journalist within a fifty-mile radius would sniff them out and be camped out for the duration, their zoom lenses invading every inch of the investigation.

'Boss?'

She turned as Chris, one of the team's younger DCs, waved her over.

'What have you got, Chris?' Jane asked, pushing herself away from the tree trunk and walking towards him.

'We've got some electrical wire, boss,' Chris said, pointing a gloved finger at two lengths of black cable resting amongst the grass and leaves.

'Okay. Track it and see where it goes,' she said.

'Hold up.' Chris shouted to the rest of the team. A shuffling noise drifted through the air as twenty paper suits rustled to a stop. Jane watched as Chris passed the wires to the officer next to him, who then passed them on to the next officer and the next, each pulling gently to release the wires from the soft earth. 'It's partially buried,' Chris said, 'but not that well. Might just have been dropped here and sunk in over time.'

'See where it ends,' she said, looking over Chris's head to see where Lockyer had secreted himself now. He hadn't said a word in the car on the drive over. Not even the traffic on the South Circular had penetrated his stupor. People had cut in front of them more than once, but Lockyer had just stared out of the window, as if he couldn't see or hear the shouts of the frustrated commuters.

'Boss.' Chris called. 'Take a look at this.'

She turned and walked along the line of officers. 'So, what have we got?' she asked.

'These sections appear to go underground,' Chris said, with a shrug of his shoulders, 'but the other end was free. One wire has an AV receptor, and the other isn't a cable at all. It's a tube – polyethylene, I'd guess – about a quarter-inch wide.'

Jane took a pair of gloves from her jacket pocket and pulled them on. She stepped forward and Chris handed her the wire and the tubing. She pulled both, but there was no give. She thought for a moment, trying to decide how much time the cable and tube warranted. 'Chris, can you give Natasha a call, over at the SOCOs' office, and see if they can bring down the GPR?' Chris nodded in response and made a quick note on his report pad. The GPR was a ground-penetrating radar they sometimes used to locate clandestine graves or buried evidence. It should be able to pick up the wire and track it to its source. 'Leave this for now – move on,' she said to the rest of the team, who obliged by dispersing, bowing their heads and resuming their shuffled walks, moving forward in unison. It was then that she spotted Lockyer.

He was standing with the perimeter officer. He wasn't talking, just staring into space. This was getting beyond a joke. She walked over to join them. Lockyer took a step back.

'How's it going?' he asked.

'Nothing so far, sir,' she said, trying to catch his eye, to see if he was really listening. 'We've found a wire with an AV receptor and some hollow tubing. I've asked Chris to get the

GPR down here. It might turn out to be nothing – fly-tipping – but we have to check, don't you think?'

'Sure,' Lockyer said, 'anything else?'

Well, at least that confirmed what Jane suspected: that her boss was barely listening to a word she said, let alone computing the information. 'No, sir,' she said with a sigh. They both turned in unison, and in silence watched the team making their way slowly towards them. 'Sir,' Jane said, searching for the right words. 'It's not looking good.' If she expected some emotion, some clue as to how Lockyer felt about his friend's disappearance, she was wasting her time. He just shrugged his shoulders and continued to stare off into the distance. 'Sir, are you all right?' Even as the question left her lips it seemed ludicrous. 'We haven't really had chance to talk properly, since you . . . since you've been back in the office.'

Lockyer turned to look at her, his eyes finally meeting hers. Jane found herself wanting to look away. There was so much pain there. What was she meant to say now? She had asked the question, but now she didn't know what to do next. He was her superior. This wasn't, and had never been, how their working relationship functioned. Without realizing it, she was seeing his face the night after they had slept together. His haunted expression the next morning had both attracted and repulsed her. She had spent years keeping her life as simple as possible. No boyfriends, no lovers beyond a few weeks – nothing that could potentially distract her from Peter or the job. In those brief seconds she had envisioned a different kind of relationship with Lockyer, and it had frightened her. She felt that same fear now. He was standing in front of her, his face open, his grief hers for the taking. But she didn't want it. He seemed to sense her discomfort and turned away. Jane felt the weight of her cowardice settle on her shoulders.

Forty-five minutes later Jane was looking at the screen of the GPR machine, her brow creased, her head cocked to one side. Lockyer was standing behind her, his face unreadable. 'What is it?' she asked Jared, the SOCO who had brought the equipment down from headquarters.

'It's an underground space – a cave of some sort.'

Jane moved her head to block out the sun and squinted at the screen, trying to see the lines: the edges of whatever lay no more than a yard or so beneath the ground. 'Natural?' she asked.

'No,' Jared said, shaking his head. 'Look at the edges here and here,' he said, pointing to two black lines on the screen. 'It's been excavated . . . shaped. It's been done well. There's nothing supporting the roof, no struts of any kind that I can make out. The pressure from the compacted earth is all that's keeping the structure intact.' He sounded impressed.

'And the cables?' Jane asked.

'There,' Jared said, pointing to two tiny dots on the screen. 'They both end at the point of entry to the area. Here,' he went on, using a pencil to indicate two small dots, one slightly larger than the other.

'What's that?' she asked, pointing to a shadow to the left of the screen.

'Hang on. I need to move the sensor – it's almost out of range,' Jared replied, already unplugging leads and shifting

the machine a few feet to the left. Jane felt Lockyer step back.
'Here,' Jared said, 'look at this.'

'Oh God.' she said, her heart thudding harder in her chest, her pulse loud in her ears.

'It's a body,' Jared said, his voice hollow.

CHAPTER SIX

Jane stood in the shower, debating how long she could delay getting out. She had managed to stay in a warm bubble since 5 a.m., when her alarm had woken her. In a semi-conscious state, curtains still drawn, she had tiptoed around the house in her fleecy dressing gown, making tea and toast in a daze. Peter was still out for the count. He didn't stir when she kissed his warm forehead. She wouldn't be here when he woke up. It was becoming a bit too familiar: seeing her son only when he was sleeping. Her mother was snoring in the spare room. Jane would see how the day turned out, before asking her to stay another night.

She closed her eyes and turned up the temperature of the shower. As she soaped her body she couldn't help but notice the differences she felt. Time and a crappy diet of late were taking their toll on her skin. Her breasts sagged more than she remembered. She would be forty soon. Well, not soon, but she was closer to forty than thirty, and the thought of middle age terrified her. She didn't want grey hair, bad eyesight and wrinkles – or, in truth, more wrinkles. A line from a film came into her head as she covered her face with a flannel: 'Time marches on, honey, and eventually it marches right across your face.' The water was beginning to cool. The tank was almost empty. If she stayed there any longer, the pipes would start to wheeze and cough, filling the system with air. She hung the flannel over the soap dish and turned off the shower.

As she stepped out, a chill raced over her skin. She wrapped her dressing gown around her and opened the door to the bathroom. The sun was making its way across the landing. She tiptoed into her bedroom and over to her wardrobe. Everything in her bedroom was white. Her own piece of New England in Lewisham. Ikea's clever marketing seemed to mock her, wherever she looked. The store in Croydon was too close. A quick trip to stock up on pillar candles and nightlights for a pound turned into a battle to find the last Hogbo mattress in their labyrinth-like warehouse. She picked out her most user-friendly outfit from the array of black, grey and brown in front of her. A silk camisole, a pale-blue shirt and a pair of tan trousers. Today wasn't a skirt day.

Once she was dressed, she took her jacket off the hook on the back of her bedroom door and padded down the stairs and into the kitchen. She kept all of her make-up and hair stuff downstairs. It aided a quick getaway, but it also meant she didn't have to sit in her room in silence for any longer than was necessary. Late nights on the job had never bothered her, but the early mornings still grated. To be awake and active when half of London was still sleeping just felt wrong. It was an eerie time of day, as if some great disaster had wiped out the population and she was alone. Lewisham was either too loud or too quiet. There was no happy medium, it seemed.

She flicked on the radio to break the silence; banging pop music filled the room. She shook her head, turned it off and opened her make-up cupboard. There was a mirror stuck to the inside of the door, not that Jane needed it. With practised movements she applied moisturizer, concealer under her eyes and foundation over her face and neck. A swipe of pinkish lipstick and a brush of bronzer and she was done. She glanced at her handiwork. She didn't look much different. With her paddle-brush she pulled her dark bob into some semblance of order, and tried in vain to get her fringe to stay down. She shrugged into her jacket, picked her keys out of the bowl that Peter had labelled 'Keys' and walked to the front door. She debated about her windbreaker for a second, before shoving it under her arm and sneaking out into the morning sunshine. As she climbed into her car she looked up at Peter's bedroom, his X-Men curtains still drawn. This was probably the best she was going to feel all day.

Jane stamped her feet, trying to encourage blood into her toes. She had been standing in the same spot for over an hour, watching the excavation team. The sun was out. It was hot and clear, only the jet-streams of passing aircraft breaking up the expanse of blue sky. She had left her jacket and windbreaker in the car. If only she had brought her sunglasses with her. She could see them now, on her kitchen counter in a bowl labelled 'Glasses'. Peter liked his bowls.

It had taken the excavation team two hours just to decide where to start the dig. They had been on site since six-thirty.

There had been lots of talking and nodding, but very little action, which further convinced Jane that her decision had been right. Once Jared had confirmed no signs of life with the GPR last night, she had postponed the dig until this morning. The thought of trying to manage all of this at night, blinded by dozens of floodlights and observed by London's press contingent, had not appealed. At least this way everyone had been able to get a good night's sleep. It was going to be a very long day – of that Jane was in no doubt.

A twelve-foot-square area had been cordoned off, screens put up, a white tent erected waiting to be put in position, another fingertip search completed and pictures taken. Only then had the team begun the excavation of an entrance hole. As she walked into the cover of the trees she thought about all the evidence that would have been lost already. Yesterday's search, walkers – in fact anyone who had visited Elmstead Woods in the past few days – would have disturbed fibres, footprints and any evidence relating to the underground cave, or tomb, as it had turned out to be. A camera flash caught her eye. The press were here. She counted four, then five lenses pointed her way. She turned her back.

'It'll be about five or ten minutes, boss,' Chris called, from his position next to the hole.

'Great,' she said, shifting from foot to foot, before rocking back and forth on her heels. She caught sight of Dave. He was attending as the on-site pathologist. She waved him over to join her. 'They'll be ready soon,' she said when he was within earshot.

'About time,' Dave replied, taking up position beside her. 'I see we have an audience,' he said, motioning towards the photographers.

'Of course,' she said with a shrug. 'We were lucky to keep it quiet this long. I'll no doubt be wanting their help anyway – depending on what we find down there.'

Dave ran his hand over his chin. 'Yeah, but I didn't even have time to shave this morning.'

'I wouldn't worry about it. They're not looking at you,' she said, gesturing towards the tent. 'They're only interested in what that tent's going to be hiding. Besides, I think the stubble suits you. You look George Clooney-esque.'

He turned his back and coughed out a laugh. 'You're a terrible liar.'

Jane smiled and nudged his arm. He was right. Dave was the senior pathologist for Southwark. His district included the boroughs of Greenwich, Lambeth and Lewisham. His work was his life, and it was etched on his face. He was also one of Lockyer's closest friends. She wondered if it was worth speaking to Dave, to see if he could offer any insight into her boss's erratic behaviour. She opened her mouth, but then changed her mind. Now wasn't the time. She had enough to deal with, without bringing him into the mix. She looked at her watch.

The body looked small, from the GPR readings, possibly female. Jane couldn't help feeling relieved. Mark was five foot eleven, and built like a rugby player, so unless he had shrunk and lost four stone, there was no way the body beneath Elmstead Woods was his. She looked around her, at the plethora of police officers and equipment cluttering the scene. Mark's trainer had been found fifty yards from the burial site. Could that be a coincidence? She took a deep breath and blew it out again. Whoever was in that tomb required her attention now. Mark's disappearance would have to wait.

'What state do you think the body will be in, Dave?' she asked, trying to pull her shirt collar away from the back of her neck. It had to be over twenty degrees today, she thought, as a bead of sweat rolled down her spine.

'Hard to say for sure,' Dave said. 'It appears to be three or four yards down. That will limit the insect life. The temperature, and the lack of moisture, will mean the body won't have decomposed, according to Casper's.' He scratched his head, the sound of his nails against his skin making Jane wince. She hated that sound.

'Right, access to air in relation to decomposition. It's when . . . ' She faltered to a stop. The page of a textbook appeared in her mind, but she couldn't recall much past the first sentence.

Dave cleared his throat. 'That's right,' he said, 'when there is free access to air, a body decomposes twice as fast than if immersed in water, and eight times faster than if buried in earth. So in this case, beneath several yards of dryish earth, we might not find much evidence of decomposition at all. I don't think we're much past the fresh stage,' he said. Terms like 'putrefaction', 'microbial proliferation' and 'anaerobic organisms' sprang into Jane's mind. 'The body looks intact – very little blurring on the GPR monitor. If we were past the fresh stage and into bloating, the gases released, putrefaction of the organs et cetera would mean enough liquid to sustain a tranche of organic life. Once they're present, things move much more quickly and the images we're seeing would look very different.'

Jane nodded. Forensics and pathology were both fields she had considered when she first joined the force. In fact, listening to Dave, she couldn't quite recall what had led her to the murder squad. Dave's job was far more technical and analytical. Far more in tune with her personality.

'Okay, boss,' Chris said, waving them over. 'We're in, just collecting and dispersing any gases.'

Jane walked forward, stepped over some equipment and stared down into the entrance hole. She couldn't see anything. It was too dark. 'Any sign of the original entrance?' she asked.

'Yes. It's at the north end of the structure,' Chris said. 'It hasn't been disturbed by the excavation. Once you're done, the team will continue on and uncover it. You be able to see it when you're down there. There's a hatch, two feet square. SOCO have marked it out for you. There's no handle or hinges on the inside. The entranceway itself was filled in with earth.' Chris scratched his head, and even on a younger scalp the sound still made Jane's shoulders tense. 'None of us even noticed it on the fingertip searches,' he said.

'Right. Thanks, Chris,' she said. 'We're ready when you are.' She turned back and looked at Dave. 'I'm not really looking forward to going down there,' she whispered, a small shiver running down her spine, cooling her skin.

'Ah, here she is,' Dave said, pointing to a petite woman walking towards them. Jane thought her own five-foot five-inch frame was small, but this woman was tiny. She didn't look much over five feet. She could see the woman's scalp. She needed to get her roots done.

'Good afternoon, David. How are you keeping?' the woman asked, not so much shaking Dave's hand as holding it, before turning her attention to Jane. She had a soft Irish accent.

'Hi, Jeanie, I'm not too bad at all. It's been a while since I've had the pleasure of your company,' Dave said, a huge smile on his face. 'Dr Jeanie Crown, this is Detective Sergeant Jane Bennett. She's running the scene.' Jane took the proffered hand, not surprised when her own engulfed the woman's tiny fingers. Jeanie reminded her of a young Jodie Foster, before *Silence of the Lambs*, but after *Bugsy Malone*.

'It's a pleasure to finally meet you, Detective,' Jeanie said, shaking her hand with a firm grip. 'Dave's told me so much about you. He's quite the fan, it seems.'

'Of course, and why not. Jane here is one of the murder squad's biggest and brightest,' Dave said, giving Jane a playful punch. She felt touched by his unabashed praise. If it wasn't so hot, she might have blushed. 'I called Jeanie in when I got the call,' Dave continued. 'As I was telling you just now, the decomposition of the body is going to be our best bet to ascertain the time of death. I don't think my talents will stretch that far. Jeanie here is our resident taphonomist. She specializes in decomposition. If anyone can tell us when the victim expired, it's Jeanie.' Dave put a big hand on Jeanie's shoulder.

'It's a pleasure to meet you, Jeanie. Dave has always spoken very highly of you too,' Jane said, the three of them moving off to the side to allow the SOCO and excavation teams room to work. She took the white suit being held out to her by one of the SOCO officers and began climbing into it. 'Taphonomy. An interesting field, I would imagine?'

'It is fascinating, absolutely fascinating – always changing.

I'm always learning,' Jeanie said, gesticulating, her face open and excited as she too climbed into a papery white suit. 'And, of course, it's well suited to your case, as it happens. "Taphonomy" comes from the Greek word *taphos*, meaning "tomb". Appropriate, don't you think?' she said, giving Dave a wink.

Jane was surprised to see the obvious chemistry between the two colleagues. From what Lockyer had told her, Dave had been married, but it hadn't lasted long. His job had taken precedence, and the end of the marriage had not been pretty. Since then he had prided himself on his single, trouble-free status. Jane found herself looking from one to the other, intrigued by this new side to Dave. It was nice. He looked happy, and the lines around his eyes seemed to have softened since Jeanie's arrival.

'Okay, boss, you lot ready?' Chris asked, holding an air indicator in his hand. The gases produced from a corpse could be deadly. No one was going down that hole before the needle read zero.

Jane turned and looked again down the dark hole. 'Yes, we're ready,' she said. 'Dave, do you want to run things from here on in?'

'No problem.' Dave's face had changed. His eyes were serious now. When it came to dealing with bodies, he showed the utmost respect, whether they were an accident or a murder victim or a gang member caught up in a shooting. 'I'll go down first,' he said, 'see what we're dealing with, and call you when I'm ready. Jeanie,' he said, touching her arm, 'you first and then, Jane, you follow. Okay?' Both women nodded.

'Great,' Jane said, feeling anything but, as Dave began to

climb down the ladder that had been put in place by the SOCO team. She felt as if a small hole had opened up in her stomach, and the closer she got to the entrance, the bigger it was getting. It wasn't claustrophobia, but it wasn't far off it, either. A cold sweat was forming on the back of her neck. She could feel Jeanie standing next to her. She forced herself to step forward and look down as Dave's head disappeared into the gloom. 'Won't be long, ladies,' he said, his voice muffled.

'He's wonderful, isn't he?' Jeanie said from behind her.

'Yes, he is,' Jane replied.

CHAPTER SEVEN

24th April – Thursday

Jane waited at the entrance to the tomb. If she could get over the confined-space issue, she should be fine. She wasn't worried about viewing the body. It was the next part of her job that she dreaded. Once the body was brought out and identified, it would be her job to inform the next of kin. Next of kin – it sounded so mundane, so detached. No amount of training or experience could lessen the impact when she told a mother that she had lost a child, or a husband that he had lost his wife. She would have no choice but to watch, helpless, as they were rocked by grief, shock, disbelief, anger, fear, hysteria. Every emotion was catered for. It was her job to be there and listen, take abuse or whatever needed to be exorcized from those who were bereaved. Her discomfort would lessen and disperse the second she left them. Theirs would last long after her departure.

'Okay, Jeanie,' Dave called from the bottom of the ladder. His face looked pale, upturned to the daylight. 'The entrance is a tight squeeze, so take your time, but there's a little more space once you're inside.'

Jeanie squeezed Jane's arm and said, 'See you down there.' Her smile said that Jane's fears had not been as well hidden as she thought.

'Thanks,' she said, aware now that her palms were sweating. It was hot and the morning's noise seemed to have distilled to a hushed whisper. She looked at her watch. It was ten-thirty. Lockyer should be here soon. She had dropped into the office on her way over this morning, with the intention of picking him up, but he had other ideas. He seemed to have his list of excuses ready the moment she stepped into his office. He had two case files to 'put to bed' and a meeting with Roger. After he was done, he would drive himself down or grab a lift with one of the team. 'Nothing will happen quickly today, I'm sure,' he said as she was leaving.

Jane wanted him here. More than that, she needed him here. She had dealt with clandestine graves before, but nothing like this one. Shallow graves, a poorly chosen site in a field, skeletal remains – all that she was used to. But this was different. This wasn't some crime of passion that had ended with a hurried burial. Someone had excavated and created a tomb. Someone had put a body down there. As the thought moved through Jane's mind, it occurred to her that maybe it hadn't been a body. Maybe whoever was down there had been alive. As the idea took hold, a large cloud covered the sun. She looked up. The sky to the east of her looked dark. She was not going down into that hole if it rained. The earth might move, crumble, collapse. Her heart began to thud harder in her chest.

'Jane,' Dave said, 'we're ready for you now.'

She put her foot out and stepped down onto the first rung

of the ladder. 'You can do this,' she whispered to herself. Only five rungs to go. Without allowing herself time to think, she began climbing down. Once she was at the bottom she bent to a crouch, pulled back a piece of heavy-duty plastic covering the entrance and looked through. She could see Dave and Jeanie beyond, their faces illuminated by the lamps the SOCO team had set up. Now that she had negotiated the ladder she felt calm, her anxiety all but gone. She slid down onto all fours and crawled through the entrance, the sheet falling back into place behind her. Her eyes were taking in every-thing: the look of the floor, the walls, the ceiling. The earth had been sculpted, its edges smooth. It looked like marble, polished to a high shine. The light from the lamps bounced off the shiny surfaces. The next thing she noticed was the smell, or rather the lack of it. She closed her eyes and took a deep breath: earth, moisture and a slightly sweet odour. It was hard to believe there was a body down here. 'It's bigger than I thought,' she said. There was very little space above her head, but it looked to be about four yards long and three yards wide.

'It's been well crafted,' Dave said. 'Someone spent a lot of time and effort creating this. Look at the edges there,' he said, pointing to the far corner.

'I know,' Jane said, 'they're perfect.' She was surprised to hear the wonder in her voice. Of all the emotions she had expected to feel, amazement wasn't on the list. 'I can't believe this is man-made.'

'But it is' was all Jeanie said, her voice low.

'The original entrance?' Jane asked, wanting to move away from the ominous tone in Jeanie's voice.

'There,' Dave said, pointing to his right.

Jane crawled forward, her head bent at an odd angle. SOCO had used a luminous pink spray to outline the hatch. It didn't look like much at all, but then from her position it was hard to see. She turned, banging her head on the ceiling, before settling on her back, her elbow bent to keep her shoulders off the cold floor. She reached up her free arm and ran her hand over the door, the joins and the compacted mud around it. She closed her eyes and repeated the action. In the light it was hard to feel the difference in texture, but in the dark it was almost impossible. She had expected the wooden hatch to feel rough, warmer somehow, but it didn't. Uniform walls, floor and ceiling. A tomb in every sense of the word. With that, she remembered the body. She still hadn't seen it. Dave and Jeanie were blocking her view. She shuffled on all fours until she was crouched next to Dave, with Jeanie on his other side. They were wedged together like sardines.

It didn't look like a body at all. It was a woman, a girl really. She didn't look much older than twenty, twenty-one maybe. She was curled up in a foetal position facing them, her legs pulled up to her chest. Her eyes were closed, her hair falling slightly over her left eye. Her hands were clasped together beneath her chin. She was wearing what appeared to be blue cotton pyjamas with a daisy pattern on them. Her feet were bare and pale in the lamplight. Her face looked wholly unremarkable. She didn't look dead. She looked as if she was sleeping. One gentle nudge and she would open her eyes, apologize for the confusion and then the four of them would climb out of the tomb together.

Dave cleared his throat. 'As I suspected – and Jeanie agrees – the victim hasn't made much transition from the fresh stage.'

'I can see that,' Jane said, still stunned by what she was seeing. 'Cause of death?' she asked, although her question felt precipitous. The girl simply didn't look dead.

'Asphyxiation would be my guess,' Dave said. 'I'll need to confirm that, but from my preliminary examination there are no other significant signs of injury. There is a contusion on the back of her head, over to the left here,' he said, pointing to the side of the girl's head; her hair was slightly matted with blood, 'but that wouldn't have killed her.'

'How long has she been down here?' Jane asked, looking over at Jeanie.

Jeanie shook her head. 'My best guess would be five to six days at the most. There's no rigor.'

'She died down here?' Jane asked, her voice hollow.

'Yes, I would say so,' Jeanie said, 'given her body position.'

Jane held her breath. What must it have felt like to be trapped down here, in the dark? It didn't bear thinking about, but part of her needed to know, needed to feel what this girl had felt. 'Can we lose the light for a second?' she asked.

'Sure,' Dave said, reaching for a radio attached to his belt. It crackled and then he spoke. 'Can you kill the lights for thirty seconds, please?' There was no response, but then the three of them were plunged into darkness.

'Oh my God.' Jeanie said. 'The poor girl.' It sounded as if she was holding back tears. The three of them were silent in the blackness.

'Jeanie and I are done here,' Dave said, gesturing over at

Jeanie as the lights bloomed back into life. 'Are you almost finished?' he asked, blinking.

Jane was about to agree when she remembered what had started this whole circus. 'You two go on up. I just want to check something. I won't be a second.'

'Are you sure?' Jeanie asked, raising her eyebrows.

'Yes, thank you, Jeanie,' she said, looking over her shoulder and smiling. 'I'm okay now.' And she was. From the state she had been in topside, Jane had half-expected to come down here and have a panic attack. But she was fine. Now it was all about the job. All about evidence, clues and piecing together threads. This was the bit she enjoyed. This was the part she was good at. She listened as Dave and Jeanie made their way out and into the excavation shaft. She crawled forward and looked up at the far north-east corner. Again, SOCO had outlined the area in luminous pink. Jane looked at the tube first. It wasn't a tube. Now that she was down here, its purpose was clear. It was an air-hose. Whoever had done this had allowed the victim air, at least to begin with. But why bring the girl down here to die and provide her with air at all, for however brief a period? It didn't make sense. Unless, of course, her suffering had provided some kind of twisted entertainment. Jane turned her attention to the wire and what she knew she would find at the end of it. A tiny camera.

CHAPTER EIGHT

I feel light-headed today. At least I think I do. It's hard to tell real from imagined down here. Even as the thought runs through my mind I realize I don't know that it is, in fact, 'today'. The word implies daytime, daylight – luxuries I no longer have. It is almost thrilling not knowing. An unexpected thrill. I want to document how I feel, to share it, but I can't. There is no light. I have no pen. No paper. There is only me and the darkness.

I should be scared, but I'm not. The silence comforts me, enfolding me in its nothingness. I feel cradled like a child in its mother's arms. A strange calm has overtaken my body and mind. I feel light, almost giddy, like I've had too much to drink. I crawl around, my hands tracing smooth walls of mud. There are no imperfections, no cracks to hold onto. I start to laugh, a childish giggle. That isn't right. This isn't normal. I begin to feel sick, to panic, but then I remember: lack of oxygen can cause a feeling of euphoria. That must be why I feel so good. Relieved to have solved the riddle, I make my way back to the centre. I know it's the centre. I know this space, but why the centre? Why do I choose to be here rather than in a corner or leaning against a wall? A shiver runs over my shoulders. The cold seeps through my clothes and dampens my skin. I pull my legs up to my chin, my arms wrapped around me. I can hear a song in my head. I only know the chorus. It's Kings of Leon – 'Your sex is on fire'. I begin to hum the tune as I push off one of my trainers and wiggle my toes. Pins-and-needles. My big toe is numb.

CHAPTER NINE

25th April – Friday

It was only nine-thirty in the morning, but Jane felt as if she had been in the office for a full shift already. She had left the house early, but not before having some breakfast with Peter and her mother, who had stayed over again. She was just waiting for a phone call from her father, requesting his wife back. Peter had chattered away while she ate her toast. He didn't want to go to school. Would the teacher let him outside at break-time? He always found it hard being back after a holiday. She had tried to reassure him, but he kept spooning his cereal up and tipping it back into the bowl over and over again. The anxiety rippled off him like a heatwave, ageing his young face. She sighed, tipped her head back and eased it from side to side, her fringe brushing against her forehead. She could smell the burning oil from the takeaway shops that lined Lewisham High Street. It turned her stomach. She couldn't fathom how anyone could eat a kebab and chips at this time of the morning.

She was waiting for a call from MISPER. A photograph and a description of the girl in the tomb had been emailed over to their office last night. Jane hoped that at least this part of the investigation would be straightforward. She needed a name. The girl hadn't looked like a vagrant or someone invisible to the system. The post-mortem was scheduled for later on today or early tomorrow, depending on the ID and Dave's workload. The Exhibits team was detailing and examining evidence gathered from the site. A headache was taking up residence in her left temple. She massaged the spot with the tips of her fingers and closed her eyes. An image of the air-hose and camera poking into the tomb came into her mind. Such benign objects in themselves, although their purpose felt anything but. She couldn't stop thinking about the girl: about her final hours, trapped in the dark, terrified, screaming. Jane ran her fingers over her eyebrows, pushing the thoughts away. She pulled her chair back to her desk and began checking through her emails.

There were several from the Exhibits team; two from Roger, her SIO; one from Despatch and a couple from the lab. There were at least a hundred more, but she didn't have time to deal with them right now. She had to focus all of her attention on the girl in the tomb. Each piece of evidence filtered out, expanding the investigation into different departments, involving more and more officers. The speed at which a case moved in the first twenty-four to forty-eight hours could be intimidating: a lot of plates spinning or balls in the air, whichever analogy you preferred. Jane had to keep a tight grip if she was going to avoid mistakes. Of course as soon as there was a name to go with the young girl's face, the investigation would explode, but for now she was in control. Her eyes were drawn to an email from Lockyer. She had already read it. Read it more than once, in fact. He was having a 'day off'. He had emailed Roger, copying in Jane and saying, 'I won't be in the office today. On my mobile, if you need me.' That was it. No reason or apology. She ran her fingers through her hair, her fringe crackling with static. He had chosen to take a day off now?

The DNA results on the blood found in Mark and Sue's utility room still weren't back. Sue had provided a sample of Mark's hair for analysis, but everything seemed to be on a go-slow. The discovery of the girl's body in the tomb had overshadowed the fact that the original call-outs had pointed towards Mark. Jane had managed to speak to Sue late last night, to reassure her that everything that could be done was being done. In reality she couldn't do much until the blood results came back and Roger, and the officer in charge over at MISPER, decided which department should run the case. Given the trainer found in Elmstead, she thought the discussion should have happened yesterday, but that decision was above her rank. She could still hear the tremor in Sue's voice. The poor woman was trying to hold it together for her children, but that couldn't last. Whatever department ended up with Mark's case, the reality was that he had been missing for three days.

Her mobile started to ring. She reached over a stack of files and answered it. 'Bennett speaking,' she said.

'Hi Jane,' a familiar voice said. 'It's Alan. I've got good news for you,' he continued, clearing his throat.

Jane pulled her notepad towards her and uncapped her pen. 'Okay,' she said. This was the call from MISPER that she had been waiting for.

'I've got two files for you. I'm emailing then over to you now,' he said. He sounded as if he had a cold, the ends of his words muffled by phlegm. 'The first one is a Margaret Hungerford, goes by "Maggie". Twenty-six years old, five foot six, Caucasian, shoulder-length hair, dark brown, hundred-and-twenty pounds, reported missing on Monday 21st April by her mother, Elizabeth Hungerford, fifty-five years old. The mother provided a photograph, which I've attached to the email. Looks like your tomb-girl,' he said.

'And the second?' Jane asked. Two possible IDs meant a delay in the post-mortem but, more than that, it meant two possible families. The last thing she wanted to do was have to put two terrified sets of parents through the ordeal of identifying the body.

'Joanna Bailey, twenty years old, five foot five, Caucasian, short red hair, dyed, hundred-and-seventy pounds . . . '

'Hang on, Alan,' she said, her pen hovering over the new description. 'I thought these were both IDs for my tomb-girl,' she went on, feeling appalled by the ease at which she had adopted Alan's terminology.

'No, sorry,' Alan said with an audible sniff that made her wince. 'Didn't I say? My brain's shot today. Hungerford relates to your tomb-girl; the second, Bailey, is the last missing girl on the Stevens case. A friend of hers saw the appeal and recognized her from the photograph. Joanna Bailey visited the station last night to confirm her identity. My team has done the necessary regarding support for her and her family, et cetera, but I've told her that your department will be in touch, as you'll need to question her in relation to the prosecution.'

Jane hadn't thought about the Stevens case in days. With Mark's disappearance and the burial site in Elmstead, the girl in the second photograph had dropped off her radar. The fact that Joanna Bailey had been found was a huge relief, but it wasn't down to her. It was dumb luck. Luck that benefited Jane: one less thing to juggle. She shook her head. She was trained to move on, tick it off the list and begin the next task, in order of priority. Her whole life was a list of priorities, but it was in a constant state of flux. She couldn't avoid the inevitable feeling that she was always on the verge of letting something slip, or letting someone down.

'You still there?' Alan asked as he stifled a bout of coughing.

'Yes, sorry. That's great news, thanks, Alan,' she said, writing and underlining Joanna Bailey's name on her notepad. 'What was she like?'

'Er, she was sweet, quiet. She was shocked, as you'd expect. Why?' Alan asked.

'No reason. Just curious, I guess,' Jane said. She couldn't help wondering how Bailey had taken the news that she was a potential target for south-east London's first-ever serial killer. The truth was that she didn't have the time or the head-space to find out. She was already onto the next case, the next victim. She put a tick next to Joanna Bailey's name and pushed her personal feelings aside.

'Files should be with you now,' Alan said, sniffing. 'I'll talk to you later?'

'Yes, sure,' she said. 'Thanks, Alan. Hope you feel better.'

'Me too, because right now I feel like death warmed up.'

She managed to smile, but her thoughts were elsewhere.

She had a name to go with the face in the tomb. She now had a dozen things to action, and a dozen more after that. 'Cheers, Alan,' she said, pushing 'End' on her phone. The emails were already sitting in her in-box. She clicked on the first one, opened it and double-clicked on the attached photograph. Maggie Hungerford. It was her – the girl from the tomb. It meant the post-mortem would have to wait. The girl's parents would have to come into the station to formally identify the body. But first Jane had to tell them that their daughter had been murdered.

CHAPTER TEN

25th April – Friday

Jane climbed into the squad car, put on her seatbelt and started the engine. 'You ready?' she asked, turning to look at Penny, a senior detective constable on the murder squad from Lockyer's team. Penny had volunteered to accompany Jane when she informed Maggie Hungerford's next of kin. Roger had provisionally signed off on five officers for the investigation. Jane didn't have full authorization to choose Penny as one of them, but with Lockyer out of the office, what choice did she have? Her investigation couldn't be put on hold, and he hadn't bothered to reply to any of her emails.

As Penny clicked her seatbelt into place and put on a pair of large round sunglasses, she turned to Jane. 'I hate this part.'

'You and me both,' Jane said, putting the car into reverse and slipping on her own Ray-Ban sunglasses, an extravagant treat for her thirty-fifth birthday. She put the Hungerfords' postcode into the satnav, pulled up to the exit of the car park and out into Lewisham's mid-morning traffic. Rain or shine, day or night, Lewisham High Street was busy. However, today's volume of traffic and the lack of blaring horns seemed to suggest that everyone who wasn't at work had decided on a jolly to a park or a pub, or both, starting their weekends early. No one appeared to be in a hurry.

Maggie's parents, William and Elizabeth Hungerford, fifty-six and fifty-five respectively, lived over in Greenwich. It was a straight shot down Lewisham Road – three miles and six minutes, according to the satnav.

It would take longer than that. Jane pulled up behind a Mazda Bongo displaying a Hot Tuna sticker in the rear window. Two surfboards were strapped to the roof. It was a strange sight. The nearest coast was an hour away. 'Have you got the list of questions handy, Penny?' she asked, flicking on the car's air-conditioning.

'Yes, I've got them on my iPad. Do you want to run through them on the way over?' Penny asked, pulling her handbag up onto her lap.

'Yes, if you don't mind. You don't get car sick, do you?'

'Not so far,' Penny said, opening up her iPad and navigating to the right page. 'Okay. I've got the standard questions: confirming the victim's age, description, where she lived, worked, marital status, income, activity in the last month and last-known whereabouts.'

'Good. When it comes to the last-known whereabouts, we need to ask when Elizabeth Hungerford last saw her daughter, and for what reasons she reported her missing. Had she noticed any changes in Maggie's behaviour in recent weeks?' She paused to allow Penny time to type the new question into her list.

'Got it,' Penny said.

'Did Maggie appear depressed, anxious, nervous – that kind of thing?'

'Yes,' Penny said, tapping away.

'Okay,' she said, pulling away from some roadworks and avoiding a bus, before settling back into the line of traffic. 'We need to prepare them for the photograph of Maggie, and arrange for one or both of them to come in and formally identify the body. Would you be able to be present for that, Pen?'

'Of course. When do you think they'll want to come in?'

'Today,' Jane said without hesitation. 'It wouldn't surprise me if they followed us back to the station with the Family Liaison Officer.' In her experience, viewing the body was the first step in processing what had happened. Despite the shock of being told that a loved one had been murdered, the bereaved needed to see the body for themselves, to know what was happening to them was real. The longer the gap between being told and seeing the body, the harder the family seemed to find it.

'Is the FLO meeting us there then?' Penny asked, pushing up her sleeves. Even with the air-con on, it was getting warm inside the squad car.

'Yes, Anne Phillips is coming over. I spoke to her earlier. She was in Blackheath, finishing up with another family. Depending on how the A2 is looking today, we should arrive at the Hungerfords' at about the same time. Anne will be on hand for the family, going forward,' she said, swerving to avoid a cyclist.

'She's fantastic,' Penny said, putting her hand out and holding onto the dashboard. 'I worked with her on the Stevens case. She worked with the Stevens family.'

Jane nodded. She couldn't help thinking about Joanna Bailey, and how lucky she was that her family had never needed Anne's services. Jane had no doubt that the Stevens case would haunt Anne. It had been a difficult case for everyone. In fact, today's job felt like a walk in the park by comparison. The banality of her thoughts made her grip the steering wheel tighter. Nothing about this morning was going to be easy for Maggie Hungerford's family. In less than an hour their lives would change beyond all recognition.

'How much are you planning on telling them?' Penny asked.

'Only the essentials. For now, anyway. The less they have to process, the better. Besides, until I've spoken to the forensic psychologist I really don't know what we're dealing with here.' And she didn't. All Jane knew was that Maggie Hungerford had received a blow to the head before being put in a tomb to die. There was also the possibility that whoever had done this had filmed her while she died of asphyxiation. It was a lot of information to deal with, and it raised a lot of questions. Without answers, Jane was feeling around in the dark, just like Maggie.

She looked out of her window at the people walking up and down Lewisham Road: groups of lads, groups of girls, families. Everyone seemed to be out this morning. The sunshine had affected people's choice of clothing. All the women, old and young, were sporting strappy tops – their bras, if they were wearing one, on show. The pavements were awash with flesh of every colour. The fairer-skinned were already pinking up, burned by too long in the sun without sunscreen. The men weren't faring much better.

At least 50 per cent were shirtless, their biceps adorned with weird and wonderful tattoos. Other than men she had slept with, and the girl who had done a spray tan for a wedding she had been to last year, no one knew that Jane had her own tattoo. It had been another thirty-fifth birthday present to herself, like her sunglasses, though slightly less pricey. It was at the base of her spine. Her birthday in Roman numerals. It was meant to be semi-permanent. The tattoo artist who had done it for her said it would only last for five to eight years. She was two years into the timeframe, and it showed no sign of fading at all. It was the only real evidence that she could be crazy and devil-may-care when she wanted to be. It represented a wild side that rarely got an airing. Lockyer had seen her tattoo.

The woman's voice on the satnav intruded on her thoughts. 'In two hundred yards turn left, then turn left . . . '

'Almost there,' Penny said, pointing at the screen. 'Ashburnham Place, number seventy-three.'

'Right,' she replied, waiting for a scantily dressed pedestrian to cross in front of her. She turned left into Ashburnham Place, looking for a door number to let her know which end of the street she was aiming for. The woman on the satnav was telling them they had reached their destination.

'There's number fourteen,' Penny said.

Jane continued up the road to a row of Victorian town houses. 'Nice area,' she said, listening as Penny called out house numbers.

As she looked at the trees lining the street, framing each house, it occurred to her that she would forget Ashburnham

Place. She had never driven up here before and, once this case was over, she probably wouldn't drive up it again. She would forget Elizabeth and William Hungerford. Not immediately, but in time their names would fade. But what she would never forget was their faces. In a few minutes she would have to inflict the kind of pain that most people only had nightmares about. The faces of all the bereaved families she had ever met were burned into her memory. The faces of Elizabeth and William Hungerford were about to join her picture library of grief.

'Let's get this done,' she said, pulling into a space. Anne, the FLO, was standing at the Hungerfords' front door waving back at them.

Jane couldn't help but be impressed by the Hungerfords' living room. It was a far cry from the kind of houses she spent the majority of her time in. The room was light and spacious. It looked like something out of *House & Garden*. Two large cream sofas faced each other, with an oak coffee table in the centre. There was an open fire, the grate immaculate, and a large gilded mirror taking centre-stage over the mantelpiece. Colourful oil paintings and watercolours adorned the off-white walls, complemented by the room's high ceilings, cornices and a rose in the centre, showing off an ornate but tasteful chandelier. Rays of sunshine shone into the room, bouncing off the hundreds of tiny pieces of hand-crafted glass. It was beautiful and serene, but she was about to tarnish all of it with her presence.

'Would you like to sit down, Mr and Mrs Hungerford?' she asked, directing them to the sofa nearest the window.

'I've made a pot of tea,' Elizabeth Hungerford said in a whisper.

Anne seemed to move with the stealth and grace of a ninja. She was at Mrs Hungerford's side in a second, taking her arm and leading her over to the sofa. 'I'll get the tea, Elizabeth,' she said, in a soothing but confident voice. 'DS Bennett and DC Groves have some questions for you and your husband. It won't take long.'

As instructed, Elizabeth Hungerford sat down on the sofa with a bump, her husband mute beside her.

'I won't be a minute.' Anne disappeared from the room as quickly and as quietly as she had entered. Jane had worked with her before, but she had never actually been present for Anne's first visit with the family. She was good. Quiet, controlled, in charge, sympathetic without being patronizing. It was an amazing balancing act, which it must have taken years of experience to master. As the door to the lounge clicked shut, Jane took a seat opposite the ashen-faced couple and cleared her throat. She waited for the Hungerfords to look up, to engage. They knew what was coming. She nodded for Penny to take over.

Penny perched on the edge of the sofa and took a notepad out of her handbag. 'Mr and Mrs Hungerford,' she said, 'could you tell me your daughter's date of birth?'

Elizabeth Hungerford looked confused, staring into the empty fireplace as if the answers had been swept away with the ashes. William Hungerford took his wife's hand and squeezed it. 'The seventh of May 1987,' he said.

'Thank you. Do you have a recent photograph?' Penny

asked. 'I know you've probably already given one to Missing Persons, but if you have another, that would be helpful.'

'Of course,' William Hungerford said, releasing his wife's hand and digging into his jacket pocket. 'Miss Phillips called ahead and asked us to have one ready.' He placed the photograph on the coffee table between them. Jane was again impressed by Anne's professionalism. If Jane was ever in the Hungerfords' position, she could only hope that the FLO assigned to her was even half as considerate and well-trained as Anne Phillips. An image of Peter's smiling face flashed into her mind. She realized that in reality it didn't matter who came or what they said. If anything happened to Peter, she would be beyond all sensible thought.

She looked down at the photograph. It was taken at Christmas time – Christmas morning, it looked like. Maggie was sitting where Jane was now. She was wearing black skinny jeans and an oversized black-and-white striped jumper. Her hair was damp, pulled over one shoulder. A glass of champagne was in her hand. She was saying 'Cheers' to whoever was taking the picture. She looked happy. Jane dragged her eyes away from Maggie's face. In the back of the shot she could see the Hungerfords' Christmas tree. It was beautifully decorated, not an ornament or piece of tinsel out of place. Everything was silver and gold. It looked more like a tree you would see in Harrods, not in someone's home.

She turned her attention back to Maggie's mother, who was wringing a tissue in her right hand, her eyes still fixed on the fireplace. She was dressed in white linen trousers and a pale-yellow cardigan buttoned up to her neck. Her make-up was perfect, but no amount of concealer could disguise the hours she had spent crying for her missing daughter.

'Thank you,' Penny said, picking up the photograph and putting it carefully into her bag. 'And if you could confirm Maggie's . . . Margaret's address?'

'"Maggie's" fine,' William Hungerford said. 'My wife loves the royals, hence "Margaret". Maggie's not so keen.' He shrugged his shoulders. He pulled another piece of paper out of his jacket pocket. 'Number fourteen Hyde Vale,' he said, moving the paper further away and squinting to read the postcode. 'I have her housemate's details here too, if you want them?'

'Yes, please,' Penny said.

Jane listened and watched as Penny noted down the phone number and email address of Christina O'Reilly, also twenty-six. They would need to talk to her, but that would have to wait for another day. According to Maggie's father, both of the girls were studying for their Masters in psychology at Greenwich Uni. They had been friends since primary school. Both sets of parents had helped their daughters purchase the Hyde Vale property two years ago. Like his wife, William Hungerford was well dressed. Dark-green cords, a blue-and-white striped shirt and a simple blue blazer. The couple looked as if they were on their way to a friend's for drinks, or out for lunch at a local restaurant. But then what outfit would Jane pick, in their situation?

'The girls want to get into clinical psychology and open a practice together,' Mr Hungerford was saying, 'something like the Priory, but for young adults and children with emotional problems, not pop stars with a drug habit.'

Jane wondered if William Hungerford realized he was talking about his daughter and her future in the present tense. His wife was now smiling, either at the familiarity of her husband's dislike of celebrity culture or at her daughter's ambitions to use her education to help others. Either way, it was clear that Maggie was loved, and her parents were proud of her. Did they ever doubt their daughter's choices or raise their eyebrows when she gushed about all the great things she was going to do with her life? Celia Bennett had never been thrilled about Jane joining the force. It was a man's job, or certainly a job for someone without the kind of responsibilities that she had.

'Maggie's working in a Montessori school at the moment,' he said.

'She loves children.' It was the first time Elizabeth Hungerford had spoken since Anne had left the room. 'I don't expect it'll be long before she has her own. We certainly can't rely on the boys for grandchildren, can we, Bill?' Her husband nodded. 'Ben, our eldest, is married. Has been for almost eight years, but there's no sign there,' she said, gazing up at the ceiling. 'Christopher, Maggie's middle brother – well, he's hopeless. Thirty-two and no intention of settling down. Doesn't like the idea of commitment, he says. Bill's always telling me that young people today are more focused on their careers. Get the job sorted first and then think about a family. Well, of course by then it's too late, isn't it?' She looked at Jane and pursed her lips. 'Live for today: that's what Maggie always says, isn't it, Bill?'

The couple's roles had been reversed. The more his wife talked, the more William Hungerford seemed to shrink, disappearing before Jane's eyes. Maggie's mother seemed unaware that she had transformed from a state of catatonia to animated chatter. But it couldn't last. Jane knew the next set of questions would bring both parents' focus back on why there were two police officers sitting in their beautiful lounge, and why Anne – a stranger to them an hour before – was moving around their house as if she had always been there. Tea and coffee had arrived on a tray, biscuits laid out, napkins folded neatly next to four teaspoons. Anne was more like a presence than actually being present. Jane had barely noticed her slip in, put down the tray and serve drinks for everyone, asking about milk and sugar without even interrupting the flow of the conversation. She was out of the room again as if she had never been there. Ninja, Jane thought. It was amazing.

'Mrs Hungerford,' Penny said, putting her half-drunk tea back on the tray in the centre of the coffee table. Jane hadn't touched hers. 'You reported Maggie missing on Monday the twenty-first of April. Can you tell me what led up to you calling the police?' Before the words had even had chance to settle in the air, Maggie's parents were back on full alert. Elizabeth Hungerford's eyes were wide, her pupils like pinpricks, and she was holding her husband's hand as if she might float away without it. 'I know this is difficult,' Penny said. 'Just take your time, and talk us through what happened.' The air in the room seemed to have dropped by several degrees.

'Maggie was meant to come for lunch on Easter Sunday,' Elizabeth Hungerford began. 'The boys were coming, and Chrissie was driving here straight from her parents' place in Stratford. I met Maggie for lunch on the Wednesday – the sixteenth, it would have been. She had some coursework to get finished, so she said she couldn't come on Good Friday, but that she might come on Saturday and stay over, so she was here when her brothers arrived on Sunday morning. I spoke to her on the phone later that day. We speak every day – well, most days. Her printer had packed up again,' she said, shrugging her shoulders. 'She said she'd call me in the morning and sort out timings for the weekend, see if I wanted anything picking up from Sainsbury's – that kind of thing. But she didn't call. She hasn't called. Chrissie hasn't seen her. None of her friends have seen her. No one has spoken to her.' A tear rolled down her cheek. She released her husband's hand just long enough to dab at her face with the screwed-up piece of tissue. 'She always calls. If she says she's going to call, she calls, doesn't she, Bill?'

The look she gave her husband made Jane want to turn away. There was a mixture of fear and longing, which was understandable; but what made Jane's heart squeeze was the unbridled hope that she could see in Elizabeth Hungerford's eyes. Despite everything – the week that had passed since she last spoke to her daughter, the police officers in her lounge on a sunny Friday morning – she was still hoping that her daughter was going to call, was going to come home.

'She does,' Maggie's father said, looking at Jane and then at Penny. 'She always calls.' His wife took a deep breath beside him and blew it out, reaching for her tea before deciding against it, her hands returning to her husband's.

'That's why my wife called the police. That's why we've been so worried.'

Jane realized that the only thing left linking her and Penny to this distraught couple in front of them was the words that had remained, as yet, unsaid. She couldn't delay it any longer. She had to put them out of their misery; or rather she had to move their misery on to the next stage. The preliminary questions were over. The paperwork side of things was all but done. She could come back to Maggie's mental state before her disappearance at another time. She would be speaking to the Hungerfords again, many more times in the coming weeks.

'Mr and Mrs Hungerford,' she began. 'On Wednesday the twenty-third of April a body was discovered in the Elmstead Woods area. It was confirmed to be that of a young woman. It has been recovered and taken to the mortuary suite in Lewisham.' She looked at Maggie's parents in turn. Neither moved or spoke. Their eyes were fixed on Jane's mouth. 'The death has been listed as suspicious. Pending formal identification, I am sorry to tell you that the description of the woman found matches that of your daughter.' She reached into her handbag and pulled out Maggie's file. She took the picture, a head-shot of Maggie taken in the mortuary suite, and handed it to the Hungerfords. Maggie's father reached for the small photograph and stared down at it. Tears flowed freely down his face, but he made no sound. Maggie's mother looked at Jane. Her eyes seemed to plead with Jane, saying, 'Don't make me do this.'

Elizabeth Hungerford turned to face her husband, her shaking hand reaching out for the picture. The next few minutes would stay with Jane for life. Maggie's mother howled and screamed at her husband, at Jane, at Penny, at the room around her. Jane looked on, helpless, as every emotion tore the poor woman apart.

CHAPTER ELEVEN

I need water. I need air.

Something is wrong. This wasn't meant to happen. I can feel the panic now. It's like razor wire inside my mind. It's tearing into my brain, the soft tissue no match for its metallic barbs. The space is closing in around me. I swear I can hear the slow grind as the muddy walls inch towards me. I can smell the friction. It's like burning coal. It will crush me. I will become part of the earth. I won't feel any more pain. It feels like madness. I lie on my back and put my hands on my stomach, concentrating on my breaths. In and out. In and out. Each rise and fall of my chest hurts. My head is heavy. My tongue sits in my mouth like a stranded fish, bloated by the sun. I have shouted. For hours I have screamed, until my body gave out, leaving me coughing, my lungs dry and raw. Where is the euphoria now?

There is a door, a way out. I know there is, but I can't find it. I have searched every inch of the space, but it is hiding from me, torturing me. I lie here, my hands shaking in the darkness, tears rolling down over my ears, tickling my skin, making me itch. I scratch. My fingers feel like sandpaper against my skin. I ache. My head, my back, my stomach, my legs. Everything aches. I have dived too deep. The pressure of the nothingness presses against me, crushing me.

I hear a sound above me. I look for it, not knowing if my eyes are open at all. I have to fight. I have to shout. I roll onto my front and push myself onto all fours. I take a deep breath and throw my head back. Nothing comes out of my mouth but a strangled hiss. I drop my head, focusing all of my strength on my lungs. I try again. Nothing. As I sit back on my haunches I begin to laugh. There is no sound, but my shoulders shake, my breath turns into ragged gasps. This is how it is meant to be. This is what I know is meant to happen. It's all part of it. The madness retreats, frightened back into submission by my rational mind. I have let the wild thoughts take over. That's all they are. Thoughts. I need to sleep. Once I regain my strength I can begin again. I reach back to massage my feet.

My right foot is numb.

CHAPTER TWELVE

25th April – Friday

Jane put her Peugeot into gear and reversed into the driveway. Her mother's car was parked in the garage, the door open. She refused to close Jane's garage door on principle. In her opinion, the world had 'gone mad' when it came to household security. Jane had spent more than a few hours trying to convince her mother that some Lewisham residents might not sign up to her particular code of ethics. She turned off the engine and used her remote to close the garage door. She picked up her briefcase from the passenger seat and climbed out of the car.

Her morning with the Hungerfords had drained her – and that was before she had visited Maggie's home, and SOCO had confirmed blood on the doorstep and pathway outside the house in Greenwich. There wasn't much, but enough to warrant the theory that Maggie had been taken from her home by force. Jane closed the car door and leaned against it, relishing the support. She felt as if she had done a ten-mile run, her legs were so heavy. The lab was rushing the blood sample through to get confirmation that it belonged to Maggie. Not that Jane needed it.

The temperature gauge in her car had read twenty-one degrees, but standing in her driveway it felt a lot warmer than that. She had an hour before she had to be back in the office. Dave had called to say he could do the post-mortem at five o'clock, and Phil Bathgate, the squad's resident forensic psychologist, would be 'popping in' to see her at six-thirty. It was a pity the two appointments didn't overlap, because if it came down to a choice between Maggie Hungerford's post-mortem and seeing Phil, she would pick the post-mortem. Phil gave her the creeps. The only saving grace was that she didn't have to deal with him very often. His kind of expertise wasn't necessary on the kind of cases she handled. If she was ever promoted to inspector, then – like Lockyer – she would no doubt get to know Phil a whole lot better. The thought made her shudder. She had seen him in action on the Stevens case. He had reacted to Lewisham's first serial killer like a kid who had been given a new bike.

She pushed her fringe out of her eyes and walked up to her front door, sliding her key into the lock. As she opened the door, the coolness of the hallway wafted over her. She smiled, closed her eyes and allowed herself to enjoy the moment. She loved this house. She loved coming home. When she was in her twenties, living in a tiny flat on Lee High Road, she relished feeling at the centre of it all. She would never have imagined that, ten years later, she would be living in a 1960s dormer-bungalow-style house in Belmont Hill with a seven-year-old son. She pushed the door closed, dropped her bag on the floor and walked through to the kitchen. Her mother should be home with Peter soon. He would be dying to get out in their garden. She remembered the first time she had watched him running his chubby little hands over the grass, the sun shining on his face. He had been two and a half. She walked back into the hallway and up the stairs into her bedroom.

The mortuary suite would be cold, and she knew from experience that the odours released during the post-mortem tended to stick to your clothes. She opened her wardrobe, took out a pair of charcoal trousers, an old green T-shirt and a light sweater. As she changed she realized this particular ensemble had become her PM outfit. She could wash it all together, it dried quickly and she never wore it socially. She laughed out loud as she sat down on the edge of her bed. 'Socially' implied a social life, and she hadn't had one of those for a while. She heard a key slide into the lock downstairs. She buttoned her trousers and walked out of her room. As she rounded the corner to go down the stairs she caught sight of Peter's head disappearing down the hallway. Her mother smiled up at her.

'I tell you, that boy just about wears me out. We weren't at the park for more than ten minutes before he was dragging me out again, wanting to come home.'

'Hi, Mum,' she said, walking down the stairs. She kissed her mother on the cheek and reached up to smooth away the flyaway hairs that had come unstuck on the walk home. Celia Bennett believed in hairspray. 'How's he doing today?'

'He's good – super. A touch hyper, but then the sun's shining,' her mother said, shrugging out of a lightweight jacket and hanging it on the banister. 'Do you have time for a cuppa?' she asked.

'Yes,' Jane said. 'I've got half an hour before I need to be getting back.' She received a cool look as her mother flicked on the kettle.

'Oh well,' her mother said, flicking on the kettle, 'I suppose it can't be helped.'

Jane walked over to the window and looked out. Peter was already in position, sitting at the top of the garden, his face upturned to the sun, his hands outstretched on either side of him, stroking the grass. He looked like a little Buddha. She knocked on the window and waited. After a second or two Peter tipped his head forward and looked in her general direction. She waved and smiled. He waved back at her, before resuming his position.

'Go out and say hello. I'll bring the tea,' her mother said.

Jane opened the back door, stepped outside, kicked off her shoes and walked up the garden. 'Hello, handsome,' she said, bending down until she was crouched in front of him. 'And what have you been doing today?' Peter kept his eyes closed, but turned his face towards her voice.

'School,' he said. A frown wrinkled his forehead. 'Mrs Porter didn't let me in the playground at break-time.' He spoke as if it was an accusation directed at her rather than at Mrs Porter.

'Oh dear. Why didn't Mrs Porter want you to play outside today?' she asked.

'I wasn't listening in class. Miss Hanson said so, so Mrs Porter said I had to eat my lunch in the lunch-room.' His whole face was scrunched up now, as if the memory was more stressful than the punishment itself.

'Oh, I see,' said Jane. 'Well, you know you have to listen

in class. Miss Hanson is there to help you, isn't she?' As soon
as the words were out of her mouth she could see that Peter
wasn't in the mood for more reprimanding. She didn't want
to get into a fight. She didn't want to spoil his afternoon.
'Don't worry. I'm sure you'll listen twice as hard tomorrow,'
she said ruffling his hair. He reacted to her touch. A casual
observer wouldn't notice, but she did.

'That's what Mrs Porter said,' he replied, settling his hands
back into the grass.

She smiled, leaned forward and kissed her son on the
forehead. His skin smelled of soap and was warm and soft
beneath her lips. 'Love you, munchkin,' she said, pushing
herself back up until she was standing over him. She
retreated to the table and took the mug being offered to her
by her mother.

'He had a hard day' was all her mother said as she sat
down. Jane nodded and reached for one of the blueberry
muffins laid out on a tray. As she went to take a napkin, her
mother caught her hand and squeezed it. 'Good days and
bad days, darling. Good days and bad days.'

She was back in the office by quarter to five and in the lift
on her way down to the mortuary suite by ten to.

She had received three emails from Phil confirming
their meeting at six-thirty, amending their meeting for
later on and then reconfirming the original time. From the
tone of his emails he sounded buoyant. He said he had
some 'interesting ideas' to discuss with her. She looked at
her reflection in the lift doors and straightened her
hair, rearranging her fringe. Why wouldn't it stay where

she put it? The doors opened, she stepped out and walked down the quiet hallway. Sue had called the office three times and left messages. Her questions and mild enquiry into 'how things were going' seemed benign, but Jane could hear the message underneath. Why wasn't Jane out there, finding her husband? Why wasn't she doing her job? Jane would have to call Sue after the post-mortem, if there was time, or after her meeting with Phil. She had put in a call to the lab to see where they were with the DNA results. With any luck, she would have an email from them when she got back to her desk. At least then she would have something new to tell Sue, rather than fobbing her off with the standard line of 'We're doing everything we can.'

'Jane, nice to see you.'

She looked up to see Patrick, Dave's senior assistant, walking towards her.

'Either I'm lost or you're going in the wrong direction,' she said, smiling.

'Don't worry; you're in the right place. Dave's almost ready,' he said, touching her arm as he passed her. 'I've just got to make a call for him. I'll be back in a second.'

'No problem,' she said. She continued down the hallway, lifting her pass to the entry-reader before pushing through two sets of doors that led into the suite. The viewing room was off to the left. The Hungerfords had been in to formally identify their daughter, after Jane saw them this morning. Even though it wasn't possible, Jane felt sure she had heard Elizabeth Hungerford's cries rising up the three floors to her office. She turned to the right and walked into the main room. The lights were bright, harsh beams bouncing off the copious amounts of steel and Formica. Maggie was already in place. She was covered by a white sheet, with only her feet exposed. They looked smaller than they had in the tomb. In fact her whole body looked tiny compared with the large steel dissection table. Jane busied herself pulling on surgical gloves and putting on an apron, tying a loose bow at her back.

'Jane, how's it going?'

She turned at the sound of Dave's voice. He was dressed in his usual scrubs and a thick apron that went all the way down to his shins. 'Hi, Dave. I'm doing okay. How about you?'

'I'll be glad when this week is over.' He looked at the cart next to the body and counted off the items, talking to himself the whole time. Jane stepped back to the edge of the room and stood in silence. 'How's your boss doing?' he asked.

She hesitated, unsure how to respond: what to say and what not to say. 'He's . . . okay,' she said, staring at the floor.

Dave turned. 'Oh, as good as that,' he said, walking to the other side of the suite and beginning to check the labels and equipment laid out in front of him. 'I did wonder. I've tried to talk to him a few times, but to be honest even getting him out of his flat has been a challenge.'

'Really?' she said, although she wasn't in the least bit surprised.

'I've just about exhausted my "good reasons to get out" list,' he said, counting off a row of scalpels. 'I even joined him on one of his runs, to see if he'd talk. Almost killed me,' Dave said, turning to her and rolling his eyes.

'The run or Lockyer?' she asked.

'Both,' Dave said. 'I'm sure he doesn't normally run that fast.'

'And?' she said, stepping forward.

'He's never been one for deep conversation, but he's not right,' Dave said, shaking his head. 'At first I kept it work-oriented and tried to talk to him about the Stevens case, about the issues he had there, but he shut me down . . . said he couldn't talk about it until it had been resolved internally.' Jane could see Dave was just as frustrated as she was. '"Resolved internally" – what the bloody hell does that even mean?' he asked, throwing a gloved hand in the air.

'He hasn't said much since he's been back,' Jane said, aware that despite Dave's friendship with Lockyer, she was still talking about her boss. 'There's been no official . . . disciplinary action, as far as I'm aware.' She felt guilty. Just talking about him made her feel guilty.

'There was never going to be, Jane, was there?' he said, turning to face her. 'It could derail the entire case, something like that. I still can't believe he'd be so bloody stupid.'

She was shocked by his candour. It occurred to her that perhaps Dave found defining his relationship with Lockyer just as difficult as she did. Lockyer was Jane's superior and he was Dave's colleague, first and foremost. But then there was the murky boundary between that and the amount of time at work, and out of work, they both spent with him.

'What can we do?' she asked.

'Another time,' Dave said, nodding towards the doors leading into the suite just as Patrick walked in. 'Here he is. Patrick, let's get things moving, so DS Bennett can get on with her day.'

CHAPTER THIRTEEN

25th April – Friday

Jane watched and listened as Dave and Patrick worked on Maggie Hungerford. Both men talked in hushed whispers, Dave speaking into a Dictaphone pinned to the strap of his apron. Before he could ask for a piece of equipment, it seemed Patrick was handing it to him. They worked together in perfect harmony. It was impressive to watch.

'So, what can you tell me, Dave?' Even though he had managed to get through the external examination in less than half an hour, Jane was aware of the time and how long the rest of the procedure would take. She didn't want to be late for her meeting with Phil; or rather, she knew being late would cause her more hassle than she could stomach. A press conference was being arranged to coincide with the evening news. She needed time to prepare for that, too.

'Okay, here we go,' he said, stepping back from Maggie's body. 'As I suspected from my initial examination on-site, the head contusion is superficial. Blunt head-trauma to the upper right quadrant here,' he said, pointing to an area behind the girl's right ear. It had been cleaned and a small amount of the hair removed to expose the wound. 'The assailant would have approached from behind, leading with their right hand. The instrument used was small with a rounded end, but with enough weight to inflict this type of injury. The victim would have been knocked unconscious, but only momentarily – a few minutes at most.' Jane uncapped her pen and made a note of the wound, its position and a description of the object used. 'Are the labs back on the blood found outside the girl's home address?' he asked.

'Yes,' Jane said, making a rough sketch of the wound on Maggie's head. 'They came in just before I came down. It's hers. Not that I'm surprised. It was a safe assumption that she was taken from her house . . . She was wearing her pyjamas, after all.'

'Right,' he said, lifting Maggie's hand. 'There was a lot of dirt and organic matter under the victim's nails, although it's hard to tell what we've got as the ends of her fingers are damaged.' He looked over at Jane. They both knew what that meant. Maggie had tried to dig her way out. 'Patrick has taken samples. We might get lucky and find something of the assailant's: fibres, blood or tissue. Have to wait and see.'

She nodded, but didn't feel hopeful. Maggie's attacker had knocked her unconscious; even if it was only for a few minutes, there would have been time to restrain her. If Maggie was tied up, she wouldn't have been able to scratch him. Him – Jane realized that her brain had automatically assigned a gender to Maggie's killer. 'Does she have any ligature marks?' she asked.

'Not that I can see,' he said, 'but if the attacker used soft restraints you wouldn't necessarily be able to. Closer examination will confirm either way if there are fibres embedded in her skin, so you'll have to wait for my full report on that one,' he said as he leaned closer to examine one of Maggie's wrists. 'I'll know more once we have the lab results back, but in my opinion – given the lack of defensive wounds, and the limited time she would have been unconscious from the head-trauma – I think a sedative might have been used to subdue and transport her.'

'That would make sense,' she said. 'Be good to have that info as soon as you can manage it, Dave.'

'Of course,' he said, not looking at her.

'Would you say the attacker was male or female?'

He seemed to consider her question, tilting his head to one side. 'Male,' he said after a few seconds. 'From the angle of the head-trauma, the attacker was tall: six foot, I'd say. Also, the amount of force required to render the victim un-conscious would have been considerable. Not to mention transporting the victim, carrying her into the tomb . . . That would be challenging for a woman, in my opinion.'

'That's what I figured,' Jane said.

'There is something else,' Dave went on, looking over at Patrick. 'From the initial examination, it looks like she had intercourse not long before she was interred.'

Jane looked up from her pad. Two words stood out to her: 'interred' and 'intercourse'. Neither was good to hear. 'Rape?'

Dave's lips turned down at the edges as his shoulders lifted in a small shrug. 'I'm not sure on that yet,' he said. 'I don't think so. I'll do a full rape-kit, but from my external exami-nation it looks consensual – rough possibly, but consensual.'

'What makes you say that?' she asked. She had written

the word 'rape' on her pad, circled it and then surrounded it with question marks.

'There's a significant amount of vaginal secretion, which suggests she was conscious and consenting. There's semen as well. There are external abrasions and swelling consistent with aggressive intercourse, but not enough to suggest forced penetration. She has a contraceptive implant in her arm,' he said.

'So there might be a boyfriend,' Jane mused, making a note on her pad. A lover killing his partner in a rage wasn't unusual, but it didn't seem to fit this scenario. The tomb suggested premeditation, but to have sex with the victim and bury her without even attempting to remove traces of bodily fluids seemed spur-of-the moment or reactive. 'How long before she died did the intercourse take place?' she asked.

'A few hours. Certainly not long before she was interred,' he said. She couldn't help cringing. There was something about the word 'interred'. A body could be interred, but it seemed wholly wrong that the same could be said for a living, breathing human being. 'Sorry,' Dave said. '"Interred" doesn't sound right, I know. But then "buried" doesn't fit, either. Not in this case.' He sighed. 'Anyway, I'll know more about timings when I do the internal examination. Sperm can survive for up to five days inside the uterus. We're working on the hypothesis that she was alive when she was placed in the tomb, and that she wasn't there for more than five to seven days. Once I've taken more samples I should be able to give you a more accurate timeline for both intercourse and time of death.'

'Okay,' Jane said, looking down at her watch. It was ten to six already.

'Somewhere else to be?' he said, frowning.

'I've got a meeting with Phil Bathgate at six-thirty, up in the conference room. I could do with ten minutes to prepare . . . ' She trailed off. Nothing could prepare her for Phil. 'And there's a press conference later on.'

'I see,' he said. 'Well, the internal will take me forty-five minutes to an hour. I've got to do the chest cavity and digestive system first, so it'll be a while before I get on to the reproductive system. Up to you.'

She looked at her watch again. 'Well, if you don't mind, I'm going to head back then,' she said, trying to ignore the disapproving look Dave was giving her. His deference to his patients knew no bounds. 'I know you'll take care of her,' she added.

Dave's face softened and he nodded. 'No problem. You'll be upstairs for a while?'

'Definitely,' she said, walking towards the exit, pulling off her apron and gloves and throwing them in the bin by the door. 'I'll be in the office until seven-thirty or eight, so if you find anything or need me for anything, just give me a buzz and I'll come back down. In fact,' she said, putting her finger to her head as if she had been struck by a brainwave, 'you could call me at about half-past six with something vitally significant . . . '

He laughed and shook his head. 'No, no, my friend. I wouldn't dream of dragging you away from such an important meeting.' He turned away and indicated for Patrick to bring over the shears for opening up the chest. 'Be sure to pass on my regards to Phil,' he called over his shoulder. 'I love that man,' he said in an exaggerated shout.

'Will do,' Jane replied, pushing open the doors and walking out into the hallway.

She turned and looked back into the mortuary suite. Dave and Patrick had resumed their hushed chatter. As she looked at them she thought they looked like mourners, standing at a graveside, respectful. Dave was a gift to the dead. She had always thought so. He was a gift to Maggie and her family, because he would care for her as if she were still living.

Jane carried her laptop into the conference room and started to set up. Maggie Hungerford's file looked slim and unremarkable on the glass table. It contained the preliminary paperwork and a few crime-scene photographs. It wouldn't stay slim for long. Penny was typing up the notes from their meeting with Maggie's parents, SOCO were sending over their report from Maggie's home address, the PM would arrive sometime tomorrow, and Jane had no doubt that Phil's notes would be extensive. All of the information relating to Maggie's case would be available on computer files but, like most of the coppers, she preferred the bulk of a 'real' file. There was something about the substance of papers, the file's increasing thickness as the case developed, that reassured her. She thought about what Dave had said in the post-mortem about Maggie's birth-control implant. The Hungerfords had told her their daughter was single, that she didn't have time for distractions. Her MA in psychology and her long-term goal of opening her own practice were her main focus. An interview had been arranged with Christina O'Reilly for Monday morning. Jane was banking on Chrissie having a different story.

'Are you ready for me?'

She looked over her shoulder as Philip Bathgate strolled into the room, a folder clasped under his arm. She wished she had set up on the opposite side of the table. Her position in the room made her feel as if she had been waiting for the headmaster. 'Yes, of course. Come in, Phil,' she said, repositioning Maggie's file in front of her.

'Good, good,' he said, walking to the other side of the conference table and sitting down as he whipped the file from under his arm with a flourish. 'Interesting, Jane, fascinating,' he said, indicating the file and tapping his lips with his fingers as he sat down. His chair was set much higher than hers, his knees grazing the underneath of the glass tabletop.

'That's good – great,' she said, finding it almost impossible to maintain eye contact with him. She cleared her throat and sat up straighter in her chair. This was ridiculous. She was in charge. This was her case. 'I could certainly use your insight here, Phil. This case isn't exactly standard.'

'Indeed, no,' he said, sniffing. 'I would imagine you were both delighted and perturbed when it was assigned to you. Quite a step up from your usual cases, I would have thought, but then your boss isn't exactly up to it, is he?' His smile wasn't difficult to read. 'I mean, spousal murders, yes. Territorial killings, sometimes. Involuntary manslaughter, certainly. Far more your speed. Within your comfort zone, if you don't mind me saying.' Before she could defend herself he continued, 'I mean, between you and me, it isn't exactly fair, is it? Because of Lockyer's error in judgement – for lack of a better word – you are left carrying the can, on probably the most unusual murder case Lewisham has seen, the Stevens case notwithstanding.' She wanted to say something, respond, retaliate, but his assassination of her career and of Lockyer's actions had left her stunned into silence. 'I can see I have offended you, Jane. I did not mean to impugn your abilities whatsoever. On the contrary. I simply felt it appropriate to let you know that I am on your side, and I will do whatever I can to assist you when conducting your investigation.' He reached his hand across the table, as if expecting her to return the gesture, to seal their bond of understanding.

She took a deep breath, glanced out of the window on the pretence that something had caught her eye. 'Phil,' she said, returning her gaze to his, loosening her jaw in order to feign indifference to his tirade of insinuation and outright insult. 'I'm sure you are aware that I am not at liberty to discuss the Stevens case or anything pertaining to it. As for my role in this particular case, notwithstanding my previous experience . . . ' She decided speaking Phil's language might assist in delivering her point. 'Roger assigned the case to me because I had the availability in my caseload and the experience to deal with this type of crime. I will certainly pass on your concerns. I am sure he would be keen to speak to you and would welcome any feedback you have. I, personally, welcome your offer of cooperation and assistance. Cases like this one need to be reviewed endlessly. To know I can call on you to revise your findings at any time is an absolute comfort.' She smiled. 'Having someone of your authority and experience "on my side" is an honour and I fully intend to utilise your expertise at every opportunity. Thank you, Phil.'

Despite the sweat collecting at the back of her neck she could see that her words had had the desired effect. She watched as Phil shifted in his seat, clearing his throat several times as if readying himself to speak, but then changing his mind at the last second. She pulled up her sleeve and looked at her watch. 'I can see that I've already eaten into your valuable time, Phil. My apologies for that. Shall we move on to your findings? I'm sure you're as keen as I am to get things moving.'

'I . . . ' he coughed. 'Yes. Perhaps it would be best to get on with it.' He stared at the tabletop, fiddling with the edge of the folder in front of him.

The warm rush of satisfaction swept over her entire body, drying the sweat on the back of her neck. 'Great,' she said, unable to keep the smile off her face. 'So, what have you got for me?' She sat back and crossed her legs, laying her hands in her lap, unclasped, relaxed.

'I will email over my full report,' he said, still not looking at her, 'but I think I have enough to assist you as of now, in as much as geographical profiling goes.'

'Good,' she said. 'Go on.'

He straightened in his chair. 'The tomb itself, its design and location are my primary points of interests. I have spoken to Dr Crown.' It took Jane a few seconds to realize he was talking about Jeanie. 'Your office passed on her findings, but I felt – as I am sure you did – that further discussion was in order. I talked to Dr Crown at length yesterday and she agreed with me that the "tomb" was not so much constructed as altered from its original state.'

'Meaning?' she asked.

'As I'm sure you are aware, Chislehurst Caves are less than

a mile away.' She nodded, despite not knowing anything of the sort. She had heard of the caves. She had watched some documentary about them being used as a music venue back in the Sixties.

'Bowie performed there once,' she said, hoping she was right.

'Indeed, him and many others,' Phil said, seemingly unimpressed. 'I think, more importantly, they were used as air-raid shelters during the Second World War. At one point nearly fifteen thousand people inhabited the caves during the worst of the Blitz. Of course it is an inaccuracy to call them caves, as they are man-made. They were originally chalk- and flint-mines, used up until the late 1930s—'

'Right,' she said, noting down the date, as if it had any bearing on the case. 'And you and Jeanie – I mean, Dr Crown – think the murder-site is an extension of these caves?' she asked, interrupting his monologue.

He sat back in his chair, opening and closing his mouth like a stranded fish. 'I . . . well, yes. Dr Crown believes it to be an aborted access tunnel, and that the individual who altered the site did so by excavating more earth from the base and then using it to cover the walls and ceiling. The entranceway and hatch are also new additions. She is confident further examination of the soil will confirm this.'

'I'll need to see detailed plans of the cave system. There must be a public record.' It left Jane wondering what came first: Maggie's death or the tomb itself. 'It must have taken months,' she said, more to herself than to Phil.

'No doubt, but I must tell you, I believe the location to be far more important than the tomb construction.'

'Why?' she asked, her pen poised.

'Elmstead Woods is a well-frequented green space, a thoroughfare; it would be difficult to go unobserved if one were engaging in unusual activities, such as excavation or body disposal,' he said, smiling. 'Therefore, in my opinion, the location must have been chosen for specific reasons. For the individual, or individuals, to choose a site where discovery was almost guaranteed is a message.'

'Right,' she said. On her pad she wrote the words 'location', 'message' and a question mark.

'You need to establish whether the victim has any connection with the Elmstead area. I suspect you will find she doesn't. In which case Elmstead Woods was chosen by her attacker for a specific reason. The individual you are looking for will have good local knowledge and will live within a five- to ten-mile radius of the site.' Jane was making shorthand notes: key words, phrases she needed to remember. 'The planning it would take to locate and alter the burial space; the patience and restraint of the attack – there is nothing frenzied or impulsive, the blow to the head notwithstanding. Each element demonstrates someone motivated and highly intelligent.' Phil's fascination with Maggie's killer was obvious, but it was his admiration that Jane was finding hard to ignore. 'The anticipation would have been incredible,' he continued, 'preparing to take the girl, executing his plan, interring the victim without discovery, watching her panic and then waiting for her to die, once her air supply had been stopped. All these factors in themselves would have been exhilarating. But imagine, if you will, the greater anticipation of waiting for the body to be found.'

'So you think Maggie was meant to be found?' she asked, frowning.

'Absolutely, yes. It had to be witnessed, like the proverbial tree falling in the forest. The murder would have been incomplete without discovery.'

'Incomplete,' she repeated the word, testing the idea that was taking hold. 'If that's true, then Maggie's death wasn't the endpoint.' Phil was nodding as she spoke. 'And if her murder wasn't the endpoint, then it was the starting point . . . ' She looked at Phil. 'But the starting point to what?'

'I don't know,' he said. 'That's what you need to find out.'

CHAPTER FOURTEEN

I feel better. I knew I would. All I needed was sleep. Sleep deprivation can drive you mad, but I have a positive outlook today. Even the space seems bigger – roomy even. I know that it can't be. If anything it should be smaller, sucked inward by my presence. I am mapping out my surroundings, despite knowing them already. It feels good to be moving again. It feels good to be awake.

'Four to the right,' I say to myself, crawling on my hands and knees. The soil in my throat has made my voice croak. I can see Kermit the Frog sitting on a wall singing a song to Miss Piggy:

> Lydia, oh Lydia, that encyclo-pidia.
> Oh Lydia the Queen of Tattoo.
> On her back is The Battle of Waterloo.
> Beside it the Wreck of the Hesperus, too.

The song fades as my head hits the wall. That's right. The same as before. I turn back to face the centre. 'Four to the middle and four to the left.' I hold my breath, waiting for the wall. My head bumps against it. There is the smallest amount of give this time. Is that the wall softening or my head? 'Four back to the middle, then six to the top.' My legs are getting tired, but I must finish my route. I lift my head a little, so that my forehead takes the impact of the far wall. I can smell clay. I shuffle backwards. 'Six to the middle and six to the back.' Kermit sings over the top of my voice. My feet hit the back wall. 'Good,' I say. 'That's good.'

Everything is as it should be. I can rest now. I have executed my cross-section. Once I have slept some more, I will repeat the process, but diagonally. In my head the space has become a Union Jack that I rediscover every time I wake up. The faint outline of the flag must be imprinted on the floor by now, where my knees have rubbed at the dirt over and over again. I reach the centre of the space just in time. My legs will carry me no further. I don't worry about my feet any more.

I can't feel them.

CHAPTER FIFTEEN

26th April – Saturday

Jane pushed her fringe off her forehead, static crackling over her fingers. She looked at the picture of Peter on her desk and started tearing up. She had missed bedtime again last night and she would be working most of the weekend. He had been pissy with her this morning and had refused to eat his breakfast. She blinked back her tears, sighed and turned back to her computer. The results were back on the blood found in Sue and Mark's utility room. It was Mark's. She had known it would be, just as she had known that the blood found outside the house in Greenwich would belong to Maggie. But knowing didn't help her, in either case. So the blood was Mark's. What did that mean? She couldn't make the suicide theory stack up, whichever way she looked at it. There was only one alternative. If Mark hadn't injured himself, then someone had entered the Leech home, attacked Mark and either taken him from the property injured or, more likely, had removed him in order to dispose of the body. She shook her head. The Missing Persons team would still liaise, but the investigation had now been officially assigned to her. It was a murder investigation. Not that she would be telling Sue that. Not yet.

'Is the blood-work on Leech back yet?'

She looked up. Lockyer was leaning on the partition, staring down at her. She hadn't heard him approach. He looked terrible: unshaven beyond the point of designer stubble. His suit jacket looked as if he had slept in it. There were stains on the left lapel, toothpaste and something darker, unknown. 'Sorry, sir. I didn't see you there,' she said, re-arranging the files on her desk.

'The blood-work on Leech,' he repeated. 'Is it back yet?'

She nodded. 'Yes. I just had the email come through this morning, sir. It's Mark's.'

'Any third-party hits?' he asked, pulling at the corner of his left eye with his finger. He looked bored.

'No, sir. The only DNA found was Mark's. Forensics are going over the rest of the trace evidence to see if they can find anything else. I should hear back next week – Wednesday, hopefully.'

Lockyer frowned, his eyes drifting around the office. 'I'll go and speak to Sue. I was planning on heading home soon anyway,' he said.

Jane felt her mouth drop open. 'Er, I was actually heading over there now,' she said. The lie was out before she could stop herself.

'I think she'd prefer to hear it from me,' he said, not looking at her. 'Don't you?'

'Have you spoken to her?' she asked.

He didn't seem to notice her tone. 'Yes. I've spoken to her . . . every day since Mark's disappearance. It still is a disappearance, Jane. Blood doesn't equal dead. It may have been assigned to my team, but that doesn't mean anything. Until Mark is found we are assuming he's alive. Aren't we?' His eyes searched her face. He seemed to be daring her to disagree with him. 'Well?' he said, folding his arms.

'Of course,' she said. 'I mean, yes, sir.'

'Good.' He turned and walked out of the office without a backward glance.

Lockyer stood staring at himself in the mirror, his hands on either side of the basin, squeezing the porcelain as if it were to blame for his actions. He turned and walked into a cubicle, locking the door just as another officer came into the Gents. He closed the lid, sat down and put his head in his hands. The last thing he needed to do was alienate Jane, but he couldn't seem to control his resentment. While his life was disintegrating, hers was coming together. Roger had made her lead detective on the Hungerford murder. It should be his case. It would have been his case, if it wasn't for the Stevens debacle. Everyone was treating him differently. Even Dave had started turning up at his flat unannounced, on the pretext of going for a beer, a run, a trip to the supermarket – anything to gain access, to give them time to 'talk'. Jane was the only one who was even attempting to act normally around him. So why was he determined to treat her like shit? He thought about the cold-cases sitting on his desk. It was dead-work. It was a punishment.

He put his hands on his knees and stood up. He unlocked the door to the cubicle and walked out – out of the Gents and over to the lifts. Maybe some fresh air would do him some good. He looked at his watch and stopped. There wasn't time. He had told Jane he was heading home, but he couldn't, not yet. He had an appointment. He had rescheduled it twice this week, in a lame attempt to avoid it, but that hadn't worked. It was in five minutes, up on the fifth floor. It wasn't a meeting he wanted to keep. As he stepped into the lift he nodded to the other officers, but then bowed his head. The last thing he needed right now was banal conversation about shift-work, the weather and the five-car pile-up on Shooter's Hill that was causing chaos. It was hot. The traffic was backed-up. It was the weekend. Everyone was pissed off. What else was there to say?

The lift shuddered into motion and climbed to the next floor. He didn't wait for the doors to open fully. He walked out, head down, towards a part of the building he had never visited before. This was his first scheduled appointment. It would be a weekly event, until such time as Roger was satisfied that Lockyer was 'back on form', as he put it.

The sign on the door in front of him made his head ache. The black stencilling on the door read: *Occupational Health – Counselling Service.*

He didn't want to be here.

CHAPTER SIXTEEN

26th April – Saturday

Jane's mobile started to ring. She was pacing back and forth in front of Boots on the high street. She couldn't stay in the office. Not after Lockyer's rant. She looked at the screen. 'Sue, hi,' she said, holding the phone to her ear and walking away from a group of teenagers. 'I was just going to call you.' It felt like a lie. 'How are you?'

'I'm all right. I'm okay,' Sue said, her voice not matching the sentiment. 'Any news?'

Jane felt as if she had two unexploded grenades, one in each hand, both missing a pin, both seconds away from blowing up in her face. One was Sue. The other was her boss. 'I was just speaking to Lockyer – Mike, I mean,' she said, correcting herself. 'If it's okay with you, he's going to come out and see you this afternoon, to update you on where we are.' She perched on the edge of a bench, trying to avoid an array of bird-shit and chewing gum. 'Will that work with the boys? Are they home?'

'Er, yes, that's fine,' Sue said. 'I'm home all day. The boys are with friends for the night,' she continued. 'I'm grateful

Mike can see me . . . at the weekend, I mean. I was hoping to speak to him. Not that I don't trust that you're doing everything you can, Jane, but I just hoped, you know, given his relationship with Mark, that he'd be more . . . involved.'

'Of course, I understand,' she said, feeling helpless as she listened to Sue crying at the other end of the line. She watched a mother pushing a pram; two girls smoking, laughing. Their days were normal. Their lives were moving forward. Sue's wasn't.

'It's been four days. Four days,' Sue said, sniffing. 'I understand how busy Mike must be, but he's Mark's friend. I thought he would at least have phoned to say . . . to say . . .' Her words disappeared into a sob.

'I'm sorry, Sue,' Jane said, feeling her face heat up with anger. Lockyer had lied to her. Again. He hadn't spoken to Sue at all. 'Listen. Let me get Mike to call you. You can sort out a time with him, and I'll give you a call later on today to see how you're doing. How does that sound?'

Sue sniffed. 'Thank you, Jane. I really appreciate everything you're doing for me . . . and Mark. The kids are a mess. I'm a mess.'

'I know, I know. I'm here, Sue. We will find Mark, I promise you.' It was the first time in her career that she had ever made a promise to a relative. It was a reckless thing to do, because how could she possibly stand by her word? She stood up and started pacing again. 'I'll call you later. Okay?'

'Thank you, Jane. Thank you.'

She hung up the phone and logged into her emails. She opened a new message and addressed it to Lockyer: 'Call from Sue Leech, 10.13. Requested update on case. Advised you would call ASAP and confirm meeting at Leech residence this afternoon to update. Did not mention blood-work results.' She pressed 'Send' and started to walk back towards the office. She couldn't believe what she was about to do, but what other choice did she have? There was no way she could allow Lockyer's behaviour to continue unchecked. Even her loyalty had limits.

CHAPTER SEVENTEEN

26th April – Saturday

'Sir,' Jane said.

Roger Westwood, SIO for three of the murder-squad teams, looked up from his desk. He was on the phone, but seemed to be coming to the end of his call. He waved Jane into his office and gestured for her to sit down. The feeling of betrayal weighed her down, her guilt compounding with each step into the room. She sat with a bump and looked over Roger's head. It sounded as if he was talking to his daughter. His tone was indulgent and firm, a combination reserved for children who were trying to get their own way. From the side of the conversation that Jane could hear, he was putting on a good show of resistance.

She crossed her legs, straightened her skirt and looked out of the window at St Stephen's church and the huge elm tree that shaded it. The sun bounced off the leaves as they swayed in a light breeze. From Roger's office she would never have guessed she was in Lewisham – or in London even. It struck her as funny how a different office, location or view could change someone's perspective, even their reality. It made her think of Maggie, of Elmstead, and what it meant to her killer. She heard a change in Roger's voice as his conversation came to an end. There was one word his daughter was waiting to hear and she suspected her SIO was seconds away from saying it.

'All right, yes. Okay,' he said, shaking his head. He looked over at Jane and shrugged his shoulders, defeated. 'Yes, yes. I'll speak to your mother,' he paused. 'You too,' he said, hanging up the phone. 'I'm sorry about that, Jane. My daughter,' he went on, gesturing at the phone. 'She wants to borrow my car to move into her new flat. Apparently her car is too small and unsafe with a heavy load.' He shook his head again. 'God, I'm a soft touch.'

'All parents are,' she said.

'There should be a course, some study group – a "how to" on parenting. How to spot emotional manipulation and avoid it.' He laughed.

'I'm pretty sure you'd still give in, sir.'

'You're probably right.' He stood up, arched his back and looked out of his window at the view Jane had just been admiring. She wondered how he saw it, and what it meant to him. 'So, what can I do for you, DS Bennett? You don't want to borrow my car, do you?' he asked, looking over his shoulder at her, smiling.

Words failed her. Roger was in a good mood, jovial even, especially for a Saturday morning. What she had to say was serious. Too serious. He didn't need to know. It could wait until Monday, until after the morning briefing. She was over-reacting anyway. She started to stand, opening her mouth to apologize.

'Right, I see,' he said. 'It's like that, is it?' He walked around his desk, put his hand on her shoulder as he passed and closed the door to his office. Once he was back in his chair he shuffled forward and looked at her. 'Let me guess . . . Lockyer?'

'Yes, sir,' she said, staring down at her hands.

'Let's hear it then. What's he been up to now?'

She felt like a snitch, a child telling on a friend. This was wrong, but it was too late. Roger was looking at her, his eyebrows raised. He was waiting for her to speak. She had no choice.

Jane stood in the lift, massaging her temples, her eyes closed. Christina O'Reilly was waiting for her down in the interview suite. Her appointment wasn't scheduled until Monday morning, but according to the desk sergeant, Maggie's best friend couldn't wait and had come into the station on the off-chance that, first, Jane would be in the office and, second, would have time to see her. She should be thinking about why Christina O'Reilly was so desperate to talk to her, but all Jane could think about was her conversation with Roger. Her SIO had been understanding, patient, considered – all the things you would expect someone in senior management to be – but she had sensed his concern. That wasn't good. She would have preferred Roger to have dragged Lockyer into his office and given him a bollocking. End of discussion. But Roger wasn't angry. He was worried. That meant her fears for Lockyer and his mental state weren't unfounded. 'Leave it with me' was all he said.

As she stepped out of the lift her phone buzzed in her pocket. She walked over to the desk sergeant on duty as she took it out. 'Christina O'Reilly,' she said, looking down at her phone. She had a new email.

'I put her in room three,' he replied, gesturing towards the signing-in register lying open on the counter.

'Great, thanks.' She signed in, turned and stopped outside the door to the interview room as she opened the email on her phone. It was from Lockyer. She held her breath as she read: 'I want to see you in my office ASAP.'

CHAPTER EIGHTEEN

The madness is back, eating away at my mind. It feels different. Not what I expected.

I can't sleep, no matter how hard I try. I rock back and forth, humming to myself, but as my eyes begin to close I am jolted awake. My stomach flips, my breath catches in my throat, a cold sweat covers my skin. It takes a second, a minute or an hour to remember my predicament. I am nowhere. I am no one. I am not missed. I am not a picture on a carton of milk. I am not missing. I have already gone, passed over into the nothingness. All that awaits me is death. There is some comfort in that thought, but if I cannot sleep, how will I slip away? Will there be pain? I cry, but my face remains dry. There are no tears.

I lie back and blink my eyes, my pupils straining to focus on the blackness. When someone is deprived of one sense, their other senses are meant to develop to compensate. It is true. More than I ever thought possible. I cannot see, but I can hear everything: my breathing, creatures burrowing in the earth, footsteps, my heartbeat, water dripping through rocks, my teeth chattering. Each sound overlaps the other, creating an almost deafening roar. I can smell the earth, the stale air, the cold on my skin. Every breath filling my head, until I think it will burst open. My fingers are constantly moving, caressing my numb skin and the glass-like walls that surround me. I taste the soil, the air and my body as it disintegrates from the inside out, but nothing can hold my attention, nothing can give my mind or body what it craves. The thing I wish for – even more than death – is daylight. Even a brief glimpse would nourish me, more than a thousand hamburgers or an entire lake of cool water. To be able to see for even a second would be enough. Then I can let go. Then I can die in peace.

I wrap my arms around my body. There is no comfort. My body is numb.

CHAPTER NINETEEN

26th April – Saturday

Jane chanced a look in Lockyer's direction. He was sitting in his office, his back to her. His blinds were closed. He was waiting for her. She ducked back behind the partition on her desk and continued with her interview report.

Christina O'Reilly had tried her best to be helpful, but Jane had learned very little. She had half-hoped that the premature visit might have meant more. But no. Jane had seen grief manifest itself in a thousand different ways, and Chrissie's behaviour wasn't really that unusual. She had just been desperate to talk about Maggie, as if it would somehow bring her friend back. However, there was one piece of information that had got Jane's attention. According to Chrissie, Maggie had dated a PhD student, Terry Mort, the previous year, but the relationship had only lasted for a few months.

Jane had just hung up the phone after speaking to the head of psychology at the university, Professor Cresswell. He was due to come in for an interview first thing on Tuesday, but had been happy to email over details of Maggie's tutors, modules, coursework and results to date. It seemed Jane wasn't the only one who worked weekends. From a brief look, the drop-off in Maggie's work was evident and was more serious than either her parents or Chrissie knew. Maggie had missed a number of classes and had been late with three separate coursework proposals. The downward trend appeared to start around the time of the break-up with Mort, the PhD student. Was that a coincidence?

Jane clicked into the 'Action' list on her computer. The head of administration was organizing class lists for Maggie's modules and a full student list, separated into degree, Masters and doctoral level, together with a map of the university detailing communal areas and where each subject was taught. Penny was making sure that got followed up, and was collating information from the interviews already carried out. William Hungerford had dropped off Maggie's laptop, mobile phone and Kindle this morning. Jane had asked the Computer Forensics team to check Maggie's email accounts, social media activity, online dating and any photographs of men taken in the last twelve months. Chris would oversee this and report back. Franks and Sasha were finalizing the door-to-door enquiries at Maggie's home address and in Elmstead, and maintaining security around the tomb. And Whitemore was liaising with the Exhibits team. Jane was going to need more help, especially after last night's press conference naming Maggie and asking the public for help. Roger had agreed to sign off on a provisional eight to twelve officers, based on her estimates, but even that might not be enough.

She put her head in her hands. There was so much to do, and she hadn't even begun to allocate duties relating to Mark's disappearance. Mind you, there was at least a ray of hope on that score. Sue had confirmed that she and the children never went away without Mark, certainly not since his retirement – something Jane had thought odd. What were the chances that his attacker just happened to choose a day when Mark was home alone? That suggested that the attack was premeditated, and that the attacker must have had access to, or at least knowledge of, Mark and Sue's schedule. Did that mean the attacker had access to their emails or telephone, or was he or she using the local resident grapevine to get information? Jane didn't know the answer to that question, but she knew where to start. Mark was bound to have made more than a few enemies during his career in the murder squad. She would need to go over his old cases, checking convictions, jail terms and cross-referencing current residence status. But that would have to wait. She pushed herself away from her desk. It was now or never.

Guilt slowed her steps as she walked towards Lockyer's office. She had almost managed to convince herself that she had no choice; that his erratic behaviour had to be reported. But it wasn't that simple. She was worried about him, but she couldn't deny she was also pissed off with him, for acting like a nut-job on the Stevens case and for lying to her about his brother. She was also running two major investigations, and the truth was that she was floundering. She needed Lockyer's help and he hadn't been there for her, so she had gone running to Roger, like a coward. She knocked her knuckles on the glass door a few times and waited. Lockyer turned and motioned for her to come in.

She pushed open the door. 'You wanted to see me, sir?'

'Yes, Jane. Have a seat,' he said, turning his back on her and opening his blinds. It was raining. Rivulets coursed down the windows, obscuring Lewisham High Street and the buildings on the other side of the street. 'I've spoken to Sue Leech,' he said. Jane remained silent. 'I have a stack of cold-case reviews, so I won't have time to get to Bromley and back. I've told Sue you'll call to confirm, but that you will go over and update her.'

'Of course. No problem, sir,' she said.

'The three cases you're winding up are still under my direct supervision, so I will need to know when they are finished.'

'I should have all three done by the end of next week at the latest, sir.'

'Good. You'll need full resources on the Hungerford case.' He looked over his shoulder at his computer screen. 'Roger has agreed to having another six members of the team, but will increase that to eight, depending on the outcome of the morning briefing on Monday.'

'Right,' she said, not wanting to contradict him.

'This lot is going to keep me pretty busy,' he said, gesturing at a messy pile of files on the edge of his desk. 'You will report directly to Roger on the Hungerford and Leech cases.'

Jane didn't know what to say. She wanted to walk straight into Roger's office and recant everything. This wasn't what she wanted.

'Did you hear me, Jane?' Lockyer said.

'Yes, sir. Of course, but I'll keep you informed. I know I'm going to need your help.' As soon as the words were out of her mouth she regretted them. She sounded pathetic, her tone whiney, like a child.

'That won't be necessary,' he said, shaking his head. 'Roger will keep me up to date, I'm sure.'

Jane swallowed hard, holding back the tears that wanted to come. If she had kept her mouth shut, talked to Lockyer directly, this wouldn't have happened. He didn't need her regrets or tears. He needed her loyalty and support.

'That's all,' he said.

She stood and backed out of the office. She walked over to her desk, numbed by the experience.

'Jane?'

She looked up. Penny was standing by her desk, waiting for her. 'Yes, Pen. What's up?' she said, without enthusiasm.

'Your mother called. She wants to know what time you'll be home. And I've got a lead on the boyfriend.'

'Mort?' she asked.

'No. Lebowski,' Penny said, looking down at a notepad she was holding. 'He's a lecturer at Maggie's uni, teaches psychology. We've had two calls on the inquiry number naming him.'

Jane raised her eyebrows. 'What do we know about him?' she asked, already thinking ten steps ahead. She was pretty sure that sleeping with a student was a sackable offence for a tutor. And therein lies a motive, she thought.

CHAPTER TWENTY

27th April – Sunday

Jane put her Peugeot in gear, turned to check the road behind her and backed out of the driveway. There wasn't a lot of traffic on the road. If her luck was in, it shouldn't take more than twenty minutes to get to Sue's house in Bromley.

There just hadn't been time yesterday. Roger had called her into his office straight after her uncomfortable conversation with Lockyer, to get updates on the Hungerford and Leech cases. By the time she got out it was gone eight o'clock – too late to see Sue.

She waited for the lights to change and then pulled onto Lewisham Road. She stopped to let two women cross in front of her. Yesterday's bad weather hadn't lasted. The sun was out, warming the pavements, creating a steamy haze around the women's feet. One held the hand of a little girl who was skipping alongside her mother in a pretty summer dress. The other woman was pushing a double stroller. A child sat in one side, but the other was crammed full of Sainsbury's bags and a picnic blanket. Everyone seemed to be migrating to their closest patch of green to enjoy the sunshine, whereas

Jane was left with the smog-stained buildings and oil-soaked roads and working on a Sunday.

She pulled up to the roundabout, indicated and then took her chance and nipped out in front of a procession of empty buses. Sunshine hit the windscreen, blinding her for a second. She leaned over and pulled down the visor on the passenger side, then her own. Peter was sitting next to her in the passenger seat, his belt pulled tight, his hands wrapped around a multicoloured Lego helicopter. It was a pre-birthday present from his grandmother. Jane suspected it was a 'good behaviour' treat. 'Let's have some music, shall we?' she said, turning on the stereo and then reaching over and smoothing down the wayward cowlick on the top of his head.

She wished she didn't have to take Peter with her. She cursed under her breath when she got stuck at the temporary traffic lights straddling Bromley Road. She had already been into the office this morning and left Peter sitting at her desk while she briefed her team. Roger had signed off on fifteen extra officers ahead of Monday's briefing, which meant she would need to go in again this afternoon to organize work schedules, and then she needed to go over Victor Lebowski's background. Penny had forwarded his details. A tutor having an affair with a student didn't surprise her, but it might explain why Maggie hadn't told her parents or Chrissie. It was the kind of thing that could ruin a man's career.

Fifteen minutes later she pulled up outside Sue and Mark's house. 'Okey-dokey. Here we are. Now you remember what

119

we talked about,' she said, unclipping her seatbelt and then Peter's as she turned to face him. 'Tom and George might be a bit sad, because they are missing their daddy.'

'When will he be home?' Peter asked. He had asked the same question at breakfast.

'I don't know, honey, but there's nothing for you to worry about.' She climbed out of the car and waited for Peter to join her. She took his hand, led him up the path, pushed the doorbell and waited. She could hear footsteps and saw a shadow appear behind the obscured glass in the front door. It opened to reveal Thomas, dressed in a red T-shirt, long white football shorts and a scruffy pair of trainers. 'Hi, Tom,' she said, taking a step back. 'I know grown-ups always say, "Oh, haven't you grown", but in this case it's true. You're taller than me.' He was a typical rangy teenager, rake-thin, all limbs, knees and elbows.

'Mum's in the kitchen,' he said, pulling the door open wide to let them in. 'Hey, Pete. How's it going, mate?'

She felt the pressure increase on her hand as Peter tensed. She squeezed back to reassure him. 'What games have you got?' Peter asked, staring at his flip-flops.

Jane couldn't help smiling. 'I happened to mention that you and Georgie have a computer. Peter wants an Xbox for his birthday,' she said. Thomas nodded and retreated into the house until he was standing on the bottom stair.

'Cool. We've got loads of games. George is upstairs. Mum won't let me play *Call of Duty* with George, but we've got *Lego Star Wars*. You ever played that?' Peter brandished his Lego helicopter as if it was a secret access device to the world of computer gaming. 'Nice. Come on.'

Peter released his grip of Jane's hand and followed Thomas up the stairs. He didn't look back.

She was about to call out when Sue appeared in the doorway to the kitchen. 'Hi, Jane,' she said, wiping her hands on the tea towel that was tucked into the pocket of the apron she was wearing. 'Thanks so much for coming over at a weekend.' If anything, Sue looked better than she had on Tuesday night. She had some colour in her cheeks and her voice had some bounce to it. The boys, Jane thought – all this was a facade, a show of normality for Thomas and George.

'It's not a problem,' she said, walking forward and putting her arms around Sue. She could have wrapped them round twice. 'How are you doing?'

'Oh, you know,' she said, patting Jane on the back as if she was burping a baby. 'Bearing up.' The two women parted and looked at each other. This part was always difficult. Was Jane here as a friend or a police officer? She could see Sue wrestling with the same dilemma, because both applied. Both *had* to apply. As much as Jane wanted to support her friend, listen to her worries and dry her tears, she had a job to do. Everything that Sue said could be important. The private details of their marriage were now evidence – indicators that could lead to Mark. 'I know,' Sue said, as if reading Jane's thoughts. 'Business or pleasure?' she added, smiling. 'Come through. I've just made some lemonade. Do you fancy some?'

'Sounds great,' Jane said, following Sue through to the kitchen. The children's drawings and attempts at pottery still adorned almost every surface and the rustic walls gave the room a warm glow, but the door to the utility room was closed, two pieces of red tape criss-crossing the entrance.

Jane was pleased to see that whoever had sealed the room had used plain tape, rather than the bright-yellow crime-scene stuff. Neither Sue nor the boys needed to see that every day.

Sue put a jug of lemonade, two glasses and a packet of biscuits on a tray. 'I've got a table set up in the back garden,' she said, picking up the tray and nodding for Jane to follow her. Sue walked back into the hallway, passed the front door and went into the lounge. It was an open-plan lounge and dining room, the table set up at the far end next to French doors that led into the garden. 'Have to go the long way round, I'm afraid.'

'Okay.' Jane felt as if her inter-personal skills had abandoned her. She was so desperate to get the 'work stuff' done that she was finding small talk impossible.

'So, where are we?' Sue asked, walking out into the garden and sitting down at a small mosaic-topped table. She balanced the tray in the centre.

Jane walked over and sat down opposite her, taking her notepad out of her handbag. There was no easy way to say it. 'The blood results are back. It's Mark's.'

'I guessed as much,' Sue said, leaning forward and stirring the lemonade with a long-handled wooden spoon.

'As you know, there were extensive blood-spatters in the utility room, which had been wiped down.' An image of the utility room bathed in the harsh spotlights settled in her mind. 'The cleaning fluids used match the products that SOCO found in the utility room, in the cupboard under the sink,' she said, turning the page on her notepad, keeping her eyes on the paper in front of her. 'No other fingerprints were found. However, SOCO did find a small amount of white residue on the trim of the back door. I've just had confirmation that the substance is consistent with the powder used in surgical gloves.'

'Are you saying someone came into my home . . . someone attacked my husband?' Sue's voice stuttered to a stop.

'I'm so sorry,' Jane said, reaching over and taking her hand. 'That's the premise we're working on.'

'But why? Who would do this?' Sue said, shaking her head, her hands gripping the edge of the table. 'Who would—?' She stopped. 'I . . . '

'What is it, Sue?' Jane asked, trying to catch her eye. 'Sue?'

Sue shook her head. 'Nothing,' she said. 'I just can't believe this is happening.'

'Sue, I need your help.'

Sue looked over her shoulder and up at the window of the bedroom where her sons were playing computer games. When she turned back, Jane could see that her face had paled. Without looking Jane in the eye, she said, 'Ask me anything.'

CHAPTER TWENTY-ONE

27th April – Sunday

Lockyer dropped onto the sofa and turned on the television. Both sash windows were wide open, but there was no breeze to shift the heat in his lounge. The back of his shirt was soaked in sweat from his journey home in the car. He and Bobby had sat in the back garden at Cliffview and played 'Happy Families'. He had spent most of the game trying to engineer the deal so that Bobby would get his favourites, Mr Pots the painter and Mr Pint the Milkman, together with their respective families.

He rested his head back and looked up at the ceiling. Cobwebs clung to the cornices. He made a mental note, not for the first time, to get a duster that extended. He closed his eyes. Bobby would be forty-six this year. Time was meant to heal, but Lockyer felt just as angry today as he had five years ago when he drove to Manchester to meet his brother for the first time. The hardest part was having no one to blame. His parents were dead and so was Aunt Nancy, Bobby's guardian. Lockyer would never understand how they could separate two brothers. How could they lie to them both? But then that was part of it. No one had needed to lie to Bobby. His autism shut him off from the world to a certain extent. He remembered faces, footfalls, smells; he didn't remember hurt or rejection. Lockyer tipped his head forward and looked at his watch. Was it too early to have a beer?

He stood up and walked down the hallway and into the kitchen. The blast of cold air as he opened the fridge felt good. He debated between a French stubby beer and a larger bottle of Corona. Bigger was better. He took out the bottle, the glass cold against his palm, and reached into the kitchen drawer for the opener, flicking the lid onto the counter. He took a long swig and let out a satisfied groan. Just what he needed to smooth out the edges. He slopped back into the lounge, his flip-flops smacking his heels with each step. He could hear raised voices. A young couple were having a row on the pavement outside. He wandered over to the windows, sipping his beer as he listened to snatches of dialogue. He turned away, pained by another wound in his life that wouldn't heal.

It should be *them* on the street arguing, bickering like couples do once the honeymoon period is over. They never had the chance to get that far. Sometimes he could still feel her. Late at night, when he couldn't sleep, he would come into the kitchen and stand at the sink staring out at his tiny concrete garden. He would hear her approach, her feet soft on the tiled floor. She would put her arms around his waist and rest her cheek against his back. He shook his head and downed the rest of his beer. He didn't want to think about her, but she was always there, a shadow in his peripheral vision that disappeared if he tried to look at her. He reached for the remote and turned off the television. He was going to have to go for a run, try and sweat out this funk.

He had been home all weekend. It felt wrong, but Roger had made it clear that Lockyer only had three options: in his office going over cold-cases, in therapy or at home. Jane's little chat with their SIO hadn't helped, either. Lockyer needed the Hungerford case. He needed the focus, but Jane had seen to it that he was shut out. What he couldn't figure out was why. Roger had told him he wasn't authorized to be 'on-scene' until he was satisfied that Lockyer could be trusted. The more he thought about it, the more angry Lockyer felt. Without the job he was blind, bumbling about, trying to function like normal people. His years with the Met had worked the 'normal' right out of him. His non-work friends thought his job began and ended with a body, fascinated by the gory details, but there was so much more to it than that. Every death was like a pebble dropped into a lake with no shoreline. The ripples kept going.

His phone was ringing in the kitchen. He walked through, picked it up and glanced at the screen. It was Megan.

'Hi, honey,' he said, turning and leaning his back against the kitchen counter. He ran his free hand through his hair. It was more out of control than usual, standing up at odd angles. If he didn't get it cut soon, either the fashion police would arrest him or Animal Control would mistake him for a Yeti and he'd end up in a science lab being prodded by people in white coats. The thought of white coats made him smile. How apt, given his current situation.

'Hey, Dad. How's it going?' Her voice had a sing-song quality that always reminded him of when she was younger.

He was still trying to get to grips with recognizing her as an adult. Her nineteenth birthday had been at the beginning of the month. 'You're at home this weekend, aren't you?'

'Yes. I'm home.' His daughter knew that he was being reintroduced to his caseload gradually, but he had told her that it was his choice. She didn't need to know everything. She would just worry and would be over here every five minutes to check he was all right.

'Your garden could do with some TLC,' she said. 'Why don't you go down to B&Q and get some pots, or whatever, cheer the place up?' The thought of going to a garden centre filled him with more dread than a hundred cold-cases. 'I could come over and give you a hand, if you like? I don't have much planned this afternoon. Was just gonna sit in the garden and soak up some rays.'

'Thanks, Megs, but I'll be fine. I'm just heading out for a run, and then I've got some work to do.'

'Okay. Are you around tomorrow at all?' she asked. 'I've got a study week, so I thought I'd go and see Uncle Bobby. We could go together. If you fancy it?'

Under normal circumstances Monday mornings were hectic. But all Lockyer had to look forward to was more cold-cases and a counselling session in the afternoon. No contest. 'That sounds great,' he said and meant it. After the Stevens case he had promised himself that Bobby and Megan would be a priority in his life. He had seen Bobby every other day, if not every day, and Megan had stayed over on a number of occasions now. He had even shifted his home office around and had bought a single bed off eBay. 'Why don't you come over tonight, if you're free? We can watch a movie – you can stay over.' He waited for her to reply, hoping for a yes.

'Okay, yeah. That sounds nice,' she said.

'Great. We can have a takeaway tonight, and I'll cook us up something special for brekkie before we head over to Bobby's in the morning?' He turned and opened the cupboards above the counter. 'I'm pretty sure I've got Hollandaise in here somewhere.' His eye settled on the posh-looking jar. A leftover from the Christmas hamper that Roger and his wife had given him. 'Yep. Got it. I'll get some muffins on my run, and I'll do us eggs Benedict. How does that sound?'

'Sounds good to me. My favourite,' she said, making a smacking sound with her lips. 'I've got some bits and bobs to finish off at home tonight, so is about eight okay?'

'Absolutely. See you later on, hon.' He hung up the phone after they had said their goodbyes. He had something to look forward to. He walked through to his bedroom and over to the chest of drawers. He took out some shorts and a T-shirt and changed. Within five minutes he was pulling on his trainers at the front door. A run would help. He needed to clear his head.

CHAPTER TWENTY-TWO

28th April – Monday

Jane stood at the water cooler and filled a small plastic cup, its ridged edges slippery beneath her fingers. She drank it in one, refilled it and walked back across the office to her desk, passing Franks and Whitemore. She nodded to Whitemore. He returned the gesture before refocusing on his computer screen. He was new to the team. New to Jane. He had transferred from the flying squad, a division of Serious and Organized Crime. She didn't know much about him or his background, but so far she was impressed. He was thorough and enthusiastic.

She turned and looked over her shoulder as Franks's throaty laugh echoed around the office. He was talking on the phone, his eyes shining with tears. If there was humour to be found – however bleak the situation – Franks found it. Lockyer had tried and failed to rein him in, and for that Jane was grateful. Office banter made a difficult day bearable. Like Whitemore, Franks had moved over to the murder squad from S&OC – Drugs division. It was a well-respected unit, despite the fact that they were fighting a losing battle with south-east London's drug problem. As soon as one faction was shut down, another four popped up to replace it. Franks turned and saw Jane looking at him. He made a funny face and winked at her. She returned his goofy grin before sitting down, the partition around her desk cutting her off from the rest of the office.

She was knackered, after spending most of the previous night going over her conversation with Sue. They had talked for two hours straight. To anyone else, Sue would have appeared to have been candid about her marriage to Mark, but Jane had known the couple for a long time and a doubt was nagging at her, blurring her focus. It was like a whisper lost at the end of every sentence, a truth not quite told. It didn't make any sense. Sue was an ex-copper. What was she holding back? Jane sighed and looked down at her scribbled notes. She picked up one of the pages of A4 and started reading. Sue and Mark had been to see a counsellor in the first year after his retirement. They had been told to work on their communication, as a couple and as a family, and Mark had been advised to get a hobby. It sounded laughable to Jane: quit the force, start knitting and all your worries would be over. She knew it was never that simple for anyone, especially someone in Mark's position. A bit of woodwork or gardening wasn't going to fill his days in the same way the job had done. Jane dreaded the day she retired. She had no idea how she would function without the routine. She pushed her fringe off her forehead.

From what Sue had said, it sounded to Jane as if Mark had suffered a nervous breakdown: days in bed, not eating, his moods swinging between sullen and aggressive. Sue believed the counselling had helped, but Jane wondered if Mark felt the same. She picked up her pen and circled the paragraph and wrote 'f/u' in the margin next to it – 'follow up'. It would be difficult. The counsellor wouldn't hand over their notes, or discuss Mark and Sue's sessions, without a subpoena. Jane doubted, given what she had so far, that she would get one.

She logged into her computer and checked through her emails. Her eyes kept drifting down to the papers spread out on her desk; a name that Sue had mentioned kept catching her eye.

Amelia Reynolds.

It was one of the cases Jane had highlighted last week: a possible stress trigger for her all-but-abandoned suicide theory. She tapped her pen on her teeth and looked up at the ceiling tiles. Amelia was the daughter of a friend of Mark and Sue's. In fact, now that she thought about it, Mark must have fought pretty hard to get the case, given his personal involvement. The case had never been solved, and Mark, according to Sue, had never forgiven himself. Sue said he had nightmares about it at the time.

It wasn't unusual for a case to impact on the subconscious. She had had her own share of sleepless nights about the Stevens case. She still did. The dream was the same every time. She would wake up in bed, frightened. She would try to turn on her beside light, but it wouldn't come on. She would stumble around the house, trying every light switch, without success. She would get to the kitchen and open the fridge. The internal light would come on and she would feel a wave of relief until she realized what she was looking at. Every shelf was empty, but in the door, standing alone, was a baby's bottle filled to the brim with blood. She shuddered. Even thinking about it now made her mouth go dry. She forced herself to keep reading. She picked up a red pen and circled the paragraph about the Reynolds case and put 'CH' in the margin. She wanted to review the full case history.

She spent the next hour going through her scribbled notes, circling each detail and giving it a letter or shorthand note. Either Chris or Aaron could type them up and add the follow-ups to the Action list. Both were due in at five. By the time she finished it was already three o'clock. Whitemore had gone and Franks looked as if he was getting ready to do the same. She craned her neck to look over at the briefing room. DI Ayres's team had been called in an hour ago to deal with a suspicious death near Brockwell Park. Their voices were muffled by the wall of glass separating them from the rest of the open-plan office. They would be here for the rest of the day. So would she, at this rate. She had been due a day off. No such luck.

Penny had dropped off a list of Maggie's tutors and class-mates, each with a brief biography. Jane took the folder out of her in-tray and scanned through the names, flicking through to Lebowski. The information on him was a bit more extensive, at Jane's request. She was loath to trust the call-in's suggestion that he and Maggie were having a relationship but, with the post-mortem evidence, it was her best lead. The first caller hadn't given a name. The second, an Oliver Hanson, had given a partial address, but had then been cut off. He was due to call back. She clicked into her computer and added

Hanson's name to the Action list. He would need to be contacted and his information verified.

She read through the basics. Victor Lebowski was thirty-nine years old, Caucasian, five foot eleven. Divorced, living alone in a flat in Greenwich – a flat he owned. His ex-wife, Emily Loxton, lived in Dulwich Village with their two children, Poppy and Petra, seven and ten years old respectively. He had been a tutor at Greenwich University for nine years. He taught psychology to undergraduates, but also cognitive and applied psychology to the MA and PhD students. There were no records of any complaints about him by either students or other tutors. Jane was interviewing the head of psychology in the morning. It would be interesting to see how Lebowski was viewed by the teaching staff. From his employment records, he appeared to be a model teacher. The achievement statistics relating to his classes were above average. He was in charge of three PhD students, and currently had ten on the Masters course. He didn't have a criminal record. He had never been cautioned. As far as Jane could tell, he hadn't so much as got a speeding ticket. A model citizen. No one was *that* good, were they? She was a detective sergeant, but she still had three points on her licence for speeding.

The ticking of the clock in the middle of the office seemed to increase in volume with each hour that passed. She pored over the details of students and teachers alike. There were no red flags. On paper they all looked the same. Normal, law-abiding individuals. No one who fitted the profile of Maggie's killer. Phil had stressed that the suspect was motivated and organized. There was a suggestion that this was an ongoing pattern of behaviour. Not necessarily that other girls had been murdered, but that the suspect – whoever he was – would have a pattern of obsessive behaviour in their past. But none of the names on Jane's list stood out. The phone on her desk started to ring. She picked up the handset. 'Detective Bennett,' she said, looking over at the clock. It was six-thirty. She had forgotten to call home.

'Good afternoon, Detective. I'm sorry to trouble you. I had intended to leave a message, but the switchboard operator said you were in the office, so I asked to be put through. I hope I'm not disturbing you?' His voice was soft. There was a crackle at the end of his sentences, like waves kicking up pebbles on a beach. It was soothing.

'How can I help you?' she asked.

'I wanted to speak with you about Maggie Hungerford.'

A pen was in her hand before he could finish speaking. 'Can I ask your name?'

'Yes, of course,' he said. 'I'm sorry. I assumed the officer who connected me would have given it to you.' Jane closed her eyes. She could listen to this guy talk all day and all night. It was like listening to a combination of David Attenborough and Anthony Hopkins. 'I taught Maggie,' he said, the crackle in his voice tickling Jane's ear. A shiver started working its way down her back. 'My name is Victor – Victor Lebowski.'

The shiver stopped. Jane opened her eyes. The model citizen.

CHAPTER TWENTY-THREE

29th April – Tuesday

Jane stood in Lockyer's office with her back against the door. He had been ranting for the past five minutes. Given the volume of his voice, she guessed he had taken the weekend to wind himself up in order to give her the full force of his displeasure. She couldn't blame him. He was essentially off active duty because of her.

'Who did you think would benefit from this?' he asked, not waiting for an answer. 'You? Me? Your career?' She decided silence was the best option. She couldn't defend herself. For the most part she agreed with him. 'Wasted time – that's all you've achieved.' A lump started to form in her throat. She thought for a second she might cry, but then she realized it was her own anger surfacing. She wanted to tell him exactly what she thought, but if she started she wasn't sure she would be able to stop. 'Well?' he said, slumping into his chair.

She swallowed and pushed the ball of anger back down her throat. 'I did try and talk to you, sir,' she said. 'More than once.' He stared at her. The colour in his face was beginning to settle, but he still had two livid spots on his cheeks. 'I felt

135

I had no alternative, sir.' He said nothing. 'You told me you had spoken to Sue Leech every day since Mark's disappearance. I spoke to Sue. You hadn't spoken to her. Not once.'

'You asked Sue?' His eyebrows disappeared under a mop of hair. He looked as if he had been to a festival for a month and had decided that haircuts were for repressed people.

'No, sir. I didn't. I told her you were going to speak to her, and she happened to mention that she hadn't heard from you. That she had hoped to hear from you.' Jane felt a tug of guilt. 'It wasn't just that, sir,' she said, levelling her tone. 'I was concerned about you. I was concerned about the amount of pressure you were under.' Now she just sounded patronizing. She sighed, took a step forward and held her hands up. 'I had no idea Roger would take it this far. He had indicated to me, privately, that he was . . . ' she searched for a different word, but couldn't think of one, 'concerned. I wanted more support for the team, not less, sir.'

That was true. She would never have said a word if she had known. Yes, she was concerned about Lockyer's behaviour. Yes, she was concerned that the Stevens case was having a detrimental effect on her boss. But that wasn't it. She could see Lockyer spiralling down and, no matter what she thought about his actions of late, she couldn't stand by and watch her senior officer – someone she had considered a friend – self-destruct. And she would not allow Mark's disappearance, or Maggie's death, to be lost in the crossfire.

'I did it *for* you, sir, not *to* you.'

He held up his own hands, mirroring her gesture. He took a deep breath as if he was about to launch into another tirade, but instead let the breath out and walked over to his chair. As he sat down he pointed to the seat opposite. Jane obliged, pulling out the chair and sitting down. The tension in the room seemed to have imploded. She felt wrung out. From the look of Lockyer, he felt the same. 'Okay, okay,' he said, pushing his hair back, before pulling his hands down his face. 'I should have—' He stopped and looked up at the ceiling. 'We should have talked sooner. You were in a difficult position – I can appreciate that.' When he looked at her, Jane felt her heart squeeze in her chest.

'I'm sorry, sir,' she said before she could stop herself. 'I didn't intend for it to go this far.'

'I know,' he said, his eyes on hers. 'I shouldn't have gone off on you like that.' He shook his head. 'I was stuck at home all weekend, and most of yesterday. I guess it gave me a bit too much time to think. Here I am, banging on about professionalism and responsibility to others, and what do I do?' He pointed out towards the rest of the office. 'I'm sorry.' She wanted to say something. To acknowledge that she knew this was hard for him. To thank him. But she couldn't. His eyes stopped the words coming. 'We should have spoken about all of this weeks ago.'

She couldn't disagree. 'Yes, sir' was all she said.

'Have you got time for a drink later on?' he asked. The question was so incongruous that she opened her mouth to answer, but shut it again. 'We've worked together for a long time, Jane. The last thing I want is for this . . . ' he pursed his lips, 'situation to have a detrimental effect on our working relationship. You have questions, I'm sure, and I think it's only fair that I answer at least some of them. That being said,

I don't think the office is the best place for us to have this conversation, do you?' He managed a half-smile.

'No, sir. I agree.' She looked at her watch and pictured the files on her desk and the emails on her computer. 'I've got two interviews this morning. I've got a follow-up with Sue this afternoon, and a few people to see after that. I should be done about six . . . six-thirty?' Another evening when something – or someone – took precedence over Peter. Jane bit her tongue for a second, pushed the thought away and continued. 'I could meet you in the Jolly Farmers?'

'I was thinking of somewhere a bit further afield,' he said, again gesturing to the office behind her. 'Half the team will be in the pub later – there's some quiz on. How about the Goose at Rushey Green?'

'That's fine,' Jane said, feeling as if she was making a date. 'I'll meet you there at six-thirty.' He nodded. 'Sir,' she said, pushing back her chair. 'See you later.'

She kept her eyes trained on her desk as she crossed the open-plan office, but she could feel everyone looking at her. There would be whispers about this for weeks. If any of the team saw her and Lockyer together in the pub tonight, the whispers would be around for the rest of the year.

Professor Edward Cresswell, the head of psychology at Greenwich University, was in interview room one with Penny. Victor Lebowski was in room two, waiting for Jane. She looked from one door to the other. As much as she was keen to get started, part of her was still deciding how to handle the interview. It wasn't being recorded. Lebowski wasn't here under caution. As far as he was concerned, this was just a chat to flesh out Maggie's university career, but Jane had other ideas.

As soon as Lebowski had said his name on the phone the previous night she had felt a buzz of adrenaline, but he hadn't called to admit his relationship with Maggie. On the contrary, he had called to express concern for his students and the university as a whole, and to give her a name. She stood at the sergeant's desk now, signing in, putting her name and the time. The name he had given her was Terry Mort's. He was one of Lebowski's PhD students and, according to Lebowski, Mort and Maggie had dated the previous year. Of course Jane knew all of this already. Chrissie had told her about the relationship in her interview at the weekend, but she said it happened over the summer and was over before the second year of their MA began, which begged the question: how did Lebowski know about it? This would be one of the questions she would be putting to him in a moment, along with several others. She said thank you to the desk sergeant, turned and paused outside the interview room. The hairs on the back of her neck were vibrating. She took a deep breath, opened the door and walked in.

Lebowski was standing at the far end of the room, leaning against the wall. He was about six foot, wearing tan Birkenstocks, blue jeans and a white T-shirt, with a David Bowie album cover emblazoned on the front. His forearms were tanned, his skin the colour of digestive biscuits. He pushed himself upright and approached her, his hand out in greeting. 'Detective Bennett,' he said, 'it's a pleasure to meet you.'

She shook his hand. His grip was firm, his hand hot and

clammy. Was he nervous or was it just the temperature outside making him sweat? She felt a blush in her cheeks. She looked down. 'Mr Lebowski,' she said, 'thank you for coming in.' She gestured to the chair on the other side of the table. 'Please, take a seat.' He sat down. He appeared calm. If anything, she felt more on edge than he looked. She took the seat opposite him. 'So, Mr Lebowski,' she began.

'Please, call me Victor,' he said. He crossed his legs, straightening the front seam of his jeans.

'Victor,' she responded. 'As I said, I appreciate you coming down to the station. I have some questions I would like to ask you. But, first, why don't you tell me how you knew Maggie.' He opened his mouth to speak. 'I know you told me a fair bit last night, but I would appreciate it if we could go over it again. I'll be making notes, if that's all right with you?' She put her notepad on the table and laid a biro next to it.

'Of course,' he said, raising both hands, palms facing upwards. 'Anything I can do to help. I really *do* want to help.'

She had heard the same phrase innumerable times in her career. She looked up and studied his face. He was telling the truth. She could tell by his eyes. He did want to help, but that in itself felt odd. She opened her pad and gestured for him to continue.

'Okay, well, as you know, I am a tutor on Maggie's MA. She was in her second year, doing very well. She was incredibly hard-working. Mature students are, by their very nature, more focused, but Maggie was exceptional. Her knowledge and grasp of psychology were enviable. As was her dedication. I wish I had been like that at her age. I had already been married a year, and was far more interested in starting a family than concentrating on my studies.' He held up his hands. 'Sorry – not relevant. Anyway, yes, Maggie was one of my students. I taught her in the first year, along with her housemate, Christina O'Reilly, and I had her for two modules this semester.'

'And they were?' she asked, noting his slight embarrassment at his turn of phrase.

'Cognitive and applied psychology,' he said, running his hand over his head.

'Go on,' she said, making a note. She listened while he elaborated on his teaching techniques, how much coursework was involved and what his students were expected to produce. He ran his hand over his head every two to three minutes. His hair was fair and cut short. It was not quite a buzz-cut, but it was close. His eyes were blue. The lack of hair, and his colouring, made them stand out. There was no denying he was attractive. Jane doubted that she would be able to concentrate in any class Victor was teaching. A flash of a scene from an Indiana Jones film popped into her mind: the adoring college student who, when Dr Jones looks at her, closes her eyes to reveal that she's written 'I love you' in make-up on her eyelids. Jane cleared her throat. 'So what is the basis of cognitive and applied psychology?' she asked, pulling her brain back to the job in hand.

'Well, cognitive psychology is all about mental processes, like speech, memory, perception and so on. If we can break down and study a mental pathway, we can devise ways in which to alter it. For example, developing ways to help drivers concentrate on the road better, or – as with cognitive behavioural therapy, or CBT – how to help someone understand and control their reactions to certain triggers: fear of heights, agoraphobia, that kind of thing.' She watched his hand move towards his head. He stopped, as if resisting the urge, returning his hand to his lap. 'That's where applied psychology comes in. The two modules work alongside each other.'

'You said before,' she said, glancing down at her notes, 'that Maggie was "exceptional". Could you elaborate on that?'

'She was gifted,' he said, without hesitation. 'Gifted.' He stopped and looked down at his hands. 'I have no doubt she would have been a brilliant practitioner. Such a waste. An absolute waste of a brilliant young woman.'

Jane listened, tapping her pen against her lips. 'Miss O'Reilly mentioned that Maggie was a bit behind in her studies. That she had planned to stay in over Easter to finish a piece of coursework.' Victor rubbed his hand back and forth over his head. 'She also said one of Maggie's tutors had given her an extension until the Tuesday after the bank holiday.' She waited. She didn't really need to ask Victor if it was him. It was clear from his expression that it was.

'That was me,' he said, stroking the end of his nose with the edge of his hand.

'Are the students in after Easter?' she asked. 'I may be wrong, but I'd assumed lectures would have finished before the break?'

'They did,' he said. 'The students have two revision weeks that straddle Easter, before their exams this week.' He seemed flustered. He was pulling at the skin on the inside of his thumb. 'The paper was due two weeks before Easter. I gave Maggie the extension because . . . well, because she asked.

She said she was just a bit behind, that was all. It happens to the best of us,' he said, with a shrug of his shoulders.

'Can you excuse me for just a second?' she asked. He seemed taken aback that she would leave now. As if the admission of Maggie's slip in performance needed further justification. 'I won't be a second.' She pushed her chair back, left the room and knocked on the door to the first interview room. Penny's head appeared around the edge of the door. 'Can I borrow you for a sec?' she asked.

'Sure.' Penny closed the door and Jane heard a murmured apology before she reappeared.

'Has Cresswell mentioned anything about Maggie's grades – her recent performance?' she asked.

'Just now,' Penny said, raising her eyebrows. 'You must have X-ray ears.' She smiled and walked a few paces away from the interview rooms. 'He said Maggie's work had been in the top five per cent until September of last year. Then she was late with three pieces of work for the Christmas hand-in and missed several classes.'

'Do you know which classes she missed?' she asked. She had a pretty good idea Maggie wasn't missing Victor's classes.

'Yes, hang on,' Penny said, opening her notebook, which she had brought out with her. 'Reeves, she missed two of his classes; and Baxter, she missed one.'

Jane nodded. 'Right, good. Thanks, Penny. Have you spoken much about Victor – I mean, Lebowski? Does Cresswell know he's here?'

'Not as far as I can tell,' Penny said, shaking her head. 'I've asked him about all of the tutors and senior members of staff, but I've not gone into detail yet. I'll come back to it now, shall I, and get some more info on Lebowski?'

'Yes, do that,' Jane said, already walking back to the interview room. 'Come and get me if you think there's anything I need to know.'

'Yes, boss,' Penny said, with a mock salute. 'How's it going with you?'

'Good,' Jane said smiling, 'I think I might be making some headway.'

Penny's expression changed. 'I hope so, boss. That girl's poor family could do with some news – any news. I went out to see them over the weekend. Anne's doing her best, but they're in bits. The mother's aged twenty years overnight. It was awful . . . awful.'

Jane put her hand on Penny's arm. 'I know. We'll get there, Pen. We're not even a week in. You know how long these things can take.'

'God, I so do, boss,' Penny replied, shaking her shoulders as if shrugging off the emotion that was trying to drag her down. 'Right, I'll come and get you if the Prof. says anything important.'

Both women stood at their respective doors, took deep breaths, dropped their shoulders and walked back into the interview rooms. They made a good team, Jane thought. Maybe she and Penny would end up like Lockyer and her. Jane the DI and Penny the senior DS. She thought about Lockyer and how he had been this morning. She couldn't imagine not working with him every day. 'Sorry to keep you,' she said, sitting down opposite Lebowski. 'Just a few more questions.'

'Of course,' Victor said. His hands were clasped together in his lap.

'Do you know if Maggie had any problems with her other classes?'

'No,' he said, shaking his head. 'Not as far as I know. If she was behind in any of her other classes, her tutors certainly didn't say anything to me.'

'You said on the telephone that she was dating one of the PhD students,' she said, opening her notepad again. 'Terry Mort. Is that right?'

'Yes. Yes,' he said. He sat up straight in his chair and leaned towards Jane. She caught the faintest scent of his after-shave. It was familiar. 'I am one of Terry's supervisors for his PhD. He and Maggie dated last year. I don't know for how long.'

'And how do you know they dated?' she asked.

'Maggie told me,' he said.

'Why?' she asked. 'Why would she tell you?'

'It's not like with degree students,' he said, sighing. 'They barely listen in class. They care far more about the drinks in the student union. They're kids, but my MA classes are different. They're adults. I get on well with them, talk to them, go to the pub with them sometimes. So, naturally, we talk. I get to know my students as individuals.' He seemed to be proud of this differentiation. Jane found it a bit sad, as if he was trying to validate his existence by saying that his students liked him.

'And why did you feel the need to come forward with Mort's name?'

'Terry's a good student, or he was. I mean, he still is. He's a bright guy, but I don't think . . . I'm not sure he treated Maggie all that well.' Victor was wringing his hands in his lap. His biscuit skin had paled. His blue eyes seemed to be pleading with her, like entities in their own right. 'Believe me,' they were saying, 'believe me.'

'Did Maggie tell you about any specific problems in their relationship?'

'No. Nothing specific. It was just an impression I got. I don't know . . . ' He looked over Jane's shoulder at the door. 'Maybe I was wrong to say anything. I just thought, you know: a girl is murdered, you check out the boyfriend. That's how it works, isn't it?' There was a hint of sarcasm in his voice, but she couldn't decipher whether his anger was about Maggie's murder or the way the police handled death.

'What was your relationship with Maggie?' she asked. They had danced around the topic long enough. If he was going to admit it, which Jane had a feeling he would, then they might as well get it over with.

'I was her tutor. Her friend,' he said. 'I was her tutor, first and foremost.'

'Okay. Did your relationship ever go beyond the boundaries of friendship?'

Victor's hand was on his head in seconds. 'I don't know what you mean,' he said. There was no conviction in his words.

'Well, as you said, Victor, when a woman is murdered – as a police officer – my first port of call would generally be to question her sexual partner, husband or boyfriend.'

'Of course,' he said. He was looking over her shoulder again.

'Do you fall into any one of those categories, Victor?' She

knew the answer. She had known the answer as soon as she walked into the room. But as she looked at him, she found herself hoping that he would say No. She didn't want the man in front of her to be Maggie's lover. She didn't want to have to stop the interview, advise him of his rights and start again – on the record, this time.

He looked straight at Jane. 'Yes,' he said. 'Yes. I do.'

CHAPTER TWENTY-FOUR

No one is coming. I know that now.

When I woke up I felt different, changed in some way. I can hear music. It surrounds me; Snow Patrol – 'Chasing Cars', Cascada – 'What Hurts the Most', Mark Ronson – 'Valerie'. It's like an iPod on permanent shuffle in my head. I hum along. It's comforting to hear the sound of my voice mingled with theirs. I was never any good at singing. I tried teaching myself the guitar once. I mastered the introduction to 'Blackbird' by The Beatles. I would play it on a loop. That was the extent of my talents. There were other things I was good at. Less creative things. Anything to do with science fascinated me. Even as a child playing with my first chemistry set, I realized I understood things my parents didn't. My father would sit with me, watching me play. 'How do you know what to add?' he would ask me, as I poured one liquid on top of another, making the mixture in the tube turn blue. 'I just do,' I would answer. I always did. There were rules. This plus that equals X. It made sense to me. I have never enjoyed variables. I have always been more exacting in my work and my life. Give me a rule and I will follow it to the letter. You can't go wrong, if you follow the rules. So why is this happening to me? How have I managed to venture so far off-course?

I am lying on my side, my knees drawn up to my chest, my hands shoved between my thighs, like an inward prayer. I haven't been able to move. The strength in my legs is fading. I no longer feel thirsty or hungry. When I really think about it – which I have had plenty of time to do – food is such a waste of time. You ingest, you process, you excrete. What's the point? Lying here, I can imagine myself in some Buddhist retreat, finding myself through starvation. Of course I know I am not starving to death. That would take weeks – maybe a month. Water is a bit trickier. I'm certain I'm on my reserve tanks for that. The 80 per cent that my body had has dried up. I know because my skin feels like paper, like the tissue that comes wrapped around a new pair of shoes. My tongue no longer aches. It just sits in my mouth, redundant.

I start to rock my head to the rhythm of a new song that has just started playing. It's not my kind of music, but the iPod selection in my mind doesn't seem to have learned my specific tastes. I thought I felt the door before. I would say 'yesterday', because that is how long ago it feels, but I am sleeping so much now I really can't be sure. It felt like wood beneath my fingers. Even now my heart begins thumping harder in my chest at the memory. I hadn't wanted to move my hands, in case when I returned them to the spot the door had gone. I held on for as long as I could before my arms tired. I slept right there, sitting up. Or rather I think I did. There was no door when I awoke. Was there ever one to begin with? I can honestly say I don't know any more.

At least 50 per cent of my body has no feeling. The numbness, once a marker of time, is now more erratic. My lower legs went an inch at a time. My thighs and stomach seemed to go together. My arms are holding on. So is my heart. I don't think I can describe the sensation of becoming paralysed one muscle at a time. It is impossible. I think I would have preferred to have gone from mobile to paralysed in one step. If I had been running one day and lying in bed the next, I think I could have coped with that, adapted somehow. But to feel your body freezing, going limp in slow motion – it is the most acute agony. Cruel.

I see my mother's face. I can hear her words in my ear. 'It's almost time to go, honey. Get yourself ready. I'll wait for you.' The colours of my parents' house blind me. I can smell my mother's cooking: roast lamb, mint sauce, apple charlotte, custard. For a moment I can taste the rich gravy on my tongue. 'Are you ready yet?' I hear my mother call out to me.

'Almost,' I reply.

CHAPTER TWENTY-FIVE

29th April – Tuesday

'It'll just take a few more minutes, Victor,' Jane said as she passed him a cup of coffee, took her seat and began sipping at her tea. Technical difficulties with the recorder meant they had been sitting staring at each other for the last ten minutes. She blew on her coffee and tried to focus on the file before her, stealing occasional glances at the man in front of her. He appeared calm, relaxed even.

As soon as he had confirmed his personal relationship with Maggie, Jane had stopped him and advised him that the rest of their conversation would need to be taped. He said he didn't think it was necessary, but he hadn't refused. His behaviour didn't make sense. She couldn't decide if he was being foolhardy or just naive. Not more than an hour ago he had told her that he knew 'checking out the boyfriend' was standard procedure. Did he think he was any different from Terry Mort? Did he think his age or status as a lecturer gave him more credibility? No matter what he thought, she wanted everything on tape, going forward. For his benefit as much as her own. She didn't believe Lebowski was a killer.

She knew it was ridiculous to make a judgement at this stage, but the more she talked to him, the more convinced she became. He had admitted dating Maggie, yes. Moreover, from what he had already told her, he was the last person to see Maggie alive. One of these factors alone would have made him a person of interest. Two made him a prime suspect. She couldn't remember the exact figures, but something like 40 or 50 per cent of female murder victims were killed by a spouse or intimate partner. He was the obvious choice.

She pushed her fringe off her face, static tickling her forehead. She could feel him watching her. 'I'm sure it won't be much—' Before she could finish her sentence, the door opened and a young PC poked his head into the room.

'All set, Ma'am,' he said.

Jane nodded. The PC disappeared, closing the door behind him. She leaned forward and pressed the button on the digital recording device, cleared her throat, stated the date and time and who was present. She debated again whether she should have one of the team in with her, but it seemed like overkill at this stage. Without looking up at Victor, she explained his rights, the reason for the interview and the overall objective. He said he understood and was happy to continue.

'Can you tell me about your relationship with Margaret Hungerford? When it began, the nature of it, and where and how often you saw or met her,' she said, jotting down each point to keep her on-track once the interview began.

'Okay,' Victor said. He was leaning towards the recorder as if he was keen not to be misheard. 'Can I call her Maggie?'

She looked up at him. 'Yes, of course.'

He sat back in his chair, crossed his legs and looked up at the ceiling. 'I first met Maggie in February 2011.'

His chin was tipped up and to the right. Jane had read a ton of literature on body language: physical behaviour that indicated when someone was lying. None of it was proven, but she found herself trying to remember the drawings detailing the probable part of the brain being accessed, judged by the direction of the individual's eyes. Victor was looking up and to the right. She was pretty sure that meant he was accessing the visual cortex.

'Me and Professor Edward Cresswell, the head of our psychology department, interviewed her for a place on the psychology MA.' She wondered if he was picturing Maggie sitting across from him in the psychology offices. She would have been nervous, keen to make a good impression. 'She interviewed very well,' he said, bringing his focus back to Jane. 'She had a first in her degree and had done a huge amount of voluntary work and research into the field she was interested in. Both Edward and I were impressed. Psychology is a complicated discipline, Detective,' he said, raising his eyebrows. 'Most of my students, even at MA level, struggle to decide where best to focus their attentions.' There was admiration in his voice – genuine, as far as Jane could tell. 'Maggie was accepted on the basis of her application and interview.'

'Who made the decision to accept her?' she asked, pen poised over her notepad. It felt like a silly question to ask – leading even. What was he going to say? 'It was my decision. I accepted her onto the course because I thought she was hot. I was going to get her to choose my modules, seduce her and then leave her to die in an underground tomb, which I just happened to have ready. Oh, and I watched the whole thing on CCTV. Do you want to read me my rights now or later?' She resisted the urge to shake her head.

'Professor Cresswell and I discussed it, and we both agreed she was an ideal candidate for the course. Our decision was handed down to Admissions, and they would have written to Maggie to confirm her place.'

'Did you speak to her in private at this time, or after the interview?' she asked.

'No. As far as I can remember, we had several candidates that day. I would have to check my diary but, as I recall, her interview didn't last very long.'

'And you didn't see her on campus after the interviews were done?'

'No,' he said, shrugging his shoulders. 'Not that I can recall. The next time we met was in September 2011, during the induction weekend.'

'Induction weekend?' she asked, glancing up at the clock.

'Yes. We like to have an informal weekend away before the course starts. It allows the students to get to know each other and their tutors and, of course, it helps them to decide on their modules for the second semester.' He was looking straight ahead, but not at her.

'What do you do on these weekends?' she asked.

'We have exercises – little role-plays to demonstrate different aspects of psychology and its applications in the real world,' he said. 'Attendance isn't compulsory, but we always have a good number of the students.'

'Did you speak to Maggie that weekend? Spend any time alone with her?'

He nodded. 'A little. I was trying – and failing – to give up smoking at the time. Maggie used to smoke, and let me nick a couple of her fags.' He smiled.

Jane could picture them now, bonding over a habit that was no longer socially acceptable. 'Do you recall what you talked about?' she asked.

'I honestly can't remember,' he said, with a shrug of his shoulders. 'We just chatted about psychology – aspects that interested her, I think.'

'Did you talk about the modules that you teach?'

'We may have,' he said, looking down at his hands. 'It was a long time ago.'

For the first time Jane had the feeling he was lying. 'Okay,' she said, looking up again at the clock on the wall behind Victor's ahead. 'Let's move on.' If he ended up being a person of interest in the case, these details – every second he spent with Maggie – would be gone over and over. She wanted to get to the meat of the interview. 'When did your relationship with Maggie change and move away from being purely professional?'

He seemed taken aback by the change of pace. It hadn't been her intention, but she was pleased to have achieved some movement. The room had felt dead.

'Not until September last year, when the new term started. I had bumped into Maggie a few times, just in town when she was out with friends, or shopping. We ended up having a drink, chatting. I don't know – I didn't expect it at all. I knew she was seeing someone else and I knew, as her tutor, that I shouldn't even be entertaining a relationship, but it just . . . ' He shook his head. 'It just happened.' He raised his hands in a pleading gesture. 'I know how that sounds. I know everyone must say the same thing. It sounds pathetic, but it's true. I had no intention of doing anything about it. I thought she was intelligent, brilliant even. I would never have done anything if she hadn't made a move.' He was tripping over his words.

Jane began to doubt herself. 'Maggie suggested the affair?' she asked. It sounded stupid. Maggie wasn't married; she was having fun at university. More than one sexual partner was expected, wasn't it? Sleeping with a tutor probably added kudos. Jane cleared her throat, ashamed by the judgement in her thoughts. She knew why. Her own life had been different. She hadn't had time to enjoy her youth. She had been working her way up the ranks, working her arse off. There wasn't any time for love, sex or affairs. The only guy she had given more than five minutes to had buggered off when she was pregnant. Left her to raise Peter alone. Left her to punish herself for all the things she wasn't able to do for him. She blinked, took a deep breath and looked back at Victor.

'Yes,' he said. 'It's not that hard to imagine, is it?' I might not be Brad Pitt, but I wouldn't say I'm Herman Munster, either.' He looked as if he wanted to smile. 'Anyway, we were having a drink. She told me she "fancied" me,' he said, using his fingers to create inverted commas. 'I'd had a few beers. I was flattered.' He looked up to the ceiling. 'No, I wasn't flattered, I was shocked. Things progressed from there.' His face changed, his mouth now a thin line. 'Maggie was a fantastic person. She had her whole life ahead of her. I was under no illusion that the relationship would last. I was a stepping stone for her. She could have made a real difference in the field of psychology. I genuinely believe that and I'm . . . ' He looked at Jane and held her eyes. 'I honestly don't know how anyone could do this to her. She was the most gentle, open person I have ever met.'

Jane tried to look away, but found she couldn't. His gaze was fierce. His words. His body language. He was telling the truth. She was more convinced now than she had been at the start of the interview. 'Tell me what happened the last time you saw Maggie,' she asked.

'She came to dinner,' he said.

'When was this?'

'The sixteenth of April. It was the Wednesday before the Easter weekend. At first she told me she couldn't come. We had been having a few problems: arguing over stupid things, like people do,' he said. He leaned back in his chair and picked up his coffee. It must have been stone-cold, but he took a sip anyway. 'Things weren't straightforward right from the start. She'd ended things with her ex a few weeks after we started seeing each other, back in August or September last year. He wasn't happy. He was persistent, trying to get her back – texting her, calling, sending her flowers, stuff like that. I know the guy. He's bad news, not right in the head. But I couldn't do anything, because Maggie and I weren't meant to be seeing each other. It was one big secret. I hated it. I wanted to tell him to back off, but I couldn't.'

'We'll come back to that, Victor, if you don't mind. Tell me about the Wednesday, the night of the sixteenth.' She wanted to try and keep him on-track. His eyes were darting all around the room. He looked as if he wanted to hit something or someone.

'This is pointless,' he said, sinking down in his chair. 'I feel like we're talking in code, talking around the subject rather than about it.'

'I understand it can be frustrating, but I need to be clear on what happened.'

'Okay,' he said, sighing. 'I invited Maggie over for dinner, to talk – make up, I guess. She said she couldn't come. That she had to see Terry, to sort things out. I insisted. She gave in. She came over about seven . . . seven-thirty. I'd cooked a chilli. We ate, had a few glasses of wine, talked.'

'What did you talk about?'

'About us – the relationship. She was feeling a bit trapped, I guess. I was ready for more. She wasn't.'

'Go on,' Jane said.

'She said we'd "see how things go", and we kissed and made up,' Victor said, his tone angry, bitter.

'What happened then?' she asked, knowing before he opened his mouth what he was going to say.

'God,' he said, rubbing his hand over his head. 'We had sex. We had dinner. We had an argument. We had sex on the table, if you must know. We broke it, as a matter of fact.' He looked angry. He held the fury in his eyes, like a wasp trapped behind glass.

'Would you like to take a break?' she asked, stunned by the words even as they came out of her mouth. What was she doing? He was rattled. If he was holding anything back, now was the time to push for the truth, but she couldn't bring herself to do it.

'No,' he said, waving away her question. 'I need to tell you about Terry. I don't care what you think of me, what you do to me. But if anyone was capable of killing her, it was Terry.'

CHAPTER TWENTY-SIX

29th April – Tuesday

'You can still talk to me, Jane,' Lockyer said as he handed over her drink. She looked nervous.

'Sorry, sir. It's just been one of those days.' She turned her glass of wine around in her hands, the condensation running down the stem.

'Okay,' he said, 'let's try something a bit different.' She looked up from her drink. If he was going to say what he wanted to say, then he would have to find a way of making her ease up, if only for an hour or so. 'No more "sir". It's just "Mike", for tonight. And you're "Jane". We're colleagues and,' he paused, not knowing if he should continue, 'friends?' It was more of a statement than a question. He hated to admit it, but without Jane by his side he felt almost lost. He knew he relied on her. He just hadn't realized, until now, how much. He sat down and took a swig of his pint.

'I can't stay long,' she said, taking a sip of her drink. 'My mother has Peter at her house. He's got school in the morning. I don't want to be late picking him up.'

She wasn't going to make this easy for him. He looked

around the pub at the other couples sitting at mahogany tables, chatting, talking about their days. Some would be work-friends, some would be friend-friends. Which was Jane, and was this 'chat' even a good idea? Someone behind the bar turned up the volume of the music and the lights dimmed to indicate the change from daytime drinking to evening. Lockyer was happy with that. He could do without a spotlight on him for the apology speech. He took a deep breath. 'I want to apologize again for my outburst this morning,' he said, feeling like a politician preparing to sidestep the blame. 'It was unnecessary, unprofessional and, above all, unfair on you.' He watched as Jane opened and closed her mouth. He wasn't known for his apologies. 'We need to clear the air. The Stevens case was difficult for everyone.'

She shook her head. 'Every case is difficult in its own way,' she said. 'The Stevens case was no different.'

'That's not true, Jane, and you know it.' His tone was more forceful than he intended and he noticed her sit back in her chair. This wasn't going well. She wasn't even looking at him.

'What do you want me to say?' she asked. She seemed to hesitate, as if she had more to say. He guessed she was going to add 'sir' or 'Mike', but had resisted both. How was he supposed to talk to her, if she couldn't even say his name? He knew there was some damage to repair, but he had not realized things had drifted this far – that it was this bad.

'I want you to talk to me, Jane. I want you to say what's on your mind. You've never had trouble doing that in the past. Sure, you tend to tell me what I want to hear, before you tell me what you really think. But you've never held back, as far as I'm aware. Am I wrong?'

'No, you're not wrong.' She hesitated again. 'It always takes the team a few weeks to settle, to move on from a traumatic case.'

'Yes, Jane,' he said, draining half of his pint, 'I know that and you know that, but we're not talking about the team. The team will be fine as long as I'm fine, and I'll be fine as long as you're fine.' He wanted to clap his hands over his mouth. That was not what he had planned to say. His speech, which he had worked on in his mind, was all generalizations about 'working together', 'moving on', 'putting it behind us' and other pointless euphemisms.

'You're worried about me?' Her voice went up, her surprise evident.

'I guess,' he said, mining his brain for the right words. 'I'm worried about you, but I'm more worried about us.' He felt his cheeks heating. This was a nightmare. This wasn't even why he had asked her for a drink. He just wanted to get back to work and have Jane in her usual position, at his side, her support unfailing. This was all emotional mumbo-jumbo. She looked as incredulous as he felt. 'I don't mean us as in "us",' he said, rushing to justify himself. 'I mean the team. The unit. Strong leadership is all about teamwork and building working partnerships that . . . ' He ran out of words. He didn't know where he was going with that sentence. 'I lied. I misled you and I shouldn't have, and I'm sorry.' He drained the rest of his pint. 'Another?' He was up and out of his chair before she could reply. He had to resist the urge to run screaming to the bar.

He joined the back of a group crowded around the bar. They didn't appear to be waiting for drinks, but it would give him some time to get himself together. He glanced over his shoulder. Jane was staring at him, her empty wine glass still in her hand. He cringed as he did a ridiculous mime of getting her a fresh glass. To say he was out of his comfort zone was an understatement. Whatever this zone was, he never wanted to be in it again, ever. A girl in front of him turned and looked at him.

'We're not waiting,' she said. Her eyes travelled up and down his body until they rested on his hair. 'Go ahead.'

He mumbled his thanks and moved around the group, trying to flatten the piece of hair that was obviously sticking up. Without thinking, he rested his elbows on the long metallic bar. He could smell the alcohol as a long puddle of beer soaked into his shirt. 'Great,' he said, lifting his arms as he examined the large, dark patches inching up his sleeves.

'What can I get you?' the barman asked, using a ratty-looking cloth to wipe the bar as he spoke.

'Bit late for that,' Lockyer said, displaying his damp elbows.

'Yeah, mate. We're short-staffed tonight. Only me on,' he said, without a hint of apology. 'What can I get you?'

Lockyer could feel the anger rising up his throat. He opened his mouth, but closed it again. He shook his head. Starting a fight with a complete stranger wasn't going to help. It might make him feel better for a second or two, but then he would be back where he started. 'Glass of Sauvignon blanc and a pint of Thatchers,' he said.

'Small or large?'

'Small,' he said, with as much venom as he could muster.

As the barman poured the drinks, Lockyer glanced back at Jane. She was texting, running her free hand through her fringe. She looked tired. He was so preoccupied with getting things sorted that he hadn't even noticed how strung-out she was. He remembered his thoughts over the weekend. She had brought this on herself – that's what he had been telling himself, and telling her. He was pushing all the blame onto her. 'Very gallant,' he said.

'Say what, mate?' the barman said, his eyebrows bunched together.

'Nothing,' Lockyer replied, shaking his head.

'That'll be nine-forty.'

He took a tenner from his wallet and handed it over. 'Keep the change. I'm sure you've got a tips jar for the excellent service.' His sarcasm missed the mark. The barman had already wandered off. Lockyer was invisible to him now. 'Thanks,' he went on, turning and walking back over to the table.

'Thanks,' Jane said, as he handed her the wine.

'No worries,' he replied, chinking his pint with her glass. 'So,' he said, taking a hurried sip, 'where were we?'

'You were worried about me,' she said, a sudden smile appearing on her face.

In that one gesture he felt all the tension leave his shoulders. She was taking the piss out of him. He could have kissed her. It was familiar – this was the kind of talking he could handle. 'Yes,' he said, in a mock-serious tone. 'Very. You look, if you don't mind me saying, like shit.'

Jane laughed. She threw her head back and really laughed. Lockyer joined her, relieved to feel normal again, to be rid of whatever phantom had taken over his brain for the last half-hour. 'So, what's up?' he asked.

'Well,' she said, with a sigh, 'I've had a pretty crappy day. My boss called me in this morning and tore several strips off me. I've got nowhere with a case involving a friend, and I'm going round in circles with a case involving a stranger.'

'So, all in all, not good,' he said, picking up his beer mat and peeling back the edges.

'That's about right,' Jane said, taking a large gulp of wine. 'If in doubt, drink,' she said, taking another swig.

'Impressive,' he said. 'Has anyone ever told you that you drink like a bloke?'

She smiled. 'Not today.'

They fell into a comfortable silence. Well, he was comfortable and Jane looked better, more relaxed. The atmosphere had changed. It was as if his trip to the bar had actually been a wormhole and he had travelled back to the time before the Stevens girl was even found. He was the boss and Jane was his dedicated and enthusiastic DS, who laughed at his jokes, took the mick out of him and essentially made the everyday feel better.

'Why didn't you tell me about your brother?' she asked.

Lockyer coughed, choking on his cider. 'What?' he asked, his voice croaking.

'Your brother. Why didn't you tell me about him, Mike?' To hear her using his first name made him feel like a small boy. 'Well,' she said, lifting one shoulder, 'you wanted to clear the air. Put the Stevens case behind us. Your brother is a part of that.' Lockyer was stunned into silence. His brain dried up. Jane seemed to read his thoughts. 'What I'm trying to say is . . . I talk to you about Peter. Not a lot, I grant you, but about how hard it can be sometimes, with his autism: the problems at school; my mother – I talk to you about all of that. I talk to you because I trust you. Bobby . . . it is Bobby, isn't it?'

'Yes,' he said, staring into his pint.

'Your father dies. You discover you've got a brother. You move him to Lewisham. You try and build a relationship with someone who is, in essence, closed off from you. And you never say a word – not a word. After your father died you carried on, business as usual. The team talked about it at the time. Figured you weren't close, or whatever.'

'My father was—' he began.

'No, no,' she said, holding up her hand. 'I don't expect you to share your personal life with me. Your family, your life – that's your business. I only mean that we could have helped each other. You know? I have no one who really understands what it's like with Peter. I mean, I've got my folks and friends, but it's not the same. I have work to deal with, and I have home.' She shook her head and pushed her drink away from her. 'It would have been nice if you had talked to me about it. I could have helped you, and in turn that might have helped me. I feel so isolated some-times; and there you are going through almost exactly the same thing and we're not talking. You're not talking. What's the point of being colleagues – of being friends – if you can't share something like that?' Lockyer opened his mouth, ready to defend himself. 'Look, I'm not trying to have a go at you. I'm not trying to make you feel bad. It's just that, with this whole Stevens case and everything that happened, it feels like the trust I thought we had is worth nothing. I trust you, but it feels like you don't trust me.' She stopped, her eyes blinking. She looked as if she might cry.

'I . . . ' he began, again feeling like a small boy standing in front of his mother when he had done something bad. 'I had no idea. I didn't think, Jane.' He searched his mind for how he really felt, what he really wanted to say. Now wasn't the time to fall back on even more euphemisms. 'I do trust you.'

'Do you, Mike?' she asked. Again, hearing his first name unsettled him. It held an intimacy that he wasn't comfortable with, not in this situation anyway.

'Of course. I chose you for my team. I chose you as lead DS. If I'm honest, I probably trust you more than I trust Roger, or even Dave.'

'Really?'

'Yes, really,' he said. He felt angry. How did she not know all of this? He had assumed it was his actions on the Stevens case that had caused the problem between them. *Bobby* . . . *trust* – it had never even crossed his mind.

'You thought this was about *her*, didn't you?' Jane said, looking over her shoulder, as if checking that no one was listening to their conversation.

'You said something about trust – about lying – a while back,' he replied, trying to recall the conversation: a few garbled exchanges that hadn't amounted to anything.

'I figured you were pissed off that I had gone behind your back, that I might have jeopardized the case.'

'He killed five women, Mike,' Jane said, her voice loud. She looked around her again. 'He would have killed five more if we hadn't stopped him, and you think I was worried about the case?' She stopped. 'I was worried about *you.*' Again she stopped, before looking up and holding his eye. 'Look, I'm not going to say you were right. You weren't. It was stupid, reckless and against every rule in the book. You know that. I know that. Everyone in the bloody office knows that. But that doesn't change anything. Those women are still dead. She died because of me, because of you.'

She might as well have smashed her glass and ground the broken shards into his face. He felt sick. 'Jane,' he said, closing his eyes and taking a deep breath before opening them again. 'He made those choices, not you. He killed those women, not you. I fucked up, and people got hurt. I have to live with that.' Jane was shaking her head. 'No, Jane, you need to listen to me now.' He waited until he had her attention. 'It wasn't your fault, any more than all the other murders we deal with. It happened – there's nothing you or I can do about it. It's not your responsibility. I am not your responsibility. Do you understand me?' She nodded. He could see her eyes were wet with tears. He wanted to comfort her, but he didn't know how. 'I didn't tell you about my brother, because I'm an idiot. I was ashamed of . . . ' he paused, 'of nothing. I don't know why, but I blamed myself for my parents sending Bobby away. As for the Stevens case, I can't defend my actions, any more than I can explain them. But we're past that now. What you need to know is that I trust you. I value you. I don't want you to doubt that again.'

'Yes, sir,' Jane said in a voice so quiet that it was almost drowned out by the music that surrounded them.

'Look at me,' he said. 'Jane.' She raised her head. 'Are we clear?' He sighed, pushing away the negative feeling. He needed to let it go, for both their sakes. 'Tell me we're clear, otherwise I'm going to have to kill you and hide the body. You know I can do it.' He smiled, willing her to let go too.

She did. She smiled, pushed her hands through her hair and shook her shoulders, as if sloughing off their entire conversation. 'Yes, sir. We're clear.'

Relief crashed over him like a wave, washing him clean. 'Now,' he said, finishing his pint, 'we can get back to work. Another?' he said, pointing to her empty glass.

'You don't have to ask me twice, but you'd better make it a spritzer,' she said.

'Spritzers are for City women – and you, Jane, are not one of those. You'll have another glass of wine, and I'll arrange for Chris to take you home, via your mother's. Cool?'

'Cool, sir,' Jane said, shrugging out of her jacket.

'And when I get back, you can tell me all about the Hungerford case. I can tell by your notebook that your interview was – shall we say – long?' She frowned. 'It's been on the table for the past hour, Jane,' he said, pointing to the book lying between their empty glasses. 'I happen to know that you number all of your notebooks, and that you start a new one for a case that you're running personally. The Hungerford case has only been yours for a week and that book's almost half-full.' He tapped the side of his head with his finger. 'Not as stupid as I look, eh? I'm not a detective inspector for nothing, you know.'

'Never doubted you for a second, sir,' she said.

'I should think not,' he said, walking away. He was smiling – really smiling – for the first time in weeks.

CHAPTER TWENTY-SEVEN

30th April – Wednesday

Jane stood listening as Professor Cresswell talked. He was in full 'selling' mode. Why? She had no idea. Two coppers from Lewisham were hardly ideal candidates for Greenwich University. There was no denying the university's academic record, and the fees were very competitive, if the professor was to be believed. She was tempted to ask if there were facilities for adults with autism. She opened her mouth to speak, but then closed it again. It was a bit premature to be planning Peter's further education. As if she could afford the fees anyway, competitive or not. She covered her smile with the back of her hand. She could just imagine what Peter would be like in his interview. *'So, Peter, what made you choose Greenwich University for your degree?'* He would frown, as if the answer was obvious. *'My mum's a detective. A girl was murdered here. My mum visited the campus to find out who killed her. She thought it looked nice.'* Factual. To the point. That was Peter, especially when he wanted something. She could hear his voice now. 'I'm hot, Mummy. Ice-cream is cold, Mummy. I want one.' You couldn't argue with that kind of logic.

She looked at the professor, still in full flow, and realized she hadn't been listening. She glanced at Lockyer and let her shoulders relax. His eyes were focused. He was paying attention, even if she wasn't. That had to be a first.

She looked around her at the manicured lawns. This area would be called the 'quad' or something similar. She would bet that most universities in London would be all but deserted during examination week. But not here. Dozens of students were sitting on the grass around her, chatting, listening to music or tapping away on their tablets. It had an Oxford or Cambridge air about it, or even Hogwarts. Beautiful stone buildings and archways leading to different parts of the university. It had taken her and Lockyer twenty minutes to find their way in. There were at least four different campuses, specializing in different disciplines. She guessed that once you were signed up, it would all become simple. She imagined it was like Vegas. To the uninitiated, it could be impossible to leave. Lockyer was asking questions about the psychology department now. She took out her notebook to jot down any new names that came up. She still couldn't believe Lockyer was here with her. After their drink in the pub, things had changed. Not quite back to normal; in fact, nothing like normal. She was going against procedure, and against Roger's specific instructions, by having her boss with her. She never broke the rules – not if she could help it. In her experience, you couldn't go far wrong if you followed the rules. But today she wasn't doing so.

After they had finished sorting out their 'issues' in the pub, Lockyer had asked for a rundown on the Leech and

Hungerford cases. It was such a familiar question that she had reeled off the information without thinking. It was only when she was halfway through talking about Victor's interview that she realized something was amiss. She wondered at the time, and now, if Lockyer knew and had pushed her for the details on purpose, keen to step back into the fray. Whatever his motives, she had to admit she was glad he was here. The Hungerford case was building momentum. Her interview with Victor had ended up taking three hours. What he had to say about Terry Mort wasn't favourable, but was it true? Victor had been Maggie's boyfriend; Mort was the ex-boyfriend and, according to Victor, deranged. Given his involvement, Victor was not a strong witness, no matter how credible she thought he was.

'If it's okay with you,' Lockyer said to the professor, 'we'll just have a wander, and chat to a few of the students, while we're waiting for Maggie's MA group to get out of their exam.' The professor muttered his disapproval. 'Don't worry,' Lockyer continued, taking the guy's hand to signify that the meeting was at an end. 'We won't disturb anyone or delay them unnecessarily. If I could have the list you were just showing us, with the timetables and registered students, that would be a big help. At least that way we can mark off who we manage to speak today, before calling anyone into the station.' It was obvious the professor wanted to protest, but Lockyer held onto the hand he was shaking and took the pages of A4 with the other.

'I'll be in my office, and in and around campus, all day today,' Cresswell said. It sounded more like a threat than a statement. 'If I can be of further assistance please don't hesitate to come and find me. I'll no doubt see you. Also, if you can go through to the office, they will provide you with ID for the day. We are vigilant when it comes to strangers wandering around on campus.'

'Very wise,' Lockyer said, nodding his head. 'If only all teaching institutions were as well organized as yours.'

If the professor noticed Lockyer's sarcasm he didn't show it. He nodded to Jane, but didn't bother to shake her hand, despite the fact that she was holding it out to him. He must have assumed Lockyer was in charge, but who could blame him? She had stood by, mute, and let him take the lead on her case. But why? This was her investigation. Lockyer said he was only here to observe and support her, but she had fallen back on old habits and stood quietly beside him while he ran the show. She had to snap out of this stupor. The last thing she needed was a disciplinary from Roger for bringing Lockyer along, and then the added insult of not having all the correct information, because she had let her boss ask all the questions. 'Thank you,' she said, as the professor walked away. 'And thank you, sir, for stepping in there. I zoned out for a second. It won't happen again.' She could feel her cheeks heating up.

Lockyer turned and stared at her. He nodded and gestured for her to enter the building first. 'After you,' he said. 'It's your show.'

Two hours and two dozen conversations later Jane felt exhausted. Students were tiring. They were so young and en-thusiastic. She couldn't keep up. The majority of the people they had spoken to were only ten years younger than her, but she felt like an old woman by comparison. As she listened to endless stories about nights out in Greenwich, clubbing up in town and all-night parties she could almost feel her wrinkles getting deeper.

'Mort's name came up a lot,' Lockyer said, pulling on his earlobe.

Jane slid her sunglasses into her handbag and pursed her lips. 'He's not popular, that's for sure.' She looked up and down the hallways. 'What I find a bit odd is that so many of the MA students seem to know him. I mean the PhD doesn't run alongside the Masters. They have some linked events, but not many, and yet eight of the people we talked to mentioned him, without prompting. What does that tell you?'

'I'm not sure,' Lockyer said, wandering up to a noticeboard and repinning a couple of A4 pages that had come loose. 'But we know where he is now, so let's go and find out.'

She nodded and they walked in silence towards the library. Terry Mort had just had a meeting with a tutor and was now, according to several of the students, in the library taking out more research material for his thesis. As they passed the lecture halls and smaller study rooms she thought over what Victor had told her about Mort, comparing it to what his fellow students had to say about the guy. It was true Mort was not popular, but none of the people she and Lockyer had talked to were quite as adamant, or as vocal, as Victor. Had his relationship with Maggie clouded his judgement, or did Victor just know Mort better?

From the university file, Jane knew that Mort was thirty-two, lived alone in Greenwich and was in his second year of his PhD. According to the curriculum, which she'd checked, a full-time PhD would take three years. But Mort had chosen to study part-time, adding a further three years. She couldn't imagine studying for that length of time. The bulk of the PhD seemed to be research-based, testing theories, finding new treatments or applications utilizing psychological theory – or so the handbook said. It all sounded like psychobabble to her. She kept thinking about a scene in the film *Ghostbusters*, where Bill Murray tests two students with Zener cards, measuring whether stimulus affects ESP. If they fail to guess the picture on the card, they receive a small electric shock. The attractive blonde gets all the questions wrong, but Murray – in his bid to woo her – pretends she's some kind of telepathic marvel. Her dorky counterpart, however, is shocked mercilessly. Jane had always found the scene funny, but as she walked towards the library she found herself wondering if Mort's experiments were similarly cruel. Victor had told her that Mort had formed an off-campus clique, and that the group was carrying out unauthorized experiments. When she had asked him to elaborate on what kinds of experiments, Victor had faltered and become vague. She slowed her pace now, allowing Lockyer to go ahead of her.

There was no denying it. She was nervous about meeting Mort. She knew it was irrational, but 'head-doctors' freaked her out. She had been referred to a psychiatrist when Peter was first diagnosed, to help her adjust and cope with her son's changing behaviour. She had felt violated, as if the therapist could read her thoughts and manipulate them. She worried that her feelings towards Peter would change, that the intrusion would damage their relationship. No one could tell her how to feel or understand the ever-changing combinations of love, anger, guilt, fear and acceptance that she dealt with every day. She had left the session and never gone back.

'Here we are,' Lockyer said, pointing to two double doors.

She looked up and saw the sign pointing towards the library. She had expected it to be in the old part of the building: a huge room with panelled walls and heavy oak doors. Lockyer pushed open one of the very ordinary-looking doors and gestured for her to go ahead of him. His expression seemed to reiterate his earlier statement. It was her show. Not for the first time, she felt unsure of herself. When Lockyer had been absent from the office – from her cases – she had coped fine. Well, maybe not fine, but she had managed to maintain both files without any major catastrophes. So why, when he was here supporting her, was she going to pieces?

'And we're not moving – why?' he asked, raising his eyebrows.

'Sorry,' she said, pushing her shoulders back and walking into the library.

Instead of row upon row of shelves filled with leather-bound books, there were banks of computers. The actual library section was relatively small, tucked away at the back of the large room. There were half a dozen students in the room, but she guessed which one was Mort as soon as she spotted him. He was seated at a desk off to one side, surrounded by large research texts. He looked like the love-child of Einstein and Justin Timberlake. His hair was wild, but Jane could tell it was styled to look like that. It was a statement. It said, 'I don't care what people think. I'm my own person.' That made her even more uneasy. If individuals operated under their own set of rules, rejecting those set by society, then they could be unpredictable.

'Bet you a tenner that's him,' Lockyer said, pointing in the same direction she was looking. 'I know we aren't meant to go on stereotypes, but for me he's ticking all the boxes, so far, of an anti-establishment academic.'

As if he could sense their presence, the young man looked up and smiled. 'Are you looking for me, Detectives?' he asked in a whisper.

'Yes,' Jane said, walking over to the table, with Lockyer close behind her. She held out her hand. 'I'm Detective Sergeant Bennett and this is Detective Inspector Lockyer,' she said, gesturing behind her.

'Good to meet you,' he said, standing up to shake Lockyer's hand and then hers. 'I heard you were on campus today.'

'Have you got a minute?' she asked, looking down at the pile of books on the table.

He seemed to consider her question. He looked over her shoulder at Lockyer and then down at the books in front of him. 'Actually, do you think you could you give me five minutes?' he asked. 'I've got a shared office down the hall, Room 407. I'll meet you in there. Grab a coffee, if you like. There's a vending machine just outside the library.'

Jane opened her mouth to respond.

'That's fine,' Lockyer said. He started walking towards the exit. Jane found herself following.

'I'm Terry, by the way,' he called after them, again in a hushed whisper. 'Terry Mort.'

'Yes, we know,' Lockyer said pushing open the double doors for Jane. She walked out without looking back. Was she invisible?

Ten minutes later Jane and Lockyer were sitting in what Mort had called an 'office'; 'broom cupboard' would have been more appropriate. There was a desk against the back wall, a small window, two plastic chairs and a rusty-looking filing cabinet. Lockyer was leaning against the door-jamb, sipping his coffee. 'Do you think he's done a runner?' he asked, an amused expression on his face.

Jane blew on what was now her second cup of tea and crossed her legs, bumping the chair opposite. 'I think Mr Mort – soon to be Professor – is making us wait. I think he wants to show us just how relaxed he is, and who is in charge.'

'You're probably right,' he said, leaning out into the hallway. 'He was a bit,' Lockyer seemed to be searching for the right word, 'intense, wasn't he?'

'He looks older than thirty-two,' she said. 'You can see why people don't warm to him. He's a condescending prick.' Lockyer chuckled at her description. Despite her feelings about therapy-types, she had tried to resist the urge to pre-judge Mort. She had failed.

'Speak of the devil,' Lockyer said in a stage whisper. He raised his hand and nodded. 'He's just getting himself a drink. He isn't portraying the grieving ex-boyfriend very well.'

'No, he isn't,' she said.

'Sorry about that,' Mort said, appearing in the doorway

and sliding past Lockyer into the office. 'The scanner's buggered again. I'll have to go back and try again later.'

'Technology,' Lockyer said.

Mort put his cup down on the filing cabinet, before dropping a pile of folders onto the desk. He waved his hand at Lockyer. 'Come in, come in, shut the door,' he said, reaching for his cup. 'It's a bit snug, I know, but at least it's all mine . . . well, for today at least.' He sat down opposite Jane, raised his cup to them both and took a sip of his drink.

'Terry,' Jane began, pulling her notepad out of her trouser pocket and placing it on the desk next to her, 'as I'm sure you're aware, my colleague and I have been talking to Maggie's MA group today, but we're also interested in speaking to anyone who studied, taught or had contact with Maggie Hungerford at the university in general.'

Mort nodded. 'Well, I'd have to say yes to all three,' he said, raising his cup again.

'What do you mean by that?' she asked.

He shrugged and said, 'Well, I guess you could say that I studied with her, in that we sometimes studied together. I taught one of her modules for a term. Teaching is a requirement of my PhD, and I obviously had contact with her at university and outside it.'

'Were you friends?' Jane asked.

Mort's brow creased. 'Er, yes,' he said, although he might as well have said, 'Duh, yeah', like a character from *The Simpsons*. 'I'm sure you already know that Maggie and I dated.'

'Terry,' Lockyer said, leaning against the filing cabinet, 'we prefer to ask the questions and get the information from the source, if you get my meaning?'

'Sure, that's fine,' Terry said. 'No problem. I just assumed you'd sooner skip the details at this stage.'

'Not the way it works, I'm afraid,' Lockyer said, as if he too found it tiresome that questions had to be asked and information repeated.

'Fair enough,' Terry replied, looking at Jane. 'So, do you want me to start from the day we met, or would you prefer to ask questions and I'll answer them?' His intention was obvious. He was managing the meeting, a further demonstration to her that he was in charge.

'Go ahead and tell us as much as you can recall, and we'll jump in with questions as and when,' Lockyer said. 'If that's all right with you, Terry?'

Jane tried not to react. This interview was going to be even more difficult if Lockyer acted as if she didn't exist as well.

'I met Maggie in her first year – nothing specific, just saw her around campus, at social events, stuff like that. I don't tend to see that much of the Masters lot, unless I happen to be in college or coming in for a visiting lecturer. Anyway we met, enough to say "Hi" when we saw each other, but that's about it. I had a party for my birthday in May last year and I invited her and a bunch of others off the MA course to come.'

'Why?' Jane asked, aware of how practised Mort's speech seemed and how, when he spoke, she felt less and less comfortable with his proximity to her.

He looked at her as if reading her mind, his eyes travelling over her face and body. 'I always think parties are more interesting if you have both sexes present, don't you?' He didn't wait for her to answer. 'She came, we got talking and things sort of happened from there,' he said.

'Can you expand on that, Terry?' she asked, indicating her pad and the lack of notes so far.

He looked up at Lockyer, smiled and then turned back at her. 'Okay,' he said, his tone indulgent, 'we hooked up at the end of the party – nothing serious, but enough to know we liked each other. She was smarter than the others. Her insights into psychology and its possible applications were quite interesting.' He must have thought he saw confusion on Jane's face as he said, 'It's not everyone's thing, but I find the whole subject fascinating, hence the PhD. So we met up for drinks and I guess you could say we were dating for most of the summer.'

'How would you describe your relationship?' Lockyer asked.

Again Mort smiled. Jane felt as if he and Lockyer were on the same team and she was the outsider. 'Not much at first,' he said, 'just casual dating, but by the end of the summer we were pretty serious – or rather I was serious.'

'Maggie didn't see the relationship as "serious"?' Jane asked, jumping in.

'I thought she did,' Mort said, shaking his head. 'But I realized there was someone else. You don't have to be a psychologist to know when a woman is lying.' He laughed, but there was no mirth in his voice.

'How do you know she was seeing someone else?' Jane asked.

'She admitted it,' he said, shrugging his shoulders, looking up at Lockyer. 'At first I ignored her behaviour. She was late turning up at my place, or sometimes not turning up at all. Mystery absences – you know how women are,' he said, again not giving Jane time to respond, to defend her sex. 'I just assumed she was trying to get my attention. I'm a busy guy. I'm only in the second year of my PhD. I have a huge amount of work to do.' He let his words hang in the air. His implication was clear. Jane was wasting his time. Just as Maggie had. 'Anyway, eventually I confronted her and she admitted she had feelings for someone else. End of discussion. End of relationship.'

'How did you feel?' Jane asked.

'Really?' Mort said, laughing. 'Is that how you're going to play this?' he asked, looking at her and then at Lockyer. He looked disappointed. 'I have a degree in psychology, Detective. I have a Masters in applied psychology and I'm studying for my doctorate. Interviewing techniques are not unfamiliar to me. Maggie was murdered, and from what I hear, the manner of her death was not, shall we say, very nice. You're establishing that I knew the victim. Now you're establishing whether I had a grudge or a reason to dislike her. Parlay that into a motive, and all you have to do is disprove my alibi and wham, bam and you're done: I'm your man. Is that how this is going to work?' The disdain in his voice made Jane sit back in her seat.

'No, Terry,' she said, choosing her words before she continued. 'We know you had a relationship with Maggie. We know she had a relationship with someone else. We know there was an overlap. You weren't happy about the situation, which – given the circumstances – is understandable. All of that is, as I'm sure you are aware, circumstantial evidence.

What we are trying to "establish", as you put it, is whether or not you have any information that can assist in this investigation. My job is to gather as much information as possible in order to ascertain who murdered Maggie and then arrest that person.' She stopped and waited for Mort to look at her. 'Does that make things clearer for you?' The shift in power was almost imperceptible, but Jane felt it, and it felt good.

'Just ask your questions,' Mort said. 'I have work to do,' he went on, gesturing at the files on his desk.

CHAPTER TWENTY-EIGHT

30th April – Wednesday

'I appreciate you're a busy man, Terry,' Jane said, ignoring the blank stare Mort was giving her. He had folded his arms and his bottom lip was stuck out like that of a petulant child. 'Detective Inspector Lockyer,' she said, gesturing at Lockyer, 'assured Professor Cresswell that we wouldn't unnecessarily detain his students.'

'I certainly did,' Lockyer said with a solemn nod, catching Jane's eyes for a second.

'So,' she said, relieved to feel in control again, 'if you would prefer to continue this discussion at a more convenient time?' She kept her eyes on Mort as she closed her notepad. 'I can arrange for you to come over to the station in Lewisham. Whatever's easiest for you?' She waited. Mort wanted to believe he was in charge, but he wasn't. He might have a degree in psychology and a Masters to go with it, but Jane had been interviewing suspects since he was in secondary school. As soon as he lost his cool she had him. And Lockyer, to his credit, had backed off.

Mort looked at her and then up at Lockyer. If he was

expecting any kind of brotherly support, he didn't get any. 'Now is fine, Detective,' he said.

'Good. Great,' she said, reopening her notepad. 'Let's get on with it then, shall we?'

'Fine with me,' Mort said, looking anything but fine.

She waited for a few more seconds and then continued where they had left off. 'Did Maggie tell you who she was seeing behind your back?'

Mort shook his head. 'No, she didn't; or rather, she wouldn't. Further demonstration of how little respect she had for me and our relationship.'

'You said earlier that Maggie was . . . ' she flicked back a few pages in her notes, ' . . . that she was smart. We know from friends of hers that she didn't date a great deal, that her work was very important to her. Would you agree with that statement?'

'That her work was very important to her? Absolutely,' he said. 'That she didn't date much? I wouldn't be the best person to answer that, now would I?'

'Of course not,' Jane said. 'As far as you know, did Maggie ever fall behind in any of her studies, lectures, assignments – anything like that?'

Mort was shaking his head before she could finish speaking. 'No. She was a dedicated student. We spent a great deal of our time together discussing theories, reading academic articles and journals. Maggie was, in my opinion, Detective, a lousy girlfriend, but she had the potential to be an outstanding academic.'

The sudden outpouring of praise made Jane pause. She studied Mort. His impassioned speech appeared genuine, not unlike Victor's the previous day. It was clear that Maggie attracted a certain type. Both men were intelligent, academic. Both men were confident, handsome and dynamic. Where they differed was in their personalities. Victor was charming, affable and sincere. Mort was aggressive, condescending and full of shit. Mort was Dr Jekyll to Victor's Mr Hyde. 'Terry,' she said, tapping the end of her nose with her pen, 'it seems obvious that Maggie's behaviour lessened your opinion of her, but even so, you don't seem at all distressed by her death. Would it be fair to say that?'

'Can I be honest?' Mort asked, leaning forward. She felt Lockyer mirror the gesture, leaning down towards them from his position by the filing cabinet. Whether that was to protect her or hear better she wasn't sure.

'Please, go ahead,' she said.

'Maggie's death was sudden, and obviously I have some feelings about it, despite the nature of our break-up. But the truth is, I am more intrigued than anything else.'

Jane saw Lockyer's eyebrows go up. He opened his mouth to speak, but she beat him to it. 'Intrigued?' she said.

Mort nodded like an eager schoolboy. 'I just . . . I have so many questions.' He looked at Jane and then up at Locker, holding up his hands. 'Now I know how that sounds, but I'm sure – given your training and experience – you can understand. In the same way you have learned emotional detachment in order to do your job, I have been trained to look at things from a scientific perspective. The manner of her death: what does it mean? What can be learned?' Jane could feel Lockyer's agitation. He was moving his weight from one foot to the other. She was pretty sure he was thinking about knocking Mort's front teeth out. She was tempted to do the same, but Mort seemed oblivious to their reactions. 'Was she alive when she was put underground?' he asked. Jane would swear his pupils dilated as he spoke. 'If she was, do you know how long she lived for? Fear has an astonishing effect on the brain. I'm sure it's not possible on an active investigation, but perhaps, once you've finished, I could speak to you again; perhaps get some more details. This kind of data could be invaluable to my research.' By the time he finished speaking he was out of breath.

Jane looked at Lockyer. He shook his head, his eyebrows high on his forehead, and looked up at the ceiling. 'Terry,' he said, his hands gripping the top of the filing cabinet, 'you need to think very carefully before you continue. Maggie Hungerford's death is not one of your school projects. She is not some guinea pig that you can dissect and study. I would appreciate it if you would keep your ghoulish thoughts to yourself.' He took a deep breath before levelling his gaze at Mort. 'And if I ever hear that you've been talking about this case – any aspects of this case – to your fellow students, I will have you kicked out of this university quicker than you can say "Freud". Am I making myself clear?'

Mort shrugged. Lockyer's position and body language were obvious, but if Mort felt threatened he didn't show it. 'Fair enough,' he said, turning back to Jane. 'Many people find some aspects of psychology difficult to understand.'

Lockyer took a step closer. 'I've had enough of this.'

'You and me both, Detective,' Mort replied, his face the picture of innocence.

Jane stood, putting herself between Lockyer and Mort.

'Just one final question, Terry,' she said. 'It has been mentioned that you run several study groups.' Lockyer huffed out a breath behind her.

'I do,' Mort said.

'Are these groups regulated by the university?' she asked. 'Do you have to submit your study programme, members – that kind of thing – so that students can be registered for extra credits?'

He was nodding. 'Exactly that, Detective.' He seemed impressed that she knew something, however banal, about academic life. Lockyer was pacing in a tight circle next to the door. Mort remained unfazed. It was as if he couldn't see him. 'I help with two of the Masters groups. I'm not involved per se, but I suggest topics, further reading; anything to help them expand on their own ideas.'

'Do you run any extracurricular groups? Outside the university, for example?'

'No,' he said. 'What would be the point?'

His answer was clear, but Jane could tell by the way he shifted in his seat that the 'can I be honest' section of the interview was over. She was remembering what Victor had told her. She was also thinking about what Lockyer had just said: 'Maggie Hungerford's death is not one of your school projects.'

But what if she was? What if that was exactly what she was?

CHAPTER TWENTY-NINE

30th April – Wednesday

Lockyer was becoming accustomed to being on the wrong side of Roger's fury. Jane, on the other hand, was not. Lockyer pulled out a chair for her and told her to sit down. 'There's no point standing on ceremony. When the boss goes, he goes,' he said, positioning himself to the side of her chair, still standing. She might be the one in trouble, but he was going to do his best to deflect as much of Roger's anger as possible. She had let him in on her case and for that he owed her one. Yes, she had, in not so many words, told him to back off at the university; and yes, he had wanted to kill Terry Mort with his bare hands. But Lockyer had felt more like himself today than he had done in weeks. 'Roger will shout a fair bit and stomp about the office, but it's mainly for show. Imagine a silverback gorilla banging about in the jungle – it's like that.' He saw Jane's face drop and realized he wasn't helping. 'It'll be fine, Jane. I'll explain what happened.'

She shook her head and looked up at him. 'Thanks, sir, but I'd prefer to handle it, if you don't mind? It's my case. Roger assigned it to me. I need to take the heat.'

'But—' Lockyer tried to cut in.

'Sir, if I let you take over again, Roger won't be able to trust me, or my judgement. The Hungerford case was assigned to me, and it's my responsibility to explain why I took you over to the uni.'

Her 'again' didn't escape Lockyer's notice. She looked nervous, her face pale. Lockyer doubted if Jane had ever been called into their SIO's office for anything other than praise. She was beyond reproach in everything she did. It was her way, and what made her such a brilliant DS. It was why he had chosen her for his team. He could only hope that the impending dressing-down didn't knock her confidence too much. 'Okay, fair enough,' he said. He would respect her wishes for now, but if things got too serious he would step in, whether Jane liked it or not.

'Great – you're both here.'

Lockyer turned as Roger walked into the office, shutting the glass door behind him. Compared to the last time he had faced his SIO's wrath, Roger looked in control. Maybe this wasn't going to be too bad after all. Perhaps it was only Lockyer who brought out Roger's crazy side.

'Boss,' he said, nodding, standing to attention and clasping his hands behind his back.

'Jane, nice to see you've made yourself comfortable,' Roger said, walking around the desk. She was out of her seat and standing next to Lockyer before he turned back to face them both. 'That's better.'

Lockyer tried to catch Roger's eyes, to let him know he was more than happy to take the blame. He couldn't stand seeing Jane this submissive. There was something shameful about it. 'Boss,' he began, unable to stop himself.

'Take it easy, Mike,' Roger said. 'You don't need to get all over-protective. DS Bennett can handle herself, can't you, Jane?'

'Yes, boss,' she said. The look she gave Lockyer needed no interpretation.

'Please,' Roger said, pointing to the two chairs facing his desk. 'Sit down, both of you. Half the office watched you walk in, so now the whole office is straining to hear which one of you I'm firing today.' He smiled, but Lockyer could see the tension in his face.

Lockyer waited for Jane to sit down, before pulling his chair closer to her and sitting down himself. He couldn't help feeling protective. Jane was his DS. She had taken him to the uni for the interviews because he had asked to go. She was following orders. Just not the ones handed down by Roger.

'So, I hear you had a little excursion today?' Roger asked, looking at Jane.

'Yes,' Jane said. 'First-time interviews on the Hungerford case. DC Groves interviewed Professor Cresswell, head of psychology, yesterday and he provided a list of all the students and tutors who would have had contact with the victim.' Her voice was level and she maintained eye contact with Roger, but Lockyer could see she was still anxious.

'And?' Roger said, sitting back in his chair, waving his hand for her to continue.

'DI Lockyer and I discussed the case yesterday and I asked him to accompany me, to assist with the questioning and—'

Roger cut her off. 'Right, I see. That all sounds reasonable, sensible even. But the problem I have, DS Bennett, is that I specifically assigned DI Lockyer to cold-cases, for reasons we don't need to go into now. Furthermore, I specifically told you that the Hungerford case was yours to run. I signed off on your team members. Why didn't you take one of them with you?'

'This is a complicated inquiry,' Jane said. 'I felt DI Lockyer's support and input would be valuable. He is the most senior officer in the squad, and my direct superior.'

If her words riled Roger's sense of hierarchy, he didn't show it. 'You don't feel you can handle the case on your own?' The question sounded genuine.

'No, boss,' she said, 'I *can* handle it. It was a judgement call. DI Lockyer was available and willing to offer his assistance. There were a lot of individuals to speak to, and I have a lot of experience of working with DI Lockyer. It made sense.'

'For the case, you mean?'

'Yes. My first priority was, and is, the Hungerford case. It's my job as lead DS to requisition and utilize all resources available to me, as long as they benefit the ongoing investigation. The case is now a week old. I am not prepared to let inter-office disputes disrupt the case.'

Lockyer was impressed. There was no need for him to be here. The confidence and authority in Jane's voice were hard to ignore. She had no intention of getting stuck in the middle of Roger and Lockyer's business. She had separated herself, and the case, with skill and poise. Lockyer could tell from Roger's expression that he was just as impressed. Both men sat in silence.

Jane went on, 'I should have advised you, as SIO, that

I was intending to take DI Lockyer with me. I can only apologize for the oversight. It won't happen again.'

Roger smiled and said, 'You wouldn't believe how many times I've heard your boss say the very same thing. You've taught her well, Mike.' He finally met Lockyer's eyes. 'Is it just me, or did she just run rings around me in my own office?'

'What can I say, Roger,' Lockyer said. 'She's the best DS we have.'

'No denying that,' Roger said. 'Thank you, Jane. You made that a lot easier than most.'

'Thanks, boss,' she said. Her shoulders had dropped by an inch, but Lockyer could tell she was still on full alert. He had a feeling that today would be the first and last time she went outside the chain of command. Lockyer stood to leave.

'Before you go,' Roger said, 'I have some news – for you both, it seems.' Neither he nor Jane said anything. Lockyer didn't want to disrupt the newly calm atmosphere. 'While you were over in Greenwich, some of the labs came back on Hungerford. Penny ran them past me to get the okay for a warrant.'

'A warrant?' Jane said, standing and pushing her chair back.

'The toxicology report came back positive for morphine. The victim had traces in her stomach,' Roger said, raising his eyebrow.

'Meaning she ingested it?' Lockyer asked, his brow creasing. 'I thought she was knocked unconscious?'

'She was,' Roger said.

'Liquid morphine?' Jane asked.

'No,' Roger said. 'The morphine was in tablet form. Dave found fragments in the girl's stomach.'

'What?' Lockyer said. 'Her attacker force-fed her morphine tablets while she was unconscious?'

'No. Dave says that's not possible,' Roger continued. 'One or two pills maybe, but the quantity required to knock the victim out: no. She would have to have ingested them herself.'

'So it's a suicide now, is it?' Lockyer said, almost amused.

'Victor?' Jane said in a whisper.

'You've got it,' Roger said. 'Victor Lebowski was the last person to see the girl alive. They had dinner. He must have crushed up the medication and put it in her meal.'

'That can't be right,' Jane said, sitting down again, her eyes darting back and forth. 'Maggie was taken from her own home. She was in her pyjamas. Her blood was found on her front steps where she was knocked out. According to Victor, they had dinner at his house, drank some wine, had sex,' she paused. 'Then Maggie went home. We're assuming she wasn't taken until the early hours. She could have eaten later on that evening.'

'Jane,' Roger said, 'are you suggesting her killer broke into her house and crushed up morphine tablets in her cereal, on the off-chance that she might have a snack when she arrived home? Then he knocked on the door in the middle of the night, got her to answer it in her pyjamas and come outside, turn round so that he could hit her on the back of the head and then, luckily for him, she'd had her cornflakes and the morphine just happened to kick in at that moment, so she was sedated for their trip over to Elmstead?' Their SIO looked incredulous. It was clear he had been expecting thanks from

Jane, not questions. Lockyer couldn't blame him. Liquid morphine or drugs administered by needle would have left things ambiguous, but the victim ingesting a large quantity of morphine pills pretty much put Victor Lebowski in the frame. Why was Jane arguing the guy's case?

'No,' Jane said. 'Of course not. But we met an individual today. Mort – Terry Mort.' Lockyer's shoulders tensed at the sound of the guy's name. He still wanted to hit him. 'He's Maggie's ex-boyfriend, and he was . . . ' She rubbed her face. 'I wasn't happy with his story, boss, and he's yet to provide an alibi. Victor told me that Mort had tried to stop Maggie going to dinner that night. That he had been trying to get her back for months: calling, sending flowers, harassing her.' She seemed in a rush to get her words out, and Lockyer couldn't help but notice that she kept using Lebowski's first name. 'What if Mort went to Maggie's flat later than evening. He was an ex, so it's feasible she would let him in, even in her nightclothes. They talked. He'd brought something with him for them to eat.' She looked up at the ceiling. 'Then he . . . he attacked her as he was leaving.'

Lockyer could tell she had more to say, but she stopped herself. She had been quiet in the car on the way back to the station. He had assumed she was as floored by Mort's attitude as he was, but maybe it was more than that. 'That's a bit of a stretch, Jane,' he said. She turned to face him, her eyes blazing.

'Are you telling me you don't think Mort's involved, after what he said to us today?' she asked.

'No, Jane, I'm not. Mort was an abomination, no doubt.

But from what Roger's just said and from Dave's findings, Lebowski's the guy – nine times out of ten.'

'But she was attacked at home,' Jane said, shifting in her seat. 'Explain that to me.'

Lockyer took a deep breath. 'The drugs suggest premeditation, Jane,' he said, putting the pieces together in his mind. 'From what you've told me, Lebowski's a clever guy. The fact that Maggie was attacked when she got home, rather than at Lebowski's house, gives him the perfect alibi.' He waited until Jane was looking at him. 'Think about it. He'll say, "If I drugged her and planned to kill her, why wouldn't I do it in the safety of my own home? Why would I risk taking her home and attacking her on her front doorstep, where people could see me, where people would recognize me?"'

Jane was shaking her head, but Roger was nodding. He could see sense in Lockyer's reasoning, even if she couldn't.

'I authorized the warrant. DC Groves is just getting the necessary signatures. She should be making the arrest shortly,' Roger said, standing up. 'Forgive me, Jane, but I thought you'd be pleased?'

She was still shaking her head. 'I am, boss. Of course I am. But there's something that doesn't fit. Why the tomb? Why put Maggie down there when she was alive? I can't explain it right now, sir, but I know Mort's holding something back. Victor . . . ' Again she stopped.

'Well, you will have at least forty-eight hours to question Lebowski before you have to worry about charging him. Put a team on this Mort character. If your suspicions prove correct, then you'll have your next arrest already lined up, won't you?'

'Yes, boss,' Jane said, nodding. 'Thank you.' She turned and walked out of Roger's office, leaving Lockyer and Roger in her wake.

'What was all that about?' Roger asked.

'Not sure,' Lockyer said. 'This is her first big case. As she said, it's complicated. It's a lot of pressure. You know Jane. She just wants to get it right.'

'Okay, well, make sure you back her up.'

'I will, Roger,' Lockyer said, turning to leave.

'And, Mike, without needing to go into detail, I need to ask: are you all right? You seem more together – more like your old self – but . . . '

'It's okay, Roger,' Lockyer said without hesitation. 'I'm good, better: back on form.' The euphemisms sounded weak, but he could tell by Roger's face that they were the words he wanted to hear.

'Good. About time,' he said. 'Off you go. Good luck with Lebowski. Let's hope Jane has her man.'

It was an interesting phrase, Lockyer thought, as he left Roger's office, closing the door behind him.

'I don't believe it,' Jane said, walking into Lockyer's office. She sat down without waiting to be asked.

'What don't you believe?' he asked, leaning back in his chair and clasping his hands behind his head.

'Victor – I don't think he killed Maggie Hungerford.' It was the first time she had said the words out loud. Just hearing herself cemented her belief.

'And what makes you think that?' Lockyer asked.

There was warning in his tone, but Jane couldn't stop

herself. 'I'm not sure.' She was embarrassed by the weakness of the statement. 'I know how that sounds, but listen. Victor dated Maggie, yes. He saw her the night she was attacked. He even admitted that they argued. But he didn't kill her.'

'Jane,' he said, pushing his chair back and walking behind her to close the door to his office, 'I'm not sure what your relationship with Lebowski is, but I think it's fair to say it's clouding your judgement in this case.'

'Relationship?' She lowered her voice before continuing. 'There is no relationship between me and Victor. I've talked to him, interviewed him. He isn't a killer.'

'Jane,' Lockyer said, holding up his hands, 'you've got to admit that you seem to be taking this personally. You only met the guy yesterday, and now you're protesting his innocence like he's a family member. It's not like you, and what I don't understand,' he continued, his eyebrows raised, 'is why. What did Lebowski say or do to incite this . . . reaction?'

She felt winded. 'He didn't. I'm not.' She didn't know what to say. She dropped her head.

'Do you realize you keep calling him "Victor"?' he asked. Jane closed her eyes. She had caught herself referring to Victor by his first name a couple of times, but beyond that, no, she hadn't realized. 'I take it that's a No,' he said, sitting down. 'Look, Jane – that aside, I appreciate your instincts, but you need to be realistic. You interviewed Lebowski yesterday for what: a few hours? That isn't enough time to observe and study a suspect's responses. You wouldn't be the first copper to form an opinion of a suspect before having all the facts.' Jane bit the inside of her cheek. 'You didn't have the morphine angle then,' he said, holding up one finger. 'Given that, and everything you told me last night, Lebowski is the obvious fit. I know you told Roger that you thought Mort might be involved, but come on. Do you really believe the Miss Marple stuff you were spouting in there?'

'I don't know, sir,' she said, feeling as if she wanted to crawl out of his office with her tail between her legs. 'But I felt something with Mort,' she said. Lockyer might be right about the Victor thing. She had taken the news of his arrest personally, but not because of any relationship. It was because of Mort. How could Lockyer be so obtuse? They had only finished speaking to Mort a couple of hours ago. Had he forgotten how unhinged the guy had been? 'There was something wrong there, very wrong,' she said, looking over at him, searching his eyes for some shred of understanding.

'I'm not going to argue with you. Mort is a major concern, on a number of levels. But, Jane, Lebowski dated the victim. He had the means, the opportunity and a possible motive.'

'What motive?' she asked.

'You said yourself that Lebowski and Maggie argued the night she was attacked.'

'Yes, but . . . '

'Hang on,' he said. 'Let me finish.' She sat back, resisting the urge to cross her arms. 'Lebowski told you that Maggie had tried to cry off that night because Mort wanted to see her, that he'd been trying to get her back for months.'

'Yes,' Jane said.

'Did Victor tell you what he and Maggie argued about?'

Lockyer shook his head. 'You've got me doing it now. Did Lebowski tell you what they fought about?'

'No, he didn't,' she said, knowing where Lockyer was going with this.

'So, isn't it possible that Maggie was thinking about getting back with Mort; that she was thinking about breaking up with Victor, and that is what they were fighting about? Jealousy, revenge,' he said, sighing. 'They're not the most exciting motives, but they're the oldest.'

Jane's brain felt as if it was misfiring. She could hear what Lockyer was saying, but something was stopping her from accepting it. 'Mort didn't say anything about trying to get Maggie back. In fact, from the way he talked about her, I can't imagine he would even have entertained the notion.'

'So now you believe Mort?' he said. She could tell Lockyer was trying to sound sympathetic, but he was failing. 'Five minutes ago you were telling me and Roger that Mort fed Maggie the morphine because she rejected him. If Lebowski is telling the truth, then you have a possible motive. If the impression Mort gave of not being interested in Maggie any more is true, then your theory about him killing Maggie out of jealousy doesn't stack up. You can't have it both ways.'

'It doesn't have to be jealousy,' she said, feeling her resolve weaken. 'What Mort said about wanting information on her death, to study it, what if that was to cover his tracks? Victor – sorry, Lebowski – said he thought Mort was carrying out unauthorized experiments with an off-campus clique: weird psychology shit.' Even to her this was sounding far-fetched, but goose-bumps had come up on her arms. 'I haven't had the time or the manpower to really look into the air-hose and CCTV angle, but think about it.' She looked at Lockyer to gauge his reaction. He wasn't laughing, so she decided to keep going. 'Maggie was drugged, but not enough to kill her. She was hit, but not hard enough to inflict serious injury. She was put in that tomb alive with a supply – however limited – of air. There was a camera lens in with her. Why? Why would anyone want to watch that?' Lockyer's mouth turned down at the edges. He was considering what she was saying. That had to mean she hadn't gone mad. 'I'm sure Phil would say that someone would need to be psychopathic, if not psychotic, to indulge in such an elaborate murder. But what if it wasn't a murder – not in the usual sense of the word? What if it was an experiment? An experiment set up by an over-zealous, mentally unhinged PhD student?'

'Jane . . . ' Lockyer began.

'I know it sounds crazy, but it's been on my mind ever since I met Mort.'

'What would he hope to gain from such an experiment?' he asked, shaking his head. 'Are you saying Maggie was meant to come out of that hole and report back on how she felt?'

'No. I don't know,' she said, and she didn't. 'He had the camera, so maybe he didn't need her to come out. Maybe she was just a guinea pig, like you said. Or,' she went on, throwing her hands up, 'or maybe I am losing it. Mort, the camera, the tomb – I can feel a link. I just can't see it.' Lockyer didn't say anything. Jane's shoulders sagged. 'I don't know,' she said, pushing her thumbs into her temples. 'Everything you've said about Lebowski makes sense. He's the one in the frame. I'm focusing on the wrong person. I've let the case . . . I've let Mort get to me. My mind won't settle.' Again it was the first time she had said the words aloud, but not the first time she had thought them.

'It's okay, Jane. It's happens to everyone. It's happened to me, more than once. It's a big case – your biggest. You met Lebowski and he seemed normal. You met Mort.' He paused. 'And he seemed nuts. It's your job to connect the dots, not tangle yourself up in knots.' She nodded. 'You're bound to be anxious,' he said, 'keen to get it right; and get it right in record time. The kind of pressure you're under would drive a normal person insane.'

She managed to smile. 'Are you saying I'm not normal?'

'I hope not. Normal people don't make very good detectives. And you, Jane, are an excellent detective.'

She took a deep breath and blew it out. 'Okay. I think I need to get some air, clear my head, before they bring in Victor . . . I mean, Lebowski.'

'Do you want me to sit in?' he asked.

'Yes, sir. I do, thank you.' The relief in her voice was obvious even to her. She needed his support; it had just taken her a while to realize how much. She needed to talk things through – that was all. To get her mind straight. She was so used to having Lockyer there as a sounding board that not having him on the investigation had left her floundering. She could almost feel the fug of confusion lifting, and for that she was grateful.

As she stood to leave she saw Penny jogging across the office towards them. 'Looks like they've got him already,' she said, opening the door to Lockyer's office. 'You back from picking up Lebowski?' Jane asked, pleased that she had remembered to call him by his surname. No matter what she thought, he was now a murder suspect awaiting charges. She needed to maintain an emotional distance if she was going to do her job, and not calling him Victor was as good a place to start as any.

'Yes and no,' Penny said.

Jane noticed that she was out of breath. 'What's up?'

'It looks like we might have another clandestine site,' she said, taking in a lungful of air. 'Over in Elmstead.'

'Another body?' Jane asked.

'Not sure yet – maybe,' she said. 'It was dumb luck, really. I was out with Chris, waiting for the go-ahead from the SIO to pick up Lebowski. Despatch called the office looking for you. Franks told them you were in a meeting, so he transferred the call to me.'

'Right,' Jane said, willing Penny to get to the point. Lockyer was standing behind her. She could feel that he was ready to move. So was she.

'A man was seen over in Elmstead.' Penny took out her notepad and read, 'The individual was seen "rooting around" at the edge of the woods. The description sounded like Lebowski, so Chris and I took the call, went over to check it out and, sure enough, there he was. We took him into custody, and I called Franks and Whitemore to secure the scene. They called in the GPR guys as a precaution. I just got off the phone with Franks. GPR confirms that another underground space has been found.'

Jane turned to Lockyer. She knew what needed to be done. He nodded. 'Penny, are you happy to process Lebowski's arrest with the custody sergeant?' she asked.

'Yes, boss,' Penny said. 'No problem.'

'Fine. Get things under way here. DI Lockyer and I are going to head over to Elmstead. Can you call Dave and let him know what's happening?'

'Already done,' Penny said. 'I phoned down to the mortuary suite earlier. Dr Simpson is just finishing a post-mortem but after that he said he's all yours, if you need him.'

'Great job, DC Groves,' Lockyer said from behind Jane. Penny thanked him and nodded to Jane, before turning and walking away, back across the office towards the custody suite. If he wanted to say 'I told you so', now was the time to do it. But instead he said, 'It's not looking very good for our boy Victor, is it?' There was no sarcasm in his voice and he had said 'our' rather than 'your'.

'No,' she said. 'It's not.'

CHAPTER THIRTY

1st May – Thursday

Jane was pacing outside the interview room. She was waiting for Lockyer to arrive so that they could question Victor
Lebowski together. So much had happened since yesterday's
arrest. Her brain was in overdrive.

'Ready?' She turned as Lockyer walked towards her, a
folder wedged under one arm. 'I've read through the file and
listened to the interview you did on Tuesday,' he said.

'What did you make of him?'

'Well,' he said, pulling the file out from under his arm, 'I
can see why you thought he was one of the "good guys". There
was nothing in his tone to suggest he was being dishonest,
but . . . '

'But what?'

'It's going to make questioning him difficult. If he was
able to appear that calm and composed only two weeks after
he took her, it's unlikely he's going to roll over and admit it
now.'

'Probably not,' she said. 'He's declined the duty solicitor.
He's called in his own. Whitaker – she's a criminal lawyer

and, if her suit's anything to go by, this isn't her first case.'

'Great,' he said.

She knew what he was thinking. Interviews conducted pending formal charges were a potential minefield. Lebowski's lawyer, if she was any good, would be advising her client to say little or nothing. The burden of proof was on Jane, and her scope of questioning was limited. Lebowski had been arrested for the suspected murder of Maggie Hungerford. All of Jane's questions would have to relate to that. So far the evidence she had was circumstantial. He had admitted to seeing Maggie the night she disappeared, and that they had had intercourse. That made all the DNA evidence moot. The morphine tablets gave her some leverage, but not much. Even if she could prove he had a prescription for the medication or had stolen it, she still couldn't prove beyond doubt that he had drugged Maggie's food. Maggie could have taken the pills herself. It was Lebowski's word against a dead girl's. Jane was going to try and establish what Lebowski was doing in Elmstead, but she had no doubt his lawyer would shut down that line of questioning. It was a public park close to his home. His presence didn't prove he buried Maggie there, nor did it prove he was responsible for the second burial site.

'How are you thinking of approaching the interview?' Lockyer asked.

She had thought about little else on the ride back from Elmstead the previous night. It had taken a few hours, but the GPR had confirmed the existence of a second underground cavity and the presence of another body. The image was still fresh in her mind. It had been too late to get started on the dig, so Jane had been forced to return to the office, by which time it was also too late to talk to Lebowski.

She pushed her thumb and finger into her eyelids, harder than she intended, a sharp pain shooting down her neck. She was due back on-site in an hour to view the remains. The excavation team had been working since the early hours. The ramifications kept piling up, scrambling her thoughts. Another investigation, more evidence, more officers. Another family torn apart by grief. She shook her head. 'I want to get him talking about Maggie, about the night she disappeared.' Disappeared – the word made her think about Sue; about Mark. Her entire week had been built around Maggie. In order to do one part of her job she had forgotten her friend's pain.

'Thinking about Sue?' Lockyer asked.

'How do you do that?'

'Because I know you,' he said, tapping the side of his head. 'Your focus is on Maggie, on this case, because that is where it needs to be, Jane. You have to prioritize your time and, more importantly, your efforts. You can't conjure up informa-tion where there isn't any.'

She ran her fingers through her hair and sighed. 'I know. I just feel like I'm letting Sue down. Letting Mark down. Sue's my friend. I told her – no, I promised her – I would find Mark.'

'And we will,' Lockyer said, steering Jane towards the interview room. 'But right now you need to concentrate on Lebowski.'

'I don't want to mention the second tomb,' she said, resting her hand on the doorknob.

'I wouldn't either. We may need it later on,' he said, his

hand on her shoulder. 'Relax, Jane. I know you know what you're doing, even if you don't.'

'Thanks.' She blinked several times, took a deep breath and pushed open the door. 'Mr Lebowski. Miss Whitaker,' she said. 'I'm sorry to have kept you both waiting.'

Jane stared into the hole, a dark throat disappearing into the ground. She wiped her palms on her trousers. It was still early, but the sun was beating down on the back of her head. Her hair felt hot as she pulled it back into a stubby ponytail. Strands fell around her face, tickling her skin. The sense of déjà vu was undeniable. Her legs began to shake as the memory of climbing down into Maggie's tomb took hold.

Lockyer was standing a little way off, talking to one of the perimeter officers. She remembered that first visit to Elmstead. She had not known what to say to him, aware that he was staring into his own abyss. She remembered his face: his eyes hollow with guilt and grief. As the image faded he looked over at her. He pointed to a white paper suit in his hand, gave her the thumbs up and smiled. Things were different this time. He was coming down into the tomb with her. They were a team again.

'Do you want to wait for Jeanie?' Dave asked, taking Jane's arm. He had been here last time too and, just like then, he seemed to sense her unease. For someone who spent the majority of his time with corpses he possessed an empathy and understanding that Jane admired.

She squeezed his hand as a silent thank you. 'How long do you think she'll be?'

'An hour maybe,' Dave said, looking at his watch. 'She was up in Camden when I spoke to her. It'll take her a while to get across town.'

Jane nodded. 'Okay, then I think I'd rather get down there and see what we've got. I've got a suspect in custody, and so far I don't have enough to charge him.'

'Yes, I heard,' Dave said, tipping his head in Lockyer's direction. 'If it's any consolation, he thinks you're doing an amazing job.' She started to argue, but he cut her off. 'Now there's no need to get all self-deprecating on me. He doesn't dish out compliments very often, and I wouldn't be passing it on if I didn't know it was true.' Dave smiled and put his arm around Jane's shoulders. It was a simple gesture, a sign of his faith in her, but Jane found herself stepping away, rejecting the intimacy. She had spent a lot of her career trying to blend in with the guys. She knew Dave didn't see her as girlish or weak, but she wasn't about to risk the rest of her team even contemplating it.

'Thanks, Dave. I'm just glad he's talking. The catatonic-boss routine was getting a bit old.' She could see he was taken aback by her attitude. 'Sorry. I just want to get this done and get back to the station.'

'You don't have to tell me twice,' Dave said with a shrug of his shoulders. 'Mike,' he called over to Lockyer, 'we're ready.'

Lockyer walked towards them, pulling on the arms of his white suit, the legs flapping behind him like a snake's discarded skin. 'Did I mention that I suffer from claustrophobia?' he said. 'Are all three of us really going to fit down there?'

'Normally I'd say yes,' Dave replied, stepping into his own

suit, 'but considering the length of your legs, I'm not so sure. You might have to leave them outside, you lanky git.'

Jane laughed under her breath, letting the banter wash over her. Any and all distractions were welcome. 'Come on, you two,' she said, zipping up the front of her suit, the paper rustling beneath her fingers. 'Dave, you go down first. Mike, you can follow. I'll come down last.'

'You're going to pull us out if we get stuck, are you?' Dave asked, smiling.

'No,' she said. 'I just want to be able to get the hell out of there if you two get wedged.' Both men turned their heads away as they laughed. Jane covered her smile with the back of her hand. The press were arriving en masse. The last thing any of them wanted was to see their pictures on the front page of a newspaper with stupid grins on their faces. Humour would help them deal with what they were about to see, but the public was unlikely to see it that way.

Dave put his foot on the top step of the ladder. 'Joking aside, this one is smaller, so watch your heads and keep your arms and elbows in.' He started to climb down.

'I'm not looking forward to this,' Lockyer said in a whisper. 'I really don't like confined spaces.'

'You'll be fine once you're down there,' Jane said, and then she added, 'I don't think anyone *likes* confined spaces.'

He stepped onto the ladder. Dave's back was visible below them. 'See you in there.'

Jane watched Lockyer climb down and bend into a crouch to crawl through the covered entrance. She patted her pocket to check the little torch was still there, attached to her keys. It was a 'Be safe' gift from her mother. Satisfied, she turned and took hold of the ladder. Her legs shook on the first step, but by the second and third they had steadied. She could hear Lockyer and Dave talking, their voices muted by the mass of mud and rock surrounding them. She was prepared for what she was about to see. Or as prepared as she could be. But she couldn't stop seeing Lebowski's face. She paused and leaned against the ladder for support, a bead of sweat rolling down the back of her neck.

This morning's interview had been as she had expected. His lawyer had put a stop to almost every line of questioning, but it was the change in Lebowski's behaviour after a night in custody that had surprised Jane. He was like a different person. He was cold, indifferent. Even when he was talking about Maggie, about their relationship, his voice remained on a monotone. His version of events hadn't changed. In fact it was almost word for word what he had told her on Tuesday.

She felt again for the torch. This time she took out her keys and put her finger through the keyring, holding them in her hand as she turned the torch on and off a couple of times. Lebowski's reason for being in Elmstead was laughable in its simplicity. 'I went for a walk.' That was all he said. He didn't elaborate and, when Jane pressed him, his lawyer intervened and told her to move on.

She lowered herself from the final rung and dropped onto her knees. As she pushed aside the plastic sheeting she had one final thought, but it wasn't about Lebowski. It was about Mort. He had told her and Lockyer that Maggie

had refused to tell him whom she was seeing behind his
back. Was that true? She sat back on her haunches as an
idea took shape. Maggie's tomb was prepared, the entrance
hatch dug out, an air-hose and CCTV installed. Maggie
was drugged, attacked, transported to Elmstead, carried
through the woods and manhandled into the tomb. For
Lebowski to achieve all that, unseen and without help, was
no mean feat.

'You need to see this, Jane,' Lockyer called.

She looked up. Dave and Lockyer were both on their
hands and knees, facing away from her. Only the soles of
their shoe covers and their white-papered backsides were
visible. She crawled in, struck by how much smaller the
space was, compared to the tomb where Maggie had been
found. She remembered how cramped it had felt and how
terrifying it must have been to be trapped there, in the dark.
But this place was even worse. It was more like an oversized
coffin, a yard or so high and not more than two, or maybe
three, yards square. The three of them pretty much filled
the space once she was alongside. Again she found herself thinking about Lebowski and Mort, and Maggie, seeing
her lying there in her pyjamas, her hair covering her face,
her feet bare.

'We should have waited for Jeanie,' Dave said.

Jane followed Dave's eye-line to the body. The legs and
feet were tucked into the corner of the tomb, the torso and
head stretched out in front of Lockyer. Jane tried to lean
forward, but her back struck the ceiling, limiting her view.
She could see tufts of hair. They looked fragile and dry, like
hay left to bake in the sun. The skull beneath was like white

marble. 'How long has it been here?' she asked, staring at the skeleton in front of them.

'A long time,' Dave said. 'A very long time.'

CHAPTER THIRTY-ONE

1st May – Thursday

'I'm not going to be able to charge him,' Jane said, kicking a stone across the gravel. They were standing in the small car park on the edge of Elmstead Woods waiting for Jeanie to arrive.

'You don't know that yet,' Lockyer said, leaning against a squad car.

'Really?' She pulled the band out of her hair, snapping it in the process. 'What are the chances of there being any useable trace evidence down there?' she said, pointing to the woods and the tent that was being erected as she spoke, the sun bouncing off the white plastic. 'I don't need Jeanie to tell me that those remains have been there for years. Dave won't even confirm the sex of the victim at this stage. It's going to take weeks to examine the whole area.'

'We'll just have to go back and speak to Lebowski again,' he said, pinching the bridge of his nose. 'Try something else. See if we can't work in this scenario. What are the team doing?'

She sighed. 'Whitemore and Franks are going over

215

Lebowski's background – everything and anything. I told them to go back five years initially, but I think today's discovery might mean pushing that back further. Penny's got six of the PCs that Roger signed off running second interviews with all of the students and tutors, and she and Aaron are doing Lebowski's family, ex-wife, et cetera. Who else?' she said, looking up at the cloudless sky. 'Sasha's reviewing Lebowski's financial history and overseeing the search of his home address. I've got some of the PSs looking at cold-cases and talking to Missing Persons about today's body. The Exhibits team are re-examining all the original evidence, preparing to add today's samples, cross-referencing any similarities . . . blah-blah-blah.' She stopped talking, shaking her head when she realized Lockyer was laughing at her.

'Not much fun being at the top, is it?'

'No,' she said. 'I can feel this case slipping away from me and, to be quite frank, I'm shitting myself.' She didn't swear very often; it was a lazy use of language, or so her mother told her, but the main reason was Peter. He picked up everything and stored it like a computer. She remembered saying the F-word when she dropped the hoover on her foot. Peter had been three, but he repeated the word and put it in every sentence for about a month before he got bored. Even thinking about him made her chest ache. She had not spent more than an hour with him all week. He had been fast asleep when she picked him up from her mother's on Tuesday night after her 'chat' with Lockyer. She had managed breakfast with him on Wednesday morning, but Lebowski's arrest and the discovery of the second tomb meant she hadn't got home until gone midnight. She had crept into Peter's room to kiss him goodnight and found her mother sleeping next to him, both of them cramped beneath his dinosaur duvet on the tiny single bed. She had left the house at six to give herself time to prepare for the interview with Lebowski. So all in all she had no idea how her mother was, let alone her son; and she had no idea what trauma had caused his grandmother to forgo the comfort of the spare bedroom.

'Peter?' Lockyer asked.

'Stop doing that,' she said, frowning. 'It freaks me out.' She tried to maintain a cross expression, but couldn't. It was unnerving when he read her mind like that, but part of her was relieved. It felt more like 'old times' between the two of them.

'Oh, come on – you know I love doing it,' he said. 'Mind you, if you'd have asked me last week what you were thinking, I wouldn't have had a clue. But this week,' he said, hooking his thumbs under a pair of imaginary braces, 'ta-dah, I can read you like a book, Jane.'

'Good for you,' she said, wishing she could say the same about him. He had changed in the past few days, regained some of his old self, but she still didn't know what he was thinking. Not when it came to things that mattered. 'What am I going to do about Lebowski?' she asked. 'I don't think I've even got enough to keep him for the full forty-eight hours. That means he'll be out by tonight. His lawyer's been calling me all morning asking if I have any new evidence to support the arrest.'

'Have you spoken to her?'

'No, because I don't have anything to tell her. She's already provided an affidavit from his doctor saying he has no health issues or reason to be prescribed morphine, so that's blown that one. Dave told me just now that he can't say whether the pills were crushed up in food or taken orally in the normal manner. All he can say is that the fragments are consistent with digestion. We can't prove they were crushed. Even if we could, I can't prove Lebowski drugged her food, because her meal was eaten at least three days before her body was found. There's no trace of the chilli con carne Lebowski claimed they ate. So unless Sasha turns up a chilli-mix laced with morphine in Lebowski's kitchen, I'm up that infamous creek without a paddle.'

'So let him go,' Locker said.

She looked at him. 'What? Just like that?'

'What more can you do? As you say, unless the house search turns up something linking him to the morphine, or the blow to the back of Maggie's head, your evidence won't hold up.'

'I know,' she said, dropping down on the bonnet next to him. 'Even the arrest has worked in his favour.'

'What makes you say that?' he asked.

'Because it means the Exhibits team has nothing to do, again,' she said, turning to face him. 'Think about it. He was dating Maggie; saw her the night she died; admitted to sexual intercourse, to cooking her dinner, to arguing. That makes all the physical evidence on the body, and whatever we turn up at his house, worthless. Everything we find he's told us about already. Now Elmstead: if the Exhibits team finds traces of soil on his shoes, in his car or on his sodding kitchen floor, we could place him at the scene of Maggie's murder. Not any more,' she said, shaking her head. 'He likes to go for walks in Elmstead Woods. Of course he has soil on his shoes.' When Lockyer didn't respond she opened her hands. 'So where does that leave my investigation?' She put the toe of her shoe into the gravel and swept it from side to side. The realization hit her as if someone had slapped her face.

'That's it,' she said, slowing her breathing as the pieces fell into place. 'He knew we were going to arrest him. That's why he told me everything – everything that had happened between him and Maggie. He wanted me to know about Mort, about the fights. He wanted to put himself at the top of the suspect list. He knew the tox screen would tell us about the morphine and that it would be enough to arrest him. He also knew it was only a matter of time before the other body was found. So he took himself off to Elmstead, made a show of scrabbling around in the dirt, knowing that the neighbour-hood would be on full alert after the discovery of Maggie's body, knowing someone would call it in. It's almost like he engineered this whole thing to prove just how clever he is.'

'There is some good news,' Lockyer said.

Jane almost choked on the laughter that wanted to come. 'There is?'

'Yes,' he continued, pushing himself up off the car. 'He might know how to skew your investigation, but he doesn't know you. He doesn't know how you think. We let him go and see what he does. It won't end here. If he's anything like the man you're describing, then he won't stop. Right now he has our attention, but in order to keep it – to really prove his superiority – he'll have to do more, he'll have to take risks.' Jane took her phone out of her trouser pocket. 'Who are you calling?' he asked.

'Phil Bathgate,' she said, already dialling the number. 'Lebowski might be clever, but no one knows the workings of a psycho's mind better than Phil. And . . .' she said, holding the phone to her ear, 'I'm starting to think Lebowski might not be alone in this. There are too many things, too many coincidences. You'll probably think I'm stretching a point with this, but I still think Mort is involved. He knows more than he's told us. I think it's possible that he and Lebowski know each other. They both seem to relish their own brilliance. They'd be the perfect team.' She saw the doubt on Lockyer's face. 'It's my case. Maggie is my responsibility. I'm not about to let Lebowski run the show. I need to show him that you don't have to have a PhD to mess with people's heads. I won't let him make a fool out of me . . . again.'

CHAPTER THIRTY-TWO

1st May – Thursday

'I'm happy to come to you,' Jane said, looking at her watch. 'About three-thirty?' She listened as Phil rattled off all the important things he had to do, debating aloud whether he had time to squeeze her into his hectic, life-altering schedule. She took a deep breath and waited. The last time they had spoken she had wanted to physically injure him. Today appeared to be no different. How could someone so useful be so annoying? 'Fine, four-fifteen works for me. Thank you, Phil,' she said, not feeling any gratitude at all. She ended the call and dropped her mobile onto the desk. She looked at her watch. It was two-thirty. Another five hours and Lebowski would be out.

How could she have been so gullible? It felt as if everything had been tailored, from his phone call on Monday night to his arrest yesterday, and she had fallen for it. Her office phone started ringing. She picked it up as she scrolled through her emails, clicking on a new message from Penny. 'DS Bennett,' she stated, double-clicking on the document attached to Penny's email.

'Hello, darling. Am I disturbing you?' her mother asked.

'No, Mum. I was just about to call you,' she said, her cheeks heating at the lie.

'I just wondered if you might have time to pick Peter up from school this afternoon.'

Jane started to read the document. She looked at her watch again. 'Well, I've got a meeting just after four, so I'd be a bit pushed to get there and back. Why?'

'It doesn't matter. I was going to take your father to . . . Never mind, I shouldn't have called. Not to worry. I'll do it. What time do you think you'll be home?'

'No, no,' Jane said. 'I can sort something out. It's fine.' She tried to disguise the sigh that accompanied her statement.

'No, honestly, darling. I'm sorry I bothered you. What time did you say you'd be home?'

'I don't know yet,' she said. 'I'll need to check.' She stopped and stared at the name in front of her. 'Sorry,' she said, looking on her desk for Mark's case file. 'Listen, can I call you back in a second?'

'Of course, of course. I'll speak to you later.'

The line went dead before Jane could answer. She replaced the phone in its cradle, found the file she was looking for and opened it, scanning her notes before turning back to her computer. She had asked Penny to find out more about Lebowski's lawyer. His choice of legal representation had been bothering Jane ever since Mrs Whitaker had waltzed into the station in her immaculate suit. That kind of representation didn't come cheap and, according to the desk sergeant, Lebowski had Whitaker's contact details with him, in his wallet. Jane now knew why. Whitaker was worth every penny. She must have pulled some hefty strings to get the details of Lebowski's previous dealings with the police sealed. Jane pushed herself away from her desk. She needed to talk to Roger.

Jane stopped running, bent over and took in several deep breaths. She had been circling the block for the past half an hour, sprinting for thirty seconds and then jogging for a couple of minutes. She had passed the gates to the station several times, but she wasn't ready to go back to the office.

After getting the necessary permissions from Roger, it had only taken her another ten minutes to find the sealed file and read over Lebowski's previous encounters with Lewisham police. The run was meant to clear her head. She sat down on the wall outside the station and rolled her neck around her shoulders.

'Hey.'

She looked up and saw Lockyer walking towards her. He sat down next to her.

'Good run?' he asked.

'I hate running around here,' she said still somewhat breathless. 'All that effort and I wind up back where I started.'

'I don't know why you don't go to the Soho gym up the road. At least you can watch the TV,' he said. 'You wouldn't be filling your lungs with exhaust fumes and you wouldn't end up smelling of . . . ' He leaned across and sniffed. 'Curry. You smell of curry.'

'Oh, sod off.' she said, shoving him away. 'I bloody hate the gym. You know I hate the gym.' She punched him in the arm, somewhat harder than she had intended.

'Okay,' he said, stretching out the final syllable, rubbing his arm. 'Might I enquire what's up with you?'

'I've got more on Lebowski,' she said, picking a piece of lint off her tracksuit trousers.

'And that's a bad thing because . . . ?'

'It isn't. It's just . . . ' She looked at her watch. Her meeting with Phil wasn't for another twenty minutes.

'It's just what?'

'Lebowski has a criminal lawyer because he's been here before,' she said, pointing at the double doors leading into the station. 'Do you remember the Amelia Reynolds case?'

Lockyer's brow creased. 'The name rings a bell, but I can't remember the specifics, no.'

'Amelia Reynolds was a university student murdered by strangulation six years ago. She was twenty-one years old. Her body was found in an allotment shed in Deptford. She had been sexually assaulted. Her killer was never found. Guess where she went to university.'

'Greenwich,' Lockyer said, turning to face her.

'That's the one,' she said, running her fingers through her hair.

'Lebowski taught her?'

'No. It's not quite that straightforward. Amelia was studying law, but according to the case file, she had an ethics module that Lebowski sat in on. He had to teach as part of his PhD. His thesis dealt with psychology and ethics apparently, so he opted to assist on a couple of modules for the credit and as part of his research. Anyway he, along with a dozen other tutors, was interviewed in the normal course of the inquiry, but Lebowski was brought back in – more than once in fact.'

'Why?' Lockyer asked.

'The DCI on the case thought Lebowski was involved.'

'And was he?'

'I don't know,' she said. 'As far as the case file reads, Lebowski had a passing knowledge of the victim. He had no alibi, but no personal relationship, no motive, no physical evidence – nothing to link him to the girl's murder. I've read through the interview transcripts, and Lebowski sounds the same. I mean, he sounds just as sincere and measured as he did when I first met him.'

'Which makes you think he was lying?' Lockyer asked.

'Yes, it does. If Lebowski's the kind of man I think he is, then I think it's also possible that Maggie wasn't his first victim.'

The sun came out from behind a bank of cloud, warming Jane's face.

'Why didn't this come up when Lebowski was first arrested?' he asked.

'His involvement in the case was sealed.'

'How?'

'Whitaker – Lebowski's lawyer. She was present at his second interview and all subsequent interviews.'

'How many were there?' Lockyer asked.

'Five,' Jane said, looking at him. 'Whitaker made a case that the DCI was heavy-handed, harassing Lebowski without cause. Which, given the information, is fair enough. She got a judge to agree that it could be damaging to his career, if future employers did a CRB or DBS check and found that he had been questioned in a murder investigation.'

Lockyer stood up. 'Come on, my arse is going to sleep. We can continue this in my office. Have you got the case file?'

'Yes,' she said getting up. They walked up to the double doors, into the foyer and over to the lifts. Her brain ached as she tried to push and pull the facts into some semblance of order. She felt chilled as the sweat dried on her skin.

'I still don't get how Whitaker managed to wangle a seal on the file, if Lebowski wasn't charged?' Lockyer said. 'His name wouldn't have come up on any checks, unless he was going for a government job or something that required extra vetting; and even then sealing the file feels like overkill to me.'

'Me too,' Jane said, pushing the call button for the lift. 'But that's what happened.' She zipped up her running jacket.

'Who was the DCI?' Lockyer asked, walking into the lift as the doors opened.

Jane waited for the doors to close before she said, 'Mark.'

'You're kidding me?'

'I wish I was.' The doors opened and they both stepped out. Jane put her hand on Lockyer's arm. 'Can I ask you a question?

'Of course,' he said.

'Do you think Lebowski killed Maggie?'

He was nodding before she had finished speaking. 'I do, yes. If you recall, it was me who had to convince you of that fact,' he said, smiling.

'I know,' she said, unable to return his smile. 'And you

believe Lebowski could have engineered the whole thing: having dinner with Maggie the night she was taken, getting arrested in Elmstead?'

Lockyer looked at her as if she had lost her mind. 'Er, yes, Jane. I told you that earlier,' he said. 'I'm yet to be convinced about Mort's involvement, but from everything I've seen and heard so far, I think Lebowski's been clever enough to cover his arse.'

Jane took a deep breath before she spoke. 'Mark was convinced Lebowski was involved in the murder of Amelia Reynolds. He just couldn't prove it. That's three bodies, Mike. Lebowski is linked to all of them: Reynolds, Maggie and whoever Dave's got down in the mortuary suite.'

'Jane,' he said, his voice hushed, 'I see where you're going with this, but what do you want me to say? None of this is going to keep Lebowski in custody. If Mark couldn't make the case stick six years ago, I don't see how we're going to fare any better. And it's not like we can ask Mark for help now, is it?'

'Exactly,' she said, relieved that he had voiced what she had been thinking throughout her run. 'Think about it, sir. Mark was the DCI on the Reynolds case. He believed Lebowski was guilty. Maggie was taken on Wednesday the sixteenth of April. Mark disappears five days later. That feels like too big a coincidence to me. Maybe Mark found something, some new evidence – I don't know,' she said, closing her eyes. 'But either way it's pretty convenient for Lebowski that Mark isn't around. If I hadn't specifically looked into Whitaker – Lebowski's all-too-fancy legal-eagle – the connection with the Reynolds case would never have come up. Whitaker was hardly going to tell me, was she?'

'No. But, Jane . . . ' Lockyer stopped.

'When Maggie's body was discovered, it was all over the news. A young student from Greenwich University murdered. You don't think Mark would have seen that and called you . . . called me? I've spoken to Sue. Mark had nightmares about the Reynolds case. He couldn't let it go.'

'Hang on,' Lockyer said. 'Are you saying you think Lebowski has something to do with Mark's disappearance?'

'I think it's a possibility, yes,' she said, pausing, not wanting to say the next words aloud, not wanting them to be true. 'And if Lebowski was involved, then I'm not sure we're ever going to find Mark . . . alive.'

'How are you going to proceed?' Phil asked.

'I'm not sure yet. I'd need new evidence on the Hungerford or Reynolds case to bring Lebowski back in. How would you recommend I deal with him?' Jane asked. Her question was greeted by silence. Phil rocked back on his chair, looked up at the ceiling and closed his eyes. She recognized the gesture. She would have to wait for genius to strike before he spoke again.

Their discussion so far had been pretty much one-sided. She had laid out as much background as she could, before Phil had dived in. He was particularly interested in the idea that Mark might have fallen victim to Lebowski. The amount of planning and intelligence required was impressive, according to Phil. She didn't let his attitude bother her. This was just how the guy operated. He must have known Mark for twenty years, yet there was no hint of regret at his ex-colleague's disappearance. Like Mort, Phil was only interested in what he could decipher and learn from the case. His musings were peppered with his stock phrases, 'That aspect is very interesting' or 'That could be significant'. He was like a textbook: dry and long-winded. He was taking deep breaths through his nose, a high-pitched whistle accompanying his outgoing breath.

'Well,' he said finally, tipping back in his chair, his eyes still closed. 'Amelia Reynolds was murdered six years ago, you said?'

'Yes.'

'Do any of the specifics of that case tally with the Hungerford victim?'

'Both female students at the same uni, similar age.' She flipped open the folder on her lap and looked down at the notes.

'Differences?' Phil asked.

'Amelia was sexually assaulted. Maggie had sexual intercourse, but we think it was consensual. They were studying different subjects. No link between them, socially speaking. Their families didn't know each other – nothing like that. Amelia disappeared in the afternoon, whereas Maggie was taken in the early hours of the morning. Found in different locations. On paper they look unrelated,' she said with a sigh.

'But this Lebowski character links them,' he said.

'A tenuous link, yes,' she said.

'Tenuous or not, I think your instincts are good here, Jane,' he said, opening his eyes and looking at her. 'However, another more experienced officer has tried and failed to make any charges stick, so it would be foolish to believe you can do any better.' She resisted the urge to smile. Only Phil could praise in one breath and criticize in the next. 'That said, you do have a few points in your favour.'

'And they are?'

'Well, when Mark tried to get Lebowski six years ago, he only had the Reynolds girl and the Deptford crime scene to work with. Whereas you have three bodies so far . . . ' He counted them off on his fingers. 'Amelia Reynolds, Maggie Hungerford and the Jane Doe down in the mortuary suite. And . . . ' he said, holding out his hands, as if in triumph, 'you have four crime scenes, if you include Mark's house. Lebowski – if indeed he is your man – is without doubt highly intelligent and resourceful, but I would have thought the chances that he carried out three or possibly four murders without leaving so much as a hair behind are slim.'

She found herself nodding. 'You're right. Thank you, Phil.' She looked down at her notes.

'We haven't discussed your other theory,' he said, sitting forward and smiling at her.

'What other theory?' She had a horrible feeling she knew where this was going.

'Mort, is it?' he said, his smile changing into a smirk, one eyebrow raised to accompany it. 'Mike mentioned it to me, in passing.'

'Terry Mort is part of my investigation, but I've neither ruled out nor confirmed his involvement,' she said with a shrug of her shoulders. 'He dated Maggie Hungerford and is . . . ' She was unsure how to describe Mort without sounding excessive.

'Nuts?' Phil offered. 'That's what Mike said: that you thought the boy was nuts. Not the most scientific diagnosis, Jane.'

'True, but as soon as I am confident that Mort is involved, I will of course want to discuss the matter with you. You are the expert, after all.' She was about to add that, in her opinion, Phil and Mort shared more than a few personality traits, but her phone vibrated in her pocket. 'Excuse me,' she said, retrieving her mobile. It was Lockyer. She pushed 'Answer'. 'Yes,' she said. She could feel Phil's eyes on her as she listened to her boss on the other end of the phone. 'I'll be right down.' She ended the call and stood up. 'Sorry, Phil, I need to go back down to the office.' She turned away, unable to meet his eye. 'If you could let me have your notes regarding the Amelia Reynolds case ASAP, I'd appreciate it.'

'Shall we book in another time to talk about—'

'I'll call you,' she said, pulling his door closed behind her. She felt as if she was leaving the headmaster's office. She could kill Lockyer.

CHAPTER THIRTY-THREE

1st May – Thursday

'Okay, let's have some quiet, please,' Jane said, waiting for her team to settle. 'We'll have our usual briefing tomorrow morning, but I wanted to get everyone up to speed.' Notepads opened, pens were uncapped.

'Do you want the screen on, boss?' Penny asked.

'No, thanks, Pen. We won't need it.' Jane cleared her throat and stood, still waiting for the murmurs to stop. 'Are we ready?' she asked, just as Lockyer entered the room. He nodded and took the seat nearest the door. She was tempted to throw her pen at him for talking to Phil about Mort, but that gripe would have to wait. 'Right. I've asked DC Wall to join us,' she said, gesturing to Chris. 'He's on the Mark Leech investigation, but there is a possible overlap that I want that team to look into.' The murmurs started up again. 'Can we leave the speculation until the end of the briefing?' She waited for quiet. 'As many of you know, Lebowski will be released without charge at eight o'clock this evening.' She held up her hand as several voices mumbled their disapproval, Penny included. 'Yes, I know it's frustrating, but we don't have enough to hold him for the full forty-eight hours. He has given a "reasonable" explanation for being in Elmstead and, without physical evidence to the contrary, we have nothing concrete linking him to the second burial site. The evidence linking him to the Hungerford case is circumstantial. Franks, Whitemore, have you come up with anything in Lebowski's background that could assist with keeping him in custody?' She shifted her body to the right so that she could see them both.

'No, boss,' Whitemore said. 'His educational background is pretty standard. His work history the same. There's no record of any disagreements with tutors or students. In fact, looking at the complaints records, he's one of the few tutors with a clean history. The majority have had a complaint filed at one time or another: a student disputing a grade, that kind of thing. Franks went through his DVLA records – nothing there. From the electoral role, it seems he lived with his wife for ten years. They divorced and he's lived on his own ever since. He pays his child support for the two minors,' Whitemore looked down at his notepad. 'Two girls. Poppy and Petra, seven and ten years old respectively. He sees them every other weekend and for a month during the summer holidays, as far as the custody settlement goes. His divorce papers cite "irreconcilable differences". There's no mention of a third party being involved.'

'Okay. You've gone back more than the five years we discussed, I take it?' Jane asked. She wasn't annoyed. If anything, she was pleased to see Whitemore and Franks using their own initiative.

'Yes, boss,' Franks said, taking over from Whitemore. 'We figured ten years should cover everything.'

'Good. Penny, you were running the first and second interviews of all the university staff and students, and local residents. Anything there?'

'Nothing new,' Penny said. 'We've canvassed her neighbours. No one saw or heard anything unusual on the night Maggie was taken, or before. None of the students had a bad word to say about Lebowski or any of the other tutors. Terry Mort's name came up a couple of times, due to his previous relationship with the victim, but other than personal opinions there's nothing concrete there.'

'Personal opinions?'

'Same as what you got. No one likes him,' Penny said. 'I spoke to three students in one of the study groups he mentors. They've nicknamed him "Little Hitler".'

'Right,' Jane said.

'A couple of students in Maggie's classes thought she might have been sleeping with Lebowski.' Penny shrugged her shoulders.

'Have you spoken to Chrissie O'Reilly again?'

'Yes. She insists she didn't know about the relationship,' Penny said. 'I believe her. She was very upset when I confirmed that Maggie was seeing someone, behind her back, so to speak.'

'It still feels strange that she wouldn't tell her best friend,' Jane said. 'How did the other students know about the affair?'

'None of them knew for certain,' Penny said. 'It was just a rumour – a rumour Chrissie wasn't privy to, I'm guessing.

Maggie sometimes stayed behind after class, and sometimes she and Lebowski had coffee together in the cafeteria.'

'What about the ex-wife?' Jane asked, glancing down at her watch.

'I spoke to her on the phone yesterday, but only briefly. I told her I needed to ask her some questions about her ex-husband, in relation to an ongoing inquiry. She sounded upset but helpful; very complimentary about Lebowski, said he was a good father, et cetera. I asked her to come in for a proper interview today. She's due in about ten minutes. Do you want to sit in?'

'I will, yes. Thanks, Penny. Did she know Lebowski has been arrested?'

'I assume so. She wasn't surprised to hear from me,' Penny said.

'Okay. Give me a shout when you're heading down and I'll walk with you,' Jane said. 'Anything on the financial side of things, Sasha?' She searched the room for the DC. When she spotted her, she saw Sasha was shaking her head.

'He's clean, boss. No debt, other than his mortgage and a credit card that he pays off in full at the end of every month. As Whitemore said, Lebowski pays his child support and a bit extra to his ex-wife every month. She's comfortable in her own right, so there's no obvious need for the over-payment.'

'He's just a generous guy?' Jane asked, looking around her at a dozen other sceptical faces.

'I don't know,' Sasha said, her mouth turning down at the corners.

Jane scratched her head. 'Who spoke to MISPER about the second body that was found?'

An officer she didn't know held up his hand. 'I did, Ma'am,' he said. 'There aren't any missing persons relating to the Elmstead area. Without more information on the body recovered, there are too many missing persons listed for the South-East to even attempt a productive search. I said I'd call back when the post-mortem was done, so that I could at least give them sex, age, height, et cetera, to narrow down the parameters. Do you have a date for it yet?' he asked.

'Dr Simpson said he should get to it tomorrow. I'll let you know, Officer . . . ?'

'Dixon,' he offered. 'I came over from DI Ayres's team.'

'Great. Well, thank you for that, Sergeant Dixon.' Jane bit her lip. She had run enough briefings to know what she was doing, but this case was by far the biggest she had ever dealt with. It was the kind of case Lockyer would normally deal with. She would usually be setting up the laptop and assisting him in the briefing, not running it. 'I've already spoken to the Exhibits team and they don't have any new trace evidence that could help us. So, as I said, Lebowski will be out by this evening.' Again there were grumbles of protest. 'I want to make it clear that we are only releasing him until such time as we have more evidence. Our job now is to find that evidence as quickly as possible. Another case has been brought to my attention, which we need to link into our investigation.'

She held up a file.

'Amelia Reynolds was found murdered by strangulation six years ago in an allotment shed in Deptford. She was a student at Greenwich, studying law. No one has ever been charged with her murder. However, Lebowski was questioned, several times.' She put the file down and held up both hands as the chatter increased in volume. 'I've asked Penny to make the file available to all of you, and I expect you to have read and digested the information before our briefing tomorrow morning. Lebowski was questioned, as I said, but he was released without charge. However, the DCI in charge of the investigation seemed confident that Lebowski was involved. This belief caused him to be a tad over-zealous. After several interviews and accusations, Lebowski's lawyer had the file sealed, and the DCI in question was cautioned not to pursue the matter. That means,' Jane said, waiting until she had everyone's attention, 'that means this case is not to be discussed with anyone outside the team. And I mean anyone. There is no new evidence to link Lebowski to the Amelia Reynolds case and, until there is, I don't want to hear anyone talking about it to the general population.' There were nods of agreement. 'The second point is that the DCI in charge was Mark Leech.' Her words were met with a collection of loud intakes of breath. 'Chris is handling Mark's disappearance.'

'Do you still think it's a disappearance, boss?' Franks asked, his voice incredulous.

'We don't know, Franks, but I want you and Whitemore to liaise with Chris and go over Mark's and Lebowski's backgrounds again. I want to know if they had any contact before or after the Reynolds case. Check phone and Internet records – everything. Penny, I also need you to go back further. Locate and question all tutors of law or psychology dating back to the time of Amelia's murder.' She turned her attention back to the full team. 'That's all for today. I want everyone up to speed with the Amelia Reynolds case by tomorrow. Unless the post-mortem on the body downstairs comes up with something concrete, which I doubt, we're going to have to do the work ourselves. Keep your paperwork up to date, and if anything feels strange or out of place, I want to know about it. It's possible Lebowski slipped through the net six years ago. I don't want that to happen again.' She was greeted with nodding heads as the team shuffled out of the briefing room.

'Good work,' Lockyer whispered, walking towards her as the room emptied.

'There were too many "possibles" and "what-ifs" for my liking,' she said, shaking her head.

He put his hand on her shoulder and waited for her to look up at him. 'That's how it works, Jane. Until you have the evidence and the case is solved, everything is a "possible". I know it can be frustrating, but you are handling yourself and the team really well. Everyone knows what they should be doing and why they're doing it. You can't do any more than that, can you?'

'No, I guess not,' she said, picking up the Reynolds file off the glass table.

'Jane,' Lockyer said, turning and walking to the briefing-room door. 'You need to prepare yourself.'

'For what?'

'For not getting him,' he said, facing her. 'If Lebowski murdered Amelia Reynolds six years ago and got away with it – even with Mark on his back – then it's going to be difficult.'

'But what about Maggie . . . and Mark?' she asked, unwilling to accept what he was saying.

'What you think, and what you know, doesn't mean shit in this game,' Lockyer said, putting his hand on the door. 'If you can't prove it, we've got nothing.' He pushed open the door and left her reeling in the wake of his statement.

She knew he was right. She had been thinking the same thing. In every case she had worked, going back to her DC days, finding the link had always been the key. Once you had that, you could use the rest of the evidence to support it, to show that only that individual or individuals could have committed the crime in question. She could link Lebowski to Amelia Reynolds, Maggie, the body downstairs and even to Mark, but she couldn't prove that Lebowski was the man who killed them. She felt her cheeks heating as she realized she was about to cry. Mark was dead. She knew it now. Perhaps she had always known, but it wasn't until that moment that she had allowed herself to believe it. He was her friend. Sue was still her friend. She couldn't let his killer walk away. She wouldn't.

Jane sat back and listened while Penny did the introductions. Emily Loxton, the ex-Mrs Lebowski, sat with her legs crossed, her hands resting in her lap. She was wearing linen trousers and a white-collared shirt. She nodded to Jane and smiled. Her teeth were straight and white. Whitaker, Lebowski's flashy solicitor, couldn't hold a candle to this woman. Jane figured she was about five foot ten, slim but not skinny, and her skin rivalled that of the girls in the L'Oréal adverts.

'Thanks again for coming in, Miss Loxton. There were just a few questions DS Bennett wanted to go over with you, if that's okay?' Penny asked.

'Of course,' she said, running her fingers through her hair. 'Victor told me to expect your call.'

The question of whether Lebowski's ex knew about his arrest had been answered. How long she had known remained to be seen. It wouldn't surprise Jane if Lebowski had prepped his ex-wife, the second that Maggie's name was confirmed in the press. She could just hear him now . . . *I'm afraid to say that one of my students has been murdered. It's so awful. I've helped as much as I can, but you know what the police are like – what they were like last time. They'll no doubt be dragging me in, to fling accusations; and, of course, they'll want to talk to you too again. I'm so sorry. I only wish they would leave me alone, for your sake more than mine.'* Of course Lebowski would get his ex-wife on board. It was amazing how his 'team' always seemed to appear at the opportune moment to defend him. Clever, Jane thought. Very clever.

'Emily – may I call you Emily?' she asked.

'Please do.'

'Emily, how would you characterize your marriage to Victor Lebowski?'

'As I told Detective Groves on the telephone,' she said, gesturing to Penny, 'Victor and I were very young when we met. Both of us had just turned twenty-three when we got married. He was still studying for his degree in psychology, and I was working flat out. We didn't see that much of each other for the first year, I'm sorry to say.'

'And what do you do, Emily?' Jane asked.

'I run a catering company with my father. He started the business twenty years ago out of our kitchen at home. To say we've expanded would be an understatement. It keeps me incredibly busy.'

'And you and Mr Lebowski have two children?'

'That's right, Petra's ten and Poppy is seven – eight in July.'

'I understand Mr Lebowski sees the children every other weekend?'

'No. Victor sees the children as often as possible. We agreed after the divorce that he could fit in his time with them around his teaching schedule. He probably sees more of them than I do,' she said.

'He's a good father?' Jane asked. She knew Emily had told Penny what a wonderful father Lebowski was, but she wanted to hear for herself. There was an edge to the woman's voice. Jane couldn't decide if it was jealousy that her ex-husband had more time to see the children than she did, or bitterness over their past relationship.

'He's a wonderful father. It was very hard on him, being separated from the girls. Poppy was only a year old. It took a year or two for things to settle down, but since then we've been very much on the same page, in terms of parenting.'

'When you say "settled down"?' Jane asked.

'Divorce isn't easy on anyone, Detective,' Emily said, wiping a finger under her eye. 'It can be very stressful, and the legal aspect can cause a lot of unnecessary friction at an already difficult time. This just brings it all back.'

Jane sat back. She had hoped to work the Reynolds investigation into their discussion, but it looked as if Lebowski's ex was going to do the work for her. She took a breath and asked, 'Would you mind telling me the reason for your separation?'

Emily sighed and looked across at Penny. 'I knew you'd ask that.' She looked down and put a hand over her chest, as if she was going to be sick or faint, or something. Jane glanced over at Penny and mouthed 'What the . . . ?' before turning her attention back to Emily. The confident, model-beautiful businesswoman Jane had appraised only moments ago seemed to have vanished, replaced by a much smaller, timid creature. Emily lifted her head. There were tears in her eyes. 'I wanted you to ask. That's why I'm here.' She closed her eyes and continued. 'Poppy had just had her first birthday. Things at home had been . . . ' she paused, 'difficult. Victor and I weren't getting along. I was taking on more responsibility with the business. Victor seemed to resent my success. His teaching had always seemed to satisfy him, but then it didn't. Nothing did.' A tear rolled down her cheek, but she was quick to wipe it away. 'Poppy had been a difficult delivery. It took me months to recover, to heal. I wasn't myself. Victor was patient at first, but then . . . '

'He raped you?' Penny asked. Jane stopped herself from frowning. She felt as if she had somehow missed the first half of the conversation.

Emily didn't speak, but she nodded. Tears were now running down her cheeks, leaving pale lines through her foundation. 'It only happened that once. A detective had been to the house to speak to Victor.'

Jane took a breath in and held it. Emily had to be talking about the Amelia Reynolds case. Why else would a detective be at their home, questioning Lebowski? Jane needed her to refer to the Reynolds case by name. Only then would she be able to question Emily about it, without having to worry about Whitaker or ramifications on the department. With the seal on Lebowski's file, Whitaker could derail Jane's entire case if she so much as mentioned the Reynolds inquiry to Emily without due cause.

'After the officer left, Victor was so angry,' Emily said. 'He slapped me, and then he . . . Poppy was in the crib next to us, sleeping. I couldn't cry out, I didn't want to frighten her or wake up Petra.' Her words rushed out of her mouth in a single breath. 'He's a good man. I still believe that. He's a good father. I couldn't ask for better for my girls. He never touched me after that. We were separated within a month. I know I should have said something, but I couldn't – I just couldn't.' She took a tissue offered by Penny, covered her face and sobbed.

Jane blinked. She felt as if someone had punched her in the stomach. She was so preoccupied with how to get Emily to talk about Amelia's murder that she had failed to hear or see the pain on the poor woman's face. Had the job finally robbed her of all her sympathy? 'Miss Loxton,' she said, leaning forward. 'Emily.' She waited for the cries to subside. 'Would you like a moment?'

Emily was shaking her head. 'No. I'm sorry, I'm all right. It's just . . . I haven't talked about it to anyone, not then or since.' She sat up, tipped her head back and sucked in a large breath through her nose. 'I'm okay. I'm okay.'

'Miss Loxton, would you be prepared to make a statement to formalize the incident?' Jane asked, fighting with her conscience. Part of her wanted to step back, allow the woman time to cry, to breathe; but the detective part of her wouldn't permit it. This could be what she needed. She would be able to rearrest Lebowski, for the rape. If she could convince a judge that the rape demonstrated a history of sexual violence, then she might even be able to get the full forty-eight hours to question him about Maggie.

Emily was shaking her head, her hair half-covering her face. 'I don't want to press charges. I'm only telling you because this isn't the first time I've been asked about my husband. I should have said something then, but . . . There's something else,' she said, dabbing her eyes with a tissue.

'Go on,' Jane urged, her mind rushing ahead.

'I wanted to say something when Detective Groves called, but I didn't want to cause trouble for Victor . . . ' Emily took in another big breath through her nose. 'I think Victor was having an affair with the young girl who was murdered.' Her shoulders dropped as she spoke, as if a burden was being lifted.

'Yes, we know,' Jane said, disappointed. 'He's admitted to the relationship. May I ask how you knew about it?'

'He never told me – not in so many words. Lying is part of his genetic make-up, I'm afraid, but I'm ninety per cent sure.' Emily looked up, her face pale. 'I knew after I spoke with Detective Groves that I couldn't pretend any more. I couldn't protect him any more. What if the girl said no; maybe she wouldn't give him what he wanted and he forced her – like he forced me – and things went . . . too far.' She took a deep breath before she spoke again. Her voice was no more than a whisper.

Jane sat forward. 'Emily. Are you saying you think your ex-husband could have raped Maggie Hungerford?' she asked.

'Who's Maggie Hungerford?' Emily asked, the perfect skin on her forehead bunched and lined.

Jane looked at Penny and then back at Emily. She felt as if she had stumbled into a parallel universe. 'Maggie Hungerford was the girl Victor was dating. Her body was found on the twenty-third of April. She was murdered.'

Emily was shaking her head, her mouth hanging open. 'He had nothing to do with that . . . '

'Emily, who were you talking about?'

'Amelia Reynolds,' she said, hanging her head and sobbing again. 'I think he could have killed her.' She looked up, her eyes fierce. 'But it would have been an accident – it must have been an accident.' She was shaking her head. 'We were having problems. He was unhappy at home. She must have initiated it and then changed her mind . . . I don't know, but Victor would never do that – not to me, not to the girls. I know him. You have to believe me. He would never do anything that could hurt his children.' Her voice disappeared into another bout of sobbing.

Jane could only imagine what Emily was thinking. Had her silence allowed her ex-husband to get away with murder? Had her desire to protect her own family left Amelia's family in torment for six years, never knowing who had killed their daughter, or why? Jane could almost see the guilt rising off Lebowski's ex-wife like steam. She turned to Penny and shook her head. No, it wasn't enough. Emily Loxton's story, the rape, her theory about Amelia's murder: it was all circumstantial. It said a lot about Lebowski's character, his behaviour towards women, but in reality it only confirmed what Jane already knew. There was no proof. This was not the smoking gun she needed.

CHAPTER THIRTY-FOUR

2nd May – Friday

Lockyer crossed his arms and leaned back against the metal countertop that ran the length of the mortuary suite. 'Are we going to be starting any time soon, Dave?' he asked, stopping himself before he took a deep breath. The caustic odour of cleaning chemicals smelled worse than a decomposing body, in Lockyer's opinion. Mind you, he wasn't sure he wanted to test his theory.

'Be patient, will you,' Dave said from the other side of the room. 'Patrick's off sick and the lab is backed up. I'm doing most of the prelim and paperwork myself. Jeanie's already been in, as a favour to me. I only have one pair of hands, you know.' He looked flustered. Without Patrick at his side he seemed somewhat unglued. 'I wish I knew where Patrick kept the bloody charts.'

'Why don't you phone him?'

'Shut up,' Dave said, turning and looking at Lockyer over his glasses – a new addition that he was none too happy about. 'One more word and you can wait until Patrick's back in the office tomorrow.'

Lockyer held up his hands. 'Okay, okay. I think Jane should be with us soon anyway, so we may as well wait for her.'

'Well, thank you. Thank you for your permission and understanding.'

'What is up with you? You're not still pissed off about the glasses, are you?' Lockyer asked. Dave turned his back and resumed his search for the charts. 'They look fine, mate. Did you think you'd have twenty-twenty vision forever?'

'Yes, Mike, I did. My father never wore glasses. Neither did my mother. In fact no one in my family has ever worn glasses, that I'm aware of.'

'Yes, but none of them does the kind of job you do, and I don't think computer work was around when your father was alive. Modern living messes with your vision. Fact of life. Nothing to be ashamed about.' Dave had been bitching and moaning about the glasses in the pub last week. Lockyer was surprised that he was still so uptight about it. 'Is there something else bothering you?' He surprised himself with the question. Maybe his sessions with the occupational-health woman had helped. Maybe he was becoming more 'sensitive to other people's feelings', as she put it.

Dave turned and walked over to the table where the body lay, covered by a sheet. It couldn't really be called a body. There were just bones and fragments of clothing. 'I wore contacts before,' he said, not looking up.

'I didn't know that,' Lockyer said. 'And?'

Dave sighed, his shoulders drooping. 'I've got type-two diabetes.'

247

'And that's affecting your eyes?' Lockyer asked, still wondering what all the fuss was about. Didn't half the country have diabetes these days?

'My GP thinks I've had it for a while. I only got referred after I went to see the optician.'

'It's not that serious, is it?' he asked. His sympathy had waned a bit, now that he knew what the problem was. Maybe the counselling hadn't helped after all.

'It's affected my vision. I think that's pretty serious, don't you?' Dave said. It was clear he was angry and upset – two emotions that Lockyer found it difficult to deal with.

'Well, I'm sorry, mate. You should have said. Can they fix it?'

'I have to take pills, go for regular check-ups, but my vision shouldn't get any worse. For now anyway,' Dave said, adjusting the sheet over the remains.

Lockyer dug deep within himself, edged closer to Dave and put his arm around his friend's shoulder. It wasn't clear who found the gesture more uncomfortable: him or Dave. 'Well,' he said again, searching for just the right thing to say to comfort Dave – and end the discussion, all in one go. 'Sounds like your doc's got it well in hand, and you'll be around long enough to buy me a drink later.'

Dave sighed and puffed out a throaty laugh. 'I've got to watch how much I drink.'

'No problem,' Lockyer said, relieved to see the tension leave his friend's face. 'I'll watch it for you. Hey, what are friends for.' He gave Dave's shoulder a squeeze, before stepping away and over to the table.

'Have you told Jane yet?' Dave asked, pulling back

the sheet and looking down at a mess of bones and fabric.

'No, I thought it might be better coming from you,' Lockyer said.

'Great. You're a real pal. Is she still questioning Lebowski?'

'She had to release him again. He was only here for about an hour. It's the ex-wife's word against his.'

'Oh dear,' Dave said.

'"Oh dear" is right, my friend. She did not look happy, when I saw her earlier.'

'I'm still not.'

Both men turned as Jane walked into the room. Her face was flushed. When Lockyer had left the office she had been in with Roger. Whatever their SIO had said, it had not improved her mood.

'So you had to release Lebowski,' Dave said, walking over and handing her an apron and gloves.

Jane snapped on the gloves and turned as Dave tied her apron for her. '"Circumstantial" is the word of the day,' she said, turning back to face them both. 'Not that I'm surprised. The ex-wife doesn't want to press charges on the rape, and she has no proof that Lebowski was seeing Amelia Reynolds. He denied the lot, and so he's out again.' She sighed. 'And if both of them were in the witness stand, his testimony would win over hers any day of the week. He's the most convincing bastard I've ever met. He should be in sales, not teaching: ice to Eskimos springs to mind.' Jane hung her head. 'But even so, I had to try. Right?'

'Of course,' Lockyer said, hoping he sounded reassuring. He knew all too well how she was feeling. To know everything, but not be able to prove anything – it was a frustrating position to be in.

'The possibility of an affair has to help, though?' Dave asked.

'No,' Jane said, walking over to the mortuary table. 'Quite the opposite. As soon as Amelia Reynolds's name was mentioned, his lawyer was all over me. She let me ask the question, let Lebowski answer, but then that was it. She's been up to see Roger and threatened to file an official complaint, which – given Lebowski's history with our department – would not be good.' She looked at Lockyer. 'I've been told I am not to go anywhere near Lebowski again unless I have irrefutable evidence relating to the Hungerford case, or our Jane Doe here,' she said, gesturing at the remains. 'If me or my team continue to investigate the Amelia Reynolds case, I could be suspended.'

Lockyer pursed his lips and whistled. 'You really are in charge of this investigation. It's usually me getting into this kind of trouble.'

'Twice,' Jane said, twisting her mouth in a grimace. 'That's twice now that Roger's called me in to bollock me. If this is what it's like at the top, I'm not sure I want to get there.'

Lockyer smiled. He had been there for her first reprimand. She had been nervous, but had handled herself well. He would love to have been a fly on the wall for the second round. 'What did you say?'

'I told Roger that, officially speaking, that was fine and any future enquiries would be handled with the utmost care, but that I'm not about to ignore a major piece of evidence, for him or anyone else.'

Lockyer found himself laughing, despite himself. 'How did Roger handle that?'

Jane smiled. 'Quite well, I thought. He didn't fire me, at least.'

'She's getting more like you every day,' Dave said.

'She wishes,' Lockyer replied. 'Now, shall we get on with the business at hand?' he said, pointing to the shrouded remains. Jane and Dave both nodded, their smiles fading.

'Yes,' Jane said. 'What have you got so far, Dave? Please tell me there's some physical evidence? Something – any-thing – that might help me nail Lebowski to the wall.'

Lockyer looked at Dave. The news he was about to deliver was going to put another proverbial spanner in Jane's investigation.

'There's not a lot to go on, I'm afraid,' Dave said. 'I've sent off samples of the clothing for analysis. You might get lucky with some trace evidence: fibres, blood. But I wouldn't hold out much hope.' He shrugged. 'I've completed the preliminary examination of the remains, which I'll talk you through in a moment. I had Jeanie consult me on the time-frames.' Lockyer listened. Jane took a notepad out of her pocket and uncapped her pen. 'There are a lot of uncertain-ties, but I can tell you that the victim was interred between three and five years ago, judging from the decomposition and condition of the bones and remaining tissue. The victim was five foot nine, aged twenty to twenty-five years of age. I've emailed the dental records up to your team, to assist with identification.'

'Can you tell how she died?' Jane asked.

'There are no obvious injuries to the skeletal remains, so

my guess would be asphyxiation, which would make sense, given where the remains were found. But, Jane, it's not a she.'

'What?'

'The victim was a young African male.'

CHAPTER THIRTY-FIVE

2nd May – Friday

Jane stared at her laptop. She felt like throwing it across the briefing room. There was a veritable sea of evidence, but Lebowski was swimming through it like an eel: nothing would stick. She had watched him walk out of the custody suite this morning, his fancy lawyer by his side. He looked as if he was leaving a friend's house after a casual supper. He even had the nerve to turn and wave, his expression contrite. If the custody sergeant hadn't been there to stop her, she would have tackled Lebowski to the ground then and there. She looked again at the post-mortem report Dave had just emailed her.

A young African male. It made no sense.

Dave had confirmed that the likelihood of finding trace evidence was slim. The body had been in the tomb for three years at least. Any evidence would have rotted away a long time ago. She had been running scenarios in her mind for the past hour. She had even braved Lewisham High Street, pacing back and forth in the sunshine, blending the cacophony of traffic and people into a white noise. It helped her to focus and lay the facts out in her mind. Amelia Reynolds had been murdered six years ago in Deptford. The allotment shed where she was found was seven miles from the burial sites in Elmstead. Maggie Hungerford and the John Doe lying in the mortuary were linked by the manner and location of their deaths, but what about Amelia? She pursed her lips. Rather than tying herself in knots trying to link the three bodies, she should try focusing on what set the three murders apart.

She scrolled through the folders on her computer and opened Maggie's post-mortem, dragging it alongside the John Doe's. Maggie had been drugged, knocked unconscious and put in the tomb alive, with an air-hose, a camera and microphone already in place. She looked again at the John Doe's post-mortem. There was no evidence of physical injury. Given that they were dealing with skeletal remains, that was hard to prove, but Dave had listed asphyxiation as the cause of death. He had sent off samples of bone marrow to support his findings, although he said that was a long shot. But that wasn't what was quickening Jane's pulse. There was no camera or air-hose in the second tomb. She closed her eyes and pictured both tombs. John Doe's was smaller, basic, whereas Maggie's was more developed: more high-tech. As she rocked her head from side to side she heard Mort's voice. *'Fear has an astonishing effect on the brain,'* he had said. She rolled her eyes and shook her head. It had already occurred to her that Mort might have been involved in Maggie's death, that her murder could have been part of some bizarre experiment. She could see his face, his boyish excitement. *'This kind of data could be invaluable to my research.'* She had never asked Mort exactly what it was that he was researching for his thesis. She had never asked his teacher, Lebowski, either.

'Have you got a minute, boss?'

Jane looked up to see Chris standing in the doorway to the briefing room. She had come in for some respite from the noise of the open-plan office. It wasn't working. Chris was the fifth person to knock on the door since she had got back from her walk. 'Yes, Chris. What can I do for you?' He walked into the room and handed her several sheets of A4.

'I've been going over the phone records for Mark and Victor Lebowski, as requested,' he said, pulling up a chair and sitting down next to her. He pointed to the top sheet, at a batch of highlighted numbers. 'You asked if Mark and Lebowski had had any contact after the Amelia Reynolds case.'

'Yes,' she said, looking down at the numbers.

'Well, two things came up that I thought you should know about,' Chris said, lowering his voice. 'It looks like Mark – I mean, DCI Leech – had trouble letting the case go.'

She looked up at Chris and then at the open door to the briefing room. 'Hang on.' She stood up and pushed the glass door closed. 'Go on.'

'In the first year after Mark retired he called Lebowski's home and mobile numbers one hundred and forty-seven times, either from the Leech landline or, more often than not, from his mobile number. We have Mark's numbers on the system, and Lebowski's home phone and old mobile number are in the Reynolds file. The calls lasted anything from a couple of seconds to three minutes.' She could see by Chris's expression that he was perturbed by the information. 'Over the next twelve months Mark made a further fifty-eight calls to a different mobile number. I've checked the file and it's Lebowski's new mobile number, the one he's using now. Again the calls only lasted for a few seconds – a minute at the most.'

'So he was calling and hanging up?' Jane asked, an image of Sue's tear-streaked face in her mind. How much of this did she know?

'It looks that way, boss,' Chris said.

'When was the last call?'

'The calls stopped about three years ago. There was a handful of calls to Lebowski's office, but other than that, nothing,' Chris said, taking the top sheet out of her hand. 'The second thing,' he said, pointing to the next A4 sheet, 'is this.' Another batch of highlighted numbers. 'These are calls to Lebowski's new mobile in the past twenty-four months. He's had over eighty-five calls from an unknown mobile number. I spoke to the Communications department, which ran a search on the number.'

'And?'

'The mobile number is registered to Gary Reynolds. Amelia Reynolds's father.'

She looked at Chris and then back at the numbers. 'Is Lebowski's mobile available on the Greenwich website?'

'No,' Chris said. 'I checked. He has a work number and a work mobile, but the number called is his personal mobile. I spoke to the university admin department, and they can't give out personal information about students or teachers.'

'Mark could have got the number from someone here, no problem,' she said. 'He was a DCI. No one would have questioned him.'

'But Gary Reynolds couldn't,' Chris said, his voice low.

'Which implies that Mark gave Gary Reynolds Lebowski's number.'

'Why would he?' Chris asked. 'That's what I don't get.'

'Haven't you read the file?' she asked. 'Mark and Gary Reynolds were friends. When I first looked at the case history I was surprised they let Mark run the investigation, given the relationship.'

'Oh, right, I see,' Chris said, looking uncomfortable.

Jane sighed. 'Mark believed Lebowski was involved in Amelia Reynolds's murder. If Gary was his friend . . . *is* his friend,' she corrected herself, 'then it's feasible he would have told Gary about Lebowski. I don't know,' she said, shaking her head. 'Something doesn't make sense to me, though. If I were Gary Reynolds and someone had raped and murdered my child, and the police had let them go, I think I'd be inclined to do more than just make crank calls.' She pushed her hair off her face. 'If Mark believed the guy was guilty, I can kind of understand him making the calls, letting Lebowski know that Amelia wouldn't be forgotten. But why tell Amelia's father? Was he trying to get Lebowski killed?'

Chris looked over his shoulder at the office behind them. 'It doesn't look good for Mark, does it?'

'No, it doesn't, and it could be very detrimental to the case. If we do manage to get something on Lebowski, this is all going to come out. His lawyer will be all over it like flies around shit. She'll make a case of police harassment, and Lebowski will walk, I guarantee it.' The frustration Jane had been feeling became compounded to an ache in her stomach. What had Mark been thinking?

'Do you think Lebowski got sick of the calls and decided

to put an end to it? The Amelia Reynolds case, the calls – they connect him to Mark. It gives Lebowski a motive.'

Jane put her head in her hands. 'Shit.' When she had spoken to Lockyer she had questioned whether Lebowski could have murdered Mark to prevent him alerting them to the Amelia Reynolds case. But what if it was simpler that that? What if it was Mark's obsession that had killed him? 'We have to go over the evidence on Mark's disappearance. We need to see if we can place Lebowski at the scene. If we can prove he was there, the harassment might not matter.'

'What about Gary Reynolds?' Chris asked.

She opened her mouth to answer him, but didn't speak. She should be saying, "Bring him in for questioning", but she couldn't. 'I don't know,' she said. 'The SIO has ordered me not to investigate the Amelia Reynolds case. There's no way I can speak to the girl's father without creating a shit-storm.' She thought for a moment. 'I need to think this through, talk to Lockyer. No one outside the team is to know about this, okay?'

'Yes, boss,' Chris said. She could see he was relieved to have passed the responsibility over to her. And who would blame him?

Mark's actions would ruin his reputation; would make people question his integrity as an officer, his state of mind even. If he was dead, Jane couldn't stand the thought of his memory being forever tarnished.

Chris pushed back his chair and stood to leave. 'There was one more thing,' he said.

'Go on,' she said.

'Sasha has been checking the calls on the Hungerford case.'

Jane frowned. 'Which calls?'

'Well,' Chris said. 'It might be nothing, but I overheard Sasha talking about it and thought . . . ' He blushed.

'It's okay, Chris. All ideas are welcome. Go for it.'

He seemed to relax a little. 'Okay. Sasha said there were two calls to the incident line saying that Lebowski was a possible boyfriend. One was from a student in her class, a Virginia Jones. The other from an Oliver Hanson. When Sasha checked, she couldn't find a record of him. The caller gave a fake name and part of an address that doesn't exist. I just wondered whether . . . ' He looked at her.

'You're wondering whether Mark made the call about Lebowski, to make sure we picked him up?' She could see how hard Chris was finding this. Speaking ill of a fellow officer, retired or not, was one thing. Speaking ill of the dead was quite another.

'Yes,' Chris said. His cheeks were bright red.

'It's all right, Chris, you can relax,' she said. 'Mark went missing on Tuesday the twenty-second of April. The calls about Lebowski didn't come through until the end of last week – Saturday, I think,' she said, running through the timeframes in her head. 'But you're right to query it. The call could have been made by Gary Reynolds. Check with Communications to see if we can get a number.'

'What will you do if it's Reynolds?' Chris asked.

Jane barked out a tired laugh. 'I would have to talk to the SIO. If Gary Reynolds made the call about Lebowski, that's a direct link to the Hungerford case. Whether Roger likes it or not, I'd have to talk to the guy.'

'So it might not be all bad then, boss?'

She stood and put her hand on his arm. 'I think we're due some good luck, Detective Constable, don't you?'

'Yes, boss,' he said. He opened the door to the briefing room. 'I'll leave the call logs with you?' he said, gesturing to the papers on the glass table behind Jane.

'Don't worry. I'll deal with it.'

She sat down as the door clicked shut behind her. She looked at her mobile. It was six-thirty. She had to pick Peter up from her mother's in half an hour. It would take that long to get through the Lewisham rush-hour. She gathered her papers and picked up her phone. She would call Lockyer on the way; see if he could come over later to talk things through. Maybe he would have some words of advice. She bloody well hoped so. She wouldn't forget Mort, either. She would be talking to him again, sooner rather than later.

Jane accelerated through the amber light and turned right onto her mother's street. It was another beautiful evening. A normal person would be getting home from work, having their dinner outside, if they were lucky enough to have a garden, and enjoying a glass of something alcoholic. Lockyer was meeting her at home in an hour, so she doubted there would be time for al fresco dining, but there was a bottle of red wine in the cupboard with her name on it. She would be enjoying that, even if she had to take it to bed with her. She turned off the radio as she pulled up next to the curb.

Her phone started to ring as she climbed out of the car.

She rifled through her handbag until her fingers closed around the vibrating mobile. It was Sue. Jane looked up and saw her mother standing by the front door. She waved and muted the call. Peter and her mother deserved her time, even if it was only for an hour. She would call Sue later, once she had spoken to Lockyer. 'Hey,' she said, walking up the driveway. 'How's it going?' She kissed her mother on the cheek.

'Good. Good. Good,' her mother said. Her voice was bordering on shrill.

'How's my boy doing?'

'He's in the lounge watching cartoons,' her mother said, stepping back.

Jane gave her mother a quick hug as she passed. '*Mr Benn*?'

'Naturally.'

She walked into her parents' lounge, a vision of cream furnishings and magnolia walls. Peter was sitting cross-legged on the carpet, no more than a foot away from the television. 'Hello, munchkin,' she said, crouching down and covering his hair with kisses. 'And how is the most handsome boy in the world doing today?' He didn't respond at first, but he smiled when she tickled his ribs with the tips of her fingers. 'Good day?'

'Yes,' Peter said, leaning towards the screen.

'You can tell me all about it in the car.' She felt Peter tense by her side. 'You can watch the end of this one, while I have a cup of tea with Grandma, and then we'll get going. Okay?' He nodded. Jane looked at the screen. 'Is this the one when he turns into a knight?'

Peter smiled and touched her hand. 'There's a dragon. It's red.' The excitement in his voice made her want to bundle him in her arms and kiss him to death. The DVD had come free with a newspaper and, according to her mother, Peter had watched it every day after school for a week. He must have seen every episode at least a dozen times, but that didn't seem to spoil his enjoyment.

'Oh, this is a good one. I'll stop interrupting.' She gave him another kiss on the top of his head, before standing and heading towards the kitchen.

'Mummy?' Peter called.

'Yes, honey,' she said, poking her head around the kitchen door.

'Grandma let me have two ice-creams after school.' He didn't turn round, and from his tone it was hard to tell whether he was dobbing on his grandma or just giving Jane the good news.

'Lucky you.' She turned. 'Two ice-creams today?' Her mother had her back to her. 'Did he eat his dinner?'

'Yes. I ate with Peter. I'll do something for your father later on,' Celia Bennett said, her hands busy in the kitchen sink.

'Where is Dad?' Jane asked. She hadn't seen her father all week.

'He's upstairs. I'll put the kettle on, shall I?'

'Please. I'll just run up and say hello to the old bugger. I was beginning to wonder if you'd bumped him off.' Jane laughed and started to leave the kitchen.

'He's resting, Jane. Leave him for now. He'll come down when he's ready.'

'Resting? What's up with him?' she asked. When there was no answer she tried again. 'Mum, is everything all right?'

Her mother shook off her hands, dried them on a tea towel, turned and sat down at the kitchen table. When she looked up, Jane could see that her eyes were red.

'Mum,' she said, sitting down next to her and taking her hand. 'What's wrong?'

Without warning her mother started to cry. Celia Bennett didn't cry. She never cried. Not in Jane's presence at least. Celia shook her head and wiped under her eyes with the tea towel. 'Now, you mustn't worry.' Jane's shoulders tensed, her stomach flipped as if she was about to be sick. 'Your father's not been feeling well.'

'Okay,' Jane said, feeling as if she was having an out-of-body experience. 'Have you taken him to the doctor's?'

'Yes, I took him last week and again today,' her mother said. 'We don't know anything yet. It might not even be anything. I don't know why I'm crying. It's ridiculous. Forget I said anything. They're running some tests. I'm sure everything is fine.'

'Mother,' Jane said, trying to keep her voice level, 'what kind of tests? Tell me what's going on.' She squeezed her mother's hand. 'Just tell me.'

Celia Bennett sighed and looked out of the kitchen window. 'He's been very tired. Well, you know how tired he gets. He's had some pain and they think he might have . . . well, they think he might have had a small stroke.'

'God, Mum. When?'

'Now don't get upset, darling. He's fine. He's just tired.'

'When did this happen, Mum?' Jane asked again.

'They're not sure. In the last month, they think. He had a whole load of tests yesterday. He's been referred to a neurologist. They took blood, did an ECG and an ultrasound scan of his heart.'

'And what did they say?' She felt as if she was pulling teeth. How had she not noticed when she arrived? Her mother's face was grey. For the first time ever, Celia Bennett looked old.

'We have to wait for the tests. They wanted to keep him in, but I said no. You know how much your father hates hospitals. It would do him no good to be in there, with strangers. He's far better off at home where I can keep an eye on him. The food in those places is enough to kill anyone – and the germs. They're always fighting off one superbug or another. Well, of course, they don't clean the places properly.' Jane listened as her mother ranted. This was more familiar. Celia had always had strong opinions about the NHS, but they tended to flip-flop: either the poor doctors and nurses were underpaid and overworked, or they were a bunch of idiots who didn't know their arses from their elbows.

'What does Dad say?'

'Oh, you know your father. He doesn't say much. The doctor said he shouldn't drink or smoke, which has gone in one ear and out the other. As if he'd give up his cigars. Your father thinks it's all a lot of fuss over nothing. Of course it probably is.'

Jane could feel her mother closing off, shutting down the emotions that had got away from her. She had offloaded onto Jane and now it was done. 'Why didn't you tell me?' she asked, wondering why she would even pose such a stupid question.

'You've been busy, darling. Your father and I know how

important this new case is to your career. We're not in our fifties any more. These things happen. It's nothing. Your father's right. I don't know what I was thinking – crying like that, worrying you. Ignore me. It must be the heat. It's sending me loopy.' She stood and patted Jane's arm. 'Now, I really don't have time for tea, darling. I need to get your father's dinner on the go, and I've got a ton of washing to do. Why don't you and Peter get off home?'

'Mum,' Jane tried, but her mother turned and shook her head.

'It's all right. If there's anything you need to know, I'll tell you. You just concentrate on you and Peter, and your case. I will look after your father.'

'Can I at least go up and see him?'

'You can see him tomorrow, darling. He's not dying, for goodness' sake. You can be over-dramatic at times, did you know that?' Celia smiled. 'Look at you. You're getting yourself into a state for nothing. Come on, off you go. Peter,' she called through to the lounge. 'Turn that off now, your mother's ready to go – there's a good boy.'

Jane pushed back the kitchen chair and stood. She felt drained of every ounce of energy. 'I'll work from home tomorrow.'

Her mother scoffed. 'You most certainly will not. I'm taking Peter to the park. It's all arranged. I've been handling your father and Peter on my own for the past fortnight. I'm more than capable, thank you.' She bent down and opened the dishwasher. 'I'll see you tomorrow. We can catch up properly at some point over the weekend, if you have time. You can come and see your father. I'm sure he'd like to see you.'

Jane opened her mouth to protest, but decided it wasn't worth the effort. The conversation was over. Her mother was back in control. 'I'll call you tomorrow,' she said, walking out of the kitchen.

'Okay, darling. Bye. Bye, Petey. Kisses to you both.'

She walked into the lounge. Peter was standing by the front door, his knapsack slung over his shoulder. 'Let's go, handsome,' Jane said, taking his hand and opening the door. They walked down to the car in silence.

'Do you think there's a shop like Mr Benn's in Lewisham?' Peter asked.

'I don't know, honey,' she said, forcing back the tears that were filling her eyes. 'It would be lovely if there was.' Right now she would give anything to be transported to another world.

CHAPTER THIRTY-SIX

2nd May – Friday

Jane turned off Peter's bedside lamp and tiptoed out of his room. He was so tired. He had been asleep before she finished reading the first chapter of *Matilda* and she knew why. He was a mood-hoover. Her mother would not have discussed Jane's father in front of Peter, she knew that, but like most children he would have sensed the shift in atmosphere. She blew him a kiss as she pulled the door closed. She padded down the stairs in her slippers. She felt as if she was carrying an elephant on her back. It had been a long day and it wasn't over yet.

Lockyer was sitting in her lounge, flicking through a magazine on home furnishings. 'I never knew lighting a room was so complex,' he said, taking a sip of wine. He had brought a bottle with him. Jane was grateful, as she was pretty sure the bottle she had wasn't going to be enough to get both of them through the evening.

'Oh yes,' she said, settling in the armchair across from him. 'You have to have the right levels to create the perfect ambience.' She smiled as she bent down and picked up her own glass. She took a sip, although she was tempted to down it in one.

'I hope you don't mind me saying, Jane, but you don't look . . . great,' he said, tossing the magazine onto the sofa next to him.

She nodded and raised her glass. 'I know. I caught sight of my reflection earlier.' She opened her mouth in mock-horror. 'A frightening sight. Feel free not to look at me.'

Lockyer laughed and rested his head on the back of the sofa. 'I wouldn't go that far.' He smiled. 'I spoke to Roger before I left the office.'

'Oh, great. What did he have to say? Am I fired yet?' For one crazy moment she hoped he would say yes. At least then she could go to bed and sleep until all of the weariness left her body.

'No. You're still his golden girl,' he said, yawning. 'He's just worried about you . . . the department. It's his job.'

'A job I wouldn't want for all the tea in China,' she said, taking another swig of her wine. 'I hate office bureaucracy. I can't imagine having to answer to as many people as he does.'

'That's why he gets paid the big bucks,' Lockyer said, rocking forward and picking up the wine bottle in one smooth motion. 'More?' he asked, holding the bottle out to her.

'Yes,' she said, without hesitation. 'Fill 'er up.' They sat in silence for several minutes before she asked, 'What did he say then?'

Lockyer seemed to hesitate before he spoke. 'He's been looking at the Amelia Reynolds case. More specifically, at Mark's handling of it.'

'Really?'

'Roger was the one who authorized the arrest of Lebowski, Jane. He wants to get him just as much as you do. As much as we do, I mean. He's got to think about the department, and the damage Lebowski's lawyer could do, if we put a foot wrong.'

'So?' she said, folding her legs underneath her. 'He hasn't said anything to me.'

'He said you need to be careful,' Lockyer replied, raising his eyebrows. 'I told him you were trying to come at it from a different angle, but I didn't go into details.'

'Thanks, Mike,' she said. 'I could do with a bit of breathing space.'

'And you'll have it,' he said, putting his feet up on the coffee table. 'Do you mind?'

She waved away his request. 'Of course, make yourself at home. Have you eaten?'

'No. You?'

'Not yet. I was thinking about ordering a pizza. Do you fancy sharing?' Lockyer looked at his watch. 'Only if you've got time,' she added.

'Go on then. I'm starving.'

'Pepperoni all right with you?' she asked, reaching for her phone. He nodded and slumped back in the chair. She called through their order. She was still thinking about her father. She had sent him a text when she got home to tell him she loved him. He had replied with a 'You too' and two kisses.

'Are you going to tell me what's wrong?' Lockyer asked when she came off the phone.

'Nothing,' she said, wiping away a tear. 'I'm just knackered. It's catching up with me.'

'Jane,' he said, sitting forward in his chair. 'I thought we were going to be honest with each other from now on?'

She looked over at him, debating how much she could say without breaking down. Who else was she going to tell? She had at least a dozen unread emails from friends sitting in her in-box. She doubted any of them would be in the mood to listen to her woes when she had not even bothered to reply to their messages. 'My father had a stroke. Only a minor one, a TIA. I checked online. It's not life-threatening. The docs just have to make sure he doesn't have a full stroke.'

'When did this happen?' Lockyer asked, moving to the coffee table so that he was sitting right in front of her.

She sighed. 'My mother said it probably happened in the last month, but she wasn't sure. They're waiting on a load of test results. I only found out today.' It felt odd talking about her father like this. It felt odd thinking about him being ill. Jane's thoughts were usually preoccupied with her mother, and the delicate nature of their relationship. Her father was the stable one. He played golf, went drinking with his buddies, played the piano, listened to opera, ate dinner – and that was about it. Everything felt out of kilter.

'Is there anything I can do?' Locker asked.

She couldn't help laughing.

'What?' He sounded almost hurt.

'Sorry. I'm just finding this new "sensitive" you a bit hard to deal with, sir.' She smiled and drained her glass.

Lockyer gave her knee a shove, stood and returned to his place on the sofa. 'You're not the only one,' he said. 'I was perfectly happy before. Before that occupational-health woman got her hooks into me.'

'Is it helping?' she asked, nervous to see if he would actually talk about himself.

He turned his mouth down at the corners. 'I don't know. My daughter's happier, I know that much. After what happened, I struggled to . . . ' He seemed to be searching for the right words, but Jane wondered if, in fact, it was the feelings he was searching for. 'I couldn't talk about it. Megan said I was shutting her out.' He laughed. 'You wouldn't believe how many times I heard the exact same thing from Clara, when we were married.' Jane realized she was holding her breath. Lockyer never talked like this. It was a new side to him. It was unnerving, but it felt good to be trusted. 'Things are getting better. We spend time as a family – as much as the job allows. You know how it is. Bobby loves Megs. He's responded to her, come out of his shell. He's like a different guy when she's there.' He shook his head. 'If I hadn't been so "emotionally retarded", as my daughter calls it, she could have grown up with an uncle, rather than an absent father.'

'You thought you were protecting your brother,' she offered. 'It's not easy.'

'Maybe,' he said, looking at the dregs in his empty glass. He took a deep breath. 'Anyway, I'm going to open another bottle and we can go back to talking about you. Nice diversionary tactic, by the way.' He winked at her.

'Let's talk about the case. I'm sick of talking about "feelings".'

'You and me both,' he said, leaving the room.

The doorbell chimed. 'Pizza's here,' she called. 'Can you bring through a couple of plates and grab the kitchen roll. It's next to the kettle.'

'Got it.'

Jane picked up her purse and went to the door. She paid the delivery man and carried the large pizza box back into the lounge. The smell made her stomach rumble. Most days she wanted to forget about work, but not tonight. Tonight she needed it.

Jane handed Lockyer another piece of kitchen roll. 'You missed a bit,' she said, pointing to his chin. She picked up the pizza box. 'Do you want a coffee?'

'Sounds good,' he said, wiping his mouth. He looked at his watch. 'And we need to get on and talk about the case, if you still want to? I need to head off in about an hour.'

'No problem,' she said, pulling open the lounge door with her foot. 'It won't take long.' She padded into the kitchen, put the pizza box in with the cardboard recycling and washed her hands. There was so much to tell him that she wasn't sure where to start. She flicked on the kettle and took two mugs out of the cupboard. As she made their coffees she tried to give some order to her thoughts. She walked back through to the lounge carrying their drinks. She handed Lockyer his, before sitting down herself, cradling the hot mug in two hands.

'Come on then,' Lockyer said. 'Let's have it.'

She looked up at the ceiling. 'Bear with me if this is a bit jumbled. I'm knackered.'

'Who isn't?' he asked, taking a sip of his coffee. He rested his head back on the sofa and closed his eyes. 'I'm listening.'

'Chris passed on some information about Mark today that isn't great,' she said. 'It looks like he was cold-calling Lebowski.' Lockyer opened his eyes, tilted his head and looked at her. 'I know, I know,' she said, 'but Chris checked the phone records and there are over two hundred calls to Lebowski.'

Lockyer put his hand over his eyes. 'You're right. That's not great.'

'There's also a possibility that he passed on Lebowski's contact info to someone else,' she said. 'Gary Reynolds – Amelia Reynolds's father. Mark stopped calling Lebowski three years ago, but then Gary Reynolds seems to have taken over in the last two years, most notably in the last twelve months.'

'What the hell was Mark thinking?'

'I don't know,' she said. 'That's part of the problem.'

'To say the least,' Lockyer replied, opening his eyes long enough to take a drink of his coffee. 'Lebowski hasn't said anything about this?'

'No,' Jane said. 'There's no way he would have brought it up, because it would have meant talking about Amelia.'

'What have you got on Gary Reynolds?'

'I did a quick search before I left the office. It looks like he and his wife split up after Amelia was killed. He changed jobs, moved to north London, Islington. I think he might have a drinking problem. He's been arrested for drunk-and-disorderly twice in the last six months. No charges, though.'

'Are you going to speak to him?' Lockyer asked.

'Well, that's the thing. Everything I have on Gary Reynolds relates to the death of his daughter and the investigation. Roger said there can't be any crossover between the Reynolds and Hungerford cases. If Whitaker found out, she could revert to the original complaint about Mark: claim that Lewisham nick has it in for Lebowski.' She leaned forward and put her mug on the coffee table. She pressed her fingers to her eyelids.

'He's right,' Lockyer said.

'I know,' she said, looking at him. 'The link is weak at the moment, but I'm hoping to change that.'

'How?'

'There are a couple of possibilities,' she said. 'One of the callers to the incident number, naming Lebowski as Maggie's boyfriend, gave a bogus name and address. I've asked Chris to find out if we can get a trace on the number.'

'You think it might be Reynolds?' Lockyer asked, resuming his position with his head resting on the back of the sofa, his eyes closed.

'If he believes Lebowski was involved in his daughter's death, but got away with it, then he wouldn't want that to happen again, would he?' Jane said. 'Whatever the reason, if it was Gary, then I have a direct link to the Hungerford case. Roger would have to let me question the guy. It wouldn't be anything to do with the Amelia Reynolds case, not initially anyway. I would simply be following up on a lead. The fact that the two would inevitably overlap is happenstance.'

Lockyer started laughing. 'You've put some thought into that excuse. Nice.'

'I've not thought about much else,' she said. Which might explain how she had missed her father having a TIA. 'But that works, doesn't it?'

'Yes, kind of. But, Jane,' he said, covering his eyes with both hands now, 'if Gary Reynolds has contact info for Lebowski, knows where he works, et cetera, why make phone calls? If I thought the man who murdered my daughter was walking around, breathing free air, I think I'd do more than call him.'

'I thought the same,' she said, 'I can't explain that.'

'Mmm, okay,' Lockyer said. 'What else?'

'Mort,' she said, knowing the reaction she was going to get.

He threw his hands up in the air. 'Jane, do you not think you've got quite enough to be getting on with. What's the obsession with Mort?'

'It's not an obsession,' she said, unable to hide her irritation. 'I'm looking at as many angles as I can find. There has to be a way in somewhere. For Lebowski to come away this clean, it's feasible that he had help.'

'Are you still on the weird-experiments vein?'

Jane took a deep breath. She hated not having the answers. 'Yes and no. Do you remember what Mort said when we met him?'

'I've tried to block it out,' he said. 'Which part?'

'Him wanting to talk to us about Maggie's death . . . that it would help his research,' she said, trying to gauge his reaction. When he nodded she kept going. 'I've asked Mort to come into the station for a follow-up interview.'

'Go on,' Lockyer said, his eyebrows inching higher as she spoke.

'I never asked him about his thesis. It never occurred to me to ask Lebowski, either.'

'Right,' he said.

'Mort claims not to know Lebowski – no more than in passing. What if that's not true?'

Lockyer screwed up his face. 'Hang on, hang on. Are

you suggesting this is some kind of master-and-apprentice thing?'

Jane's shoulders sagged as he spoke. It sounded ludicrous. 'I don't know,' she said. 'Shit, I don't know.' Every time she felt she was making some headway, it felt as if reality slapped her back down again. 'There's something about Mort. I just want to see if I can rattle him. If there's nothing, then there's nothing. I'll drop it, I swear . . . But I need to speak to him before I can.'

'Okay,' Lockyer said, holding his hands up. 'No harm in trying. I assume you want me there with you?'

'I was hoping you'd say that,' she said. 'He's coming in tomorrow morning.'

'Saturday?' he said, rolling his eyes. 'You're keen.'

'I offered him an appointment on Monday, but he said he wanted to get it over with,' she replied. Lockyer nodded, shrugging his shoulders. 'Do you think I'm nuts?' she asked.

'That's a leading question,' Lockyer said, laughing. 'I'm not prepared to answer that at this time. However, I will help you question Mort. I have one request.'

'What?' she asked.

'I want to be there when you tell Roger.'

'I'm glad this amuses you.'

'Something has to,' Lockyer said. 'Given the amount of shit your case is buried under at the moment, I think hysteria is the only option.'

CHAPTER THIRTY-SEVEN

3rd May – Saturday

Lockyer could see that Terry Mort, despite his desire to 'get it over with', was none too pleased with being called into the police station. At the university he had been confident, arrogant and psychotic. Now, sitting here in the interview room, he looked nervous, younger somehow. 'DS Bennett will be along in a moment, Terry,' he said. 'She was just getting some files together.'

'I don't have a lot of time, Detective,' Mort said, taking a mobile phone out of his trouser pocket. 'Every day is a work day when you're attempting my kind of research.'

'You'll need to switch that off in here, I'm afraid,' Lockyer replied, shrugging his shoulders in a 'not my rules' kind of way.

'There's a common misconception about students at my level. I might have six years to complete my PhD, but I would wager I work more hours in a day than you do, Detective,' Mort said, as if Lockyer hadn't spoken.

'I've no doubt.' Lockyer tried to look impressed. His desire to hurt Mort was still strong, but Jane had asked for his help, which meant that he would try, if it was possible, to ingratiate himself with the wacko. 'I can't imagine studying for that long. How do you maintain focus?'

'It can be difficult for some people. I have a goal – a purpose, Detective. Research takes time and patience. If break-throughs are going to be made, someone has to have the resolve to stick with it, make sacrifices. I don't see my work as studying. I see it as discovery. The university is a pre-school: kids wandering around stoned or hungover. I only foster the association because it benefits my research. Besides, I wouldn't get funding without the board backing me.'

'So who pays for your PhD then?' Lockyer asked.

'I do, in part, but the extent of my work requires further funding. I'm an investment, if you like. To be published – to become a leading voice in a certain field – you have to know the right people. Fortunately for me, Detective, I do.'

There was no doubt the guy was arrogant. He talked as if he was single-handedly curing cancer. 'My ex-wife had cognitive behavioural therapy once,' Lockyer said, in order to keep the conversation going.

'CBT is an interesting field and has its uses. My work is a touch more complex,' Mort said. 'Did it work?'

Lockyer could tell Mort wasn't really interested, but the fact that he had bothered to ask meant they were forming a rapport, of sorts. 'I think so. She suffered from anxiety attacks when she was driving. A fear of crashing, I assume?'

'It could be,' Mort said, stroking his chin as if he was Freud. 'Some practitioners are better than others. I would have said it went deeper than a simple fear of crashing. We are predisposed to fear injury or death. It is rarely the root of such problems. If I had been treating her, I would have been interested to know if there was a particular trigger.'

'I don't know about that, I'm afraid,' Lockyer said. 'We were separated when it happened.'

'Interesting,' Mort replied, smiling. 'Separation anxiety is a classic disorder.'

Lockyer laughed. 'I don't think I'll mention that to her,' he said. 'Another thing she can blame on me.'

'Indeed. Relationships can be very trying,' Mort said, rolling his eyes.

'Women.' Lockyer said. 'More trouble than they're worth sometimes.' He was surprised the 'boys together' tactic was working so well. It was clear Mort was beginning to relax, get comfortable with his surroundings. In Mort's mind, Lockyer was on his side, and that is exactly how Lockyer wanted him to feel: safe and secure. There was a knock on the door. 'That'll be DS Bennett,' he said, standing and opening the door for Jane.

'Sorry I'm late, Terry,' Jane said, walking in and taking Lockyer's seat. He looked at Mort and rolled his eyes as he took the chair next to her. Mimicking body-language was the quickest way to put someone at ease and, as with their conversation, it was working. Mort smirked.

'Not at all, Miss Bennett,' Mort said, looking at Lockyer rather than Jane.

'Great. Shall we get started?' she said.

'By all means,' Mort replied, folding his arms. 'Fire away.'

'Well,' she said. 'This might sound a bit odd, but can you tell me the subject of your thesis?'

Mort was looking at Jane. Lockyer was looking at Mort, studying his reactions.

Mort shrugged. 'The converse relationship between fears and phobias.'

'Ooo,' Lockyer said, tapping his head. 'Sorry to appear dense, but . . . what?'

'Another common misconception, Detective,' Mort said, as if he were talking to a child. 'Most people believe fears and phobias are the same thing when, in fact, they are anything but.'

Lockyer looked at Jane. 'I don't know about you, DS Bennett, but I could do with a lesson in layman's terms, couldn't you?'

'If you wouldn't mind, Terry,' she said, taking out her notepad.

'I really don't have time for this,' Mort said. Lockyer sat back in his chair. Jane did the same. They had run through a mock-interview at her house after their pizza. This was all part of the plan: unsettle and agitate Mort and see what transpired. He looked from one to the other and then at the table. 'Okay, fine. A fear is based on something rational – an individual might be fearful of flying, spiders or heights. Yes?' Lockyer nodded. 'These fears are based on rational deductions. If a plane crashes, there's a high probability you will die. The bites of some spiders can kill. If you fall from a great height, again you can injure yourself or die.'

'Right,' Lockyer said, watching as Jane noted down what Mort was saying.

'A phobia is by no means rational. It cannot be explained or controlled. People can be phobic of the bows of ships, birds, outdoor spaces or crowds, men, flowers, numbers . . . Need I go on?'

'Why would someone be frightened of numbers?' Lockyer asked. He couldn't deny he was curious. He felt Jane looking at him. This wasn't part of her plan.

'Your question, as banal as it sounds, Detective, is the basis of my study. There is no reason . . . I'm sorry, I mean there is no *rational* reason for an individual to fear numbers. In layman's terms, as you put it, fear is rational. A phobia isn't.'

'How do you study either?' Jane asked.

'That, Detective, is part of my study and not something I am prepared to go into detail about . . . with you.'

'Why is that?' Lockyer asked.

'My research and findings have long-term scientific importance in the world of psychology and cognitive therapy, Detective. I am already in talks with several parties about a publishing deal for both my research and the history behind it. Competitors would love to poach my work. I don't intend to let that happen.'

'Have you ever heard of taphophobia?' Jane asked. Mort opened his mouth and shut it several times like a stranded fish. Lockyer had to give her credit. Her hunch about Mort was spot on; he was hiding something. 'Am I saying that right?' she asked, looking down at her notepad. 'It's the fear of being buried alive, isn't it?' Mort's expression remained static. 'I only ask because a colleague mentioned the origin of the word to me. It comes from the Greek, *taphos*. It means tomb.'

'Terry,' Lockyer said, sitting forward. 'You still with us?'

Mort's eyes seemed to clear. He tipped his chin up and said, 'Yes, I've heard of it.'

'Is it part of your study?'

'No,' he said, without hesitation.

'That's a shame,' Jane said, pursing her lips. 'I was hoping you might be able to help with the inquiry into Maggie's death. I guess I was hoping,' she said, sucking air through her teeth, 'that we might be able to help each other. After all, you are the expert.'

Mort sat back and puffed out his chest. Despite some obvious effort, he was unable to hide his glee. A smile played at the corner of his mouth. Lockyer resisted the urge to shake his head. The guy was a preening idiot. One hint of praise and he was on his back, as it were. 'What happened to Maggie was appalling,' Mort said. 'However, I won't deny that the circumstances of her death do interest me and would, given enough information, make a significant addition to my thesis. With that in mind, I would be willing to assist you, where I can.'

'That would be great,' Jane said, nodding. 'Of course, the investigation would have to be concluded before I could talk to you at length. I can speak to the powers that be and see if you would be able to have access to the file, even.'

'What do you need to know?' Mort asked. He was fidgeting in his chair with what appeared to be excitement.

'Well,' Jane said. 'Is there anywhere I could find research on the subject, to add to the file? I've had a look on the Internet – Wikipedia and such – but there's not a lot there . . . just basic definitions and that kind of thing.'

Mort crossed his legs and unfolded his arms. He cleared

his throat. Lockyer could swear he could hear the cogs in the guy's brain turning. 'Well, I think I remember reading a paper on it a few years ago, when I was completing my Masters. I could dig it out for you, I suppose, if you could bear with me?'

'Not a problem,' Jane said. 'In the meantime, what can you tell me about the phobia itself?'

'Taphophobia dates back to the 1800s. At the time it was not the irrational fear that it is now, as there were numerous cases of accidental live burial. People had coffins fitted out with air-hoses, glass lids or bells attached. The practice led to familiar phrases such as "saved by the bell" and "dead ringer".'

'Really?' Lockyer said. 'I always thought that bells on coffins was an urban myth.' For someone who claimed not to be studying the subject, Mort's recall was impressive.

'No, Detective. There was a genuine demand for safety coffins among those with the means to pay for them. Anyway, I digress,' Mort said, as if he was lecturing a room full of students. 'I'm not surprised you had trouble locating much information. There has been no significant research into the matter.'

'Other than the piece you read?' Jane said.

'No, no,' Mort replied, his agitation obvious. 'That was nothing – just the bare bones really. Nothing has been *published* on the subject.'

'The thing is,' she said, 'there are other factors in the case that suggest premeditation, alteration of the environment, prior knowledge of—' She stopped. 'I'm afraid I am not at liberty to discuss those matters with you, at this time.'

'Not until the case is finished,' Lockyer said, looking at Mort and giving him a small nod.

'I understand,' Mort said. He was intrigued, that much was obvious, which meant he was either an exceptional actor or he had no knowledge of the camera and air-hose in Maggie's tomb. Jane's theory blurred in Lockyer's mind for a second. Mort was not an average student. He was nowhere in the neighbourhood of normal, for sure. He knew more about taphophobia than he should, but despite some anxiety he wasn't displaying the signs of someone who had been complicit in the murder of his ex-girlfriend. Lockyer wondered if he should ask Jane to step outside, to reassess how she should continue with the interview.

She put her fingers to her chin as if she were deep in thought. 'Thinking about it, this isn't going to work. You wouldn't be able to publish any findings on taphophobia.'

'Why the hell not?' Mort asked, staring at Jane.

'Sorry, it's my fault,' she said, looking over at Lockyer. He wasn't sure where she was going with this. 'I've already asked my team to look into it, and any and all research on the subject . . . Once there's an arrest, our findings rather than yours will no doubt be published in the wake of the case,' she said, looking at Lockyer. He nodded his agreement, not knowing what she was talking about. 'After all, in this instance we would be the experts, not you.'

Mort looked as if he was going to cry. 'That's impossible. It's my research. There are no other works worthy of publication,' he said.

Lockyer shook his head. 'I wouldn't worry about it, Terry. As you said, you hadn't intended to include tapho . . . whatever it's called in your thesis, so the publication of your research won't be affected at all.'

'But I—' Mort stuttered.

'Not to worry, forget it, Terry. Let's move on,' Jane said as if Mort had not spoken. 'Victor Lebowski is a supervisor on your PhD. Is that right?'

'Yes,' Mort said, staring off to one side.

'Do you know him well?' Jane asked.

'No. I told you that.'

'Were you aware that Lebowski was dating Maggie?' Jane asked.

'No. I suppose it makes sense that it was him. A watered-down version of myself,' he said. 'I really don't have time for this.' He didn't look upset or surprised.

'Just a few more questions,' Jane went on. 'We received information that you had been in contact with Maggie, as recently as the night she was murdered. That you had, in fact, been trying to get her back for several months, sending flowers – that kind of thing.'

'Whoever told you that is lying. Maggie had contacted me to see if there was a chance of reconciling. I made it very clear there was not.' Before Jane could interrupt him, he went on. 'Check my phone records, my email account, my bank account. You will find no record of calls, emails, flowers or anything of that nature.'

'We appreciate your candour,' Lockyer said. 'If you speak to the desk sergeant before you go, he can arrange for you to surrender your phone, et cetera.'

'Fine,' Mort said. 'Now if you don't mind . . . I have work to do.'

'Of course,' Jane said. 'You've been very helpful.' She closed her notepad.

'Terry,' Lockyer said, pushing his chair back. 'I'm not gonna lie to you. I feel like there's something you're not telling us.' Mort started to shake his head, but Lockyer held up his hands to silence his protests. 'That said, I think it's only right to make you fully aware of the implications.'

'And they are?' Mort asked.

'If – and I stress the word *if* – you have information that in any way relates to Maggie's murder and you withheld it, the consequences would be serious,' Lockyer said. 'You would be breaking the law. If you were found to have withheld vital evidence, you could be charged with the obstruction of justice. If that happened, Terry, I can't imagine many publishers willing to take on your thesis at the end of your PhD, or ever.' Mort looked as if he wanted to jump over the desk and hit Lockyer. 'I think it's something you need to think about, Terry. Seriously.'

Mort didn't move.

'As I said,' Lockyer walked over to the door, 'if you can give your details to the desk sergeant, he can arrange for your phone and email records to be checked.' He opened the door and gestured for Jane to go first.

'Wait.'

They both turned and looked at Mort. 'Yes,' Lockyer said, his face impassive.

'Okay, there is something. I'm not saying it's important, or even relevant. I don't know . . . But I want written assurance that my PhD will not be affected,' Mort said.

Lockyer walked back over to the table. Jane followed,

giving him a triumphant shove as they sat down. He could feel her looking at him. 'Let's hear it,' he said as Jane reopened her notepad. He didn't need to look at her to know she was smiling.

CHAPTER THIRTY-EIGHT

3rd May – Saturday

Jane pulled into Sue's driveway, took off her sunglasses and turned off the ignition. Her mouth felt dry, as the bottle of wine from the previous night caught up with her.

The information she and Lockyer had managed to drag out of Mort was good, but it wasn't enough to rearrest Lebowski. She needed proof. 'Circumstantial' seemed to be the word of choice for this case. She was fed up with hearing it. As she sat looking at Sue and Mark's suburban home, she thought about Mark and how he must have felt when Amelia was murdered. To run an investigation into the death of a friend's daughter was one thing. But to know who killed her and not be able to do anything about it must have been torture. Jane could sympathize with that. She had read over the Amelia Reynolds file until her eyes hurt. If she swapped a few details, changed the names and dates, she could have been looking at Maggie's file. The differences between Maggie and the John Doe had given Jane a new avenue to explore. However, she couldn't say the same for the differences between Maggie's and Amelia's murders.

Maggie's death had been cruel, quiet. Amelia's, on the other hand was very different. Her young body had been bruised and battered. The man who had raped and then strangled her over in Deptford had left evidence of his rage over every inch of her. Jane had asked Phil to have a look at the two files side by side, to see if he could find anything to suggest that the same man, Lebowski, had committed both crimes. She was waiting to hear back.

'Jane?'

She looked up to see Sue standing by her driver's door. 'Sorry, Sue,' she said, taking her keys out of the ignition as she opened the door. 'It's been a busy morning. I was just taking a second to . . . ' She shrugged. 'I'm sorry to disturb you at the weekend.'

'Don't be silly,' Sue said. 'It's fine. Come in. You look like you could do with a coffee.'

'Is it that obvious?' she asked, feeling as if giant boulders were crashing around inside her skull.

She followed Sue up the front path, squinting against the sun. She hated people who complained about the weather, especially when it was good, but she could do without the sunshine today. The news was full of stories about potential droughts which would result in lengthy hosepipe bans in the coming months. Londoners, it seemed, were never happy. It was always too wet, too cold or too hot. The Tube was overcrowded and badly ventilated. People were fainting on train platforms. An old woman over in Ealing had collapsed on a bus, after witnessing another motorist beating the driver of said bus unconscious: road rage. It was ridiculous. Jane was dealing with three, possibly four murders and all everyone was talking about was how heat did funny things to people. She realized Sue was talking to her.

'Sorry, Sue. I missed that.'

'I was just saying that Mark used to be just the same. A difficult case – a couple or three whiskies in the evening. He walked around like a wraith when things were tough at work.' Sue turned and took Jane's bag from her. 'You need to get your rest. The job's a marathon, not a sprint.'

'I'm okay,' Jane replied, feeling guilty that Sue was counselling her when it should be the other way round. 'How are the boys coping?'

'Not so good,' Sue said, pausing for a second at the front door. 'I'm trying to keep things as normal as possible, but it's hard.'

'I wish I could do more.'

'You're going to find him,' Sue said. 'I know you are. You'll bring him home and everything will be fine.'

Jane didn't answer. She followed Sue into the kitchen, sat down and pulled out her notepad. She pushed a stack of papers to one side in order to clear a space. A glass paperweight was balanced on top of the pile. She steadied it as it bounced, pushed upwards by the mound of paperwork Sue was yet to deal with. It was obvious that holding herself together was as much as Sue could manage. The sink was full of dirty dishes and the surfaces were covered in crumbs and cereal boxes. She needed help – someone to come in and deal with the mundane aspects of life, so that she could concentrate on herself and her sons. Jane watched as Sue made coffee and cut up a piece of dry-looking fruitcake, folding two napkins into triangles and putting them onto pretty china plates. There was an echo of the home-maker Sue used to be, but it was clear that everything had changed. As her friend, Jane should do something, but as a police officer she didn't have time.

'I need to ask you some questions about one of Mark's old cases,' she said, deciding it was better to get started. Maintaining the small talk felt like an insult to Mark.

'Of course,' Sue replied, bringing the plates and coffees to the table. 'My memory isn't up to much these days, but I'll do my best.'

'I know you will,' Jane said, putting her hand on Sue's arm. 'Sit down.' She looked down at her notepad. 'You mentioned before that Mark struggled with one of his last cases, Amelia Reynolds?'

Sue broke off a corner of cake and held it between her fingers. 'Mark was distraught. It's the worst I've ever seen him. We all feel responsible, whatever the case, but with Amelia it was different.'

'I've read the file. You knew the family?'

'Yes. We met Gary and Liz when we moved here,' Sue said. 'Mark met Gary in the pub. They really hit it off. Such a lovely family.' It was like listening to a robot. Sue's words were filled with regret, but her voice was empty. The pain of Mark's disappearance had numbed her.

'Were you surprised when Mark took on the case?' she asked.

'No,' Sue said. 'He had to fight hard, but he convinced the SIO that his personal relationship with Gary and Liz wouldn't cloud his judgement.'

'And did it?' she asked, softening her voice.

Sue looked up at her, the piece of cake in her hand now crumbled into nothing. 'I . . . Mark found it difficult, yes. It didn't stop him doing his job, but the weight of the responsibility to Gary and Liz was too much.'

'I can well imagine,' Jane said, thinking that she herself was feeling something similar with Sue. It took experience to create emotional distance from a case. She had not slept well since the night Sue had called to say Mark had disappeared. 'Did he talk much about it?'

Sue sighed. 'Not as much as he should have. There were a lot of complications on the case – I know that much. Leaving the case open when he retired was torture for Mark.'

'Were there ever any suspects?'

'Yes,' Sue said, 'but no one was ever charged.'

'Did Mark ever mention a man called Victor Lebowski?' she asked.

Sue sat back in her chair, as if the name had been a physical blow. 'Do you want another coffee?' she asked.

Jane looked down at her still-full mug. 'No. I'm fine.'

'I'll just top mine up with hot water. I need the caffeine to get me through the day.' Sue pushed back her chair and went to the kettle, her back to Jane.

'So did Mark ever mention Lebowski to you?'

Sue looked up at the ceiling while the kettle boiled. 'Er, no. The name doesn't ring any bells. Mark was careful to keep the details of the case to himself. It was too difficult for me. Liz and I were close. She was here most days; she needed support and Gary was falling apart. I couldn't stand lying to her, keeping things from her. I told Mark it was easier if he didn't tell me.'

She was lying. Jane would have known even without Sue's reaction to Lebowski's name. 'Mark never told you about any of the suspects, never discussed them with you?' She tried to keep the disbelief out of her voice, but it was difficult.

'He talked about it, of course, but never any specifics. Gary and Liz were desperate for details, for anything to cling onto. It wouldn't have been fair on them, or me, if I knew too much about the case.' Sue's reasoning sounded rehearsed.

'I can understand that,' Jane said, trying to think how to proceed. 'Are you still friends with the Reynolds now?'

'I hear from Liz at Christmas. She sends birthday cards to the boys. But Gary, no. He started drinking when Amelia was murdered. By the time Mark retired, Gary was pretty far gone. I know Mark tried, but it was no use. Gary was in a self-destructive pattern. I spoke to Liz. We tried to get him help, but he wouldn't listen. In the end Liz had no choice. She left him.'

'He lives in north London now, doesn't he?' she asked.

'I've no idea,' Sue said, taking her time, it seemed, with the kettle. 'When Gary and Liz split up, Mark lost touch with Gary. I tried my best with Liz, but I was just a reminder of what she had lost, I think. Her Christmas card always has a little note in it. She got remarried two years ago, to an airline pilot.'

'Do you know if Mark ever spoke to Gary, over the years?'

'No. Not that I know of, and he would have said.'

'Did you see them together much during the case?' Jane asked.

'Not really. Mark would take Gary to the pub. A bad idea, in hindsight, but Mark wasn't to know that, was he?'

Sue turned and looked at Jane. 'It wasn't his fault. He did his best.'

'Of course he did,' Jane said, taking a sip of her lukewarm coffee. 'Do you know if Mark ever discussed the case with Gary?'

Sue put her drink on the table with a bang. The paperweight finally lost its battle as the pile of papers fell, scattering everywhere. Sue didn't even react, she just looked at Jane. 'I can't believe you would even ask me that, Jane. Mark was on the force for over thirty years. He would never do that.'

'I'm sorry, but I have to ask, Sue. You know I do,' Jane said, leaning down to gather up the pages that had fallen on the floor.

'You don't have to, Jane, but you are,' Sue said. 'What are you doing to find Mark? Where is he, for God's sake? Here I am telling you everything, and you're not telling me anything. But of course you can't, can you? Even if you wanted to, you can't tell me.'

Jane abandoned the papers, sat up and pinched the bridge of her nose. 'Sue, I'm doing everything I can,' she said.

'You promised me,' Sue said, her voice nothing more than a whisper.

'I know,' Jane said. 'I know.'

'Mark promised Gary he would find Amelia's killer. He never did. How do you think that made him feel?' Sue looked up, her eyes filled with tears. 'Don't make the same mistake, Jane.'

'I will find him,' she said as her mobile started ringing in her jacket pocket. She reached in to silence it, but then saw the call was from Chris. 'Sorry, Sue. I have to take this.

I won't be a second.' Sue waved away her apology. Jane walked into the hallway as she pressed 'Answer'. 'Chris,' she said. As she listened her head thumped, blurring her vision for a second. 'Okay. Thanks, Chris. I'll speak to you when I'm back in the office.' She hung up the phone and walked back into the kitchen. 'I have to go,' she said.

'That's fine,' Sue replied, standing up and collecting the mugs and plates. 'Keep in touch,' she said, not looking at Jane. 'Thanks for popping in.'

It broke Jane's heart to hear her friend sound so defeated. The robot had returned and taken over Sue's brain. There was no emotion left to give.

Two hours and a phone call later Jane and Lockyer pulled up to the address on the file. Lockyer had driven, and for that Jane was grateful. Her meeting with Sue was still fresh in her mind and so was the lie. Sue had recognized Lebowski's name. There was no doubt in Jane's mind. But why lie? Did she know about the phone calls?

'You ready?' Lockyer asked.

'Yes,' she said, unclipping her seatbelt. 'Thanks for driving. I couldn't have handled the traffic around the Leadenhall monster today.'

'I think you'll find it's called the Cheesegrater,' Lockyer said, smiling.

'Whatever,' Jane said, unamused, climbing out of the car. Her head wasn't getting any better. As soon as the adrenaline from the Mort interview had abandoned her, she had been left with nothing but her wine headache. 'What is it about London and construction? Ever since the Gherkin and the

Eye went up, the planners have gone bonkers.' She held up her hands counting off on her fingers. 'We've got the Broadgate Tower . . . '

'Walkie-Talkie,' Lockyer said.

'The Strata in Southwark . . . '

'Electric Razor.'

'The Shard . . . ' she said.

'I think that's just called The Shard,' he said, shrugging.

'St George's Wharf, the Heron Tower . . . '

'I give up,' Lockyer said, shutting his car door.

'It's ridiculous. I never know where I am any more, other than the fact that I'm sitting in traffic as yet another behemoth goes up.'

'You're in a great mood.' He looked as if he was going to say more – no doubt some comment about the saddlebags under her eyes – but whatever it was, he resisted.

They walked up to the block of flats. It was a four-storey building. Each flat had its own bay window. It seemed obvious which were owned and which were rented by the window hangings. The two ground-floor flats, either side of the main entrance, had dirty net curtains covering even dirtier windows. The first and second floors were much the same, except that one had a navy-blue bed sheet slung up over the window. The top-floor flats both had expensive-looking internal shutters, one white, the other natural pine.

'Which is his?' Lockyer asked.

'Guess,' Jane said.

Lockyer pointed up to the window with the blue sheet. 'That one?'

'That's the one,' she said, stepping up to the buzzers and

pressing number five. There was no name in the space next to the button. She waited a few seconds before pressing the buzzer again. Lockyer stepped back and looked up at the window.

'Can't see any signs of life,' he said. 'Oh, hang on, there's someone in. The sheet just moved. Press it again.'

'Can I help you?' a voice said from behind them.

She turned to see a man, who looked to be in his late fifties or early sixties, carrying a Lidl bag of shopping. He was unshaven and his eyes looked as if his lunch had been of the liquid variety.

'Yes,' she said. 'We're here to see Gary. Flat five.' The man nodded, stepping around Jane and Lockyer and putting his key in the lock.

'Do you know him?' Lockyer asked.

The man smiled. 'I do,' he said. 'I am him.' He pushed open the door. 'It's a bit of a trek up, I'm afraid. No lift.'

Jane followed in behind him. The three of them climbed the stairs in silence. She kept throwing occasional glances back at Lockyer. Was Gary Reynolds expecting them? Not many people would let two strangers into their home without at least asking who they were. Unless, of course, he had guessed they were coppers. Some people – usually those who had regular dealings with the police – seemed able to spot a plain-clothes officer in two seconds. Whatever the reason, Gary Reynolds didn't look bothered or even interested.

The Communications team had called to confirm that the bogus call from an 'Oliver Hanson', naming Lebowski, was in fact from a mobile phone registered to Gary. The same mobile that had been used to make repeated calls to

Lebowski. Without the actual phone, Jane couldn't do much and she didn't have enough evidence to requisition it, but that didn't matter. The call from Comms was the break she needed. It had brought her here. It was enabling her to question the man who linked Lebowski to both murders: Amelia and now Maggie.

'Do you live alone?' she asked.

'Not at the moment, no, but don't tell the council that,' he said, swinging the bag at his side as if the momentum was helping him with the ascent.

When they reached the third floor, Gary, who was out of breath, put his key in the lock and opened his front door. 'After you,' he said, stepping aside. 'The lounge is to your left.'

The smell of cat urine and faeces hit Jane the second she crossed the threshold. She put her hand to her mouth and looked over her shoulder at Lockyer, who was doing the same. 'That's enough to make your eyes water,' he whispered.

'Go on and make yourselves comfortable,' Gary said. 'I'll just dump this in the kitchen.' He shuffled off.

'How old is he?' Lockyer asked.

'Forty-eight,' she replied, raising her eyebrows.

'The years haven't been kind,' Lockyer said under his breath as they walked into what was meant to be the lounge.

There was a three-seater sofa against one wall. It was, at one time, beige, but now looked almost black, with stains covering the arms and the trim. A black leather armchair was next to it, a portable television opposite, resting on a tiny glass table. Jane flicked on the overhead light, as the bed sheet was all but blocking out the daylight. Two mangy-looking cats scrambled underneath the sofa, disappearing from view.

'Looks like he emptied a skip to furnish this place,' Lockyer said. He seemed to be deciding where to sit, before taking a place by the window and putting his hands behind his back.

Jane decided the leather chair was the best bet. She pulled her jacket around her and sat down. 'So who was twitching the sheet before?' she asked, but before Lockyer could answer a young girl walked into the room.

'Gaz wanted to know if you want tea or coffee?' she asked.

'Nothing for me,' Lockyer said.

'I'm fine,' Jane said, thinking she could murder a proper cup of coffee. 'Do you live here?'

'Kinda,' the girl said. She didn't look much older than nineteen, maybe twenty. She was wearing jeans and a black T-shirt. Her hair was dyed. Jane had seen the hairstyle advertised. It was the kind where the top was bleached and the ends were dark. She looked as if she had been hung upside down and dipped in oil.

'What's your name?'

'Phyllis,' the girl said. Jane looked at Lockyer. He rolled his eyes.

'Phyllis what?' she asked, taking her notepad out of her pocket and resting it on her knee.

The girl thought for a moment. 'Phyllis Pitt,' she said, grinning.

'Right,' Lockyer said. 'Good to meet you. It must have been hard losing Brad to Angelina, but I'm afraid we don't have time to dick about. Can you get Gary for us, please?' The girl sniffed and sloped out of the room. He peered behind the makeshift curtains. 'It's a glorious sunny day out there and we're stuck in here with Wayne and Waynetta.'

Jane could hear muttered talking, and then Gary Reynolds shuffled into the room and fell, rather than sat, on the sofa. 'What can I do for you?'

'My name is Detective Sergeant Bennett and this is my colleague, Detective Inspector Lockyer. We would like to ask you a few questions, Mr Reynolds.'

'He hit me,' Gary said, touching his forehead. 'Damn near knocked me out.'

'Who did?' Jane began, and then hurried on before he could answer. 'We're not here about an altercation, Gary. We would like to talk to you about Mark Leech.' Gary sniffed and scratched his beard. The sound made Jane's toes curl up in her shoes.

'Yeah,' he said.

'Do you know him?' Lockyer asked.

'Obviously. You wouldn't be here if I didn't, would you?' Gary said, without bothering to look at Lockyer or Jane.

'Can you tell us when you last saw him?' Jane asked, opening her notepad.

'Not seen him for years,' Gary replied. He bent forward and hooked a carrier bag that lay underneath a wonky coffee table. He pulled out a can of lager. 'Do you mind?'

'No, go ahead,' Lockyer said, shrugging when Jane looked at him.

She supposed it didn't really matter if Gary Reynolds had a drink. It was clear it wouldn't be his first of the day and she doubted it would make him any more incoherent. He opened the can, took a swig and then slurped from the top of the can. As he continued to lick every last drop off the rim, 'Phyllis' strolled back into the room and plonked herself down next to him. She snuggled into him like a child, but from the position of his hand on her upper thigh, Jane guessed he was anything but fatherly.

'It would be helpful if you could be more precise, Gary,' Lockyer said.

'Four, five years,' he said, taking another swig of his beer, his eyes glued to the girl's legs, his thumb rubbing up and down her inner thigh.

Jane looked away. 'Have you had any contact at all with Leech in that time?' she asked.

'Leech?' the girl said. 'Isn't he that copper friend of yours that's missing? There was something about it in the papers,' she said to Lockyer. 'We get the paper on a Sunday, don't we, babe?' She turned to Gary. He didn't answer.

'So you know Mr Leech?' Jane asked the girl.

'Only met him once when—' She didn't get to finish her sentence. Jane saw Gary's grip on her leg tighten.

'She hasn't met Mark,' he said. 'You're thinking of Martin, babe. He used to be a copper.'

The girl nodded her agreement. 'Oh yeah, you're right,' she said. 'I'm crap with names. Sorry.'

'I've not seen Mark in five years at least,' Gary said. 'Anything else I can help you with? Cindy and me are heading out soon.'

'Does the name Victor Lebowski mean anything to you?' Jane asked, making a note of the girl's real name.

Gary blinked a few times. 'Nope. Means nothing to me.' Cindy was shaking her head.

'Do you have a mobile phone?' Lockyer asked.

'No,' Gary said, refocusing his attention on Cindy's thigh. Her mouth opened, but she shut it again.

'We have a number here,' Jane said, reading out the mobile number from her notepad and showing it to him, 'that's registered to you, purchased in 2005. There are a few calls we would like to discuss.'

'Must be a mistake,' Gary said. 'I told you. I don't have a mobile. Search the place, if you want.'

She looked at Lockyer. He nodded and left the room. 'Have you ever had a mobile phone, Gary?'

'Yeah, but not for ages. I've not really got the money for a bloody fancy phone, have I?' he said, throwing his arm out and pointing at the mess surrounding them. 'The landline works, but only for incoming calls. Check it for yourself,' he said, pointing to the doorway.

She looked and saw an old-fashioned plug-in phone that had once been white. 'Thanks,' she said, standing. 'What's the number?'

'Dunno,' he said. 'It's written on it somewhere.'

Jane walked over and bent down, picking up the receiver with the tips of her fingers. She would need to wash her hands after this. She turned it over, noted down the number and listened to the dial tone, without letting the smudged plastic touch her skin. 'I'll check it when I get back to the office. Thank you,' she said. Gary shrugged. 'My colleague won't be long,' she said, gesturing in the direction Lockyer had left. 'You've been very helpful, Gary. We might need to speak with you again, if that's okay with you?'

'No problem. Any time,' he said. 'Cindy'll see you out

when you're done.' He put his hand under the girl's buttocks and pushed her up. 'Off you go now.' He patted her behind. The gesture made Jane wince.

Lockyer joined them at the front door and shook his head. Jane turned and said to Cindy, 'How long have you and Gary been together?'

She shrugged. 'Two years, on and off.' She leaned towards Jane and whispered, 'He can be a bit of a handful when he's had a few.' The alcohol on her breath forced Jane to turn her face away. 'You know how guys can be?' she said, nodding at Lockyer.

'Not all guys are like that, Cindy,' Lockyer said. 'You should do yourself a favour and find someone who's nice to you.'

'Gaz is nice,' Cindy said, sniggering. 'Just sometimes he's too nice. If you know what I mean.'

Lockyer looked at Jane and shook his head. 'Are we done?'

'Yes,' she said. 'Thanks, Cindy. Here's my card.' The girl took it without so much as glancing at it.

As they walked towards the car Lockyer said, 'The place was a shit-hole. I'd need half a dozen officers to search it properly, but given that he offered up the search and didn't seem surprised to see us, he's clearly not that stupid. He makes the phoney call about Lebowski, then stashes the phone, knowing it's only a matter of time before we're knocking on his door.'

'Why not use a different phone – a clean SIM card?' she asked.

'As he said, he's not exactly flush, is he? It's an old phone, running on old credit. He used what he had to hand, I guess,' Lockyer said. Jane stopped and took a deep breath. 'What did you give that girl your card for?' he asked.

'She can't be more than nineteen,' she said. 'It makes me sick to see girls like her giving themselves to a guy like him.'

'Gary Reynolds wasn't always like this,' Lockyer said. 'His daughter was murdered. He's lost his wife and he's clearly an alcoholic. What do you expect?'

'I know,' she said. 'It's not his fault, but he's taking that poor girl down with him.'

Lockyer shrugged. 'Come on. Let's get back to the station and, if you're lucky, I'll take you to Bella's for a coffee and a piece of carrot cake.'

'I love carrot cake,' she said, rubbing her stomach.

'I know you do,' he said.

Jane waited for him to unlock the car. She looked up at Gary's flat, before getting into the car. 'Cindy had met Mark.'

'No doubt,' Lockyer said, 'and the timeframe fits in with the phone calls to Lebowski.' He started the car.

'Does he seem like the kind of guy to rely on the justice system to you?' she asked.

'Not really, why?'

'It's the calls and the tip-off about Lebowski. It's still bugging me. If Mark told Gary that Lebowski had killed his daughter, why just call? Why not take the law into his own hands?' As she spoke she wondered if that could be part of the puzzle she was missing. Maybe killing Lebowski wasn't enough for Gary. Maybe he wanted more.

'I don't know, Jane, and I think it's fair to say Gary's in no hurry to tell us,' Lockyer said.

'Or Sue,' she said, flicking down the visor and looking at herself in the mirror. She snapped it shut at the sight of her haggard face. 'She's obviously trying to protect Mark. I get that. But if she won't tell me about Lebowski, it's another door slammed in my face.' Her phone buzzed in her pocket. She had remembered to put it on vibrate before they got to Gary Reynolds's flat. She answered the call. 'Bennett.'

'Boss,' Franks said. 'We've had a package arrive, addressed to you.'

'And?' she asked, shrugging when Lockyer mouthed 'What?' to her.

'It looks like what Mort was telling you checks out. As soon as I realized what it was, I bagged it and sent it to the lab. They said they'll put a rush on it, so you can have it by the time you're back in the office.'

'We're on your way,' she said, ending the call.

'Good news?' Lockyer asked.

'Maybe,' she said. 'Let's go.'

Lockyer pulled away from the traffic lights and put his foot down. Jane rested her head back and said a silent prayer that Lebowski's luck had finally run out.

CHAPTER THIRTY-NINE

5th May – Monday

Jane blinked her eyes several times before refocusing on the computer screen. The tranche of Monday-morning emails was intimidating, even for her. Lewisham nick didn't stop for bank holidays. Nor did she, it seemed: weekdays and weekends had blurred into each other. At least she'd had yesterday off. After Saturday, seeing Mort, Sue and Gary Reynolds all in one day, she needed the bloody rest. She had kept an eye on her emails for anything relating to either the Hungerford or Leech cases, but other than that she had managed to switch off, unplug and actually spend some time with her son. They had been to the swimming baths, which Peter had loved, and the cinema to see the new Pixar film. She had almost cried when her son had cuddled her, unbidden. It was as welcome as it was unusual. She had held him and breathed in the soapy smell of his skin and hair. When she had dropped him at her parents' this morning his face had been relaxed and happy. She smiled as she looked at the picture of him on her desk. He had her father's nose. She hadn't noticed it until now.

The lab had been unable to process the package as fast as they had hoped. She was expecting someone to drop it in for her this morning. The anticipation was driving her nuts. All she knew, from Franks's assessment on Saturday, was that the documents had Lebowski's name on them and seemed to contain research material and details of an experiment. She had tried calling the lab yesterday, after the cinema, to ask if they could read some sections out to her, to end the suspense, but they had not been receptive to her request. Patience, she was finding out, was not her strong point. Of course she had a good idea what she would find, from Mort's statement at the weekend. The implied threat that his PhD and future publication could be affected, if he withheld evidence, had made him much more cooperative. Within ten minutes he had admitted to snooping, stealing and lying.

According to Mort's statement, he had nosed through a paper that he found in Lebowski's office several years earlier. It related to a study of taphophobia and mentioned proposed experiments in Elmstead and other locations. Mort had approached Lebowski to ask if he could assist with the study. Lebowski had refused and told Mort that he had misread the document and there was no such project. When Mort had persisted, which Jane had no trouble in believing, Lebowski threatened to have him thrown off the course for being in his office without permission, et cetera. Mort had taken Lebowski's denial as tacit approval to break into Lebowski's office, make a copy of the papers and pass them off as his own. He had, however, made it very clear that in no way should his actions be perceived as stealing. Mort's works, then and now, were his own form of genius and no one would convince him otherwise. Even now Jane found herself rolling her eyes. The guy was unbelievable.

And why hadn't Mort come forward after Maggie's body was found in the tomb in Elmstead? His answer had been simple in its selfishness. He couldn't risk his work being tainted by the incident. Those had been his exact words. Whether the 'incident' referred to Maggie's murder or the 'borrowing' of Lebowski's research he hadn't clarified, but given his narcissistic nature, Jane could make a guess. When she asked him if he thought Lebowski could have killed Maggie, Mort claimed not to have given it much thought. He supposed – given the research, and the manner and execution of Maggie's murder – that it was possible, but he was not qualified to give an opinion on the matter, he said. Jane thought she was going to have to physically restrain Lockyer, who looked as if he wanted to knock the guy out there and then. She was still trying to decide if she could charge Mort with obstruction of justice. She rubbed her eyes, remembering too late that she was no doubt wiping mascara all over her face.

Roger had given her the go-ahead on Saturday to prepare a warrant for Lebowski's arrest, on the strength of Mort's statement and Franks's notes on the package received. However, he had made it clear she could not go to the judge for sign-off until she had examined the documents herself. She had never seen her SIO look so on edge. He had approved her own and Lockyer's visit to Gary Reynolds's flat on Saturday, but then what choice did he have, after Comms confirmed that the phoney call naming Lebowski in the Hungerford case came from Gary's phone? The possible backlash from Lebowski's lawyer had been written all over Roger's face.

'Have you got it yet?'

She looked up as Lockyer approached her desk, resting his arms on the partition. 'Not yet,' she said. 'I called the lab an hour ago and they said I should have it this morning. Although when this morning, who knows.'

'What did Mort say?'

'Says it wasn't him,' Jane said. 'I'm inclined to believe him. Why bother leading us on a merry dance if he had already posted the original research to me? The last thing he wants is more copies being made . . . endangering his research,' she said, raising her eyebrows.

Lockyer smiled. 'Good point. What about the CCTV?'

'Still waiting. The owner of the post office said her cameras are old and unreliable, but I've sent Chris down to pick up what she has for Friday. I also spoke to the Comms team and they said there is a CCTV camera on the street, but it only covers one side. It'll only capture an image of whoever posted the package if he or she left that way.'

'You thinking it could be Gary?' he asked, scratching his cheeks.

'Could be,' she said, looking around her desk for the paracetamol she had bought on her way into the office. 'Obviously whoever sent it wanted to implicate Lebowski. He's a fit for that.' She pictured Gary Reynolds sitting in his flat with Cindy. 'But . . . how would he get hold of it in the first place?'

Lockyer's mouth turned down at the edges. 'Good question. Who knows. Are you going to charge Mort with obstruction of justice?'

'I'm considering it,' she said, 'but I don't want to waste

any more time on the arrogant prick right now. When Lebowski is locked up and the case is airtight, then I'll worry about Mort. He's a parasite, but Maggie's more important. I need to focus on her.' All the evidence surrounding Maggie's case felt like blood diluted in too much water. The patterns, the connecting tracts, were not visible to the naked eye. For every answer she found, a dozen questions crushed it. She ran her fingers through her hair and sighed.

'What about the boy downstairs?' Lockyer asked, putting his arms above his head and stretching. He looked as tired as Jane felt. She wondered what he had done with his Sunday, as he had been off too. She wanted to ask, to maintain the level of 'friendship' they had developed in the past week or so, but now wasn't the right time. There never seemed to be a right time to really talk to anyone. Her father was recovering well. She had popped over with Peter yesterday after the cinema. Her mother's house had been on emotional lockdown. As soon as Jane opened her mouth to ask a question, Celia Bennett had scowled at her. 'Jane,' Lockyer said, looking at her. 'The body?'

'Sorry. Another wait and see. MISPER have all the details, and the dental records are being checked.' As she spoke an email came up on her screen from Dave. 'Oh, hang on,' she said, clicking on it. 'An email from Dave.' She read aloud. 'We've got an ID. Kieran Affiku. Twenty-five years old. Reported missing in 2009.' She double-clicked one of the attached documents. As she scan-read the contents, her heart started to beat faster in her chest. 'He was listed as a runaway. He was . . . a student at Greenwich University . . . studying for a Masters in psychology.' She continued to scan. 'One of his tutors, would you believe it, was . . . '

'Lebowski,' Lockyer said, his hands gripping the partition.

'None other,' she said, feeling the adrenaline quickening her pulse.

'Was he questioned?' Lockyer asked.

Jane clicked and opened another document and ran her eyes down the page. 'Doesn't look like MISPER did that much at all,' she said, clicking and opening another document. 'Kieran had a history of running away – the head of psychology made a statement, but that was it. It's been an open case ever since, no progress, no movement whatsoever . . . No reason to believe it was anything other than another runaway.' She blew out a breath. 'His poor parents.'

'Come on,' Lockyer said, standing. 'This is enough for the warrant. You don't need the documents. Let's go and see Roger,' he said, already walking away. Jane pushed back her chair and followed him.

As they passed Franks's and Whitemore's desks, Whitemore's hand shot up as if he was in school. 'Boss,' he said.

'Yes,' she and Lockyer said in unison. Whitemore looked from one to the other until Lockyer stepped back and gestured to Jane.

'I've got some more information on the Amelia Reynolds case. The allotment in Deptford.'

'Yes,' she said. She was itching to get into Roger's office, to call the judge, to finally arrest Lebowski with information that even his fancy lawyer would struggle to explain.

'At the time of the murder the land was owned by a Barry

Endecott. He died recently, but he sold the plot two years back.'

'Yes, yes,' Jane said, rolling her hands over each other.

'DCI Leech bought it,' Whitemore said, his expression confused.

She stopped and looked at Lockyer.

Another answer, another question.

CHAPTER FORTY

5th May – Monday

She knew she was holding her sister's hand, but she couldn't see. Her eyes felt itchy and it was very dark. 'Daddy?' she called out. He didn't answer. She bit her bottom lip to stop herself from crying. She was a big girl now. Daddy had said so. 'Pet,' she said, squeezing her big sister's hand. 'Petra. Wake up.' It was very quiet, like when they stayed at Grandma's house. It was dark at Grandma's house, but she had a nightlight that stayed on all the time. 'Petra, wake up.' She tugged on her sister's arm. 'Mummy said you're not allowed to play tricks on me. You're not allowed,' she said, her voice cracking.

Poppy sat up, still holding her sister's hand. She banged her head, just like at Grandma's house on the bunk beds. Daddy had given her a drink in the car when he had picked them up from Susie's mummy's house. They had been playing on Susie's trampoline. She was very tired because she had jumped up and down so much. That's why she was so thirsty, Daddy said. You had to drink a lot when you were jumping around. It stopped you getting too hot. She wasn't hot now. She was cold. So was Petra's hand. It felt wet.

'Pets,' she said again, trying to pull her sister up. 'The night-light is broken, Petra. It's broken. I need the toilet.' She could feel the tears coming. Sometimes she could stop them and at other times she couldn't. Grown-ups didn't cry, that's what Daddy always said. Petra never cried. She was a good girl. Without letting go of her sister's hand she wiped her face. She felt silly. She went to the bathroom on her own at home, but she didn't like to at Grandma's. The floors were creaky and the string for the light was too high for her. Mummy said next time they went to stay she would make it longer, so that Poppy could go on her own.

She started to jiggle her legs. She really needed to go. 'Petra,' she said, crying now because she couldn't help it. 'Petra, please come with me. I'll let you have some of my stickers.' She pinched Petra's arm hard – harder than she should – but Petra didn't wake up. 'I'll tell Daddy,' she cried. 'I'll tell on you.' She wailed and called out to her grandma, to her mother, to her father, but no one came. She could only hear her own voice, her own breaths. She lay back down and snuggled into her sister's back, wrapping her other arm around Petra's tummy. She would be in trouble if she wet the bed. Only babies wet the bed. She felt her wee then. It was warm under her bottom. She cried and pressed her face into Petra's back. She cried and cried, but no one came. She cried and cried, but Petra didn't wake up.

CHAPTER FORTY-ONE

5th May – Monday

'There has to be something here that can help,' Jane said, looking over at Lockyer. 'Have you got anything?'

'Nothing yet,' he said. He could feel her frustration. Her face was flushed. 'There's a lot about phobias and those safety coffins Mort was telling us about.' He shrugged. They had been reading through the notes contained in the anonymous package that had been sent into the office on Saturday. As soon as Kieran Affiku's identity had been confirmed, Roger had given Jane permission to go to the judge and a warrant had been issued for Lebowski's rearrest. Whether he had always planned to run, Lockyer didn't know, but within an hour of the warrant Victor Lebowski was gone and so were his two children.

'Any news?' Lockyer turned as Roger walked into the briefing room.

'Eric Williams confirmed that Lebowski picked up the girls from his house at four-thirty,' Jane said, lifting her note-pad out of the mess of papers on the glass briefing-room table. 'They were attending a birthday party for Susie Williams,

Mr Williams's daughter. He said Lebowski was driving a Volvo V40. Emily Loxton arrived ten minutes later, but didn't raise the alarm as she figured she'd just forgotten her ex-husband was picking the kids up. She called Lebowski on his mobile, but it went to voicemail. We've checked and the Volvo is registered to him. I've already alerted Traffic. Sasha called ten minutes ago to say that Lebowski's passport might be missing. It's not with the rest of his documentation in his house. I've put out an All-Ports Warning, just in case. His closest international airport would be City or maybe Stansted, but his ex-wife says she has the children's passports with her, so he wouldn't be able to take the kids with him if he is intending to run.'

'How is she doing?' Roger asked.

'Not good,' Jane said. 'She's threatening to go to the press, call her MP – everything and anything really.'

Roger shook his head and looked at Lockyer. 'We're in serious trouble here,' he said.

'You don't have to tell me,' he replied.

'We'll find Lebowski,' Jane said. She put her face in her hands. Lockyer shifted in his chair. He couldn't let her falter now. She had to stay in charge. He opened his mouth to say something, to give her the time she needed to recover. She dropped her hands and looked at him and then at Roger. 'I let that bastard go. I knew he was guilty and I let him go.'

'You had no choice, Jane,' he said. 'Whitaker was all over you the second Lebowski was arrested.'

'If anyone's to blame for this mess, it's Mark,' Roger said, looking down at the floor. 'If he hadn't gone off the reservation on the Amelia Reynolds case, this wouldn't be happening.

Our hands were tied from the second Lebowski's name was mentioned.'

'You're blaming Mark?' Lockyer tried to control his anger. 'He knew Lebowski was guilty back then, and he didn't have the support or the evidence he needed to do his job. Yes, he went too far; and yes, he hasn't helped Jane's case. But you can't blame him. The man was a cop for over thirty years. He was your friend, Roger.'

'"Was" being the operative word,' Roger said, not making eye contact with him.

'So, because you think Mark's dead, you're happy for him to take the blame – to besmirch his entire career to save your own arse?' It took every fibre of Lockyer's being not to shout. He wasn't sure how he was still sitting in his chair. He felt like throwing it across the office. Or at Roger's head.

Roger held up a finger, turned and closed the door to the briefing room. 'Watch your tongue, Mike,' he said. 'I have known Mark and Sue Leech a lot longer than you, but it is my job to protect this department. Mark's behaviour has jeopardized that.' Roger shook his head. 'Look, Mike, I am not trying to pass blame, or even assign blame at this stage. But I can't ignore the possible impact on the department, even if you can.' Lockyer didn't trust himself to speak. He stared down at the floor. 'Jane, what else do we know?'

'Not much,' she said. 'We've got units at Lebowski's house, the university, the grandmother's, the ex-wife's and Elmstead. I've got additional units checking local restaurants, parks and anywhere else that Lebowski might have taken them. His ex-wife said it's not unusual for him to pick the children up, and the message she left him wasn't panicked. She just asked him to call her and let her know whether he was planning on feeding the girls before dropping them home. I've asked her not to call him again for the time being. I don't want Lebowski to know we're looking for him. If he's preparing to run, then he may well be close by.'

'That's what you're hoping,' Roger said. 'That's what we're all hoping.' He sat down next to Jane. 'Have you spoken to Phil?'

'He's on his way in,' Lockyer said, not quite able to look at Roger.

'We need to get a better idea of Lebowski's state of mind, of what he might do,' Roger said. Neither Lockyer nor Jane said anything. 'Are you still going over the documentation sent in on Saturday?'

'Yes, sir,' Jane said. 'I'm hoping there will be something in here that could tell us where Lebowski might be headed.'

Roger stood and put his hand on the door to the briefing room. 'Fine. Keep me up to date. If he isn't found in the next hour I want you to speak to Air Support.'

'Yes, sir,' Jane said, nodding.

Roger turned to leave. 'And, Mike,' he said, looking over his shoulder at Lockyer, 'I will not expose individuals in this team, past or present, to scrutiny unless I have to.'

Lockyer waved away the comment. 'I know, boss,' he said. 'I know.'

Jane reread the two pages again. 'I think I know what happened to Kieran.' She looked over at Lockyer, who was leaning back in his chair with his eyes closed. Phil had done the same when she had met him. Maybe it was a guy-thing?

He tipped forward. 'Go for it,' he said, rubbing his eyes. They had been reading for several hours. For everything Jane could say about Lebowski, she couldn't criticize his initial research. It was thorough in every sense of the word. No wonder Mort had pinched it.

'There's a description for a proposed experiment on taphophobia,' she said. 'He wanted to excavate a site on the university grounds. He intended to refit a coffin with the appropriate safety measures and lower it, with an occupant inside, into the site, before covering the area with a rectangle of contained soil that could be lifted in and out of the site easily.'

'Contained?' Lockyer asked.

'He doesn't go into specifics on that. I assume he means that the excavated soil would be stored in a bag or container of some kind, to prevent the need to dig and refill the hole at each stage of the experiment.'

'He would have needed a crane to transport that much earth,' Lockyer said. 'I like this guy less and less.'

'I know. He talks about the "occupants" as if they were lab rats, nothing more,' she said, pointing at the papers. 'Anyway, from what I can tell, he couldn't get permission from the university for the dig, let alone the experiment, so he looked for other sites that would meet his requirements.'

'Did he tell the university what he was planning to do?'

'No. He gave them a basic overview of his requirements, but didn't tell them about the taphophobia angle. If Lebowski is anything like Mort, he was probably paranoid about people poaching his work.'

'Nutters,' Lockyer said, holding up his hands.

'He did some research into suitable sites and stumbled

on Elmstead because of Chislehurst Caves. There were details of aborted entrance sites, et cetera. He must have used ground-radar equipment to locate them.'

'And no one noticed?'

'He was studying for his Masters back then, full time, so this research was not only off-campus, but out of hours. He was going down to Elmstead at night.'

'And he's documented all of this?' Lockyer's mouth stayed open.

'Yes, down to every last detail, pretty much.' She turned to the next page. 'He then spent two months adapting the site: digging down to create the access tunnels, installing the hatch, camera, air-hose, and ensuring the internal walls were fit for purpose.'

'And he did all of this at night?'

'Looks like it,' she said, just as astonished as Lockyer seemed, that Lebowski had managed to accomplish such a feat of engineering without anyone noticing.

'Hang on, there wasn't a camera or air-hose in Kieran's tomb,' Lockyer said.

'I know. He adapted two sites,' she said, raising her eyebrows when Lockyer looked at her. 'I told you he was thorough. He prepared two burial sites, both fitted out with the same kit. He must have removed the wires and tube after things went wrong.'

'What do you mean?'

'I'm assuming Kieran was the first guinea pig,' she said. 'Lebowski doesn't mention him by name, but he does talk about subjects . . . subject A, B and C.'

'Does that mean we need to start looking for two more bodies?' Lockyer asked.

'I don't think so,' she said. 'His notes stop halfway through the experiment with "subject A". I think what happened to Kieran was an accident.'

'Oh, come on, Jane,' Lockyer said, standing up. 'Give me a break. Lebowski raped and murdered Amelia Reynolds six years ago. Kieran disappeared less than a year later. And we both believe he killed Maggie Hungerford. Not to mention Mark. Do tell me how killing Kieran was an accident?'

She waited for him to stop pacing. 'Listen. Subject A,' she said, looking down at the papers in front of her, 'agreed to go down into the underground tomb for five separate sessions of two, four, six, eight and twelve hours at a time. There are notes here on the exact timings, dates – everything. The sessions were filmed with a night-vision camera and the subject was monitored. I've asked Franks to check Lebowski's residence and the university for DVD footage. The subject was allowed food, water, a torch for emergencies or, I suspect, in case they freaked out, and a Dictaphone so they could record their physical and emotional reaction to being under-ground. Lebowski listed all of the initial experiments as a success, but decided the food, Dictaphone and torch under-mined his overall goal. So he set up another session, and this is where I think something went wrong,' she said, trying to ignore Lockyer huffing and puffing on the other side of the room. 'The subject agreed to a longer stint underground: forty-eight hours without water, food or the torch. Nothing.'

'Why would anyone agree to that?'

'I don't know,' she said. 'I'm just telling you what's here.'

'All right, all right,' Lockyer said, sitting down. 'Go on. I'll stop interrupting.'

'Like that's even possible,' she said, sighing. Lockyer pulled an imaginary zip across his lips. She managed a smile, but her heart wasn't in it. 'Okay. Lebowski had the camera hooked up, but he had to be on-site to view it. He couldn't be there during the day or at any time when he might be seen, so he was only able to monitor the subject—'

'Can you call him Kieran, please?' Lockyer asked. 'The "subject" sounds bloody awful.'

She raised her eyebrows. She knew Lockyer wouldn't be able to keep his mouth shut. 'Fine. Lebowski monitored Kieran the first night. From his notes, it looks like Kieran struggled with this burial far more than he had with the others. He was showing signs of stress, and at one point Lebowski thought he might have had a fit.'

'And you don't think leaving him down there after that is murder?'

She didn't bother to answer him. She was going to get this all out even if she had to talk over him for the rest of the evening. 'Lebowski continued to observe, and satisfied himself that Kieran was okay, before leaving.'

'I'm still failing to see where the "accident" part comes in,' he said, pushing his fingers through his hair. Jane wished he would get a haircut. It was like talking to one of those troll-dolls that were popular in the Eighties.

'On all of the previous sessions Lebowski had a strict routine. He checked the camera and the air-hose, taking pictures. Again, I've asked Franks to search for these, as they're not included in this bundle. Anyway, when Lebowski had to leave the site, he cleared away any mud or leaves that might impede Kieran's air supply. The last entry, when he left Kieran, he didn't check the air supply. Looking at the times, Kieran would have been unattended from five in the morning until gone midnight the next night. In that time it's entirely possible that the ground around Kieran's air-hose was disturbed. The woods are frequented by walkers, dogs, local wildlife. Any one of these could have covered the air-hole.'

'Or Lebowski did it,' Lockyer said.

'The remaining air in the tomb would have lasted for five or six hours, maybe a few more, given the size of the tomb – but not until the next night, no way. Lebowski comes back, sees that Kieran is dead and panics. He takes out the air-hose and camera and pretends it didn't happen.'

Lockyer's eyebrows were disappearing into his thatch of hair. 'What about the other tomb? Why leave his equipment there?'

'I don't know. As I said . . . he panicked, cleared the evidence away from Kieran's tomb and then legged it. He couldn't risk going back, could he?' Lockyer was shaking his head. 'Look, it's an idea,' she said. 'There's no motive to kill Kieran. From the paperwork, it was a simple experiment.' Lockyer's eyebrows went even higher. 'I don't understand it any more than you do, Mike, but that's how it reads. It's dry, boring research. Even I remember some of the terms from school: having a "control" environment, that kind of thing. The point is, everything is catalogued and documented from the beginning, right through, but everything stops the night he left Kieran in there. There's nothing after that. Whether it was an accident or not doesn't really matter. I'm just telling you what I think. Amelia Reynolds was raped and murdered. I don't doubt that. Lebowski put Maggie in the tomb to die. I don't doubt that, either. The tomb in Elmstead was the perfect place to hide the body, and he was the only one who knew it was there.' She finished speaking and stared out of the window at the buildings opposite the station. An image of Maggie's parents appeared in her mind, followed by an image of Gary Reynolds. The death of his daughter had ruined him, but Maggie's parents were just at the start of that road. Jane had to find Lebowski. She had to get justice for them, to stop them ending up like Gary.

'And what about Mark?' Lockyer asked. 'Where the hell has Lebowski stashed him? We've checked Elmstead. He's not there. Is there anything in Lebowski's notes about other sites – places we can look?'

Jane's focus seemed to come back to her all at once. 'There are,' she said. 'Lebowski had two possible sites further out. I'll speak to Jared and ask him to get the GPR over there and see if he can find anything.' She thought again. 'And I need to speak to Sue. She must know Mark bought the allotment plot in Deptford. I have to make her understand that whatever she's hiding could be crucial to finding Mark and Lebowski.'

'You need to prepare yourself, Jane,' Lockyer said.

'For what?' she asked, looking at him. She had already resigned herself to the fact that finding Mark alive was never going to happen.

'Lebowski knows about the second tomb. He's not stupid. He'll know it's only a matter of time before we ID Kieran.

He'll know we're going to get him; that he's not going to slip through the net this time.'

'What's your point?'

'My point,' Lockyer said, resting his hands on the table, 'is that if he thinks it's over, suicide might seem like his only option.'

'Don't say it,' she said, trying to ignore the smiling face of her son that was pushing its way into her thoughts.

'Come on, Jane,' he said. 'We all knew it was a possibility, the second we found out those kids were missing. If Lebowski decides to end it, he may well take his kids with him.'

Jane felt a wave of nausea. She knew Lebowski's children were in danger. She knew she had to find them before Lebowski did anything stupid, but she couldn't bear to think about what that really meant. If she had let him go and those two children died, because of her, she would never forgive herself. Never.

CHAPTER FORTY-TWO

5th May – Monday

The Monday-evening traffic was heavier than Jane had anticipated as people drove home after the bank holiday. She weaved in and out of the bus lane, much to the chagrin of her fellow road-users. A red light at Tesco's brought her progress to a halt. She pulled her handbag onto her lap and rooted around for her phone. She wanted to call her mother, to check on Peter. She swerved around a bus and accelerated away. She hadn't told Sue she was coming. Despite their friendship, she couldn't afford to give Sue time to prepare. She needed the truth. At Catford gyratory she turned left onto Brownhill Road, joining a long line of traffic. 'Shit,' she said, flicking on her lights. After a few seconds a path opened up and she pushed her way through.

All she could think about was Lebowski and where he had taken his children. The question made her stomach tighten. She had to keep her focus on the immediate future, on speaking to Sue, finding out what she knew and going from there. If she thought too much about what was happening to Lebowski's children, she would go mad. How must

Lebowski's ex-wife be feeling now? The turn for Mark and Sue's road was up ahead on the right. She waited for a line of cars to move off from the traffic lights. There was nothing coming in the other direction, so she flicked on her lights again and darted out into the opposite lane and made the turn.

She pulled up to the curb outside Sue's house. There were no lights on. 'Damn it,' she said, turning off the engine and getting out of the car. The air temperature had changed. It was muggy. The air around her felt heavy. She turned and leaned into the car doorway to grab her handbag off the passenger seat. There was a noise behind her. As she turned towards it, she saw something black out of the corner of her eye. At the same time the back of her head exploded with pain. Her knees crumpled beneath her, her vision blurred. She blinked again and again. As her world went black, she thought she could hear someone breathing.

CHAPTER FORTY-THREE

5th May – Monday

Lockyer looked down at Lewisham High Street. The scene in front of him was incongruous. It was past nine o'clock, the street lights casting their orange glow over the traffic, but people were still wandering around in shorts and T-shirts. He let his blind fall back into place, walked over to his desk, picked up his mobile and dialled the number Jane had given him. As far as she was concerned, Gary had sent the package containing Lebowski's research. She had asked Lockyer to get confirmation, but as he listened to the phone ringing he wondered whether, in the scheme of things, with Lebowski on the run with his kids, it really mattered.

'Yeah,' a female voice said.

'Hi, Cindy. It's DI Lockyer. How's it going?'

'Who?'

'DI Lockyer,' he said, resting his forehead on his free hand. 'I was over on Saturday with my colleague, DS Bennett, talking to Gary. Remember?'

'Oh, right, yeah. You're that tall copper,' she said, her words slurring into one another. 'Crazy hair.'

Lockyer couldn't help smoothing his hair down. 'That's right. Can I have a word with Gary, please?'

'Not here,' Cindy said. She sounded as if she was about to pass out.

'When will he be back?'

'I don't know,' she said, sniffing. 'We went out Saturday after you were here. Haven't seen him since.'

Lockyer sat up straight in his chair. 'What do you mean? Where's he gone?'

'How should I know?' Cindy said, sniffing again. Lockyer realized she was crying. 'He just walked out of the pub and didn't come back. Guess he was sick of me. My mum said he'd get bored. I figured if I came back here, he'd come home eventually and we'd make up, you know?' Lockyer didn't say anything. Something about this didn't feel right. 'I don't have any money. I can't go back to my folks. They don't want me. He was the only one . . . Gary was the only one who ever wanted me.' She was sobbing down the phone.

'All right, Cindy.' What could he say? He couldn't very well say that he thought Gary leaving her was probably the best thing for all concerned. 'Look, I'm sorry, but I need to find Gary. Do you have any idea where he might have gone?'

'No,' Cindy shouted. 'If I did, I wouldn't be sitting here waiting for him, would I?'

'Listen, I need you to get him to call me as soon as he comes back. Okay?'

'If he comes back,' she said.

'Call your mum, Cindy,' Lockyer said, feeling useless and guilty. 'I would want my daughter to call me if she was in trouble, no matter what had happened.'

Cindy sniffed again. 'Okay,' she said. 'I've gotta go. I need some bog-roll.' She hung up before Lockyer could say any more.

'Nice chatting with you,' he said, dropping his mobile onto his desk.

He looked at his watch. He had texted Jane twice with updates on the search, but hadn't heard back yet. Air Support had been called in, but so far there was no sign of Lebowski's car. With a few clicks he opened his address book on his computer. He scrolled through until he came to Sue and Mark's details. The home number was listed. He dialled and waited.

'Hello,' Sue said.

'Hi, Sue. It's Mike,' he said, leaning back in his chair. 'Sorry to bother you, but could I have a quick word with Jane, please?'

A brief silence greeted his question.

'She's not here, Mike,' Sue said. He could hear papers shuffling at the end of the line. 'I had a text from her a little while ago saying she was coming over. She must be stuck in traffic.'

'What time did she text you?' he asked. Jane had told him she wasn't going to tell Sue she was coming; that she didn't want to give Sue time to prepare. So why would she text Sue?

'Hang on,' Sue said. He heard the papers being moved. 'It was only fifteen minutes ago. She said she was on her way.' Lockyer looked at his watch. Jane had left the office well over an hour ago. 'She didn't say why she wanted to speak to me. Is it Mark?'

'No, Sue. I'm sorry. Jane just needed to ask you some

questions about a guy we've been talking to on the Hungerford case. There's a possible connection.'

'Is Lebowski a suspect?'

Lockyer paused, unsure whether to continue. 'You know him?' he asked.

'I know of him, yes,' Sue said. 'Jane asked me about him last week.' There was a silence at Sue's end. Lockyer held his breath. 'I didn't tell her . . . I didn't think it was relevant. Mark was . . . ' She stopped speaking.

'We know about the phone calls, Sue,' he said, looking around his desk for his notepad.

'Oh God,' she said, her voice muffled. He pictured her covering her mouth with her hand, hoping to stop the words. 'Who else knows?'

'Only a select few,' he said, not wanting to lie to her, but not wanting to subject her to any more anguish, either. Jane had managed to keep the bulk of the information from the team, but that couldn't last. Roger knew and so would the higher-ups. It was only a matter of time before it drifted into general circulation.

'Mike, I swear I didn't know anything about it until I checked the phone bill. When I confronted him, he broke down . . . He cried, Mike. I've never seen him cry, except when the boys were born. He was distraught. He felt like it was his fault.'

'Like what was his fault?'

'Amelia's murder. He tried everything, but nothing would stick. He told everyone – his SIO, the chief, everyone – but no one else believed Lebowski was guilty.'

'Why was Mark so sure that Lebowski killed Amelia?'

331

'I wish I could tell you,' Sue said. 'He wouldn't talk to me about it, not really. He interviewed Lebowski again and again and just said he knew, from the way the guy acted, that he'd done it – like he was showboating, hoping they would catch him.'

'What else did Mark say about the phone calls?' Lockyer asked.

'He said he owed it to Gary . . . Amelia's father. Gary and Liz were our friends. Their marriage went down the pan not long after Mark retired. Gary couldn't handle not knowing.'

'Did Mark tell Gary about Lebowski?' He knew he was taking a risk asking Sue the question. If anything was going to make her clam up, it was incriminating her missing husband, but her silence answered the question for her. 'When?' he asked.

'He didn't feel like he had a choice. Gary started drinking. He wasn't the same man we had known. He called all the time, made threats, came round. He even started a fight with Mark in the pub. It was awful to see him lose it like that. Gary said Mark had promised him he would get whoever killed Amelia. He said Mark's retirement was an excuse to cover up his own incompetence; that he was as guilty as the man who had killed Amelia. Mark was crushed.' Lockyer could hear Sue trying to control her voice, trying to stop herself from breaking down.

'Why didn't you call me? Or Jane?'

'How could I, Mike?' she said, sniffing. 'You would have had to intervene. There's no way you could have just swept that kind of information under the carpet. He's my husband, Mike. I'd do anything for him, to protect our family. Mark thought if he told Gary that he knew who was responsible and that he hadn't forgotten Amelia, it would give Gary some kind of closure.'

'But it didn't,' Lockyer said, unable to believe that Mark could have been so short-sighted.

'No. If anything, it made Gary worse. He came to the house. He was drunk. He threatened Mark, said he would hurt me and the boys if Mark didn't tell him who had killed his daughter.'

Lockyer felt as if someone had just walked over his grave. The Gary Reynolds that Sue was describing was not the man he and Jane had met on Saturday. He tried to piece together what it could mean. Lebowski was on the run with his two children. There was a warrant for his arrest in connection with the murders of Amelia Reynolds, Kieran Affiku, Maggie Hungerford and Mark Leech. Now Gary Reynolds had gone AWOL. Lockyer needed to speak to Jane. Now.

CHAPTER FORTY-FOUR

5th May – Monday

Jane touched the back of her head with the tips of her fingers. They came away wet. There was a throbbing pain behind her right eye. A memory floated around her consciousness: a noise, then nothing. She took a deep breath, inhaling the scent of water and soil mixed together by the rain. She opened her eyes. The blackness that greeted her pupils jolted her out of her stupor. She sat up, her head connecting with a solid surface. The impact turned her stomach. She vomited between her legs. 'No,' she groaned. 'Please, no.' She coughed and retched again as the pain in her head increased. Her throat burned as she hung her head between her knees. She pictured Peter in her mind, sitting in the garden, his face upturned to the sun, a small smile on his face. Her heartrate slowed. She held onto his image and started to shake her head. Neither Lebowski nor her own panic would prevent her getting home to her son. She would fight until her last breath.

She resisted the desire to move, to scrabble to freedom. Instead she waited, counting each breath, each beat of her heart, until she was calm. She remembered climbing down into Maggie's tomb: the moment the lights had been turned off, to allow her to imagine how it must have been to wake up in such a place. She realized now that her imaginings hadn't even come close. The blackness, the smell, the cold, the feel of the frigid earth beneath her fingers and the silence – each element pushed her mind towards madness, towards losing control. She felt it like warm hands on her cold skin. It was as if the tomb wanted to possess her, to absorb her into the earth. 'No,' she said, shaking her head again, dislodging the thoughts before they could take hold. 'Peter.' Just hearing his name calmed her mind. 'Peter,' she said again, turning until she was on all fours. She pictured Maggie's tomb in her mind and then Kieran's. The hatch had been in the top right-hand corner of both. She almost laughed. There was no way to tell where in the tomb she was: which end, which side, anything. Like Maggie and Kieran before her, she would have to feel her way.

With slow, deliberate movements she reached down and patted her pockets and the earth around her. She felt something in her left pocket. Her keys? It seemed to take an eternity to navigate the material of her trousers and find the opening. She pulled them out, her hand closing around the gift her mother had given her. 'Thank you, Mum,' she whispered. She twisted the end of the miniature torch and a thin beam of blue light appeared under her fingers. As relief washed over her, she thought again about Maggie and Kieran. She felt tears welling up in her eyes. She held the torch to her chest, closed her eyes and said a silent prayer. If she got out, if she escaped, maybe somehow a part of them would too. She allowed herself to cry for a moment, but then swallowed her emotions and looked around her. The beam of light was small, but she moved it over the ceiling ahead of her. Nothing. She turned, her head throbbing, and looked behind her. The light changed as it moved over something. Was it the hatch? She tried to focus. Her heart seemed to stop in her chest as the light flickered for a moment, fading to nothing before springing back to life. 'No way,' she said, pushing her body to move. She was getting out of here right now.

As she moved towards the hatch, her light settled on something beneath it. It was a body. A man. Her head was screaming. Mark. She retched again and again, but there was no more liquid in her stomach. She leaned over his body and shone her light onto his face. There was a lot of blood. She listened. He was breathing. She leaned further over, resting her hand on his chest. There was a deep wound over his left eye. Her head pounded. It wasn't Mark. She was looking at the bloodied face of Lebowski. 'Victor,' she said, shaking him, his head lolling backwards, limp. She looked up at the hatch. He was directly beneath it. With a strength she didn't know she possessed, she managed to push him out of the way. Her keys and the torch were wedged between her teeth, the metal tasting sour against her tongue.

She turned and lay down. With both hands flat, she pushed upwards, the floor hard and cold against her back. It didn't budge. She pictured the earth on the other side of it, weighing it down. If she managed to break it open, would she be able to dig her way out? 'You bet your life I will,' she mumbled to herself. She glanced at Victor and listened. He was still breathing. Where were his daughters? She lay back again and brought her legs up, until her feet were resting against the hatch. There wasn't much room, but she pumped her legs and kicked as hard as she could with her heels. The contact made her head spin. She rested her head on one side as she retched, but she didn't stop. She pumped her legs and kicked again. And again. Spatters of earth fell onto her face.

Without warning she was plunged into darkness. She reached for the torch and twisted it back and forth, but nothing happened. 'Oh God, no.' She could stand anything – anything but the darkness. Her breath caught in her throat; her lungs seemed to freeze. She opened her mouth, but couldn't get any air. Her pulse hammered inside her skull. 'No,' she whispered. She couldn't give up now.

She lifted her legs again and kicked with every ounce of her strength. She would not stop. With each kick she willed the hatch to break, but fear was holding her back, weakening the impact. She was terrified a landslide of mud would rush in and suffocate her. 'Come on,' she said, angry with herself now. She pushed the thought away and kicked again. A loud crack echoed around the tomb. She screamed and pummelled the door with one foot, then the other, over and over again until she was kicking at nothing. Exhausted, she let her head fall back into the deep bed of soil surrounding her. She blinked her eyes, shaking the dirt away, holding her hands over her face. Her breath hitched in her throat. She could see her hands, her fingers. There was light. It was faint and delicate, but it was there. 'Thank God,' she said, letting the moonlight wash over her face.

CHAPTER FORTY-FIVE

5th May – Monday

Lockyer took off his jacket and threw it over the back of his chair. He had been trying to get hold of Jane for over an hour. It was past ten o'clock. There was no sign of Victor Lebowski or Gary Reynolds, and now Jane was missing. He looked up as Chris was passing by his office door. 'Chris,' he called after him.

'Yes, boss,' Chris said, poking his head around the edge of the glass door to Lockyer's office.

'When was the last time you spoke to, or heard from, DS Bennett?'

'I haven't spoken to her since she left the office, boss,' he said, looking over his shoulder at the clock mounted on a column in the middle of the open-plan office. 'About half-six or seven-ish, I'd say.'

Lockyer stood and pushed past the young DC. 'Has anyone heard from DS Bennett since she left the office?' Several heads turned in his direction. 'Anyone?' A room full of shaking heads gave him his answer. 'Who spoke to her last?' There was another silence, as Jane's team looked at each other, shook their heads and then looked back at Lockyer.

'I saw her in the car park when I was coming on duty, boss,' Whitemore said, standing up at his desk. 'Seven o'clock.'

'What did she say?' Lockyer asked, trying to control the volume of his voice, which was increasing with each question.

'That she was driving over to Bromley to see Sue Leech,' Whitemore said.

'Was that it?'

'She said she'd be on her mobile, and to call if there was any movement on Lebowski,' he said, looking down at his feet like a scolded child. 'I think that was it, boss.'

'Has anyone received a text or any communication from her since then?' Another barrage of shaking heads greeted him. 'Chris,' Lockyer said, turning. 'Call Traffic and tell them to keep an eye out for Jane's car. If she hasn't called in by,' he looked at his watch, 'ten-thirty, I want Air Support.'

'Half the team is out on the Lebowski warrant,' Chris said, not seeming to grasp the gravity of Lockyer's request.

'DS Bennett has been out of contact for over three hours. No one has seen or spoken to her. She is the lead investigator on the Hungerford case. Lebowski is under warrant, in relation to that case. He is missing with his two young children. Jane is missing. Do you understand what I'm telling you?' His words elicited the reaction he needed. Everyone was looking at him. Everyone was focused. 'Unless she walks back into this office in the next half-hour, finding DS Bennett will be your top priority. Is that clear?' A chorus of 'Yes, boss' and 'Yes, sir,' rang out around the office. He jogged back into his office, grabbed his car keys and ran back across the room to the lifts. 'I'm on my mobile. I'm going to drive over to Sue Leech's and see if Jane's been delayed en route. Franks,' he shouted.

'Yes, boss,' Franks said. He was standing by the water cooler, looking somewhat shell-shocked.

'You're in charge until I get back. Clear?'

'Yes,' Franks said, nodding.

'And call the SIO,' Lockyer shouted from the hallway, stabbing the 'Call' button for the lift. 'Ask him to come in, and call me when he gets here.' The lift pinged to indicate its arrival. Lockyer was inside and pressing the button for the ground floor before the doors were fully open.

Lockyer raced through the traffic, ignoring the blasting horns and shouts of protest as he accelerated through red lights and swerved onto the wrong side of the road. He was concentrating on the road ahead, as well as flicking his eyes from side to side in search of Jane's car. His back was slick with sweat. He should have taken a squad car. Roger had signed off for his Audi to be fitted with lights and a siren, but Lockyer had not had time to get the work done. He slammed his hand down on the steering wheel. 'Come on,' he shouted, leaning on his horn, waving his arms in frustration as dazed faces looked back at him in their rear-view mirrors. 'Get out of the bloody way,' he mouthed to a woman in an Espace loaded with kids.

He reversed, almost hitting the car behind him, and nosed out into the oncoming traffic. A truck pulled out in front of him, missing his front bumper by inches. He braked, swerved to the left and darted around it before the driver knew what was happening. His mobile began ringing on the dashboard. He grabbed the phone, swerving his car onto the curb. 'Lockyer,' he said, ramming the phone against his ear.

'Mike,' Jane said. Her voice sounded far away. Lockyer's muscles started to bunch up in his shoulders.

'Jane, where the hell are you? Are you all right?'

'I'm okay,' she said, but she didn't sound like she was okay at all.

'Talk to me. What's happened?' He felt as if he wanted to get out of the car, to start running.

'I'm in Elmstead,' she said. She was coughing. Her lungs sounded dry, her voice hoarse.

Lockyer sat back. 'Jane,' he said, taking a deep breath. 'Are you hurt?' The numerous coffees he had drunk in the afternoon were working their way up his throat.

'I'm fine . . . I went to Sue's. She wasn't there . . . someone hit me. When I woke up I was in one of the tombs – Kieran's, I think.' Lockyer tried to process what she was saying.

'Lebowski?' he asked.

'No. No, Mike, Lebowski's dead. He was in the tomb with me when I woke up. Someone had caved in the front of his head.' Jane was coughing again. He waited. 'I managed to get out . . . ' She was breathing hard. ' But when I went back in for Victor, he was dead. I can't find the children. They're not here. I don't know . . . ' Her voice drifted away as if she had dropped the phone. He could hear other voices in the background.

'Jane?' Lockyer said, gripping his mobile. 'Are you there? Jane?'

He heard her retching. 'I'm okay,' she said. 'Concussed, I think, but I'm okay.'

'Listen, I spoke to Cindy. Gary Reynolds hasn't been home since we were there on Saturday,' Lockyer said. 'I spoke to Sue. She knew about the phone calls, and Lebowski. She said

Gary threatened to hurt her and the children if Mark wouldn't tell him who killed Amelia.' There was silence from the other end of the line. 'Jane?'

'It's Gary,' she said, her voice quiet. 'Now I get it,' she said, clearing her throat. 'He's been planning to take the children all along.' She retched again. 'He's going to kill them, to punish Lebowski. He's going to kill them because Lebowski killed his daughter.' As he listened to her words, everything fell into place.

'I'm coming to get you,' he said, ramming the Audi into gear.

'No, no,' she said, 'Sasha and Aaron are already here. I managed to get this phone off a couple out walking their dog. I called the office, after I'd called an ambulance for Victor. Mike, you need to get over to Deptford. The allotment where Amelia was killed. That's where he'll have taken them. Gary is going to kill them in the same place that his daughter died. I've already requested backup. But, Mike, we can't approach until we know what's happening. We can't risk him seeing us and hurting those kids.'

Lockyer realized he was nodding, but not speaking. 'Okay. All right. It'll take me ten minutes to get over there.' He could hear an engine revving at the other end of the phone.

'We'll be there in fifteen, twenty minutes. Meet us at the south end of Brockill Crescent. I'll get the rest of the team to take up position at the north end, on St Norbert Green. The railway line will pen him in on the east side.'

'See you there,' Lockyer said, dropping his phone onto the passenger seat and mounting the pavement, as he swung the Audi round and accelerated away.

CHAPTER FORTY-SIX

5th May – Monday

Jane ran her hands through her hair. She was standing at the southern end of Brockill Crescent, stamping her feet. She couldn't stay still. They had been waiting for Lockyer for almost ten minutes. She looked up and down the street, lined with 1960s terraces. Other than a group of teenagers on skateboards, it was quiet. Pockets of light from the occasional street lamp bathed the empty pavements. She looked at her watch. 'What the hell is taking him so long?' she asked, turning to Sasha and Aaron, who were still sitting in the squad car.

'He said the ambulance should be there any second,' Sasha said, leaning out of the car window. 'Traffic haven't turned up yet . . . the guy in the car is going in and out of consciousness . . .'

'Lockyer needs to be *here*.' Jane had to stop herself from shouting.

'He said he'll be another five minutes, ten max,' Sasha said.

'We can't wait,' Jane said, shaking her head. 'Those kids can't wait.'

She closed her eyes. The pain was beyond anything she had ever experienced. She was pretty sure adrenaline was the only thing keeping her conscious. The twenty-minute drive from Elmstead had been tense, and neither Sasha nor Aaron had said much. Jane had been unable to speak. All she could think about was Poppy and Petra. They were seven and ten. Innocent pawns in Lebowski's and Gary's twisted histories. She looked at her watch again. Every minute she waited put those kids in danger. She had met Gary. He was an alcoholic, a wreck of a man. The death of his daughter had robbed him of his life, but would he really hurt two little girls? 'I'm going over there,' she said, striding off towards the cut-through to the allotments.

'Boss,' Sasha said, getting out of the car and jogging after her, 'you can't go over alone. We don't know if the guy's armed, or what he's planning to do.'

'I know that,' she said, pausing at the entrance to the alleyway. 'But the longer we wait here, the longer he has to make up his mind. I've met him. He didn't strike me as a violent man, just a broken one. I don't think he would want to hurt those kids. Not really. He's doing it because he thinks he has to. I let Lebowski go. That's twice he's had to watch the guy walk free. If I can talk to him – convince him that hurting the children won't help – maybe he'll give himself up.'

'And what if he's armed?' Aaron asked, joining her and Sasha on the pavement.

'With what?' Jane asked. 'The guy's broke. He doesn't have a gun, that's for sure. I don't know what he hit me with, but as long as I don't turn my back on him . . . and give myself

344

room to run, I'll be fine. I'll take Sasha's belt with me, so I've at least got pepper spray and a baton. I've got my radio. If he makes a move, or even looks like he might be a threat to me or those children, I'll call you. Besides, we don't even know for sure that he's here. It's a hunch. My hunch. If he is, I'll try and talk him round. If he isn't, then . . . '

'We'll come with you, boss,' Sasha said, unclipping her belt and handing it to Jane.

Jane took the belt and slung it around her waist. It was heavier than she remembered. 'Okay, bring your radios, but put them on silent. I don't want to risk spooking him. That's if he's even here.' She was beginning to doubt herself. 'Hang back, out of sight, and wait for my call. Understood?' They both nodded. She waited for Aaron to run back to the car, pick up the radios and lock the squad car, and then the three of them walked down the alleyway in silence.

When they reached the end of the allotments Jane stopped. She indicated where she wanted Sasha and Aaron to wait, before opening the small gate and stepping onto a gravelled path. There was no way she could approach on that without being heard. She side-stepped onto a runner of grass and moved forward with almost no noise. From the map they had at the station, the plot where Amelia's body was found was about three-quarters of the way down. She couldn't see any light ahead of her. Maybe he wasn't here. She checked her radio and continued on the grass, looking around her every two to three steps. Her head was throbbing. She stopped and listened. A train was coming. She waited for it to pass, holding her breath as the almost deafening noise reverberated around the allotments. She was surrounded by turned earth.

It looked black in the moonlight. A shiver ran down her back as the tomb appeared in her mind.

Another sound made her stop. She ducked behind a lean-to shed. She could hear laughter. It was then that she saw the light, very faint, about fifty yards in front of her. She peered around the edge of the wooden structure. It was coming from a full-size shed standing in the middle of a large plot. There was no way to tell if the laughter had come from inside. She turned and looked back. She couldn't see Aaron or Sasha. She must be about 150 yards into the allotment. She checked her radio again. If she raised the alarm it wouldn't take them more than a minute to get to her.

Without giving herself time to think, she started forward, being careful where she put her feet. She could hear someone coughing as she approached the shed. There was a window in the door and one on the side facing her. She crept forward, hunched over until she was beneath the side-window. She held her breath and inched her head up until she could just see over the ledge. Gary was sitting with his back to her, a balaclava rolled up on his head. She risked standing up another few inches to get a better view. Her breath caught in her throat. He was looking at a small television screen. The picture was black-and-white. The image was blurred, but she could see two small figures huddled together. One of the girls was moving, but the other was still. Too still. He was watching them die. But where were they?

She ducked her head and rested down on her haunches. She had to get to those girls. Without making a sound, she moved crab-like to the front of the shed. The earth was freshly turned. Her stomach clenched. Had he buried them, like

Lebowski's other victims? She stood up and approached the door. She put her hand on her belt. If Gary wouldn't talk, she could spray him in seconds and have him cuffed before he had time to recover. She rested her hand on the doorknob, took a deep breath and pulled the door open. Gary turned at the sound, but didn't move from where he was sitting. Jane opened her mouth to speak, but words failed her.

Lockyer could see the lights of the ambulance in the distance, but it seemed to be taking an age to get to them. 'Almost here, mate,' he said to the man, who was still sitting in what remained of a Nissan Micra.

'My back,' he moaned.

'You're all right,' Lockyer said, looking at the mess that was the guy's face. 'The ambulance will be here any second. They'll sort you out.' The man, who was called Geoff, tried for the tenth time to get out of the car. 'No. You stay put. They'll want to check your back and neck before they move you. You're going to be fine. Not sure you'll make your anniversary dinner, but I'm sure your wife will forgive you.'

'Are you married?' Geoff asked.

'Not any more,' Lockyer said, craning his neck to watch the progress of the ambulance.

'So, you should know that wives don't forgive. They tell you they do, but that's bullshit. They just hold onto it for the next time you have a row, then it'll get thrown back in your face.' Lockyer couldn't help smiling. It had been a long time since he had experienced the wonder that was married life, but Geoff's description rang true. 'She'll say I was driving too fast, or texting, or drinking, or looking at another woman.

It'll be my fault. I can tell you that much.' Geoff stopped speaking and grimaced. 'Shit, this hurts. I can't see.'

'Nothing to worry about, Geoff. You've got a bit of blood in your eyes, that's all. Head-wounds bleed like nobody's business, even with a small cut.' He didn't think Geoff needed to know that his head was cracked down the middle like a melon. 'Here they are,' he said, as the paramedic jogged up the road to meet them. Lockyer stepped back and put his hand on Geoff's shoulder as he briefed the medic. 'Traffic should be here any minute,' he said. He bent down into the car. 'Right, Geoff. I'm going to leave you with the ambulance crew. They'll look after you.'

'Thank you.'

Lockyer patted the guy's shoulder. 'And don't worry about the missus. Send her my way if she gives you any trouble.' He turned and ran to his car before Geoff could respond. If the crash hadn't happened pretty much in front of him, he wouldn't have stopped at all. He didn't have time for this. He put the Audi into gear as he looked at the clock on his dashboard. All he could think about was Jane waking up in one of those tombs. She had sounded confused on the phone. She should be at the hospital, not chasing down Gary Reynolds. Lockyer should have insisted she go – that he would go to the allotments with the team. He thumped the steering wheel. He needed to get there.

'What are you doing?' Jane asked, taking a step back.

'I'm finishing what he started,' he said.

'I . . . ' She couldn't fathom what she was seeing. Mark was sitting on an old office chair, turned to face her, the

348

balaclava askew on his head. He was holding a Starbucks takeaway coffee cup. It was as if she had opened the door to another reality.

'You let that bastard go,' Mark said, taking a sip of his drink.

'Lebowski?'

'Of course Lebowski. He got away with murder before. I couldn't let him get away with it again, could I? He was so arrogant . . . He didn't even blink when I knocked on his front door this afternoon. He certainly blinked when I knocked him out, though,' Mark said, chuckling.

'He's dead,' Jane said, her voice numb with shock.

'Good,' he replied, turning away from her to look at the screen. 'You are meant to be dead too, Jane,' he said, tutting and wagging his finger at her as if she was a disobedient child.

'What have you done with the girls, Mark?' she asked, taking a small step forward, her hand resting on the pepper spray in her belt.

'They're here,' he said, pointing to the screen. 'He took my child – my heart. Now I'm taking his.'

'Your child?'

'Amelia,' he said.

'Amelia was your daughter?'

Mark started to laugh. He looked at Jane as if she was losing her mind. At that moment she thought he might be right. 'No, Jane. Amelia was not my daughter. She could have been, perhaps should have been, but she wasn't. Gary Reynolds – I know you've met him. He isn't much of a man, is he? He never was, even back then. Useless husband. Hopeless father.'

349

Jane rested her thumb and forefinger on the pepper spray. She should have called for backup before she opened the door. The man in front of her was not the Mark she knew.

'I had to promise that useless son-of-a-bitch that I would find the man who killed Amelia,' Mark said. 'What did he care? He cheated on Liz. Not once or twice, but as often as he could manage it. Amelia idolized him. She was heartbroken when I had to tell her that her father was a waste of space.'

'What made you think Lebowski killed her?' she asked, taking another minute step forward.

'I could tell by his eyes,' Mark said, putting his coffee down next to the television screen. Jane couldn't see the girls from where she was standing. She didn't have time for this. 'He was so smug. Well, you know, you've met him. He's like a snake, slithering away on his lies. He wanted Amelia. He even tried it on with her. She told me. He wanted her. She was disgusted. *Disgusted*. She didn't want him, so what did he do? He took what he wanted and then killed her.' He spat out the words, saliva spraying over his jacket. Jane could see a bandage poking out of the top left-hand side of his collar. He followed her eyes. 'I know. A bit of a struggle working with a duff arm, but it's almost healed now. I trained with the paramedics for a few months in my twenties. It's amazing what you remember,' he said, as if proud of his achievements.

'I . . . ' Jane began.

Mark laughed. 'You look confused,' he said. 'Well, I guess that shouldn't surprise me. It certainly took you long enough to follow the breadcrumbs, no matter how many I threw your way.' He shrugged, as if her inability to understand was a mere annoyance in what was otherwise a perfect evening.

'I tried every which way I could think of to plan this without me having to leave – to leave my boys – but I knew it wouldn't work. I know Lebowski, know how he operates.' Mark smiled. 'And I know you, Jane, you and Mike. I needed to create just the right kind of motivation. If you believed I was missing, presumed dead . . . ' He shrugged. 'Given the blood, the wipe-clean, the glove marks and powder residue, what other conclusion could there be?'

Jane didn't answer.

'Well, I knew as soon as Lebowski's hidden past with Amelia came out – and, therefore, my own – you'd have all the pieces you needed to take him down.' Mark shook his head, narrowing his eyes. 'But no.'

She couldn't speak. She felt as if her brain was going to explode out of her skull. There was a pain behind her right eye that was radiating down her neck and into her shoulders.

'You don't look too good, Jane,' he said, cocking his head on one side. 'Head injuries can be nasty.' He gestured to his injured arm. 'I'll admit that doing this hurt like hell.'

'Mark,' she said, holding out her hand in what she hoped was a passive gesture. She hoped he couldn't see that she was shaking. 'I don't understand any of this.' If she could keep him talking, keep him calm, she might be able to get close enough to spray him.

'Of course you don't,' he said, his tone indulgent, soothing. 'I gave you everything you needed and it still wasn't enough.'

Jane steadied her back against the door to the shed. She had to spray him soon. She wasn't sure she could stand up for much longer. 'I didn't have enough to hold him, Mark.'

Mark stood up, shoving the chair across the room. 'How?'

he said, staring at her. 'Let's look at the evidence, shall we? Lebowski was dating the victim. He was having sex with a student – or should I say *another* student.' He scoffed. 'He had intercourse with the victim hours before she was buried. He drugged her. He attacked her on her front doorstep. He buried her in a tomb that only he knew about. He buried her in the same way he buried that boy years ago.' He was holding up his fingers to demonstrate each piece of evidence that Jane had failed to utilize. 'He studied taphophobia, for God's sake. I gave you his research. And I was missing, most likely dead.' He moved forward, forcing her to back out of the doorway. 'That should have been enough, but you still let him go.'

She took a deep breath, trying to hold her hands still. 'Mark,' she said. 'How do you know about Maggie Hungerford? How do you know she was drugged? How do you know she was attacked outside her house?' Mark stared at her, his eyes black. 'And, Mark, how do you know about Kieran?'

'Doh,' he said, mimicking Homer Simpson. 'How do you think?' he asked, as if she was missing the obvious. 'I waited for Lebowski to kill again. I knew it was only a matter of time. When I saw what he did to that boy, I called and called. I even tried to talk to Lockyer about it, but no one would listen to me. I wasn't a DCI any more. I had retired for all of five minutes, and all of a sudden there's no respect. I told them that he had killed again, but they wouldn't listen. I was just some nutcase with a grudge against Lebowski. It should have ended then, when he killed that boy, but no one would listen. Tell me,' he said, opening his hands to her in a suppli-cant gesture. 'What should I have done?'

'You killed Maggie?' Jane said, feeling an icy chill run down her back as she started to feel the pieces of the puzzle shift and come into focus.

'Well, yes – I had to,' he said. 'She was the key. I had to get you to reopen the investigation into Amelia's death.'

Jane didn't know what to say. He was explaining away Maggie's murder as if it was nothing, as if it didn't matter. 'You murdered an innocent girl, Mark.'

He seemed to recoil from her words. 'I did not,' he said, breathing hard. 'I would never hurt Amelia.' Jane took another step back as he stumbled forward. He held onto the side of the shed. He was hyperventilating. 'I didn't kill her. Lebowski did. It was him: he wanted her, but she refused. She refused him, so he killed her. Then, when he knew I was onto him, he killed that boy. He was laughing at me. I knew he would kill again. I watched him. I waited, but he thought he was too clever for me. When I saw him with the girl – with Maggie – I knew what I had to do. He would have killed her, Jane. He couldn't help himself. He's sick.' Mark put his head in his hands as he started to cry.

Jane pulled the can of pepper spray from her belt and held it behind her back. 'Victor Lebowski didn't murder Kieran. He died because of an experiment that went wrong. Victor didn't mean for Kieran to die. He left him there, yes. He covered it up, yes. But he didn't murder that boy.' She swallowed. 'And he didn't kill Amelia, either, did he, Mark?'

He looked up at her, his eyes bloodshot. He shook his head.

'It was *you* who wanted her, wasn't it, Mark? It was *you*

she rejected. You killed her, Mark, didn't you? You killed Amelia.'

Before she could react he was out of the chair, barrelling into her stomach. She crashed to the ground, the wind pushed out of her lungs by the weight of his body on top of her. She tried to pull her arm from under her, but he was too heavy. He put his hands around her throat. Thousands of white lights burst behind her eyelids. She opened her mouth to scream. His fingers pushed into her neck. She writhed and kicked, but she couldn't take a breath. Her head throbbed. She looked up into his face, into the face of a killer. She could feel the darkness taking hold, pulling her under. Her eyes rolled back in her head. She bucked her head one last time, and then there was nothing.

Lockyer pulled up behind the squad car. He looked around him at the quiet street. Where were they? It was then that he noticed the alleyway on the other side of the road. He climbed out of the car and shoved his radio into his trouser pocket and jogged towards the entrance, continuing on down the path. There were six-foot fences on both sides. As soon as he came to the end he spotted Sasha and Aaron, both crouching behind a three-foot-high white picket fence.

'What's going on?'

They both jumped.

'DS Bennett's gone to check if Gary Reynolds is here,' Sasha said in whisper.

'She's done what?' Lockyer asked, not even bothering to lower his voice.

'It's all right, sir,' Aaron said. 'She's got Sasha's belt, pepper spray, baton and cuffs. She just wanted to check he was here, so we wouldn't waste any time.' If he meant to insinuate that Lockyer's tardiness had wasted their time, he didn't show it. 'She said she wanted to see if he was here and, if he was, try and talk to him first. DS Bennett felt confident Gary didn't really want to cause harm to Lebowski's kids.'

'Oh, did she?' Lockyer said, wanting Jane to be here right now so that he could strangle her. 'So far today Gary Reynolds has assaulted and killed Victor Lebowski, kidnapped two children and attacked a police officer. I think it's fair to say he's past the talking stage, don't you?'

Aaron and Sasha looked at him like scolded school-children.

'When did she go in?'

Sasha pushed her sleeve up and looked at her watch. 'Nine minutes ago, sir.' As she spoke he could see her thinking what she and Aaron should have been thinking five minutes ago. It didn't take nine minutes to ascertain whether Gary Reynolds was here. It didn't take nine minutes to know whether or not she would need backup. Either way, Jane should have radioed them.

Without speaking, Lockyer shook his head, pushed open the gate leading into the allotment and started to run.

The mud and gravel from the path were sticking to his shoes. The moon had come out enough for him to be able to see where he was going. He swerved to avoid a low fence. He could see a light up ahead. He pushed his legs faster and squinted to make sense of what he was seeing. Someone was lying on the ground. They weren't moving. He jumped over another squat fence and landed on his knees at Jane's side.

It took several seconds to make his hands move, to do anything but sit there and look at her. He felt for a pulse, pushing his fingers into her neck. She was alive. He positioned himself at her side, interlocked his fingers and placed them on her chest. He was about to start compressions when he was knocked sideways, rolling over several times in the dirt.

Without time to think, he jumped to his feet like a surfer mounting his board. He turned, crouched and ready to pounce. When his vision cleared he was staring into Mark's face. Mark stared right back at him. The moment of indecision was enough. With a keening sound like a wild animal, Mark launched himself at Lockyer, sending them both sprawling back into the dirt. He sat on Lockyer's chest, hitting him over and over again, but his punches were weak and misplaced. With a grunt of effort Lockyer lifted his knee between their bodies and pushed Mark away. He rolled and managed to pin Mark face down. Lockyer twisted Mark's arm behind his back, pushing his knee into the other man's spine with every ounce of strength. With his left hand he held Mark's face down in the mud.

Everything seemed to stop. He could see Jane lying a few feet away. She wasn't moving. He held firm until Mark stopped struggling. He could hear voices. Aaron and Sasha were speaking, both at the same time, neither one registering in Lockyer's mind.

As he pushed himself off Mark's body, he saw Aaron pumping hard on Jane's chest, counting. Sasha was on her radio, shouting instructions. Everywhere around Lockyer there was noise, but Jane was still. He stumbled over to the shed and rested his shoulder against the damp wood for support. He saw the flickering television set. Without knowing what he was looking at, he walked into the shed and stared at the screen. Two bodies. Two little girls. Adrenaline rushed into his system, awakening his brain. He looked around the shed, saw the hatch and lunged for it, pulling it up and open in one movement. Instead of a hole there was mud, a smooth, flat layer of mud.

'I need a spade. Someone get me something I can dig with.' He didn't know if Sasha could hear him, if she understood what was happening, but he didn't have time to waste. He reached forward and started pulling at the earth, gouging out huge handfuls of loose mud. He threw it over his shoulder and kept going, burrowing, pushing, pulling – anything to get it out faster. He looked over at the television screen. Neither of the girls was moving. 'Petra, Poppy,' he shouted, yelling into the ground. He shouted their names over and over again as he redoubled his efforts and threw every inch of himself into clearing the hole. His hand came crashing down on something solid. 'There's a door,' he shouted. 'Petra, Poppy,' he yelled again. 'I'm coming, girls. Hold on.' He felt as if he was screaming. His muscles ached, his tendons straining as he scooped more and more mud from the hole.

At last he saw the handle. He forced his fingers around the small ring of metal and pulled. There was still a lot of soil blocking the hatch, but with another wrench the door popped open. 'Sasha, get in here,' he shouted. The entrance was too small for him. There was too much earth blocking the way. He turned as Sasha ran up behind him. 'Get down there,' he said, grabbing her arm and lifting her legs from under her until he was cradling her like a baby. He shoved her feet into the hole and pushed down on her shoulders. 'Get in there and get those girls out.'

Sasha crouched, her head and arms disappearing out of sight. 'I can't see,' she yelled up at him.

'Just feel around – feel around,' Lockyer shouted. 'They're in there.' He waited, holding his breath, feeling sick, his head aching, his heart pounding in his chest. 'Hurry.'

'I've got a foot,' Sasha called up to him. 'I think I've got a foot.'

'Pull, for God's sake, pull.'

He watched, helpless, as Sasha's head and shoulders appeared. She flattened her body to the edge of the opening. She was pulling at a pair of little pink trainers. Lockyer dropped to his belly and grabbed hold. He pulled, using one hand to protect the small girl's face as it popped out of the hole like a cork. 'Get the other one,' he said, laying the girl down next to him. He felt for a pulse and let out a cry of relief when a strong beat pushed against his dirt-covered fingers. 'She's alive,' he said. He bent down and put his ear over her mouth. Her breathing was shallow, but it was there; he could feel it, warm against his skin. He looked around for something to wrap her up in, to keep her warm. He grabbed a piece of sackcloth and threw it over her.

'I've got the other one,' Sasha screamed. 'Help me. I can't lift her.'

Lockyer turned and sprawled onto the floor again, leaning his head and shoulders over the hole. 'Pass me her foot,' he said, straining to reach another pink trainer. His fingers grazed the cold plastic, before he finally managed to get a good grip. He pulled as Sasha fed the girl's body up through the opening. 'Check on the younger one,' Lockyer said, pointing to Poppy who was wrapped up behind him. He turned back to the girl in his arms. There wasn't enough room to lie her down flat. He crossed his legs and placed her across his knees. He felt for a pulse. He felt again. Nothing. 'We need an ambulance, now.' He held his fingers on the girl's throat. 'She isn't breathing,' he said. Still holding her in his arms, he pushed himself up, using his elbows to lever himself up. He stepped over Sasha and the girl's sister and pushed out into the night.

He dropped to his knees and started to pump hard and fast on the little girl's chest. 'Come on, Petra,' he said. 'Come on.' He said her name with each pump, wincing when he heard a crack. He had broken one of her ribs, but he couldn't stop. He had to keep her heart going until help arrived. Without thinking, he looked up and saw Aaron a few feet away. He was pumping on Jane's chest.

CHAPTER FORTY-SEVEN

9th May – Friday

Lockyer drained the last of the vending-machine coffee and threw his cup in the bin. He looked through the doors into the Toni & Guy Ward. Poppy and Petra Lebowski had been brought to King's College Hospital by ambulance on Monday night. The doctors said they were both doing well, considering they had been buried for almost six hours. Much longer and the outcome would have been very different. Apart from Petra's concussion and her broken rib, the girls were unharmed.

Lockyer had been in to see them every day since he had pulled their small bodies out of the tomb that Mark had created for them. Petra had been kept in intensive care for the first twenty-four hours on oxygen but, like all children, she had bounced back with amazing speed. He smiled as he watched them squabbling over whose go on the iPad it was. He wasn't sure what had come over him: when he had walked into Lewisham on Wednesday to pick up a little gift for the recovering sisters, a lolly or a colouring book just hadn't seemed enough. He turned and walked away, safe in the knowledge that the girls were okay.

No Place to Die

He had been to see Sue first thing on Tuesday morning, before the press got hold of the story. The repercussions of Mark's actions would be far-reaching, not only for his family, but for the murder squad as well. A never-ending line of colleagues had been into Lockyer's office searching for an explanation – something to help them understand how one of their own was capable of such atrocities: rape, murder, kidnap. What could he say? Mark was in intensive care on life support, by Lockyer's own hand. He didn't know and, if he was honest, he didn't care about Mark's motives. The man had strangled Jane with such force that he had broken her hyoid bone. He hadn't told Sue that part. How could he? She had just been hit with the news that her missing husband was in fact not missing, but had kidnapped and tried to kill two little girls, in an act of revenge – an act of lunacy. The reasons and motives were trapped inside Mark's head. Even if he did regain consciousness, the doctors said he could have brain damage. He would never again be the man he was. In a way Mark was the lucky one. He would never have to face up to his actions.

Jane had not been so fortunate. Lockyer's dreams had been filled with images of her body lying on the black earth in the Deptford allotments. Her pale face would interchange with Aaron's stricken expression as he pumped again and again on her chest. The team had been in a state of shock, but with all the new evidence to process there hadn't yet been time for a full debrief.

He arrived at Cheere Ward and smiled at the nurses. They were used to him by now. Several times they had explained that visiting hours prevented him staying the night. They had given up; he had no intention of going home. He had spent the last three nights sleeping on a chair. On the second morning he had woken to discover that someone had covered him with a blanket.

His shoulders dropped as soon as he saw her. Jane was lying on her side, her back to him. She was bruised and battered, but alive. Her broken hyoid would heal, or so the doctors told him. They had needed to operate to repair some tissue damage that had been obstructing her airway, but apart from that, she would heal on her own. The consultant had said she would make a full recovery. He pulled up a chair and sat down, not wanting to wake her. A full recovery . . . The bone, the bruises, the swelling: that would all heal; but what about the psychological damage? Maybe she would end up with the same therapist he was seeing. Two damaged detectives together. He smiled.

'Hey,' Jane said, turning over in the bed, her voice raspy and hoarse. 'How's Mark?'

'Still alive,' Lockyer said.

'That's good,' she said. 'You don't want his death on your conscience, Mike. If he wakes up, he'll have to answer for what he's done.'

'The docs reckon he might have brain damage from the lack of oxygen.' Lockyer knew he should feel more, but he couldn't bring himself to care. Mark had crossed over – become one of the people Lockyer had spent his life trying to catch.

'How's Sue . . . and the boys?'

'She's gone away. France. Her parents have a timeshare out there. She doesn't want the boys in the country when the story breaks.'

'It's not been in the papers yet?' Jane asked, wincing.

'No. Roger's managed to pull some strings to keep things quiet, for the time being, until we have the complete report.' He wanted to ask some more about what had happened, but it seemed an insult to make Jane relive what had happened in Deptford while she was still lying in a hospital bed. She hadn't been able to speak until late yesterday, because of the bruising. Since then she had been focused on her family, as she should be. She had spoken to her son on the phone, but he hadn't been in yet. Jane's mother, whom Lockyer had met in the corridor on Wednesday, didn't think it was appropriate for Peter to see his mother in this state. Lockyer shuddered. Celia Bennett was a formidable woman, and then some.

'I can do my statement now, if you want?'

Lockyer shook his head. 'There's no hurry. Mark's not going anywhere.'

'I know but I'd prefer to get it out. If only to stop it going round and round in my head,' she said, tapping the side of her temple.

'Okay, tell me then. But we'll leave the official report until you're back on your feet . . . Deal?'

'Deal,' Jane said. She rolled onto her back and pushed herself up the bed a few inches. Lockyer wanted to help, and even reached out, but she waved his hand away. 'I can manage.'

He sat back and looked out of the window at the end of the ward.

'Lebowski didn't kill Amelia Reynolds,' Jane said.

He turned and looked at her. 'Say that again?'

'I know,' she said, taking a deep breath. 'Now, some things

I know, and some things I *think* I know, so you're going to have to bear with me. Okay?'

'Sure, go for it,' Lockyer said, sitting forward. He was a detective: curiosity was part of his DNA.

'Mark killed her. I think Amelia rejected him and he reacted – raped her and then strangled her.'

'How do you know?' he asked, unable to process what she was saying. 'Did he admit it?'

'No,' she said, her expression pained as she swallowed. 'But Mark kept telling me that Lebowski had tried it on with Amelia, that she had rejected him. He said Lebowski wouldn't take no for an answer, that he raped and killed her because she had rejected him. Mark seemed obsessed with Amelia. Said she should have been his daughter – all sorts of weird stuff, like telling her what a cheating nobody her father was.'

'That doesn't mean—' he began, but Jane held up her hand and stopped him.

'I confronted him, I asked him. I saw it in his eyes, Mike. When I said it again – accused him of killing Amelia – that's when he lost it, when he tried to . . . kill me.'

Lockyer was shaking his head. 'If Mark killed Amelia, then what's all this been about? What's all the shit with Lebowski been about?'

'That's where I get a bit hazy,' Jane said. 'You'll need to talk to Phil, but it sounds like transference or psychological projection. I've read about it. Basically, rather than accepting his own guilt and facing what he had done, Mark transferred all of his guilt, confusion and rage onto Lebowski, when he interviewed him. It's a common process – like kids blaming their siblings for something they did themselves – except that in Mark's case he took it to a whole new level. I think once he had transferred the blame to Lebowski, Mark was convinced, genuinely convinced, that Lebowski *was* the man who had killed Amelia. He told me as much himself,' she said, adjusting her position.

'You should rest,' he said.

'No, I've got to get this out,' she replied, dropping her head back on the pillow. 'Mark also killed Maggie.' Lockyer felt his mouth drop open. 'He waited for her to come home. He took her from outside her own house. He drugged her – I don't even want to think how. He buried her. She was just collateral damage. Mark only killed her and buried her in Elmstead to set up Lebowski.'

'None of this makes any sense to me,' he said.

'You're telling me.' She started to cough, her face scrunched up in pain. 'I'm not sure any of us will ever fully understand,' she said, taking a sip of water from the cup he had just handed to her. 'Madness, revenge, spite – they're just meaningless motives. But Mark killed Amelia and Maggie; he admitted the latter. I'm not sure knowing all the whys and wherefores will help Sue, or anyone else, deal with what's happened.'

Lockyer could only nod. To see her so weak was one thing, but to hear the defeated tone in her voice was too much. 'Sue will cope somehow, Jane. She's tough. Now,' he said, standing, 'I'm gonna go for a wander. Let you get some more sleep.'

'Okay,' she agreed, taking a deep, shuddering breath. 'Mike, I never said thank you.'

'Thank Aaron,' he said.

'No, thank you for saving those little girls. I couldn't have lived with myself if anything had happened to them. Without you, they would have died.' Her eyes filled with tears.

He took a tissue from the box next to her bed and wiped the tears off her cheeks. 'Now listen. That's enough of that, Detective Sergeant Bennett. I order you to get some sleep.'

She smiled, but only for a second. 'Will you be here when I wake up?'

'You bet,' he said, backing away from her bed. 'Now get some sleep.' She smiled and closed her eyes. He did the same.

CHAPTER FORTY-EIGHT

9th May – Friday

'You mustn't wake her,' a voice whispered. 'Let's go for a little walk and come back in a minute.'

'No,' a determined voice replied. 'It's raining.'

Jane opened her eyes. 'Hey, munchkin. Are you giving Grandma a hard time?'

'No,' Peter said, screwing his face up, his fingers playing with the blanket that was hanging over the edge of Jane's bed. 'I don't like walking. I don't like the rain.'

'I'm sorry, darling,' Celia Bennett said, trying and failing to take Peter's hand. 'He's not in the best of moods today.' Peter shook off his grandmother's hand and stomped over to the nurses' station, where he started organizing pens, lining them up on the end of the desk. 'You need to rest,' her mother said. 'We'll come back – go to the canteen or something. We shouldn't have woken you.'

Jane covered her mother's hand with her own. 'It's okay, Mum. He's okay. I'm all right.'

'Huh . . . all right,' her mother huffed, pacing back and forth next to Jane's bed. 'You're hardly all right. I knew this job was too dangerous. It was only a matter of time. First you break your leg chasing some ruffian, and then some madman almost kills you. Well, if that's all right, I don't know – I just don't know.'

'Mum,' Jane said, trying to ignore the pain as she swallowed. 'I broke my leg when I was training in Hendon. That's almost fifteen years ago.'

'Well, that may be . . . But that's two serious injuries. You're not as strong as you think you are.'

'That's why she has us, love, so stop badgering the patient.' Jane turned. Her father was standing on the other side of her bed. He looked thinner. Her eyes filled with tears as he smiled, bent and kissed her cheek. His lips were warm and dry, his moustache soft against her skin. She could smell his cigars. 'Dad,' she said, her voice cracking.

'Hello, poppet,' he said, taking her hand and squeezing it. 'How are you doing?'

'I'm okay, Dad.' It was the first time she had seen him since the previous weekend. He looked tired. 'How are you?'

'I'm absolutely fine,' he said, looking around him, before touching his head, 'touch wood.'

'Of course he won't listen to me,' her mother chimed in, still pacing. 'I can't get him to do anything I say. He won't stop, won't rest . . . I see now who you take after.'

'How's Peter coping?' Jane asked, craning her head around her mother to see him.

'He's miserable,' her mother replied.

'He's fine,' her father said, squeezing Jane's hand again. 'He's a bit out of sorts with you in here, and the rain is making him fidgety, but he's fine.' He looked down at her. 'He's fine, and we're fine.'

'Can we go now?' Peter called from the other side of the room.

Jane had to resist the urge to laugh. Her ribs were killing her. Aaron's determination to bring her back to life was evident in the bruises that covered her torso. 'You guys go,' she said. Peter skipped over, kissed the back of her hand and then skipped off again, disappearing out into the hallway. It was all Jane needed.

'Oh Lord, where's he gone now?' her mother said, running after him.

'It's all go,' her father said, walking around the end of the bed. 'I'll bring you back something nice,' he said, smiling. 'Carrot cake?'

She nodded, swallowing back her tears. 'Carrot cake would be perfect.'

As she watched her father walk away she thought about William and Elizabeth Hungerford. They had lost their daughter. Their lives had been forever altered. Jane had felt their pain from the moment she had found Maggie in the tomb. That was how the job was, with her. It had been the same ever since her days as a fresh-faced trainee. Finding Maggie's killer had been all-consuming. And now Mark would face justice, in whatever form that took. It wouldn't bring Maggie back. It wouldn't erase the grief the Hungerfords felt, but it would, Jane knew, bring them some peace.

Her job meant she spent her time focusing on other people. Other people's families. Other people's grief. She wouldn't change it, but lying here – seeing her son, seeing her mother and father – she realized that she couldn't do any of it without them. They were her peace. Her eyes felt heavy. As she closed them, letting the pull of sleep take her, she smiled. She must remember to thank them.

ACKNOWLEDGEMENTS

No Place to Die is only my second novel, and yet the list of people I need to thank grows by the day.

I am indebted to my editor, Trisha Jackson. She is a wonderful editor and, moreover, a good friend whom I have loved getting to know over the past year. Long may it continue. By her side is Hellie Ogden, my tireless agent. You have an energy and tenacity that never fails to astound me. Thank you for everything you have done and continue to do for me.

I would also like to thank everyone at Pan Macmillan for their efforts in making *Never Look Back* a success and *No Place to Die* a breeze, considering it's a second novel and I'm told the hardest to write. In particular, thanks go to Natasha Harding, Becky Plunkett, Harriet Sanders, Sam Eades, Kate Bullows, Eloise Wood, Stuart Dwyer, Neil Lang and Mandy Greenfield.

I'm delighted to say that *Never Look Back* and *No Place to Die* have been picked up by the US, Italy, Germany and the Netherlands. So I would like to say a huge thank you to Kelley Ragland and Elizabeth Lacks at St. Martin's Press for all of their efforts in the US. Your enthusiasm and belief in my writing has been overwhelming, and the hardback for

Never Look Back was beautiful! Thanks also to Ulrike Gerstner, my editor at LYX in Germany, Fanucci Editore, my Italian publisher, and De Fontein, my publisher in the Netherlands. I hope DI Lockyer and DS Bennett keep all your readers guessing!

Audible have done a fantastic job with *Never Look Back*, with *No Place to Die* to follow. Thanks to Stacy and the amazing performances from Karl Prekopp and Imogen Church.

Mark and Sue, thank you, as always, for your guidance, police know-how and homemade curries.

None of this would be possible without the love and support of my family and friends. My mother is the stalwart, attending every event and signing, and in some cases forcing me to sit on the street to ensure I am seen by passing shoppers! My brother Chris, for being my first-look reader and for giving me the best feedback. My brothers Roger and Stephen for supporting me and spreading the word in the UK, New Zealand, Italy and beyond. As for my friends, you know who you are and I value you all. Extra big hugs go to Rachel, Eve (my long-suffering writing buddy), Clare and Jo who are ever-present.